# BELLA MAFIA

# BELLA MAFIA

*Lynda La Plante*

William Morrow and Company, Inc.
New York

Recognizing the importance of preserving what has been written, it is the policy of William Morrow and Company, Inc., and its imprints and affiliates to have the books it publishes printed on acid-free paper, and we exert our best efforts to that end.

Library of Congress Cataloging-in-Publication Data

La Plante, Lynda.
    Bella Mafia / Lynda La Plante.
      p.  cm.
    ISBN 0-688-09242-X
    I. Title.
PS3562.A635B45   1991
813'.54—dc20
                                            90-42384
                                               CIP

Printed in the United States of America

First Edition

1 2 3 4 5 6 7 8 9 10

BOOK DESIGN BY M. C. DEMAIO

*To Jeanne F. Bernkopf*

# Bella Mafia

# Prologue

At ten o'clock in the evening on the second day of the adjournment of the biggest Mafia trial in history, one of the chief prosecutors, Giuliano Emanuel, received a telephone call at his office. It was Mario Domino, an old legal adversary from Emanuel's early court days.

Domino wasted no time in pleasantries. He announced that he wanted a private meeting with Emanuel, and if it could take place immediately, it would be to Emanuel's advantage.

"I am parked outside your office. Please tell your security guards to expect me." The car phone went dead.

Emanuel slowly replaced his receiver. He decided he had no option. He warned his guards of the impending visit and returned to his desk.

The trial, intended to be the exorcism of the Mafia's stranglehold on Sicily, had been adjourned almost before it had begun. An open file on Emanuel's desk showed the gruesome reason. On top of it lay a black-and-white photograph of Emanuel's prize witness for the prosecution. He had been murdered. Lenny Cavataio's mutilated body had had the desired effect;

witness after witness had withdrawn statements against the most important prisoner, Don Paul Carolla. The prosecution was very much aware that many more might die before Carolla could be brought into court.

Domino entered minutes after his call, and the two old friends clasped each other in greeting. Domino held the embrace to whisper in Emanuel's ear, "I am trusting you, Giuliano. Pray God you do not abuse my trust."

Refusing a drink, Domino sat down and opened his briefcase. "It is of the utmost importance that no one overhears our conversation."

"Mario, I assure you that you can talk freely. My office is checked every day." He watched as Domino withdrew a large manila envelope from his briefcase, opened it, and took out a photograph.

"If you recognize this man, just nod your head. I do not want his name mentioned. One cannot be too sure."

When Emanuel looked at the black-and-white photograph, the hairs on the back of his neck began to prickle. It was Don Roberto Luciano, *Il Papa*—the real "Boss of Bosses," a leader from the past, when the Mafia was considered a force for poor people unable to fight for their rights. He had been a part of the organization for more than fifty years, and no one knew if he was still active. But he was still honored, even revered, in Palermo.

Emanuel handed the photo back to Domino. "I know who it is."

"He is a close friend of mine, and I have acted on his behalf on numerous occasions. He wishes to meet with you but is well aware of the danger to his family should it become known."

Emanuel's mouth felt dry, and he swallowed. "Why does this client of yours want to meet with me?" he asked.

"He will tell you that himself. I think you will find it beneficial, if you can arrange top security for his family and him."

The two men shook hands on their agreement. Domino's client would arrange the meeting place. Emanuel was to expect a call and was to do exactly as instructed. If he deviated from the arrangements, the meeting would not take place.

\*　　\*　　\*

The call came two nights later. Emanuel was to leave his home immediately and drive to a warehouse on the waterfront, leave his car there, and walk to the end of Pier 3, where he would be picked up. Alone.

Emanuel obeyed. His stomach churning, he waited on the pier for almost half an hour.

At last a man appeared, seemingly from nowhere, moving soundlessly, and instructed Emanuel to follow him. A second man slipped into place behind them. A third man was waiting in a car a short distance away, with the engine running.

Emanuel was searched before he climbed into the car. No one spoke as they headed back toward town.

The San Lorenzo, a small restaurant, seemed closed, the ground floor in darkness. Emanuel's nerves were in shreds as he followed his two escorts among the neat tables toward an archway. The two men then stood aside, gesturing for him to continue up the narrow linolcum-covered staircase.

A gray-haired man in his sixties was waiting at the top. With a curt nod he ordered Emanuel to raise his hands and proceeded with a body search. Satisfied, he motioned Emanuel to follow him up to the next landing and into a small, elegant dining room hung with red curtains.

There was no one else in the room, but the single table was set for three. The gray-haired man seated Emanuel at the table, poured him a glass of wine, then left.

It was fifteen minutes before Emanuel heard the quiet, unhurried footsteps on the stairs. The door opened, and Domino entered, bowed to Emanuel, and sat down. Without saying a word, he picked up the wine bottle, examined the label, and poured himself a glass.

The moment the glass was full, the curtains were moved aside and a waiter appeared with an elaborate tray filled with silver dishes. His movements were deliberate as he placed the tray on a serving table. Emanuel looked at his watch, then at Domino, and was about to speak when the curtains were drawn aside again and Don Roberto Luciano entered the room.

The photograph had not conveyed the man's aura; even at seventy he was impressive. More than six feet tall, he stood erect, his white hair framing a face with dark, heavy-lidded eyes and a slightly hooked nose.

The waiter hurried to remove the camel-colored cashmere coat draped casually about Luciano's shoulders. Luciano was wearing a pale fawn linen suit, cream silk shirt, and dark blue silk tie in which a diamond pin sparkled.

Luciano went first to Domino, placed both hands on his friend's shoulders, and kissed his cheek. Then he turned to Emanuel, his right hand outstretched. His grip was strong.

Luciano seemed concerned that Emanuel approve of the menu. As they ate the seafood rolled in fresh pasta, Luciano murmured his own pleasure. Throughout the meal the conversation was simply polite, Luciano complimenting Emanuel on his handling of a number of cases, then discussing a mutual friend with Domino, as Emanuel studied *il Papa* more closely.

Luciano's large, strong hands made almost hypnotic gestures. On the little finger of his left hand he wore a ring with a circle and moon picked out in gold on the blue stone. The nails were square-cut and polished. These were not the hands of an old man.

Brandy was served in balloon glasses, and cigars were lit as the waiter disappeared behind the curtains. Emanuel heard a door's lock click into place. He straightened in alarm, but Luciano placed a comforting hand on his arm. "It is just a precaution. I apologize for this theatricality, but it makes me feel more secure."

The old man who had searched Emanuel now entered the room from the stairs and nodded to Luciano. This door, too, was locked as he left.

From his pocket Luciano took a fob watch, checked the time, and replaced it. Then he rose from the table and sat in a deep, comfortable chair, with a high, winged back. He crossed his long legs and leaned back on the red velvet cushions.

"You must have some idea of why I asked for this meeting. I am prepared to be your main witness for the prosecution, on condition that you protect my family. They must have safe houses, armed guards. I must have your word on this before I give you the evidence that will, I assure you, mean the death sentence for Paul Carolla." Luciano spoke with the confidence of a man used to having his orders carried out.

Domino tapped the ash from his cigar. "Would it be possible for you to arrange such security without divulging my client's name? It is imperative that no one know his identity until the time comes for him to take the stand. This is not just for his protection but for your own. Can you, in your position, organize such security?"

Emanuel knew he could not make such a promise on his own, but he gave his solemn oath that the evening's conversation would remain secret. He coughed to ease his constricted throat before he spoke.

"Signor Luciano, providing safety for you and your family will require negotiations with the judges and police chiefs, and time is obviously of the essence. When will I be able to assess the evidence you are prepared to divulge?"

Luciano laughed a deep, guttural laugh and shook his head. "You think I have documents? Papers I can give you? No, no— I am your evidence, me. Dates as far back as 1928, all recorded, but not on paper—here, in my brain." He tapped his temple with his finger, then leaned toward Emanuel. A chill entered his voice. "Come, my friend, do you really think I would put anything on paper to substantiate my offer? What do you take me for? You are looking at a seventy-year-old man who would not be alive if he made notes."

Emanuel persisted. "You must understand it from my point of view. The government will require some kind of physical proof before it will release funds for total surveillance, around-the-clock guards, safe houses—and for a man whose name I cannot divulge."

The dark eyes flashed, but there was a half-smile on Luciano's face. "I brought you Lenny Cavataio. If the protection given to him is what I am to expect, my friend, we have no deal."

"That was unfortunate."

Luciano sneered and leaned foward. "No one will gain access to my villa, but in court I am vulnerable. In meetings with you I am vulnerable. Lenny Cavataio was the most valuable witness you had against Carolla, and you let him die like an animal. But my family is my life; my sons are my blood. They will need your protection more than I will."

Emanuel's nerves were beginning to show. "I understand, signor, but you have to give me something that will prove without doubt that I have a witness worth protecting."

Luciano closed his eyes and thought for a moment, then leaned forward and spoke softly. "Paul Castellano, head of the Gambino family, and his driver, Thomas Bilotti, were shot to death in front of Sparks Steak House in New York. Neither man was carrying a gun. There was no backup team to protect Castellano. Yet until that moment he had always been protected, insulated by his men. He was losing sight, not comprehending anymore the world in which he had been raised. He had refused to have his food distribution companies used as covers for drug couriers. He was not prepared to take the risks of drug running, and the main importer, the main dealer in heroin to the United States, was Paul Carolla. I have evidence that will give you Paul Carolla as the man who ordered the murders." Luciano's eyes were like slits. He cocked his head to one side as if to say, "Is that enough?"

But Emanuel knew that it was not. What Luciano had given him was evidence that any number of men could give. Emanuel rose to his feet and stood by the big velvet chair. "I'm afraid it is not enough to ensure your protection."

Luciano looked up at him, then at Domino. After a moment he, too, rose to his feet and placed his hand on Emanuel's shoulder. The big hand felt like a dead weight. The room was eerily quiet.

Emanuel was afraid of this man, and his relief as the hand slowly lifted made him gasp.

"Lenny Cavataio gave you a statement regarding the death of a young Sicilian boy. Cavataio was prepared to take the stand and name Paul Carolla as the instigator of the murder." The eyes didn't flicker. They held Emanuel's attention as he whispered, "The dead boy was my eldest son."

Nowhere in the soft, cultured voice was there a hint of what Don Roberto Luciano was feeling. He continued. "Now, my friend, I am not prepared to talk with you further. It is up to you. You say time is of the essence. Then so be it. You have two weeks. I will wait to hear via Domino. I have arranged the marriage of my granddaughter, which will take place on February the fourteenth, two weeks from today. It will be the first time the whole family has been gathered together for many years—my sons, my grandchildren. If you can guarantee the protection I need, it will be easier to accomplish with my entire family under one roof. The danger to my loved ones is obvious, and will be more so when, if, I take the stand. My sons will not approve of my decision; but my mind is made up, and I will not retract my offer. Thank you for coming to meet me. It has been a pleasant evening."

The door opened without any obvious command, and he was gone, leaving behind him the sweet smell of fresh limes.

Domino drained his glass. "Don't underestimate what he is offering you. You will make your career on his back. You will become a very famous man, or a dead one."

Emanuel snapped, "He wants protection for his family. Dear God, what about mine? As it is, they balked at giving me two personal around-the-clock guards. You'd think I'd asked for a private army, and that is what Luciano will need—an army."

"Then get it. Step up your own security because I warn you, if it were ever to leak that Luciano is your witness, he would not live to take the stand. Believe me, I am against this madness."

Emanuel's mind was reeling, but he had to take one last shot at Domino. "Why? Just give me one good reason why he's doing it."

"He told you—for his son, for Michael Luciano."

"Is that it?"

Emanuel was not prepared for the rush of anger that made Domino's cheeks flush.

"Paul Carolla saw to it that Michael Luciano was introduced to heroin while the boy was studying in the States. Then, when he became an addict, they shipped him back and flaunted him like a beaten whore to the father who worshiped him. Carolla did that to a beautiful boy because Michael's father refused to deal in narcotics." Domino's hand clenched into a fist. "Yet the don never gave way. You have the proof now; the man who was in this room tonight is one of the most highly respected legitimate exporters of goods from Sicily, and he paid the price. He paid for it with the life of his son."

Domino paused, shook out a silk handkerchief, and wiped his mouth before continuing. "Michael was his father's son, and he fought back. At the time of his death he was cured of his addiction. But his killers injected him with enough heroin to kill five men. Even that did not satisfy them; they tortured him, beat him, until even the mortician could not repair his features. Don Roberto carries all this in his heart; he blames himself for that broken body, for the terrible things that were done to his beautiful son."

Emanuel watched as Domino wiped his eyes. The old man was speaking as if the tragedy had just occurred.

"Why, if he knew all this, did Luciano wait? His son has been dead more than twenty years."

Domino gave Emanuel a disdainful look. "Because he has two more sons."

"Yet now, all these years later, he is prepared to jeopardize his life and the safety of his family. I don't understand."

Domino tucked his handkerchief away and smiled, but his eyes were ice cold.

"You are not one of us, you could not understand. Call it revenge, call it the end to a vendetta, but I guarantee that Paul Carolla is finished if you get Luciano on the stand. *Capich'*?"

Domino excused himself, and again the door opened to some unseen signal. The two men who had brought Emanuel to the meeting were waiting for him.

Emanuel arrived back at his apartment to find one of his guards washing down, yet again, the main entrance. Red stains could be seen on the cloth as the man wiped the door. Emanuel sighed. Once or twice a week a dead cat was pinned to the door, its guts hanging out, pitiful legs pinned as if crucified.

"Another cat? They carry on like this, and there won't be one left in the neighborhood."

The guard shrugged. "This one's a bit different," he said.

Emanuel looked, not even sickened anymore. "Oh, yes?"

"Yes, it's yours."

# 1

Sophia Luciano sat beside her husband, Constantino, watching the road, knowing that within moments they would reach the brow of the hill from which they could see the sprawling Villa Rivera.

The elder son of Don Roberto Luciano, Constantino had handsome features and blue-black hair that were reminiscent of his father as a young man. But only reminiscent; there was a shyness, a gentleness to him that were even more evident when he spoke, for he was afflicted with a slight stammer. Sophia waited for him to tell their children they were "home"; it annoyed her that her husband always referred to his father's house as "home" when they had lived in Rome for the past eight years, but she said nothing.

Below them now, sparkling in the February afternoon sun, the Villa Rivera seemed bathed in golden light, which spread across the tiled roof, the swimming pool, and tennis courts. White curtains billowed from the painted shutters and caught the breeze along the veranda.

Constantino stopped the car on the brow of the hill. They

could see the striped awnings of the marquee, already erected
for the wedding. Constantino stared down while his two sons
grew impatient, urging their papa to hurry.

"Is something wrong?" asked Sophia.

"They must be workmen, see them? On the roof, around
the gates."

Sophia shaded her eyes and replied, "There'll be a lot of
people, darling. You know Mama will want only the best."

Graziella Luciano was waiting on the porch, her gray hair
coiled in a bun at the nape of her neck, her tailored dress concealing her extra weight. Her face, with no trace of makeup,
was still, at sixty-five, hardly lined. Her excitement was held
in check; she appeared almost austere, but her pale blue eyes
were sharp, watchful.

The guards were opening the fifteen-foot-high wrought-iron
gates. As Constantino's car continued up the long driveway,
she waved, acknowledging their arrival, but at the same time
she gave a curt order to the florist to space the floral displays a
little farther apart and reminded him that everything had to be
completed before five o'clock.

The boys ran from the car and into their grandmother's
arms. Her face softened by smiles, her blue eyes warm and
brimming with tears, she hugged her grandchildren. Constantino followed, arms outstretched, to kiss his mother. She smiled,
touching his face lovingly.

"Are you well?"

"Mama, you saw me a month ago. You think I'd change?"

Graziella linked her arm through her son's and smiled a
welcome to her daughter-in-law. Sophia blew a kiss with her
fingertips and instructed the maid to take care with the wedding gown, which was draped in sheets to keep it clean. When
Sophia came to her, Graziella reached up to stroke her cheek.

"You have been away too long. I have missed you."

The car was full to bursting with their luggage. Graziella
ordered one of the men to unload it and take the suitcases upstairs.

Making no effort to help, Constantino asked after his father. Graziella replied that he was in town but would be back
by five. She then turned her attention to her beloved grand-

sons, saying that if they hurried to their rooms, they might just find something underneath their pillows.

Sophia could hear the boys in the bedroom below. She would have preferred them to be on the same floor that she was, but she knew better than to question Graziella's arrangements. She began to unpack the cases, which were already neatly stacked at the foot of the bed.

The room was filled with fresh flowers, perfectly arranged, as was the room itself, though Graziella's taste was a little old-fashioned and austere for Sophia. Much of the heavy carved furniture had come from Graziella's family home; it was whispered that her ancestors had been titled aristocrats. Nowhere in the house was there a photograph of these mysterious relatives, and Graziella did not look like a Sicilian. In her youth she had been very blond with piercing blue eyes, looks that only her firstborn child had inherited.

Sophia snapped open the locks of her case, angry with herself because every time she came here she was reminded of Michael Luciano. Although there was not a single photograph of Graziella's mysterious family, her dead son's face was everywhere. Over the years Sophia had deliberately learned where each silver-framed image was placed, so she could never be taken unawares, never be shocked by seeing him.

At that moment Constantino walked in, making Sophia even more angry with herself. She hated being caught talking to herself.

He closed the door and watched her, smiling. Her curvaceous body was usually hidden beneath her perfectly cut and draped clothes; now she was barefoot and wore only a silk slip. It never failed to arouse him when he saw her like this.

"You need any help?"

"No, just watch that the boys don't get too unruly."

"Mama's with them, she's bought them new Action Men."

"She spoils them." Sophia inspected an outfit she was thinking of wearing for the wedding.

"She loves them."

She smiled. "I love you."

He went to her, but she sidestepped him, laughing. "No, let me unpack. Your papa will be home shortly."

Constantino caught her in his arms and kissed her neck. "Take your hair down."

"No, just let me do what I have to do."

He released her and flopped across the bed. "It's going to be a full house, and guess what? They are actually using Michael's room."

Sophia almost dropped a coat hanger. "What?"

Constantino put his hands behind his head and smiled. "Yeah, the groom is to be in Michael's room."

"I hope they've aired it. It's been closed for years."

"I peeked as I came up. Most of Michael's stuff has been put away. They couldn't really keep it closed, not with a full house. You know, this will be the first time in God knows how many years that we all are together. Maybe it'll lay a few ghosts to rest."

"You mean Michael?" Sophia could have bitten her tongue.

"Michael? No, I wasn't thinking of Michael. I know Filippo and his wife feel slighted that they don't play more of a part in the business, but with the wedding, no doubt Teresa will feel happier."

"I'm sure she will, but it's all been arranged in such a hurry. Is there a reason?"

"It's what Papa wanted."

"I see. And Papa always gets what he wants. Sometimes I feel sorry for Teresa."

"Why's that?"

"Filippo may be handsome, but he's still a child and behaves like one."

She caught sight of her husband's face in the wardrobe mirror, saw the flash of anger. He was always this way if she said a word against any member of his precious family. "Where is Don Roberto?" she asked.

He rolled off the bed. "Mama said he was caught up with some business in town. Should be home by f-f-five." He stuffed his hands in his pockets and frowned. "Something is going on. I've tried to c-contact Papa. He's selling off some of the companies; it doesn't make sense."

Sophia noted the stammer and watched him. He rarely discussed business with her, but she knew he had been worried lately. "Well, now is your chance to talk to him."

He nodded and changed the subject. "You think Mama looks okay?"

"Yes, why? Don't you?"

Before he could answer, they heard the sound of a car horn. Sophia went to the window.

"It's Filippo and Teresa. They almost ran into Mama's flowers."

Constantino said, "I'd b-better go down," but he stood there, his hands still deep in his pockets.

Sophia went to him and wrapped her arms around him. "Your mama is fine. She's maybe a little nervous. This is a big occasion, and she has a lot to think about."

He rested his head on the nape of her neck. "You always smell so good, you know that? Sometimes I look at you when you don't know I'm there, and I still can't believe you're mine."

She ran her fingers through his hair and cupped his face in her hands. "If you like, I'll wait up here for you, and I'll let my hair loose—"

He drew away as the car horn sounded again, loudly. "No, you'd better dress. Mama will want you downstairs."

He hurried out, and she heard him calling to his brother. From the bedroom window she watched as her sister-in-law, Teresa Luciano, climbed out of the Rolls-Royce. The driver was already unloading their pieces of ill-matched luggage.

Teresa called to her husband, but he paid no attention; he was running to greet Graziella. He had film star looks but didn't seem to care how he dressed; he wore a leather jacket and a T-shirt, and his hair was long. Sophia noticed that he wore a pair of high-heeled cowboy boots.

Filippo had lived in New York for years, hardly ever making the trip home, so it was no wonder his mother was so extravagantly pleased to see him. She was so overjoyed that she ignored Teresa and her granddaughter, the bride-to-be.

Rosa Luciano was still collecting her things from the back of the Rolls-Royce. The driver held the door open for her as she got out. Sophia was surprised at how attractive the girl had grown; it had been years since she had seen her. Rosa had inherited her father's dark eyes and black, curly hair.

Teresa was older than Filippo, and to Sophia's eyes she

looked more like a spinster schoolteacher than ever, her pinched face, sharp nose, and tight mouth accentuating her bad temper as she tried to organize the luggage and her daughter while waiting to be welcomed by Graziella. It amused Sophia to see how nervous her sister-in-law was as she made an embarrassed gesture toward her crumpled skirt and jacket.

"Aunt Sophia . . . Aunt Sophia . . ." Rosa Luciano rushed into the room. "Can I see my dress? Can I see it?"

Sophia moved quickly away from the window. "Can you wait until it's pressed? I want you to see it at its best. . . . You know, Rosa, you have grown into a beauty. Let me see you close."

Rosa beamed, then tossed her head. "Maybe you should wait until later, when the creases are out of me. We were delayed hours at the airport, and then Mama and Papa argued all the way because Papa insisted on driving, so Mama nearly had heart failure—"

Sophia kissed Rosa's lips. "When one is as young as you, and a bride-to-be, there are no creases. They come with age, my darling, and you are as pretty—"

Rosa hugged her tight. "Oh, Aunt Sophia, I am so happy I don't know what to do with myself. Look, have you seen my ring?"

Sophia made all the right noises as she examined the emerald and diamond ring. Rosa was to marry Don Roberto's nephew, a boy the same age as she, just twenty. Sophia knew he could not have afforded the ring; *il Papa*, the don himself, had bought it, as he had Sophia's engagement ring. She could tell at a glance that it was worth thousands.

Rosa threw herself on the bed. "You know, Aunt Sophia, sometimes I have to pinch myself to believe it's all really happening. Two months ago I didn't know Emilio existed. He came to New York on business for Grandpa and we met—it was love at first sight, he proposed to me on our second date. It was so romantic."

"Your mother must be very happy."

Rosa sat up and gave a lopsided grin. "Are you asking me or telling me? You'd think it was Mama getting married, she's made such a fuss. She's even started telling me the facts of life, keeps bringing me books on the reproductive organs, checking that my periods are regular. In the end I said, 'Mama, I'm getting married, not going into labor.' "

Just at that moment Teresa walked in. She pursed her lips.

"Shouldn't you unpack, Rosa? You must take everything you want pressed down to Adina in the kitchen."

Rosa jumped off the bed and winked at Sophia as she loped out of the room. Teresa sighed and crossed to Sophia; they kissed.

"She can never walk from a room, she's so clumsy. I hope you haven't made a dress with a long train; she'll trip over her feet."

Sophia laughed and assured Teresa that the dress would be perfect.

"Can I see it?" Teresa asked.

"Mama has decided that the women will spend the evening alone while the men go out. We can see the dress then."

Teresa pushed her thick glasses back to the bridge of her thin nose. "You look very fit, slim as ever. Are the boys well? I hear they spend a lot of time here. How is Constantino?"

"Well, very busy . . . And you?"

Teresa ignored the question and continued. "It's strange Don Roberto was not here to meet us. He usually is. Was he here when you arrived?"

"No, just Mama."

"She looks very well."

"Yes, I thought so, too,"

"But then, you see her more often than we do." Teresa's shortsighted eyes flicked around the room, noting everything, the clothes on their hangers, the neat array of shoes.

Sophia said, "I expect you'll see more of Mama now that Rosa is marrying. Will she live at the villa?"

Teresa smiled, unable to hide her pleasure. "Oh, I think so. Don Roberto treats him like a son." She was almost out of the door when she stopped and closed it. "It is not an arranged marriage. They are in love."

"Yes, Rosa told me."

Teresa had never been sure how many of the family knew the background to her own marriage. She had never known why the don had chosen her, but she had never argued. The first time she had set eyes on her handsome husband she had wanted him more than anything else in her life, except to conceive a son. Rosa was her only child, but with the forthcoming marriage she was confident that she and Filippo would no longer have to feel like poor relations.

"We are on the top floor," Teresa complained. "It's inconvenient what with having to help Rosa dress. I would have thought we'd have the room below yours, the big guest room."

"Mama put the boys in there. We can keep an eye on them, hear them if they wake in the night."

"Yes, she told me. Well, I'll unpack, not that it'll take me long. I see you have brought a veritable wardrobe. Perhaps if my suit is not good enough, you could lend me something?"

"You are welcome to choose anything—"

Teresa interrupted her curtly. "Thank you, but I'm sure what I've brought will suffice." She left the room.

Next to arrive was Emilio Luciano, the groom, his young face bright pink with nerves. Constantino leaped down the stairs two at a time and clasped his nephew-to-be in his arms. Filippo, with shaving cream on his face and wearing only his trousers, appeared at the top of the stairs and then, amazingly, glided down the banisters to land in the hall. The children attempted to emulate him by sliding, belly down, on the polished wooden rail.

Amid the congratulations, the backslapping, the shouting and teasing, Graziella stood bursting with happiness. These were her boys, her sons, her grandsons. She seemed unaware of the mayhem, of the fact that Filippo wore only his trousers; she just clapped her hands, hunching her shoulders coyly when one or another of her boys paid her an outrageous compliment.

"Who is this young woman? Where's our mama, eh? You telling me this beauty is our mama? How come you don't age, huh?"

As Graziella gestured ineffectually for them all to go into the living room, Rosa hurtled into Emilio's arms. They kissed, to a round of applause. In mock desperation Graziella brought out a gong, as she had done when the boys were little. She banged it, laughing, and one by one they drifted in.

Graziella served espresso, and once they all were settled and the initial excitement was over, she made an excuse to get more coffee.

"I'll do that, Grandmama."

"No, no, Rosa, I have to check on supper."

Graziella crossed the hall, but instead of going toward the kitchen, she entered the dining room. Alone, she let out a long, deep sigh; the tension of having to hide her feelings had exhausted her. She pushed the shutters open slightly and checked her watch. He should have been home by now. He had said no later than five, and it was already past that. The florists, the builders and decorators had all gone, the family had arrived, and still, there was no sign of him. He always phoned if he was even fifteen minutes late. Why hadn't he called today of all days?

The telephone rang shrilly, and Graziella gasped with shock. She hurried into the hall as Adina replaced the phone.

"It was a message for you, signora. Don Roberto should be home in a few moments. He tried to get through earlier, but someone must have been using the telephone."

Graziella crossed herself. "Thank you, Adina. Make some fresh coffee, and check that all the extensions are unplugged. Leave only the phones in the hall and the study connected."

Adina nodded. Something was very wrong. She had felt it in her mistress days before the arrival of the family. But she dared not ask; she could only pretend she was unaware of it.

Graziella joined her family, sitting together in the cozy living room. Smiling, she passed around cakes and pastries.

"This is the first time we are all at home together, so that is what we celebrate tonight, the family."

Constantino became aware of his mother's frequent glances at the gold carriage clock on the big mantel. She kept a small smile on her face, but her eyes betrayed her nervousness.

"Are you worried about something?" he whispered, kissing her hand.

"Your papa is late. Next thing I know, dinner will be ruined."

Filippo, eating a slice of cake, asked loudly, "Mama, what's with the army of guards out front of the house?"

Graziella ignored the question. "If you all wish to change, bathe, then we must come to some arrangement about the hot water. Sophia, you want to go first, see to the boys?"

Don Roberto Luciano's two sons looked at each other.

Something was definitely wrong. Constantino gave Sophia a small nod of his head to take the boys out; putting her half-full cup down, she called them and immediately left the room.

Filippo looked hard at Teresa. She frowned, not understanding.

"Take Rosa up to finish unpacking, will you?"

It was not a request. Teresa put her cup down and beckoned to Rosa to go with her. Filippo closed the doors behind them while Graziella fussed with the tea tray.

"Papa w-w-worried about this trial, Mama?" asked Constantino.

Graziella nodded.

"The papers in New York were full of it," Filippo said. "Mama, you okay?"

Graziella was close to tears. She wanted to tell them there and then but could not bring herself to go against her husband's wishes. Constantino placed his hand on his brother's shoulder as a signal not to question her further.

"Maybe we should talk about this with Papa. Mama must have a lot of things to do before dinner."

With a grateful look, Graziella excused herself and left her sons together. Constantino walked slowly to the great stone fireplace and leaned against the mantel.

Filippo shrugged. "So what was all that about? The way she acted I thought she wanted to talk to us—"

Constantino gave his brother a guarded look. "Emilio, you wanna do me a favor? My cigars, I left 'em in my room. Get 'em for me, would you?"

The young groom knew he was being asked to leave the brothers alone, and he obeyed without question.

Constantino stood up and drew the curtains aside, looked out at the drive, the guards on duty at the gate. "What's going on? You think this trial business's getting to the old man? There're more guards out there than at the National Bank."

"They get any of our guys?" asked Filippo.

Constantino snorted. "They got the rubbish, small-timers. Cages are filled to breaking point with every bum in Sicily. Nice way of cleaning up the garbage."

"Paul Carolla's no small fish."

Constantino dropped his easy manner. "Eh, you think I

don't know that? Word's out the bastard hired someone to hit the prison cleaner's nine-year-old kid. He put pressure on the guy, wanted him to take messages out; when he refused, his son's head was shot off. Did you read about it?"

Filippo shook his head no.

Constantino stared from the window, apparently in deep thought. "Papa organized this wedding in one hell of a hurry. Is there some reason? Rosa's not having a kid, is she?"

Filippo sprang to his feet, his face twisted with anger, but Constantino soothed him. "Take it easy. . . . But you've got to admit it's a bad time for a wedding, unless that's the intention. We're all here, all under one roof; maybe he knows something we don't. You taken a look out there? Papa's hired what looks like an army to guard us. Maybe he's worried. I know he was blazing about Lenny Cavataio. The whole trial's ground to a halt."

Filippo, calmer now, lit a cigarette. "Who's he?"

"Cavataio, used to deal in junk for Paul Carolla."

Filippo shrugged. He had never heard Cavataio's name. Constantino realized that the stories about his brother must be true; rumor had it that he was nothing but a front in New York, that their father had virtually maneuvered him out of the business. Now he wondered if the reason the marriage was taking place was that their father intended moving young Emilio up to look after New York. The wedding had been organized too fast. The question was why. But as always, the don had kept his plans to himself.

Constantino kicked at the grate, his hands stuffed deep in his trouser pockets. "Papa's sold two companies without even discussing it with me. . . . It has to have something to do with this Cavataio business."

Filippo was more confused than ever. "You still haven't told me about Cavataio."

"What've you got upstairs, a set of marbles? Lenny Cavataio was the guy who fed Michael the bad junk that killed him. Papa searched for him after Michael's murder. There was no trace of him, not till he surfaced in Atlantic City. Papa sent me over to get him."

Filippo waited impatiently while Constantino puffed a cigar alight.

"Lenny wanted to make a deal. He'd been hiding out in Canada for a decade, finally crawled out from the gutter to try and blackmail Carolla. He surfaced because he was broke, been pumping his veins full o' the shit himself. But Carolla wasn't taking any crap; he tried to get Lenny wiped out. Last thing Carolla wanted was old history raked up, especially as he'd got so high up in the organization. But Lenny was running scared, and he came to us. Cavataio came straight to the very people Carolla was desperate to keep him from."

He looked at Filippo, who sat, head bowed, his manner so defeated that Constantino couldn't help growing more expansive.

"I got him back here; let's say he was my gift to Papa. Lenny talked, understand? And at last we got the evidence that it was Carolla who'd instigated Michael's murder. Lenny was the last, the only, surviving witness. We needed him alive, because through him Papa knew he could really nail Carolla, not only for narcotics trading but for the murder."

Filippo still looked confused. Constantino paused, irritated. "You following me? This getting through? Carolla was going to be charged with Michael's murder. Lenny was singing his head off, not only about the murder but everything else to do with Carolla's rackets. The feds, the New York drug squad were on to Carolla, and the asshole ran right back to Palermo, hid in the mountains. . . ." He laughed, shaking his head. "Man, did he choose the wrong place, because he ran right into the arms of the law. They were hunting him like crazy dogs over here. When they've got through charging him here, they'll ship him back to the States. He's looking at one hundred years behind bars."

Filippo still didn't quite understand. "So why have they dropped the murder rap?"

Constantino shook his head at Filippo. "You don't have newspapers in New York? Lenny Cavataio was wiped out four months ago. He was found in a sleaze hotel here in Palermo with his balls cut off."

Filippo stared at the thick carpet, dug the toe of his cowboy boot into the pile. "You should have told me."

"You know how Papa works, Filippo, he likes to k-keep secrets."

Filippo sprang to his feet. "Secrets? Jesus Christ, secrets!"

"I only got to know because Lenny came to me in Atlantic City. Doesn't mean anything that you didn't know—"

"What do you take me for? We've all been living with Papa's obsession about Carolla, and you tell me it doesn't *mean* anything. . . . Jesus Christ. Why didn't you contact me, why? *Why didn't Papa contact me?* I had a right to know. This is family business—"

Constantino sighed. "I g-g-g-guess you know why. You been slack, Filippo. Your wife kept appearing at the company; she was handling certain contracts. Papa didn't like that."

"She's a *lawyer*! Teresa knows the import licenses better than me!" He sighed, knowing he had no comeback. "Ah, what the hell, I never wanted to be in New York. You think this kid Emilio's gonna take my place?"

His brother gave no answer.

Filippo was close to tears. "Papa never contacts me. He's been in New York and not even called to see me, and now this . . . No matter what I've done wrong, I should have been part of this Lenny business." He began to weep. "I remember, I remember that night when he told us . . . about Michael."

Filippo was referring to the night six weeks after Michael's death, when their father had discovered Constantino's intention of marrying Sophia. Constantino had begun to call on her without his father's permission and, while Don Roberto was away from home, had brought Sophia to the villa. None of them had been prepared for their father's rage.

His fury terrified them and centered on the fact that they had allowed a stranger, albeit a young girl, into the house. It was against the rules; no one outside the immediate family was ever allowed within the walls of the family home. The don's anger had become a tirade against his sons. Apparently out of control, he had ranted and raved until, finally, he had told them the truth about their adored elder brother, Michael.

The two brothers sat silent now, immersed in their memories of that night. Michael had been their hero, their champion, their shining example. He was not only athletic but academically brilliant, and to his father's pride he had won a coveted place at Harvard. But then he had, mysteriously, re-

turned home halfway through his second year. They had believed he was suffering from a virus. On the night of his return
he had collapsed and been rushed to the hospital. Weeks later
he was sent to the mountains to recuperate, but he never came
back. The virus, they had been told, had killed him.

He had been buried with a funeral befitting the eldest son
of a don. The grief had consumed them all and darkened the
house. Their mother had been bereft, and their beloved papa
had changed before their eyes. His head of thick black hair had
turned gray overnight; the lines of his face had deepened with
pain. But worst of all was his frightening silence. It had lasted
until the night they both remembered, the night he had released before them such anguish it had struck them dumb
with fear.

He had told them at last that Michael Luciano had been
murdered. The so-called virus was a heroin addiction, carefully
arranged by Paul Carolla because Don Roberto Luciano had
persistently refused to cooperate with him, refused to use his
legitimate export company as a cover. Luciano had told Constantino and Filippo that they were as vulnerable as Michael.
Michael was a warning.

The don had initiated his sons that night, teaching them
the codes of the Mafia. He had told them, without emotion,
how many had already paid the price for their involvement in
Michael's murder, had urged them to keep their brother's soul
alive in their hearts, never to forget the need to make his killers
pay. He had made them promise never to tell their mother what
had taken place that night or how her beloved firstborn son
had died.

In confirmation of their obedience, they had kissed the ring
worn by their father, the ring that Paul Carolla coveted. But
when he had drawn them into his arms, they had felt only
terror.

Filippo's shoulders shook as he wept. Constantino tried to
comfort him.

"Look, they got Carolla banged up on so many charges
the odds are stacked against him. He'll never get free. They'll
drop the murder rap against him, but in the end he's finished.
Maybe it'll let Michael's ghost rest in peace. I hope so be-

cause if you want the truth, I've had him on my shoulder too long."

"I thought I was the only one who felt like that, like I had to live up to him and I was never good enough. I thought it was just me. . . . You know, it got so bad I hated him."

Constantino opened the liquor cabinet and poured himself a whiskey. He downed it in one swallow. "I guess we both were in competition with him. Just take a look at the family album perched on the piano. You see me, Sophia, the kids; there's you, Teresa, Rosa . . . and there is Michael, always Michael, the biggest frame, the biggest photograph."

Filippo chuckled. Then his face lit up in a grin. "I used to put his photo at the back. Every day I did that. And every time back it would go, and there he was smiling at me, like he was saying, 'Fuck you, you don't get me out of your life that easily. . . .' "

Laughing, Constantino poured two whiskeys, and they clinked their glasses together. "To Michael, may he rest in peace and leave us in peace."

They drank, and Filippo threw his empty glass into the stone fireplace. Constantino followed suit. They both stared guiltily at the shattered glass.

"Holy shit, Mama's gonna hit the roof. That was her b-b-best crystal."

Paul Carolla was led into the small interview room. He went to the counter and pressed his hand against the bullet-proof glass partition. On the other side his son gave a slow smile that made him appear younger than his twenty-five years. Luka laid his hand flat against the glass, his long, fine fingers with their perfectly manicured nails tanned to a golden brown. Carolla's own stubby fingers and square palm rested against his son's. They both reached for the communicating phones.

Carolla was guarded day and night because his life had been threatened over the murder of the jail cleaner's child. Luka had arranged the hit, and Carolla had instructed him to leave Sicily lest anyone make the connection between them. Seeing him made Carolla shake with rage.

He looked at his two guards, then back to his son, and

whispered hoarsely into the mouthpiece, "I told you I want you out of Palermo."

"But I have something for you."

The sweat began to trickle down Carolla's face. "You get out and you stay out, you hear me, Luka?"

Luka held the phone loosely. The only indication that he had heard his father was a slight arching of one of his fine, almost invisible blond eyebrows.

When he spoke, his soft voice was a strange echolike whisper. "I know the name; I have the name; everything is going to be all right."

Puzzled, Carolla watched as Luka took out a pencil and wrote on a piece of paper. He looked up and smiled, then spoke into the mouthpiece again. "I got it for you. I had to pay ten million lira for it."

"What? What?" Sweat streamed down Carolla's face, and the hand holding the telephone was clammy. "You are fucking insane, you hear me?"

Luka's pale blue eyes narrowed, the pupils turning to pinpoints. He waved the scrap of paper and spoke in a singsong voice, "I have what you want, but you tell your man to pay me."

Carefully Luka straightened the piece of paper and laid it flat against the glass. In his strange, old-fashioned spidery writing he had scrawled the name of the witness for the prosecution.

Carolla's stomach lurched, and his bile rose. He tasted it as he retched uncontrollably, but his eyes were riveted on the name: his old enemy Don Roberto Luciano.

Don Roberto's driver radioed to the guards at the gates that they were arriving in minutes. The message was passed by walkie-talkies to the men on the roof, and the last part of the journey was closely monitored through field glasses.

The gates opened, and the gleaming black Mercedes headed toward the villa. The don sat between two bodyguards in the back, with his faithful driver up front.

The villa was ablaze with lights. As the car stopped, Don Roberto sat for a moment, waiting for the door to be opened. One of the bodyguards adjusted the cashmere coat to sit perfectly on the don's shoulders, then handed him his kid gloves and hat. He had been giving statements to Emanuel since ten o'clock that morning; it had been a grueling, painstaking day, a day when memories flooded back, old wounds opened, but he stood straight, inches taller than his bodyguards, and smiled. The front door opened as he walked up the white steps and onto the porch.

There was not one of them in the sprawling villa who did not know, could not sense the presence. Don Roberto Luciano was home.

# 2

Don Roberto's family were seated in the living room, awaiting his arrival. His sons, his daughters-in-law, his grandsons,
his granddaughter, his nephew—all sat and talked loudly among
themselves.

His appearance silenced them all. His sons rose to their
feet to shake his hand. He kissed each one and then welcomed
his daughters-in-law. He looked at Rosa and gave her a private
smile. "The beautiful bride, Rosa, and my nephew Emilio,
welcome." The two little grandsons stared up at him, openmouthed, and he cupped each face in his big, strong hands and
kissed them on the lips. "And last but not least, welcome to my
special boys."

Graziella lifted her glass in a toast. "To Papa . . ."

They toasted their papa and were surprised by his tears.
"You make me happy. It is good to have you all here. Now we
eat before Mama's food goes cold." He took out a clean handkerchief and blew his nose loudly.

The don had a private word to say to everyone, making
each feel special, while the wine flowed freely. By the time the

ice cream and sweets were served, the don had one grandson on his lap and the other on the arm of his chair, his small arm around his grandfather's shoulders.

Constantino watched his wife, Sophia, as she passed a dish along the table. She looked exquisite in a flamingo red dress, her thick black hair coiled in a bun at the nape of her neck. She was talking animatedly to Rosa, telling her how she had worked on the design of her wedding dress.

"I wanted it to be like a fairy tale. I used all my girls. Some of them should have been working in the shop, but I had to use everyone to get it ready in time. Nino, my designer, was furious, but I said, 'Rosa Luciano is going to be the most beautiful bride in Sicily.'"

Constantino nudged Filippo and whispered, "You know, I will never be able to repay you. After all, if it weren't for you, I would never have met my wife. Isn't she the most stunning woman in the world?"

Filippo, flushed with wine, looked at Sophia, who turned and smiled at him. He sighed, "Ah, if I had been just a few years older, I doubt that you would have stood a chance." Then he whispered to Constantino, "You want to trade? Anytime, any day."

Teresa pursed her lips suspiciously. "What did you say?"

"He wouldn't trade you any day," Sophia interjected, then exchanged grins with Filippo.

"Exaaactly!"

Nothing in Don Roberto's manner gave a hint of his intentions. He would inform his sons the following night, when the men dined alone together. They would know then that he was to be the major witness for the prosecution, then and not before. Tonight he wished to enjoy his family. He brought out his vintage brandy and a treasured box of Havana cigars.

The little boys began to tire, but would not leave their grandfather's side. They vied with each other for his attention, demanding stories.

Puffing on his cigar, the don began to tell them about an incident in his own childhood, when he was no older than Nunzio. He had climbed into an orchard and stolen two big rosy apples. He needed his hands free to climb back over the wall, so he stuffed the apples down the back of his pants.

"Well, there I was, half over the wall, when the farmer

caught me. He pulled at my boot. . . ." He made a face and
stuck out his bottom lip. "Caught you, you thieving little beggar!" He raised his eyes in a show of innocence. "Me, sir? I
have not taken anything. I was just looking over the wall at
your beautiful orchard and thinking to myself how nice it would
be to have one of your big rosy apples."

Constantino slipped his arm around his mother's shoulders. Everyone was listening as the don continued, spreading
his hands wide. "Look, sir, I haven't stolen anything. I'm innocent."

He blinked and gave a clownish grin. Constantino whispered to Graziella, "I have never seen him so relaxed. He never
told us stories."

Graziella patted her son's hand and looked up into his face,
saying very softly, "You forget. . . ."

" 'Well,' said the farmer, 'I am sorry. Now you be on your
way and count yourself lucky I didn't box your ears. Go on,
off with you.' So I began walking away from him, backward,
because if I turned around, he couldn't help seeing just where
I had hidden the apples. Then he called out, 'Wait a minute,
wait a minute!' and he reached into his basket for a big, *big*
apple, and held it out. Just as I reached for it, can you guess
what happened?"

Two little faces peered up at him, and two little heads
shook from side to side.

"Why, the two apples I had stolen fell to the ground and
rolled right up to his feet. He chased me down the lane, shaking his fist, and then can you guess what he did? No? He was
so angry that he threw the apples after me, and guess what
then? Later that night I went back and picked up the apples. I
was so pleased with myself that I ate them all, every one. And
*then* can you guess what happened? No? *No?*" He roared with
laughter. "*I got a bellyache!*"

Everyone rocked with laughter. Tears rolled down the
children's cheeks. When they finally subsided, Don Roberto gave
his wife a private, intimate look. Their house burst with life
and energy, and it felt so safe. He knew he was right not to tell
them, not tonight.

The following morning the Villa Rivera reverberated with
the sounds of the family. Gifts for the bride and groom were

being stacked in the living room as they arrived, a profusion of wedding bells and horseshoes, but only the don and his wife knew that each one had been carefully inspected and rewrapped before being brought into the house. Only they knew why, as the family gathered for breakfast, every door was guarded. There were men on the roof, men in the orchards and in the stables, and more checked everyone who entered or left the premises against the list of staff hired to complete the wedding arrangements.

The same tight security enabled the prosecuting counsel, Giuliano Emanuel, to feel secure in his own house. He was still tired from the previous night, having worked late over the Luciano tapes in the privacy of his own home. It was after ten o'clock when he drove to work, where security was even more in evidence. It was a considerable time before he could enter his own office, but he could not complain as the guards checked his identity papers. He was the one who had instigated the security measures. He had told Mario Domino the day after their meeting in the restaurant that he had arranged to have fifteen guards allocated to the Luciano household. The don and his family would be protected as requested.

Closing his office door, he tossed his briefcase on the desk. He and Roberto Luciano had been working together for almost eight days, recording the don's statements. Luciano had asked for a weekend break, to be with his family. Emanuel agreed; he needed the time to write up all his notes.

The past eight days had been exhausting; the precautions that had had to be taken to keep the don's identity secret and to ensure his safety bordered on the obsessive. Every meeting place was guarded; cars were changed, locations switched at the last moment. Even finding safe houses had proved a nightmare. And all the tapes had to be transcribed before they went into court.

Emanuel had also prepared a list of problems arising from the statements. Don Roberto would take the stand as soon as the adjournment was over. Emanuel had let it be known that he had a powerful new witness for the prosecution, but he was confident that no one could discover the don's identity.

Emanuel pulled the tape recorder closer and loaded Tape 4 from the last session. The volume was too high, distorting the don's voice, and he turned it down. Then he opened his notebook and switched on his word processor.

The statements went back as far as twenty years, to the death of Michael Luciano. Although he had listened to the man for days on end, the don's voice impressed him with its strength and clarity, his choice of words. He never rambled; he was concise, meticulous about dates and facts, and when he mentioned a name, he spelled it out carefully so there could never be any confusion. Rarely was there any hesitation, and then only when Luciano, aware of implications against himself, sidestepped issues that would entail naming names he did not wish to disclose.

Emanuel typed onto the screen: "Roberto Luciano, Statement 3, Tape 4. February 12, 1987." He worked solidly until after twelve, rewinding the tape when he wanted to confirm or query something Luciano had said, continually cross-referencing and checking against statements he had already compiled from previous days. He tapped the "Execute" key, tapped again; the screen had locked out. He could neither execute nor exit from the program.

Suddenly the screen flashed: "Power failure." He sat in mute fury, refusing to believe the hated words, desperately wishing them away because against all instructions, he had not backed up his disks or saved the changes he had made. The only thing he could do was shut down the system to clear the hang-up; all the work he had just done would be lost.

Swearing at his own stupidity, he reached for the switch as the telephone rang. The bell cut through his anger, startling him. As he reached for it, he knocked over a mug of cold coffee from the night before. In trying to save it from falling to the floor, he dropped the telephone receiver. It smashed against the side of his desk.

He could hear his wife's voice from the dangling phone, asking if he was all right. Yelling for her to hold on, he picked up the mug, then grasped the telephone cord to pull the receiver up. The curly flex hooked on the edge of his desk, and he swore yet again as he ran his fingers along the desk to release it. Suddenly he reacted as if he had been given an electric shock. He pulled his hand back.

His wife was shouting, "Hello? You there? Hello?"

Emanuel quickly picked up the receiver. "I'll call you back.
. . . No, I'm fine, nothing's wrong. I'll call you later."

*Nothing wrong? Jesus Christ* . . . He slammed the phone
down and felt along the side of the desk, heart thudding. He
trembled as he touched it again; he knew exactly what it was.
He ran to the door and yanked it open.

The guards were at the far end of the corridor, holding a
whispered conversation.

"Get in here! Move it!" Emanuel yelled.

His office was bugged. How it had been done was immaterial; the most important thing was when. How much of the
Luciano tapes, his own phone calls, had been recorded? His
face white with fury, nerves on edge, he stared at the word
processor. Could someone have tampered with it? Even worse,
accessed his disks?

Sophia and Teresa were in the hall of the Villa Rivera,
waiting for Graziella. They were going to do some last-minute
shopping. Rosa, who had refused the invitation, was sitting in
the garden with Emilio.

As the car left the villa, Teresa was close to tears. There
was the ornate marquee, the drive bedecked with flowers, all
given an air of fantasy in the brilliant sunshine.

Sophia felt it too, and clasped Teresa's hand, turning back
to smile at Rosa. Only then did she see the car moving into
position behind theirs. She didn't realize that they were being
followed until they had left the villa and passed the guards on
duty at the gates. All Graziella would say to their questions
was that it was what Papa wanted, that the extra hands could
be useful for carrying their purchases.

"They had a guard sitting up front with the driver, and
then another car trailing them with two more guys. Okay, so
Papa's uptight about the trial, but they're all around the place.
It's like Fort Knox."

Constantino shrugged. Like Filippo, he had been very aware
of the security measures.

They could not discuss it further as their father appeared.
To his sons' astonishment he was wearing a pair of carpet
slippers.

"Filippo's discovered that old motorbike of his," Constantino told his father. "Do you know, he's got that engine turning over! It was rusty, not been used for ten years, but he's fixed it."

The don sat down in the wicker bucket chair; his long legs stretched out. "I was never very good on the mechanical side. You remember that time I tried to repair your mama's spin dryer? Her best linen tablecloth was spun into shreds." He laughed, shaking his head.

Filippo nudged his brother to broach the subject of the guards. Constantino opened his mouth to ask.

Don Roberto leaned on the rail of the veranda and spoke as if talking to himself. "Strange, during the war I worked in the bomb disposal unit, yet I ruined Mama's tablecloth. They taught me to blow men apart, to destroy buildings, defuse bombs, but I couldn't fix a spin dryer. . . ."

His voice trailed off. Neither of his sons remembered the incident, but he seemed almost unaware of their presence. The days spent recalling the past with Emanuel had made him remember things he had long forgotten. Now he could hear a child's voice calling him: Michael's voice, no older than his grandsons'.

"Papa, Papa . . ." The don could see the white blond hair, the brilliant blue eyes peering at him over the veranda. "Papa, Papa, come for a ride with me, ride with me! Look, it's my very own bicycle!"

"You want a ride on my bike, **Papa**?"

Filippo didn't dream that his father would agree but asked as if it were a dare, not really caring one way or the other. When the don did agree, he became protective, suggesting that perhaps his father should just watch. But nothing would dissuade the don. Lifting his leg, he positioned himself awkwardly on the pillion. "You think I'm too old? I ever tell you about the time Michael and I rode into town on his Lambretta?"

He saw the way Filippo's face changed as he turned away and snapped, "I am not Michael, Papa, and this is a motorbike. You want a ride or not?"

Gently the don put his arms around his son's waist. "You take care for me, now. . . ."

Around and around the garden went the old Harley. Their

papa, his hair standing on end, clung to Filippo, yelling with sheer enjoyment, waving as they passed the veranda for the third time. "This is wonderful! It's wonderful!"

At four-thirty in the afternoon the women returned from the town to find Constantino sitting on the veranda while Filippo played tennis on the lawn with the two little boys and their grandfather. Graziella noticed that one of her beribboned floral arrangements looked very bedraggled, with telltale loose soil around the base, but she said nothing.

Nunzio saw his grandmother and ran to the veranda steps. "Grandpa's been on the motorbike, Grandmama—and he fell off!"

Graziella gasped, and Constantino laughed. "He's fine, Mama. . . ."

Don Roberto called the boy back and demonstrated a service, scattering balls all over the lawn. It was all so relaxed that one of the guards had been cajoled into acting as ball boy. The don tapped Filippo on the head with his racket and called to Graziella, "You know, this boy is a brilliant mechanic. He repaired that old motorbike!"

Filippo twisted his racket, tossed it in the air, then caught it by the handle. He saw the name on the side, "Michael Luciano," just as his father put an arm around his shoulder.

"You don't tell Mama about racing those bikes, that a deal? But the next race you get me a seat, okay?" He looked closely into his son's face and pinched his cheek. "Is it a deal?"

They shook hands. Then Don Roberto pulled his son into his arms. "I love you. . . . Maybe I've been too hard on you, but we'll work it out. You are my son."

Filippo could not remember ever feeling happier.

It was almost six o'clock. The men were dressing to go out to dinner. The women, who were staying home, sat together sorting out the wedding gifts. They had decided to display them on the dining-room table.

Sophia had fussed over the wedding dress, nervous that Rosa would not like it. It was ready to be tried on but was still shrouded in white sheets.

Bathroom doors banged; their husbands called to each other.

The more the brothers were together, the noisier and more boisterous they became, behaving like young boys, reverting to shouting nicknames and joking.

Graziella smiled at her immaculately dressed husband as she carefully tied his bow tie. "You'll tell them tonight?"

"Yes, tonight."

She held him in her arms. "I feel it, the house open-ing. . . . Having everyone here has done it, even using Michael's room. We should have filled the house before this. . . . It's over, I know it. It is over, isn't it?"

He kissed the top of her head, which smelled of the sweet violet perfume he always bought her. "I feel it, too, Mama."

She patted the lapel of his dinner jacket into place, even though it sat perfectly. "You have been wonderful with the boys, especially Filippo. He loves you so. They all do, and maybe what you've decided has made you feel free to show your love."

"It is time Michael rested in peace. Maybe they won't love me too much once they know of my decision." There was a hardness to his face.

Her throat felt dry, and she blinked back her tears. "They were his brothers. They'll understand. And they will stand by your decision, as I do."

"They have no option." Gently he cupped her chin in his hand. "Don't be afraid, Mama, and don't tell the women, not yet. Let their men, my sons, tell them. That is the way it should be."

Graziella called to the women that the men were about to leave. Chattering and laughing, they waved casual good-byes, in a way anxious for the men to be gone so they could unveil the wedding gown.

Rosa, wearing a robe, blew Emilio a kiss from the landing. He was about to run to her when Filippo grabbed him.

"Don't you know it's unlucky to see the bride half naked before the ceremony?"

"I'm not, I'm not!" shrieked Rosa. She rushed to Emilio and flung her arms around him. Barefoot, her hair hanging loose and her face flushed with happiness, she kissed his crimson cheeks.

He looked fearfully toward Don Roberto, but the don was

admiring Filippo's rather flamboyant dinner jacket. Turning, leaving his arm around his son's shoulder, he called to his grandsons, who peeked through the banister rails. "Sweet dreams, little ones! Now, is everybody ready? My sons ready? Come, we'll leave the women in peace."

Seeing his sons still at the top of the stairs, dressed in matching pajamas and with their faces scrubbed, Constantino could not resist. He leaped up the stairs two at a time, clasped them in his arms, kissed them both good night, and made them promise to be good.

Filippo called from the porch that the car was waiting, and Constantino hurried out. He was the last to leave the villa.

Sophia took Rosa upstairs to try on the gown while Teresa unwrapped the gifts and put them on display in the dining room. Graziella settled the two boys into the big double bed, tucking the sheets around them and listening to their prayers.

The evening was warm, and she left the shutters open slightly, noticing as she did so that the guards were gathering at the gates. She checked her watch. It was eight-fifteen; they were not due to change over until after ten o'clock.

Rosa's excited voice called out that she was ready. Teresa and Graziella hurried to the hall and waited for Rosa to come down the stairs.

Sophia ran down ahead and confided, "I think she likes her dress!" Then she called up to Rosa, "We're waiting, Rosa!"

Slowly Rosa walked to the top of the stairs. The waiting women gasped. The bodice was low-cut with a wide, scooped neck, the long, tight sleeves reached a point at her wrists, and her tiny waist was emphasized by tight lacing and a full, hooped skirt. The deeply ruffled hem was cut slightly higher at the front, trailed on the floor at the back. The cream satin fabric shimmered with thousands of tiny seed pearls stitched into a daisy pattern; a daisy headdress supported the veil. It was a fairy-tale gown.

Brimming with happiness, Rosa came down the stairs. The skirt swayed, moving with her; there would be no problems with the train.

She lifted her hands to her flushed cheeks. "Oh, Mama, I feel so good."

*    *    *

Emanuel insisted that his wife and little daughter leave Palermo that night under top security; he had arranged accommodation for them in Rome.

His office was swarming with police officers trying to discover how the bug had been planted despite the tight security net. They began to sift carefully through the records of every police officer who had been on duty in the past few weeks. Emanuel had given orders that they all be suspended from duty and a new team put on the case.

Emanuel took the head of the security force aside. Since his prize witness's identity was now known, it was obvious the don was in great danger. Emanuel insisted that every guard assigned to Luciano be checked thoroughly and, if necessary, replaced that same evening.

Satisfied for the time being that he had done everything humanly possible, he returned to calm his hysterical wife and to assure her that she and her daughter would be safe. He wished he could believe it.

It was after nine that evening when Emanuel received a detailed list of the men allocated to protecting Roberto Luciano. They all were trusted men, but the extra guards brought in by the don could not be vouched for. Emanuel had already emphasized the dangers of discussing the situation with anyone but the don. He would speak to Luciano personally, and together, they would come to some decision about the protection of him and his family.

Three times he called the villa and spoke to Graziella, who at first refused to tell him the name of the restaurant the men had gone to, even though she knew who he was. He kept his voice as calm as he could, while he told her that it was a matter of grave urgency that he contact the don personally.

When he finally obtained the number of the San Lorenzo restaurant, the line was constantly busy. Frustrated, he decided that the safest, to his mind the only, choice left to him was to go speak to Luciano in person. By this time it was ten-fifteen.

The don had chosen his favorite restaurant for two reasons. He was, in fact, the owner and knew the staff; he also knew that the private upstairs room was easy to guard. The main part of the restaurant was closed for the night, and the doors would be locked after their arrival.

Don Luciano had ordered that only a skeleton staff be on duty. The bodyguards would eat downstairs, and the drivers were to return for them at twelve-fifteen. They were not to wait outside because the cars were well known.

The men did not enter the private dining room until the bodyguards had searched it carefully. They sat down to dine at nine o'clock.

Emanuel had a long drive ahead of him, but after only ten miles one of his back tires blew out. The car careened out of control, and Emanuel fought it onto the hard shoulder. His hands shook, and he had to sit and calm himself. He was convinced someone had taken a shot at him.

His heart beating fast, he eased the door open. His mouth was dry, his breathing heavy. Then he sighed with relief. It was just a tire.

Graziella carried the tray into the living room and said she would go up to see the children, but Sophia told her it was not necessary. If they were still awake, the women would certainly have heard them.

Graziella sat down and sipped her coffee, but she could not join in the banter about who was wearing what for the wedding. She went over and over her conversation with Emanuel. Why was it so urgent? Then she pushed it from her mind. She was tired; it had been a full day, and tomorrow would be even busier. The caterers were due at seven in the morning. She wanted to be there to greet them and oversee all that had to be done.

The clock on the landing chimed again and Graziella checked her watch, then collected the coffee cups and stacked them on the tray. Sophia told her to sit down and relax, offering to clear up, but Graziella insisted.

It was past eleven. Adina took the tray from her mistress and told her that the don's driver had left, so the men would be returning shortly. She offered to put a fresh pot of coffee on the stove, but Graziella shook her head. She doubted if they would want to stay up late. She told Adina to go to bed after she had tidied the kitchen, then gave a little smile and put her finger to her lips. She was just going to peek in on the children.

At fifteen minutes past eleven a truck driver stopped to help Emanuel. They eased the ruined tire off the car and examined the spare by flashlight. It looked very flat.

Quietly Graziella opened the door of the children's bedroom. The boys lay facing each other, Nunzio's arm resting protectively across his brother. They looked so tiny in the big double bed, so peaceful and innocent that she couldn't help smiling.

She was about to close the door again when she heard a sound as if a slate were falling from the roof. She crept to the window and found that the shutter was open wider than she had left it. She glanced across the lawn toward the main gate.

In the darkness she could see the tips of the guards' cigarettes like small, glowing dots. They were waiting for the don's return. As she closed the shutter, the latch banged, and she caught her breath, afraid she had wakened the boys. She turned toward the bed.

Neither child had stirred; they lay in exactly the same position. In the dim light she could see a dark area on the pillow between their heads. Puzzled, she moved closer, until she was standing over the little boys.

The dark stain was seeping into the pillow, between their faces. Her lips formed a scream, but no sound was released. As if in slow motion her hand reached out. . . .

Rosa was at the open living-room door when the terrible scream tore through the house. She was the first to see the stricken, terrified face of her grandmother, eyes wide with horror, at the top of the stairs.

Sophia pushed past Rosa and was halfway up the stairs before the girl could move.

"Mama, *Mama, what is it?*"

Graziella dragged at Sophia's arm, trying to stop her, pleading, sobbing for her not to go into the room. Teresa ran into the hall and up the stairs. Rosa hung back, shaking. Sophia pushed Graziella aside and entered the room.

"What is it, Mama? What is it?" Teresa was trying to follow Sophia when the awful, low moan erupted into a high-pitched shriek: *"My babiessss!"*

Sophia lay across the bed, the limp bodies of her sons beneath her. They each had been shot in the temple, and the killer had turned their little faces toward each other to hide the bullet wounds, had even slipped Nunzio's arm around his brother.

The blood matted their hair, drenching their mother as she sobbed uncontrollably, willing them to be alive, shaking them, fighting Graziella away. She would let no one near her, let no one touch her.

The guards, hearing the screams, were running down the path. One man, on the roof, was sliding, skidding down the slates. The men banged on the front door of the villa as more guards converged on the house and the men at the gates turned on their high-powered flashlights.

The garage mechanic watched the air gauge, bent down to feel the tire. Satisfied, he began to unscrew the pump. Emanuel paced up and down, checked his watch. It was almost eleven-thirty.

The don's driver banged on the restaurant door. He could hear a recording of Pavarotti singing Puccini's *Turandot*. He stepped back to look up at the brightly lit second-floor windows.

The second driver arrived and waited while the first knocked again. They knew something was wrong; one of the bodyguards should have opened the door by now.

The back door of the restaurant was locked. Lights streamed from the kitchen windows. The Pavarotti tape continued, seeming even louder as panic rose in the two men. They kicked at the main door, then fired shots into the lock until it gave way.

The door swung open. Nothing in the empty restaurant seemed out of order; the checked tablecloths and the cutlery were ready for the next day. No chairs were overturned; nothing was disturbed. But there were no bodyguards, no staff.

The drivers stood together with guns drawn. The first man inched toward the door marked "Kitchen." It swung back and forth on its hinges as he kicked it.

Pans of sauce had been drawn off the still-lit burners as if the chef had left them for a moment. Dirty dishes were stacked in a large stone sink, and black refuse bags were half filled, as if someone had been in the process of clearing the rubbish. It seemed that any moment the chef would walk in, brandishing a wooden spoon and singing along with Pavarotti, whose recorded voice still echoed around the kitchen. The two men's panic grew with every second. The back door was bolted and barred from the inside. The pantry was empty. The cellar was empty.

Emanuel inserted the coin. At last there was a ringing tone. His fingers drummed on the window of the phone booth, willing someone to answer. He waited.

As the two drivers came up from the cellar, the telephone was ringing, but it stopped before they reached it. One behind the other, they made their way up the narrow staircase. The beaded curtain clicked as they pulled it aside.

Emanuel pounded the side of the kiosk with his fist. Unable to get an answer from the restaurant, he had again tried to reach Luciano at the Villa Rivera, but the line was busy. Frustrated, he ran to the car and drove out of the garage, heading for the San Lorenzo restaurant.

The Pavarotti tape ended as they reached the door of the private dining room. The door was locked from the outside with an old iron catch. The men stood shoulder to shoulder as they inched the latch up, eased the bolt back. They waited a beat, and then, with a small nod of confirmation, they were ready.

Guns drawn, they kicked the heavy oak door. It creaked, swung open, then started to close. The first man pushed with his shoulder, his breath hissing. Then he whispered, "Oh, sweet Jesus. . ."

The dining room was lit by two candelabra on the table and dimmed electric candles around the walls. The red velvet curtains matched the dark red carpet. Permeating the room was the pungent smell of garlic and almonds. The heavy high-backed oak chairs threw shadows on the rough white walls and on the men still seated in them. Facing the guards as they entered was a terrible, frozen tableau.

Don Roberto Luciano, at the head of the table, was slumped slightly to one side, his body propped up by the wings of the chair, his hand clutching an upright glass of wine. His lips were drawn back in a grimace. On his right, Constantino was sitting well back in his chair, his head turned as if he were speaking to his father, but both his hands were frozen in a clawlike grip on the table edge. Vomit glistened on his chin, over his black silk-lapeled jacket.

On the don's left, Filippo had fallen across the table, his red wine staining the white cloth, mingling with his vomit.

The young bridegroom, Emilio, had managed to rise from the table before he died, his face contorted with agony. He had fallen forward and slipped to his knees. His glass of wine lay smashed at his feet. One hand still grasped at the tablecloth.

The don's driver forced himself to check each body. He knew they were dead, but he made himself do it before he broke down, sobbing.

Mario Domino arrived at the restaurant at the same time as the police. Sitting in his car, the door wide open, was Giuliano Emanuel, his face ashen. He had called Domino, but now as Domino approached him, Emanuel had to lick his lips before he could speak.

The two men made their way up the narrow staircase, Domino leading the way. The bodies awaited the arrival of the medics and forensic officers, so the tableau remained intact. Domino bowed his head and sank to his knees. He would remember afterward how everyone there followed him, how, to a man, they knelt in prayer.

Luciano, in death as in life, was a powerful sight. His open eyes seemed to blaze with a terrible anger, as if his twisted mouth were about to scream the name of his killer. Domino looked from his beloved don to the faces of his sons; the stench of their vomit, mixed with the garlic and the sinister sweet smell of almonds, forced him to cover his face with his handkerchief. He turned and hurried away, knowing he had to be the one to tell Graziella.

As Domino approached the villa, he could see police patrol cars surrounding it. Lights blazed from every window. He put on speed, afraid someone had told Graziella the tragic news before him.

When Domino learned from the police about Luciano's grandsons, the shock was too much for him, and he broke down. How could he tell her there was even more death?

The ambulance doors were open, and two tiny figures on stretchers, covered with sheets, were being carried from the house.

Domino walked into the house without being stopped or questioned. He stood in the brightly lit hall; every room seemed filled with men, every door stood wide open. Totally disoriented, he looked helplessly for a face he recognized and was relieved to see the don's physician walking slowly down the stairs.

The man's face was gray. Seeing Domino, he gave a sad shake of his head. "Why?" he said quietly. "Who could do such a thing?"

Domino took his arm and drew him to one side. "You'd better stay. They'll need you. Where is Graziella?"

"Mario." It was Graziella's voice.

Domino turned to see her standing halfway up the staircase. He held the doctor's arm a moment before going to the foot of the stairs. "I have to speak with you alone."

She walked down the last few steps. Domino held his hand out for her, and she clasped it tightly, giving such a sweet, sad smile that it broke his heart.

"Thank you for coming. I need you here. But I want everyone else to leave before Roberto gets home. There is no answer from the restaurant. I've tried to call so many times—"

They went into the don's study, and she closed the door behind them. He was at a loss how to begin.

Graziella went on. "They went to dine together, you see. He was going to tell them about his decision; he wanted to speak with them alone. Oh, God, Mario, . . . the little boys are dead."

Her eyes were blank with shock and so pale it was as if the color had been drained from them.

"Graziella . . ." His whisper was strained, barely audible. "There is more. . . . So help me God, I don't know how to tell you."

She looked at him, so distressed that only now did she really see him. She saw his fear.

"More?" she said.

He nodded, and his face twisted as he tried to stem the flow of his tears as they streamed down his face.

Her voice was like steel, loud, harsh. "Look at me, tell me. . . . *Tell me!*"

He gripped the back of a chair, and with his head bowed, his eyes closed, he told her. He fought hard to control his own emotions to enable himself to comfort her, but it was she who gently patted his arm. Her hand felt feather-light.

He turned to take her in his arms, but she stepped back. She gave a strange sigh, then patted her chest as if her hand registered her heartbeat. He had no words of comfort; there were no words. He stood in wretched misery.

Slowly she walked behind the don's desk, stood staring at the row of photographs. To Mario's consternation she sat down, almost businesslike, and picked up a pen, pulled a piece of paper forward, and began to write. She wrote quickly, covering the entire page, then calmly reread what she had written before handing it to him.

"Would you please contact everyone on this list? The marquee must be taken down."

"Graziella—"

"No, please listen to me. I want the flowers taken away, the caterers and the guests informed. No one must come to the villa. Tell the guards; then ask everyone to leave. We must be left alone, do you understand? We must be alone."

Domino was in awe of Graziella's self-control. It was her decision to tell each woman separately; she asked only that the doctor accompany her.

She chose to see Rosa first, sat holding her hand while the doctor sedated the shocked, hysterical girl. The wedding dress was still hanging on the wardrobe door, and Graziella was the one who removed it; but Rosa would not let go of the veil. She clung to it tightly, even when she finally slept.

Teresa repeated her husband's name. The terrible confusion of trying to accept not only the deaths of the children but of all the men was beyond her. She smoothed her skirt constantly, chewed her lips, whispering, "I don't understand, I don't understand . . ." She looked past the doctor to the waiting, silent Graziella.

"There'll be no wedding, no wedding?" her eyes, behind

the thick-rimmed glasses, were magnified like a china doll's, blank eyes that slowly, as Graziella waited, began to register. . . . As the facts hammered at her dulled senses, her breath caught in her throat, then quickened until she was gasping. Her eyes blinked rapidly, and at last, she wept. She asked, after a while, to be left alone.

The doctor warned Graziella to take care, that she must rest, but she went across the landing to Sophia's room and inched open the door. Sophia was sleeping, facedown, her arms splayed out, one hand dangling over the side of the bed. Graziella closed the door softly.

"Doctor, please leave some tranquilizers, in case my daughters need further sedation. I shall administer them, I shall take care of them. Good night, Doctor, thank you for being here. You, too, Mario. Good night."

Domino watched the taillights of the doctor's car going down the drive. Then he slowly pulled on his coat. There was nothing more he could do for Graziella tonight. He stood forlornly in the empty hallway for a few minutes, then let himself out. But he couldn't leave; he sat on the stone steps, head in hands, and wept.

Rosa remained deeply asleep. Teresa was grateful; her own sense of loss was too much to share. She wanted nothing but to lie in a dark room, alone.

Graziella persuaded Teresa to sip a little brandy. She had still not told Sophia, although she knew she was now awake. She had seen the light beneath her door.

For Sophia she had to steel herself, clench her hands until the nails cut into the palms. . . .

Sophia was sitting at the dressing table, her long dark hair hanging almost to her waist, her hands folded in her lap. The aftereffect of the tranquilizers made her feel woozy. Her eyes were heavy-lidded, slightly puffy from weeping. Her lips moved soundlessly, as if she were whispering to herself or praying. She did not turn when Graziella entered the room and stood quietly behind her. She did not even acknowledge Graziella's hands on her shoulders.

Graziella reached over and picked up the silver-backed hairbrush, began to stroke the thick, silky hair. A few strands crackled with static, and Sophia closed her eyes.

"Mama, tell me it is a nightmare. Tell me that any moment I will wake up and it will all be over."

Graziella continued the long, slow strokes. Suddenly Sophia turned sharply and gripped her mother-in-law's wrist. "Where are they? Why aren't they here? Where is Constantino?"

When she was told, Sophia began to wail, and her wails echoed and hung on the air as grief itself.

The shutters were closed, the curtains drawn. The workmen came and went until there was no trace left of the wedding preparations. The gifts were repacked in their boxes; the cards and telegrams that arrived were stopped at the gates. The ornate, brilliantly colored floral displays were thrown onto the rubbish heap, but the fallen petals remained to blow about in the cool night breeze and brown to a crisp in the heat of the day.

The Villa Rivera was shrouded. Like animals caged, the press gathered at the wrought-iron gates, hands clasping at the bars, but they remained closed.

Graziella insisted that she alone identify the dead. Wearing mourning, a veil covering her face, she clung to Mario Domino's arm as he guided her through the groups of camera-flashing photographers. Scuffles broke out as the carabinieri pushed the photographers out of the way.

As soon as they entered the morgue, Graziella withdrew her hand, determined to stand alone. Silently she allowed Domino to walk ahead, following the white-coated policemen along corridor after chilling corridor. They entered the white-tiled cold room.

The mortician's hands, encased in fine yellowish rubber gloves, slowly withdrew each cover, lifting each just enough for Graziella to view the face. She moved from corpse to corpse, crossing herself and calling each one by name, the only words she spoke. She made no attempt to touch the bodies.

"Roberto Luciano . . . Constantino Luciano . . . Filippo

Luciano . . . Emilio Luciano . . . Carlo Luciano . . . Nunzio Luciano . . ."

Then Graziella once again took Domino's arm, and he helped her back to the Mercedes; but she refused his offer to accompany her to the villa. As he closed the door carefully, a feeling of helpless inadequacy again consumed him.

Slowly her window slid down. Her face was a shadow behind the veil.

"I will bury my dead. There is not one Luciano left alive, and I want everyone in Sicily to know, to demand justice. You will arrange for me to meet Giuliano Emanuel. You are to tell him he has a new witness for the prosecution, do you understand? *Grazie*, Mario, *grazie*. . . ."

She raised her black-gloved hand a fraction to indicate that she wished to leave. Before he could say a word, the window closed, the car drew away from the sidewalk, and she was gone.

# 3

Hours after the Luciano murders were discovered, the bodies of the chef and one of the waiters were found. They had been bound and shot with a Heckler & Koch P7M8 pistol, the sign of a professional gunman. The bodies of the don's guards were not discovered for another week. The stench of rotting flesh led the carabinieri to a well twenty yards from the restaurant. They had been shot with the same gun. The second waiter had disappeared without trace.

Cyanide was the cause of the Luciano deaths. There were traces of it in every dish they had eaten and even in the wine.

As the investigation continued, it was calculated that three or possibly four men were involved. Casts of footprints were taken from the damp earth around the well. Fingerprint experts began assessing the hundreds of prints taken from the restaurant. A week after the assassinations there were no suspects.

Luka Carolla traveled by train to the northwestern tip of Sicily, sixty miles west of Palermo. He was heading for the walled town of Erice, which rises half a mile above sea level, a virtual citadel, looking out over the Egadi Islands with a clear view to Tunisia and the North African coast.

The walk from the station was long, and the steep, recklessly curved road was deserted. He had chosen to arrive so that he made the climb in the cool of the evening. He carried a small overnight bag and a long, thin leather case. His shoes were scuffed and white with dust. He had removed his jacket and slung it over his shoulder, but his straw hat made his head sweat, soaking his white blond hair and dripping on his shirt. The heat was exhausting, and his mouth was dry; but when a donkey cart passed him, he made no attempt to obtain a lift.

He kept climbing, higher and higher, until he came to the Chiesa Matrica, the small church of the Mother of God. He gave a small bow of his head as he passed. Continuing along the narrow cobbled lanes, he reached the rough track he knew so well. It was not far now, perhaps another two miles.

The sky darkened. The heat gave way to a cool, light breeze from the sea. Luka took out a handkerchief and dusted his shoes, then put his jacket on. Soon he could see thick, hand-built walls with dark green moss between the stones, and he knew that he would soon reach the high monastery gates.

He was not expected, yet he knew that he would not be turned away. The heavy iron ring and old, frayed bell rope were exactly as he remembered them, and he could hear the bell ringing in the courtyard. He knew it would take a few moments before anyone could reach the door and open the small, carved peephole.

Father Angelo was painfully incapacitated by arthritis, but when he was told Luka Carolla was at the gate, he was so eager to see the boy he forgot to use his walker.

Father Angelo wrapped the boy in his arms, weeping with pleasure, making him so welcome that Luka himself was close to tears. Brother Guido, a monk Luka did not recognize, hurried to assist the father. He bent to pick up Luka's bag and was taken aback when it was snatched from his hands. Luka apologized quickly, explaining that the bag was light and he could carry it himself. He never let the long, narrow case leave his grasp.

Brother Guido took Father Angelo's arm, and the three walked slowly across the courtyard into the cool stone corridor.

The father's slow, shuffling steps halted, and he patted Luka's arm. "You shall have your old room, remember it?"

"Yes, Father, I remember it." Luka replied in English.

"They closed the orphanage, did you know? Did I write that to you?"

"Yes, Father, you did. Would it be okay if I stayed a coupla days?"

"My, my, Luka, you are American now."

Father Angelo's sandals made a familiar shushing sound on the flagstones as he leaned heavily on Brother Guido. He seemed frail to Luka; his flesh hung on his bones, and small tufts of downy white hair sprouted on his otherwise bald head. The younger man felt such a longing to hold the old man that he moved farther into the shadows, afraid of the depth of his emotion.

Father Angelo called to two other brothers across the courtyard.

"It's Luka . . . *Luka*! You remember Brother Thomas, don't you, Luka?"

Thomas was almost unrecognizable. His girth had shrunk to almost nothing, and his once-thick, curly black hair was white above his wizened face. He smiled and waved as he came toward them with a brother who seemed even more elderly. Luka stared hard; it could surely not be Brother Louis, and yet . . . The two old men shuffled closer, and Luka realized that it was indeed Brother Louis, but it was soon clear that the old man did not know his identity. His mind was as vacant as his small, washed-out eyes.

Brother Thomas wrinkled his nose and nodded. "Luka? Well, well, Luka . . . Welcome, welcome. What a fine young man you have grown into, and so smart. You look wealthy; you look like an American through and through."

He bent his head to Brother Louis and shouted, "It's Luka, Louis, do you remember? Luka!" Brother Louis sucked in his cheeks and smiled, exposing his pink gums. Thomas repeated at a bellow, "It is Luka!" Then he shrugged. "He can't hear; he's deaf. He's over ninety, you know. Well . . . welcome, welcome." The two old men shuffled off.

Luka, Father Angelo, and Brother Guido turned a corner. Brother Guido opened the door to a cell-like stone room and ushered Luka inside. The room contained an iron bedstead, a

folded mattress and pillow, a small chest of drawers, and a
wardrobe. While Father Angelo leaned against the doorframe,
Guido carefully removed a pressed white sheet and pillowcase
from one of the drawers and placed them on the bed. Then he
picked up a large white china jug, excused himself, and went
to get some water.

Luka put his bag down and laid the smaller case on top of
the chest. He turned, and Father Angelo smiled at him, a sweet,
loving smile. Luka's mouth trembled, his eyes filled with tears,
and he took the old man gently in his arms.

"Oh, my son, my beloved boy, how happy you make this
old man. I began to believe I would not see you again before I
die. I give thanks to God."

Brother Guido returned with the jug of water.

"Thank you, Guido," Father Angelo said, "and if you will
assist me back to my room, I shall leave this boy in peace.
There's a robe and sandals, Luka, should you wish to change,
and mass will be in one hour. At supper we shall hear all
your news. . . ."

Luka whispered a soft thank-you as they left, then waited,
listening to their footsteps, until there was silence. He closed
his eyes and sighed; he had come home.

The wooden shutter creaked as Luka pushed it open. There
was his old vegetable patch, sadly neglected. He remembered
how much he had raised there, how he and old Brother Louis
had toiled there. . . . Beyond was the small walled garden,
and beyond that the wild, open fields. Beyond that was the
sea. . . . He used to believe they were on the edge of the world.
The faint, musty smell of incense that always clung to the monks'
robes, the rooms, still lingered.

He stripped quickly, wanting to be naked, wanting to be
cleansed. He poured the cold water into the bowl and picked
up a wooden nail brush, its bristles tough and hard. Without
soap, he scrubbed himself until his white skin was red raw.
Finally he slipped the robe over his head, tied the sash, and
slipped his feet into the sandals.

He unpacked his clothes from the soft leather bag: two fine
cotton lawn shirts and a pair of pants identical to those he had
been wearing. Then he took out two pairs of black socks and

carried them to the paper-lined drawers. He produced a cloth and polished his shoes, which he placed neatly at the bottom of the wardrobe, next to the empty bag. His shaving equipment, in its matching leather bag, he placed on the chest of drawers, next to the long case he had brought with him. He could not resist touching the case lightly before lifting the mattress and stowing it underneath.

He made the bed carefully, tucking the rough white sheets tightly at the corners, turning over the top six inches. When he was satisfied, he looked at his Gucci watch and smiled. He would not be needing it here; he would know the time by the ringing of the bells. He laughed to himself as they began pealing for the seven o'clock mass, and for a moment he wondered whether to join the brothers. He decided to make the excuse that he had fallen asleep, though sleep was the last thing he could think of. He climbed silently from the window and headed for his old vegetable patch.

He walked between the rows of dried and rotting lettuces, noticed the tangled beans and the strawberry patch that had been allowed to run wild. The potato patch was wretched. He sighed. . . . How many hours had he spent digging and hoeing, cutting and planting? He was deep in thought as he made his way to the low stone wall, lifted his robe, and in one fluid movement landed on the other side. He surveyed the fields that stretched far into the distance, seeming to merge with the sky-line. He reached the top of the slope, stood caught between earth and sky, and there was the dark, glittering sea. The breeze tugged at the edge of his robe. He tilted his head to feel the coolness on his face. Then, as if in slow motion, he fell to his knees, lifted his hands, and stretched his arms high.

"Forgive me, forgive me, I have sinned, I have sinned. . . . Hail, Mary, Mother of Jesus . . ."

The bells ceased, leaving only the sound of the sea and wind.

He would give himself a penance; he would not leave the monastery until he had sown and reaped; he would not rest until he had made good the neglected vegetable garden.

Luka joined the brothers at the long refectory table in the cavernous dining hall. There had been fifteen or sixteen monks when he had last been there, but now their numbers were depleted. Brother Guido was the youngest, and he sat with two others whom Luka had not seen before.

Father Angelo patted the seat next to him and bowed his head in prayer, thanking the good Lord for bringing their son Luka to visit. Supper was always eaten in silence, the only sound the scraping of the spoons on the thick-rimmed white bowls. A basket containing thick chunks of homemade crusty bread was passed; but the bread tasted stale, and the thick, congealed soup was tasteless. Still Luka ate ravenously. His last meal had been many hours ago.

Supper over, the plates were cleared by Brother Guido, who placed a bowl of bruised pears and apples in the center of the table as a signal that the meal was at an end and conversation could begin. Some of the brothers helped themselves to fruit, but the heavy red wine was relished more. Luka refused wine but accepted a glass of water.

"So, Luka, how was America?"

Beneath the table Luka's hands were tightly clenched, but he answered with a shy, sweet smile, "America was very different."

"Did you go to college?"

"Yes, but as you no doubt recall, studies were never the top of my list. I learned English. Sometimes I have to think twice before I speak Sicilian now. Do I sound American?"

Father Angelo nodded, his eyes bright points.

"I lived with my father in New York City," Luka continued.

Their attention was unwavering, unnerving. He could think of nothing to tell them, no anecdotes, no amusing incidents. He flushed, his cheeks so red that Father Angelo touched his face.

"You are tired, I can tell. Perhaps we should wait to hear your news another time?"

Luka gave him a grateful nod, his hands beneath the table twisting frantically. But Brother Guido studied the visitor closely.

"I have a brother in New York. What part of the city did you live in?" the monk said in English.

Luka's body tingled as he said quietly, "We moved around, my father and I. We never stayed in one apartment too long, but I think I liked Manhattan the best. Have you been in New York, Brother Guido?"

The blue eyes met Guido's in a direct stare. It was Guido's turn to flush; Luka had spoken in English, and he had been unable to follow all of the words. "I have never been in America. London once . . ."

Guido had not meant to pry, but he thirsted for knowledge of the outside world. Only he among them was an avid reader and had been to a university. He was fully aware of the trials taking place in Palermo, although it was frowned upon to read newspapers so he had no one to discuss them with. There was neither radio nor television in the monastery.

Guido was about to ask another question when Brother Thomas turned to him and said, "When Luka was here as a boy, we had an incident. A chicken was stolen from the pantry and consumed, and we were determined to discover the culprit. We knew it was one of the boys, but which one? They were told they would be denied all their privileges until the thief was caught: no football, no games, no country walks. Do you remember, Luka?"

Luka's face bore a childish, puzzled frown, his fine pale eyebrows slightly raised. "A chicken?"

"Yes, yes!" Brother Thomas rose to his feet, leaning farther across the table. "And I found a chicken leg under your pillow! You must remember, I took it into class."

Luka's laugh was high-pitched, almost girlish. His whole demeanor altered. It was such a light, fresh laugh that it surprised and charmed Guido.

Thomas pressed on. "Tell me, Luka, you got away with it then. Little Antonio accepted the blame, but you put him up to it, didn't you?"

Luka's smile showed his perfect, small white teeth and a dimple in his right cheek. "Brother Thomas, let me swear on my father's life, on the life of our benefactor, who we thank for the new roof, the plumbing . . . I did not, Brother Thomas, ever steal a chicken leg. Pencils and books, I believe I did, but never that chicken."

Thomas sat back with a sigh. Angelo patted Luka's shoulder.

"There, Thomas, at last you have your answer. Now may I suggest we retire? Our young guest must be tired. He has come all the way from America."

They rose from the table, Luka assisting Father Angelo, but Guido hurried toward them, carrying the walker. Having made sure that the father was firmly on his feet, he turned to Luka.

"Your father, Luka, he is Paul Carolla, no?"

Luka spun around, and Guido stepped back. "I am sorry, I do not wish to intrude. I am just interested. I have read of the trials."

"Read, Brother Guido?"

Guido, flushing, gave a furtive look to right and left before continuing. "Newspapers are frowned upon here, but they are often displayed at the grocery store."

Luka hesitated, then gave him that sweet smile. "Sadly my father is held in jail, but he is an innocent man, Brother Guido. I am here to pray for him, pray for his release."

Luka's heart was beating fast. He had not expected anyone here, in this sanctuary, to know. "Guido, I am a very good gardener. Would I be permitted to work on the vegetable patch?"

Guido nodded and said he would be more than happy to assist.

"That will not be necessary. I need no help, and I know where all the tools are kept."

Guido remained standing in the shadowy corridor until he heard Luka's door close. He was excited. He had no desire to garden, but he wanted to know more about the trials. They were, so the papers said, opening a new era in Sicily, the end of the Mafia.

In the safety of his room Luka stripped off his robe. Naked, he dragged at the mattress, checking that his precious bag was still there. Satisfied, he lay naked on top of the cotlike bed. His body felt light now, and cool.

He smiled, recalling old Thomas and his chicken leg. Luka had stolen it and had threatened Antonio to make him plead guilty. He wondered what Brother Thomas would make of the secret hidden under his mattress: a custom-made .44 magnum. He could not resist getting off the bed and taking it out. He caressed it, feeling the hard coldness against his skin. He touched the special bullets, the ones into which he had bored the minute holes to ensure that they would shatter on impact, fragmenting, dispersing. He gave a contented sigh and carefully replaced the gun in the velvet-lined case. Then he lay facedown on the bed.

The shutters were partly open, and the breeze soothed him

into a dreamless sleep. His skin was like white marble, yet across his back, down to his tightly rounded buttocks, were shining zigzag scars, some almost half an inch in width.

When the bodies were released by the police, they were taken to the funeral home. Graziella, accompanied only by Mario Domino, carried two suitcases of clothes for the dead to wear.

She carefully examined each body while two embalmers followed her at a respectful distance. When she stood by the two children, she asked if their wounds could be concealed. They assured her that the plastic they used would most certainly disguise them. She astounded the men by remaining with them through every stage of the embalming, sitting silently as they washed the corpses and pumped in the embalming fluid.

Don Roberto was the last to be embalmed. She came to stand at the table. "Can I do that? I have been watching. Please allow me to do it."

The fluid, after being pumped into the veins, makes the body seem almost alive. But the deceased's hands often have to be massaged until the fluid reaches the fingertips and turns the skin from deathly blue to pink. Graziella rubbed and squeezed Roberto's hands gently until they once more looked alive, then bent her head and kissed them. Next she insisted on washing his thick white hair, drying it, and combing it the way he did, swept back from his high forehead. She sat down then, while the men worked on his face, threading clips from his jaw to his nose to keep the mouth firmly closed.

"Signora Luciano, we are ready now. Would you like to see them?"

Graziella moved from one son to the next, checking their appearances. She stood looking at the two angelic faces of her grandsons, then turned, calling one of the men to her side. "He has too much color. Nunzio is always very pale. A little more powder, perhaps?"

She nodded her approval when the child's face was finished, then stood again beside her husband. She seemed completely in control of her emotions, but the embalmers felt moved to tears as she bent and kissed her husband's lips. Then she thanked each man for his care and attention and gave them envelopes containing more money than they earned in a year.

"Thank you for allowing me to be with my family. I came

for a reason. My firstborn son died tragically. When he was brought home, it was as if I were burying a stranger. My grief was indescribable. My daughters must see their loved ones as they were; they have suffered enough. Thank you again, gentlemen."

By six o'clock, the first mass, the crowds had begun to gather. Men, women, and children came from the villages, came from the mountains.

They came by train, by boat, by bus, in horse-drawn carts, to bid farewell to *il Papa,* to show their last respects to their beloved don. Hundreds gathered in the square in front of the cathedral.

The carabinieri had withdrawn their guards from the villa, but as a show of respect sixteen motorbike riders moved ahead of the procession. Many off-duty police came of their own accord and joined the silent crowds that lined the road all the way from the Villa Rivera to the cathedral square.

The cathedral choir was joined by a string quartet, a harpist, and four leading singers from La Scala Opera Company. There were white lilies in such profusion that the cathedral was heady with their perfume, and hundreds of candles lit during the mass shimmered.

The first pew awaited the widows. The purple velvet hassocks had been embroidered with a gold *L* by nuns from the Lucianos' local church.

By ten-fifteen the motorcycles were in position outside the villa. The gates were opened wide, and they were given the signal to move on.

A black stallion, draped in purple and with a black-plumed headdress, was led out by a young farm boy to walk at the front of the procession. The stallion tossed his head nervously, and the boy held on to the wide black ribbons while he took a harmonica from his pocket. The horse calmed as the boy began to play, and they moved forward.

A murmur went through the crowd as the first hearse, pulled by six men in mourning dress, turned into the street. The hearse was more than a hundred years old and was carved in the ornate Sicilian fashion. White roses spelled out "Il Papa" in letters eighteen inches high. The coffin was laden with white flowers and a single red rose. Black, billowing silk draperies were caught at the corners with white roses.

Following Don Roberto Luciano came the hearse of his elder son, Constantino. In third position came Filippo's hearse, followed by Emilio's, each smothered in white with one red bloom.

Twenty village children between the ages of six and eight, wearing white confirmation clothes, walked ahead of the two small white-flowered coffins. They carried roses, and the veils of the girls were crowned with white flowers. One small girl at the head of the little procession began to cry, her high-pitched sobbing making the sight of the small coffins even more poignant.

Moving very slowly to the mournful sound of the boy's harmonica, the procession wound along the silent streets. The streets were full of people, but it was the silence that everyone would remember.

To everyone's amazement, the widows walked. Led by Graziella, with Sophia and Teresa together four steps behind, Rosa another four slow steps behind them, they walked slowly, heads held high in their black mourning clothes and flowing black veils. Each held her black-gloved hands clasped as if in prayer. They seemed bound together, yet separate, facing directly ahead, and even when Graziella led them into the cathedral, no one turned.

A boy soprano rose from the choir and sang "Ave Maria," his clear voice soaring, as the women took their seats and knelt in prayer.

During the service, when the congregation filed up to take communion, a wizened old woman swathed in black inched past the children's coffins to lay a small, worn crucifix on the don's coffin. She sobbed loudly, and no one attempted to stop her; it was as though she wept for everyone there at the loss of this, their beloved don, his sons, and two innocent grandsons.

The ground was thick with floral displays, covering the small area outside the family mausoleum, hanging from the iron railings surrounding the white-pillared entrance and carpeting the lane leading up to the gates. The crowds remained standing; dark-suited men held them back, their arms linked to allow the four black-clad women privacy for their last good-bye.

As they entered the mausoleum, a flash went off. Graziella, the last to enter, turned, her expression hidden beneath her veil, and pointed at the press photographer responsible. One of the guards, without any apparent coercion, was immediately handed the offending roll of film. The doors closed behind the women.

In the gloomy interior of the tomb the coffins were already in their final resting places on the shelves, though they had not yet been cemented in. The highly polished wood glinted in the flickering light of a single torch.

The women prayed together until Graziella said, quietly, that it was time to leave. Rosa clutched her grandmother's hand, and Teresa inched the door open; but Sophia's body was rigid. She could not move. Unable to look at the coffins of her husband and children, she focused on the picture of Michael Luciano. The photograph had been there for more than twenty years, protected by the glass and the airtight tomb; it could have been placed there the day before. Michael's angelic face and soft, sweet smile made Sophia's dulled senses scream awake. Hands clenched, the scream surged through her, the single word "No!"

Graziella released her granddaughter's hand, and her voice was hoarse as she ordered the women out. She caught Sophia as she fell to her knees.

"Get up, Sophia. Up on your feet."

Her grip cut through Sophia's skin, pressing against the nerve in her elbow and making her whole body jerk, but Graziella held on. The others stood waiting at the half-open door. Graziella took Teresa's handkerchief, lifted Sophia's veil, and wiped her face.

"Let me go first." Satisfied that Sophia was all right, Graziella almost pushed past her daughters-in-law and led them out to face the watchful crowd.

There were further agonies for the widows to endure; they now had to greet and thank the many mourners who were invited to pay their respects at the villa. Rolls-Royces, Mercedeses, Maseratis, and Ferraris lined the route.

A row of gilded red velvet chairs had been placed in the living room, replacing the coffins. For five hours the women sat, still veiled, to receive the condolences of the mourners. When it finally ended, the villa seemed to die: no voices, no sound.

The women, exhausted, numbed by the day's events, retired to their rooms.

At nine o'clock they were to dine with Graziella. They entered the room one by one to find her sitting in her husband's chair; they noticed that she also wore his ring. They hardly touched the food that was placed in front of them by Adina, who had been in service with the Lucianos since she was a young girl. Her eyes red-rimmed from weeping, she moved silently and unobtrusively, serving and clearing.

They spoke little. Teresa held her daughter's hand, murmuring softly that she should eat just a little. But Rosa seemed drugged, stupefied, and stared vacantly ahead. From her handbag Sophia took another of the little yellow pills Graziella had given them all and swallowed it with a sip of ice water.

There was an air of expectancy, and at last Graziella spoke.

"Mario Domino will be executor of my sons' and husband's estate. He will let us know when he is ready to read the will. In the meantime, you might prefer to return to your homes until you hear from me, though you are welcome to stay. There is little more that can be done here. I have made arrangements to attend the trial every day. We will get our justice. The man responsible for our loved ones' deaths will be convicted." Graziella hesitated, now obviously nervous, and took a black-bordered handkerchief from her pocket to wipe her eyes, although she did not appear to be weeping. They turned dull eyes to her.

Finally she said, "There is something you all should be made aware of, something I have not told you. . . . Papa had begun making statements for the prosecution." She looked at them, expecting a reaction, but received none. It was as if they had not heard. She continued. "Papa believed in his decision and trusted that we all would be protected."

Suddenly Teresa snapped, shaking with shocked rage, "Protected! Jesus Christ, protected! He must have been out of his mind! It was his fault then, his fault this happened!"

"Do you think I have not thought, every minute, every hour, every day since? You blame Papa, then you must blame me. I knew of this decision. I approved and believed what he was doing was right."

Teresa's face was tight, her mouth a thin, vicious line. "You knew, you *knew*, and you welcomed us with open arms? You brought us over here, and we saw the guards, we saw them. . . . Jesus Christ, Sophia even asked you why! Why was the car trailing us on a shopping expedition, and what did you say? *You said it was what Papa wanted!* You should have told us then. You think Sophia would have left her babies for a second if she had known? We were all in danger, and you never told us—"

Rosa's chair fell over as she stood up. "Is that why I was to be married? To get us all here? You arranged it, you arranged my wedding?" She turned ferociously on her grandmother, her hands clenched. "And you killed Emilio. . . . I blame you, I hate you. Here, Papa bought this, put it on his grave . . . *take it!*" She flung her ring across the table and ran from the room.

Sophia slapped her hand down on the engagement ring. "*Stop this!* Rosa, come back in here. Rosa!"

Rosa stopped in the hall. She had no intention of rejoining them, but there was something in Sophia's black eyes . . . When she repeated a whispered "Rosa, come back and sit down," Rosa obeyed.

Graziella twisted her lace handkerchief in her hands as she turned to Teresa. "He wanted to tell you, wanted you all here. He didn't want you to be afraid."

"So you arranged my daughter's wedding, your granddaughter's wedding, as an excuse?" Teresa had to strain to hear Graziella's reply.

"I make no excuses. Yes, Papa chose the wedding. He chose it because if anything happened to him, we would have been together. He did what he felt was right. Paul Carolla murdered Michael—"

Sophia's deep voice was calm as she interrupted Graziella. "Michael died, Mama, more than twenty years ago. Are you saying that Papa jeopardized the entire family because of him? I have lost my husband and my babies because of *Michael*?"

They all looked to Graziella for an answer. The tension in the room was heightened by Rosa's muffled weeping. Graziella's handkerchief twisted and twisted in her hands.

"Papa did what he felt was right. Who are we to say now that he should not have—"

Teresa screamed it, her face red with pent-up anger. "I'm saying it! I don't give a fuck what anyone else wants to say, *I'm saying it, my husband is dead*!"

Graziella looked at Teresa with contempt. "Hate the men who did this, not Papa. All of you honored him to his face, took from him whatever he gave. All of you carried the name Luciano, carried it, benefited from being the wives of Lucianos."

Teresa interrupted, swiping at the table, hitting out in anger. "Rosa was never allowed the chance to become a wife. He used her. Listen to her. . . . You tell me who is to blame? Tell me!"

Graziella rose to her feet. "You have no right, here in this house, to abuse him. He will have provided for each of you, provided so that you may live well, live as Lucianos, live in the luxury none of you, not one of you, knew before you were welcomed into this family."

"This family doesn't exist anymore because of him. He, and he alone, is to blame, and you know it." Teresa's head jerked back as Graziella slapped her face.

"I wish you to leave. When the lawyer is ready, you may return, not before then. . . ." They watched her walk from the room. Her slow footsteps crossed the marble hall.

Teresa rubbed her cheek, shocked, hardly able to believe what had happened. She asked no one in particular, "Michael? He did it for Michael? Justice for Michael? My daughter's, my life, destroyed because of a boy we never even knew! Well, I spit on his memory because if it weren't for Michael Luciano, our men would still be alive. I will be glad to leave this house, leave her to her justice. . . ."

Sophia folded her napkin carefully. She felt empty, drained, unable to argue. "If you'll excuse me, I'm going to bed."

Teresa burst out. "Don't you have anything to say? Don't you think we should talk about this? I mean, she's asked us to leave. Are you going?"

"What is there to say, Teresa? No words can bring back my sons, my husband. I don't care about justice, about Paul Carolla. My babies, my beautiful babies, are dead."

The room was empty when Adina came in to clear the table.

\*     \*     \*

Sophia moved silently down the stairs. In the darkness the house itself appeared to be mourning; strange creaks and groans emanated from the staircase and the shutters.

She inched open the door to the living room, crept to a cabinet, and poured herself almost a tumbler of whiskey. The pills she had already taken were making her feel woozy. As she turned to go back to her room, the fringe of the shawl that draped the piano brushed her arm. She gasped. There he was again, smiling at her. Michael's photograph always stood in front of the others.

She whispered, "I curse you. I curse the day I met you." The sound of her own voice frightened her, and she drank, wanting to escape into oblivion. But a small voice inside warned her to be careful.

Somewhere a shutter banged. She turned to see Graziella standing in the doorway, her long hair braided, a woolen shawl around her shoulders. She walked silently into the room and took the glass from Sophia's hand.

"You should not drink if you have taken sleeping pills. It is dangerous."

"You mean I could sleep and never wake up? Then give me the glass."

"I'll take you back to bed."

Sophia backed away, remembering that viselike grip at the mausoleum, but Graziella kept on coming.

"Stay away from me, leave me alone."

"Very well, if that is what you want."

"I want to leave this house."

As silently as she had arrived, Graziella turned to leave, but Sophia blurted, "Why didn't you warn me? Because you knew, you've always known."

"Known what?"

"What this family is, what it was . . . You've always known. Is that why you are so strong, why you don't weep? Is that why?"

"You are being foolish. Don't say things, now, Sophia, that you will regret later."

Sophia made the mistake of gripping Graziella's arm and was shoved off her feet. The older woman's strength was awesome.

Graziella stood over her, eyes blazing. "*You* didn't know?

Don't play the innocent. It doesn't become you. Yes, I have known, just as you have, but perhaps my reasons for accepting it were different. What were yours, Sophia? What made you return to this house? For my son? Was it for Constantino or for what you saw here?"

Sophia remained huddled on the floor. "I loved him. You know that. He was a good husband, he was a good father, but—"

"But he was a Luciano."

Sophia put her hands over her ears. She wanted to shout, to curse the name aloud.

Graziella relaxed, as if the flash of icy anger had been someone else's. "You know, I was about the same age as you were the day you were brought here when I first set eyes on my husband. Oh, I knew what he was, Mario Domino knew what he was, but neither of us could say no to him. I could never say no to him, in my entire life with him. I mean no disrespect, but my family were well-to-do, my life mapped out. . . . Did you know I almost married Mario Domino?"

"No, I didn't." Sophia rose slowly to her feet, took a cigarette from the box, and lit it.

Graziella pushed the shutters slightly open to let the cool night breeze into the room. "How different it would have been. A nice, respectable lawyer in a good, reputable firm . . . My father would have approved. He would turn in his grave if he knew I chose Roberto instead. But you see, it was the only choice I could have made, because without him, without him . . ." Her voice trailed away.

"Don't get cold, Mama."

"I tried not to see, not to know. It was all hidden from me. I could pretend that what went on outside could never affect me, and as I chose not to know, Michael died. I blamed Roberto. I tortured him with my grief, and I hated him for being what he was. But perhaps if I had been more aware of my husband's world, Michael need not have died. You see, Roberto tried to play the game both ways; he wanted to be a good man, an honest man, but it was impossible. When I realized what I was doing to him, when I realized there was a side I didn't know, I made it my duty to know. Mario Domino would have been shot if it had ever been discovered, but I made him keep me informed of everything he could possibly tell me. So yes, I did know, I knew more than my dear, beloved husband could ever have dreamed, and I stayed by his side. If he was guilty, then so was I. . . ."

Sophia looked up. The chill had returned to Graziella's voice. "I wanted him to destroy Paul Carolla."

"Did he ever discover how much of his life you knew?"

Graziella shook her head and pulled the shutters closed. "No, I was far too clever. He never knew. He knew most things about all of you. Remember how he delved into your past when you wanted to marry Constantino?"

Sophia's breath caught in her throat. She couldn't speak. She was suddenly afraid of Graziella; did she know everything? Could it be possible? She stubbed out her cigarette, desperate to get out of the room, away from her.

The quiet voice continued. "He always said you were his favorite. You must forgive, Sophia, not blame him. You are not like Teresa; she is nothing."

"What about Rosa, Mama? Is she just a nothing? Was the marriage really arranged, or did Emilio love her?"

Graziella's eyes were like stones.

Sophia sighed; she knew then that the don had arranged that marriage just as he had arranged Teresa's. "Don't tell her, don't let her know. At least give her that."

"I will take care of Rosa," said Graziella.

At that moment Sophia loathed Graziella. "I'll return to Rome in the morning."

"You must do whatever you think best. I'm sorry that we are so divided. Together we would be stronger."

"For what? There's nothing left, Mama."

Graziella lifted her arms as if to embrace her, but Sophia hurried out, not wanting to be touched.

Left alone, Graziella took stock of the elegant room. Her eyes were accustomed to the darkness, and she noticed a cushion out of place. She straightened it deftly, picked up Sophia's glass and the used ashtray, then paused, looking at the array of family photographs. Michael's was out of line. As she pushed it back into its place, she said to the empty room, to the faces of her dead, clearly and quietly, without emotion, "It is with me now."

# 4

The widows had returned to their homes, and Graziella was alone in the villa. The rooms were kept dark and airless, the shutters over the windows, every door closed.

Graziella's entire adult life had been taken up with caring for her family. Now she thought only of the end of Paul Carolla.

Mario Domino, worried that the strain would be too much for Graziella, had tried to dissuade her from going to the trial. He made the excuse that there was not one spectator seat available, but she had told him curtly that she would arrange it herself. "The guards are paid a pittance. I will make sure that they have a seat for me every day, no matter what the cost."

The first time she saw Paul Carolla she was shocked by his arrogant, audacious manner. She could not take her eyes from him. He became aware of her attention and, calling a guard over, pointed her out. When she lifted her veil, Carolla gave a low, almost mocking bow of recognition, but he turned away as if she meant no more to him than any of the other spectators.

The eye-to-eye contact made Graziella recoil as if she had been punched in the heart, a reaction so strong that she snapped the silver crucifix chain in her hands.

Even after she returned home, she found no release from the shock. The choking feeling—as if she were being squeezed physically—persisted until she lay in her bed, hugging her husband's pillow. She prayed to Roberto, begged him to give her strength, and as if he were still alive, his strength encouraged her not to give up.

From then on Graziella hardened herself to sit through all the hours of the preliminary trials. And day by day Paul Carolla became more of an obsession with her; she had no interest in any of the other defendants. She sat, shrouded in her widow's weeds, waiting only for the day when Carolla would be brought to the stand. He joked to his guards that she was like a praying mantis, but she was getting to him. He turned his chair so that he could not see her.

Emanuel had made many excuses to delay the meeting with Graziella, but eventually he could no longer put it off. When she appeared at his office, he was impressed by her calmness. He assured her that Carolla would be convicted.

She removed her gloves carefully, straightening each finger, and folded them neatly in her lap. "Will he also be accused of destroying my family?"

"Signora, there is no evidence so far that he was involved in that tragedy. At the time he was in jail."

"He was also in jail when the little Paluso child was murdered, yet I believe he is suspected of ordering the killing. Is that not so?"

"I understand he has been questioned, yes."

"So is he to be accused of my family's murders?"

"If evidence is produced, it will necessitate a separate trial. You must realize, when it became known that Don Roberto was to testify, there would be many who would want to stop him."

"Did my husband's evidence incriminate others?"

Emanuel twisted the cap of his fountain pen on and off, then spoke with care. "He made no accusations against any other named party. He chose only to tell me the pertinent facts surrounding your son's death. He incriminated himself more than anyone else."

"Are you able to use the statements he made?"

The pen twisted and turned in his hands. "Without Don Roberto's presence the statements could be dismissed as circumstantial evidence. This also applies to the statement made by Lenny Cavataio. As I explained to your husband, all the evidence contained in the Cavataio statement was contested by the defense counsel as hearsay. . . . Don Roberto knew this; it was the sole reason he chose to offer himself."

Graziella leaned forward, her black-gloved hand resting on the edge of his desk.

"First, I would like to have the tapes my husband made. Would that be possible?"

Emanuel nodded. They had been transcribed to computer files. But he was not prepared for her next words.

Sitting upright in her chair, her hands folded in her lap, she said, "I wish to offer myself in my husband's place. I am prepared to be a witness for the prosecution."

She paused, searching his face for a reaction, but all she saw was that the nervous hands twisting the fountain pen had become still. Emanuel rose from the desk and walked to the window. He parted the slats of the blind a fraction and peered out.

"Did you discuss the statements with your husband, Signora Luciano?"

"I did not need to. I am fully aware of the facts. I am prepared to be your witness; I am prepared to repeat in court everything my husband told you."

"You mean, repeat his statements?"

"No, I mean, tell the truth as I know it."

He turned and scrutinized her. He wondered how much she really knew. "These facts, signora, would you be prepared to discuss them with me now? Or would you require access to your husband's taped interviews first?"

"Are you asking me if I would perjure myself?"

He blushed and returned to his desk. "I am in the middle of the case. The time required to discuss everything with you would mean my asking for a stay of at least one week. If I were to ask this of the judge and be awarded it, only to discover that your evidence was not—could not be used against Paul Carolla, then my time would have been wasted, and my time, right now, is my primary consideration. These men have been held in jail for almost ten months. We cannot afford further delays—"

"The murder of my entire family is just a delay? How long did my grandchildren's deaths delay the court proceedings, signor? One day? One hour?"

"Please, I mean no insult, but we have already discussed the fact that to date the police have discovered no connection—"

"*No connection?* My husband was the main witness against Carolla; is that not a connection?"

Emanuel was angry but very controlled. "I am unaware, as are the authorities, who it was who organized, arranged, whatever term you wish to use, the terrible tragedy that occurred. I am prepared to accept you as a witness if, and only if, you have evidence that stands up by itself without your husband's tapes."

"I know Paul Carolla instigated the death of my son. I know he, and only he, benefited from the death of my family—"

"But forgive me, signora, without proof—"

"The proof is in the graveyard."

He sighed. "Trust me, I give you my word—"

"Your word means little to me. My husband trusted you, trusted your word that there would be protection for himself and for his sons. . . ."

Emanuel took out his handkerchief and blew his nose. There was no denying that the leak had come from this very office, his office. After a moment he asked if she would be prepared there and then to answer certain questions in front of a witness. If he believed she had valuable evidence, he would accept her for the prosecution.

Hesitantly Graziella agreed. A secretary brought them coffee while they waited for a stenographer. Emanuel sifted through his notes, preparing questions. Graziella slowly approached his desk.

"Would it be so wrong to allow me to listen to my husband's tapes? Would it be so wrong to allow me to say the words he died for? In the end what we both want, what you want, is justice."

"I cannot, signora, no matter how much I want, no matter how much I believe in the man's guilt, go against the law. I cannot do this for you—or for the animal Paul Carolla."

Graziella remained with Emanuel and the stenographer for an hour. Emanuel was as tough on her within the confines of his office as he knew the defense would be with her in court.

"Would you state your relationship with Paul Carolla?"

"I have no relationship with him."

"How well did you know the defendant?"

"He came to my home, to visit my husband."

She could not recollect the exact date but knew that the first time she had met Carolla was in the late fifties. She explained that there had always been friction between Carolla and her late husband.

"What exactly do you mean by friction?"

"When Paul Carolla's father died, his will did not name his son as head of the family. Instead, he chose my husband. Paul Carolla always bore a grudge against my husband because he felt usurped."

Emanuel tapped the side of his desk with his foot. "So you were aware of ill feeling between the two men as far back as the early fifties?"

"Yes. Paul Carolla came to my home wanting my husband to release him; he no longer wished to work for him. He wanted to start his own business."

"And what business did Paul Carolla wish to begin?"

"I believe it was narcotics."

"You believe? Do you have any evidence to substantiate this statement?"

"No."

"I see. So let us move on to the ill feeling between your husband and the defendant. . . ."

"The second time Paul Carolla came to my home, he wanted my husband to assist him, to use the Luciano export companies as a cover for shipping narcotics. He had become very wealthy, and he threatened my husband."

"Were you a witness to any of these threats?"

She hesitated, and he knew before she spoke that she was lying. "I heard them shouting at each other. I heard Paul Carolla say that he would make my husband pay for abusing his friendship. My husband refused to assist him in any way. He had always maintained his companies legally, had spent years building up a good name. My husband was a man of honor, and he hated drugs of any kind."

"Signora Luciano, when you say a man of honor, do you accept the fact that your husband was, up until the time of his death, a known Mafia—"

She interrupted angrily. "My husband was a man of honor, a war hero, decorated for bravery, a man who despised the trade in drugs, despised Paul Carolla."

Emanuel was already certain that it would not work, but he had to continue. He changed the subject, asking gently, "Tell me about Michael Luciano."

She seemed grateful, giving him a half-smile. "He was my firstborn son."

Emanuel listened patiently as she described Michael's academic history, his acceptance into Harvard. Eventually he interrupted her. "Would you tell me what happened to this young man, a boy with such a tremendous future ahead of him?"

"He came home, in the summer of sixty-three, halfway through the second year at Harvard. He was very sick; my second son collected him at the airport, and Michael could hardly walk unaided. His hair was matted, and his clothes . . ." Her eyes filled with tears.

"He was ill, you said?"

"Yes. He collapsed, and my husband took him to the hospital. He remained in the hospital for a few weeks. Then he was taken to the mountains to recuperate. He came home once, looking well and fit, full of life. He was a very handsome boy, his blond hair bleached silver by the sun. He was better, but my husband felt he should stay in the mountains a few more days until he was completely recovered."

"What happened to your son, Signora Luciano?"

She tried to say it matter-of-factly but could not. "My son was . . . murdered."

"Did you witness his death?"

"No, I did not. My son was shot, killed as a warning to my husband not to stand against Paul Carolla. My son's return, signor, coincided with Carolla's threats, and my husband took my son into the mountains in the belief that he would be safe there."

Emanuel was kicking the side of his desk with small, light taps of his shoe. "These threats, signora—did you actually hear Paul Carolla say that he would . . ." He paused, knowing that Michael Luciano had not been shot, and chose his words carefully. The stenographer waited, the persistent, soft clicking silenced for a moment.

"What was the development of this tragedy? Was anyone ever charged with this brutal killing?"

Slowly Graziella shook her head. "No, but it was Paul Carolla."

"Was he ever arrested? Was he ever charged? Did anyone, signora, have any evidence to prove that Paul Carolla had anything to do with this tragic death?"

There was a helplessness to her. She shook her head. "No . . . but there was a witness."

"Do you know the name of this witness?"

Her eyes filled with tears, and she gave a pleading look to the stenographer, as if she could help. In the end she lowered her head and whispered, "No, I do not know, signor."

Sophia sat in the cool, empty church. She had been sitting there for almost two hours. She wore a lace veil over her face and clutched her rosary.

She had tried to pray, but her mind had blurred. She could do nothing but listen, her face cupped in her hands as she knelt. Footsteps came and went; voices echoed; there were whispers from the confessional. Twice she had risen and moved closer, only to stop and kneel down again. She had no tears left, and the small yellow pills Graziella had given her wrapped everything in a distant haze.

She had asked the maid to clear the children's toys away and take them to a children's home along with their clothes. Constantino's clothes had also been removed. The large apartment was empty, desolate, and she was so lacking in energy that she spent most of her time in bed, the blinds drawn, the pills giving her deep, dreamless sleep.

The church was the only place she went to, and for three days she had come, needing to confess, needing to tell someone, but had been unable to enter the confessional. The priest knew who she was and knew of her loss, but he did not approach her, did not intrude on what he believed were her prayers.

The candles she had lit for her sons and her husband were flickering, almost at an end, and she quietly got three more. She lit them and stood staring into the flames beneath the Virgin's feet. Two women knelt, praying, the clicking of their rosaries like small hammers to Sophia.

The confessional was empty, and she inched closer, closer. . . . Then she moved quickly to swish the curtain aside. Once in the small dark booth she forced herself to speak, but her voice was so low that the priest had to ask her to speak up.

"I have sinned, Father."

He leaned closer. Her voice was so husky he could barely hear her. He encouraged her to continue.

"I have sinned, Father."

The priest scratched at a gravy stain on his cassock, then folded his hands. "Ease the pain in your heart; say what you feel you need. There is time. Take your time. I am just here to comfort you, to pray with you."

"I had a child, a son. I was very young. I left the baby in an orphanage. I intended . . . I wanted to go back for him, but first I needed to tell his father, explain to him."

The priest waited. He saw her hand, a delicate white hand with blood-red nails, the fingers threading through the grille. He touched her fingers, gently. His hand felt warm, soft. She withdrew her hand.

"Did you tell the father of your baby? Tell him of his son?"

"I couldn't, Father. I couldn't."

"Were you afraid? Afraid of rejection?"

"No . . . no, you don't understand—"

"I can only understand, be of help to you, if you tell me everything."

"He died, he died. . . . I couldn't tell him. I couldn't tell anyone."

"So the father of your baby was dead. What did you do then?"

She gave a short, humorless laugh, then sat silent for more

than five minutes. The priest's stomach rumbled loudly, and he looked at his watch.

"I married his brother, Father."

"And what of your child?"

"I never went back for him. I left him. I never told anyone he even existed. I left my baby in the orphanage. I left him. . . ."

He heard the brass curtain rings clicking and peered through the grille as Sophia ran from the church.

Emanuel watched Graziella being driven away in her car. The stenographer asked if he would need her further, and he shook his head. He was tired; he didn't want to continue working.

He had done what had to be done; if it appeared hard, cruel even, it would in the end prove a kindness. Graziella would have been put through worse on the stand, and she had, as he had known to begin with, no evidence that he could use. He had simply wasted his valuable time.

Sophia kicked off her shoes while pouring herself a vodka. She took two Valium and lay down, fully clothed, on her bed, and drained the glass. But she could not forget. She found herself reliving all the emotions she had felt when she stood in her cast-off shoes, her cheap hand-sewn dress, waiting outside those huge wrought-iron gates of the Villa Rivera, only to be told that Michael Luciano, the boy she had loved, was dead and buried.

The guilt descended like a black cowl; her body felt as if she were drowning in a swamp of emotion. The guilt she had never allowed herself to face began to emerge, and she fought it, twisted it until it surfaced as rage. Michael Luciano, the father of her bastard child, Michael Luciano was to blame for everything. If it hadn't been for him, her husband, her sons would be alive. . . . She hurled her glass at the wall.

"*Bastard! Bastard! Bastard!*" she screamed. Her rage was out of control. She tore the duvet from the bed, the pillows, hurled everything she could lay hands on across the room. She swiped her perfumes and creams from the top of the dressing table, then opened her wardrobe and started dragging out her clothes, ripping at them in her frenzy, kicking the rows of shoes until exhausted, she fell to her knees. Clinging to the side of the bed, she wept uncontrollably, asking God to forgive her, repeating over and over, "It was not my fault. No one can blame me. . . . It was not my fault. . . ." But she knew there was no one to answer for her sins but herself.

Sophia returned to the confessional. *"Don't you understand what I have done? Don't you understand?"*

The priest quieted her, said he understood, could understand her heartache.

"No, you cannot, you can't understand."

"Well, my child, tell me what I cannot understand."

The white hand, the red-painted fingernails, again scratched at the grille.

"I wanted so much to be a part of the family. I wanted everything they had. I wanted to be—" As disturbed as she was, Sophia still held back, still could not say the name Luciano. "I wanted everything I had never had. I was so poor, Father. My mother scrubbed floors. It was all I saw for myself, scrubbing, washing other people's clothes. That was all I saw ahead of me. When I had the baby, I was sure, so sure, that they would accept me. I was sure he loved me."

"Do you know what became of the child?"

"No . . . I made myself forget him. I had to forget him to survive. . . . And then, after I was married, how could I tell them? Do you think I would have been allowed to marry the son of—" Again she would not speak the name. If she explained further, he would know who she was; the deaths of the Luciano family had made headlines.

"Do you now want to find your child?"

She leaned back. She could smell the mustiness of his robes just as he could smell her distinct, heavy perfume. She answered on a long, low sigh. "Yesss . . . yes, that is what I want."

"Then that is what you must do. Trace this child you harbor such guilt, such deep guilt for. Your sense of betrayal is natural, you know what you have done in the past, and you know the reasons. Find him, ask his forgiveness, and God will give you the strength. Now together we will pray for his soul, pray for you, my daughter, and pray for God to forgive your sins."

Graziella looked toward her husband's study. She could hear the murmur of voices. She handed Adina her veil and black lace gloves.

"It's Signor Domino; he said it would be all right. He has three gentlemen with him, signora."

"In future, Adina, no matter who it is, no one is allowed here, especially not in my husband's study, unless I have given you authority. You may go."

She waited until Adina had returned to the kitchen before she moved closer to the study door. She paused, listening; she could hear Mario Domino speaking.

". . . Panamanian companies. Listed alongside are the U.S. state bonds. We were recycling the proceeds through our bank to Switzerland—"

Graziella walked into the study, and Domino froze in mid-sentence.

"Graziella, I was not expecting you to return. . . . I apologize for the intrusion, but . . . Please allow me to introduce these gentlemen. They are from America and are handling the legal side over there for Don Roberto."

Graziella did not offer her hand but remained standing at the open door. Domino made the introductions, first gesturing toward a tall, well-dressed man in a dark gray suit. His eyes were small but accentuated by heavy, horn-rimmed glasses.

"This is Eduardo Lorenzi from New York."

Lorenzi gave a small bow. "Signora."

The next man was squat, his face shining with sweat, his collar stained. His plump hands clutched at a large white handkerchief. "I think you have met Signor Niccolò Pecorelli, a very old and trusted friend, now taking care of the don's interests in Atlantic City. And last, Giulio Carboni, also from the East Coast, who has been assisting me here."

The latter was very much younger than the others but stockily built. He was wearing an open-necked casual shirt and rose-tinted glasses. Graziella glanced around the study; drawers and even the safe door were wide open. Stacked around the desk were files neatly tied with string, obviously ready for removal.

"I shall be in the dining room. If you wish refreshments before you leave, please call Adina." Graziella walked out, leaving the door open and making it obvious that she wanted the men to leave.

She sat in the cool dark dining room in her husband's chair with her back to the shuttered windows. She could hear the men preparing to leave, their hushed voices sounding to her like those of conspirators. Then Mario himself appeared in the dining room.

"I am sorry, Graziella. I was hoping to have everything completed before your return. Don Roberto was conducting international transactions. I am not the only lawyer involved with the businesses, so we had a lot of work to do. They will be handling all the American issues."

She had never seen Mario so hesitant. He looked guilty, mopping his brow with a silk handkerchief. "They have removed only the files necessary—"

She stared at her folded hands. "Perhaps in the future you would be kind enough to warn me if you require access to my husband's study."

"Of course, but I doubt if I will have to intrude again. Forgive me."

He bent to kiss Graziella's cheek, but she averted her face. Hurriedly he retrieved his briefcase from the study, his eyes darting around the ransacked room, making sure there was no trace of incriminating documents. There was not one room in the villa that had not been thoroughly searched. Now he would begin the marathon job of assessing the Luciano holdings, knowing that many of the territories had already been taken over, that someone had already stepped into Roberto Luciano's shoes. He had known the moment he had been approached by the three men Graziella had just met.

Graziella watched Domino drive away before she picked up the heavy package of her husband's tapes. She carried it to the study desk and looked around. The room smelled of the men's cigar smoke and of charred papers. . . . Sure enough, there in the grate were the telltale blackened scraps of paper.

Adina entered with a tray. She had prepared some soup

and a small side dish of pasta. "You must eat, signora, just a little."

Graziella nodded, taking the tray and putting it down on the desk. "You may leave now. I can take this back to the kitchen."

"No, signora, I'll stay, if just to make sure you at least take a little soup."

"That will not be necessary, please leave me. And, Adina . . . in the future you show no one into my husband's study, no one, is that clear? This room will remain locked, no one is allowed in, do you understand?"

Adina closed the door quietly behind her. She paused, listening for the sound of cutlery being used, knowing that Graziella had not eaten for days. As if a ghost crossed her soul, she froze, hearing clearly the deep, warm tones of Don Roberto Luciano. She could not help crying out, and the study door opened.

Graziella's face was white with anger. "Leave me alone. Leave the house now."

Graziella stood in her husband's study, eyes closed, feeling the evening breeze as it dried the tears on her cheek, tears she made no effort to wipe away, as she listened to the don's voice.

"My name is Don Roberto Luciano. I give this statement on the eighth of February, 1987. I have certified evidence to prove that I am of a sane, healthy mind and have a witness to prove that these statements are given freely without any undue harassment or pressure from any quarter. I make these statements of my own will. . . ."

His voice hurt her, pained her. But she had to listen, had to know what her husband knew and what she did not. She would hear exactly how her son had been murdered; she would hear, in those same, warm tones, another side of the man she thought she knew and loved.

# 5

Teresa looked down into the New York street and watched Father Amberto hail a cab. He was carrying two heavy suitcases filled with her husband's clothes. She remained standing at the window until the cab merged into the stream of continuous traffic on Thirty-fifth Street, then turned back into the small room she and Filippo had used as a study. She went to the desk where she had stacked all Filippo's unpaid bills and company papers in preparation for work that evening, but now nothing could be further from her mind. She was so angry she was still shaking. She pressed her hands to her cheeks, flushing at the thought of what her daughter had said to the priest. Suddenly she yanked open the study door and walked into the narrow corridor.

"Rosa, *Rosa!*"

Her daughter's bedroom door remained firmly closed. Her radio blared, the volume turned up to earsplitting level.

"Rosa, *Rosa, come out of there!*" Teresa hit the door with the flat of her hand, kept on hitting it until the music was turned off. Then she stepped back, hands on her hips, as Rosa opened the door.

"How could you do that? How could you say that to Father Amberto?"

"What?"

"You know perfectly well what. How dare you! I have never been so humiliated in my life."

"Didn't faze him, he was too busy stuffing the suitcases with all the clothes."

"I want you to apologize to me, you hear me?"

"Sure I hear. So can half the block. There's no need to act so hysterical. You think he's never heard the word before? All I said was—"

"I know what you said: 'Check the pockets for rubbers!' For *rubbers*! What in God's name possessed you to say such a thing? Search your papa's suit pockets!" Teresa put her hands over her face. "What will he think of us?"

"I don't think he'll be saying Hail Marys over it, Mama. It was nothing, forget it."

"*Forget it*? Why did you say it, Rosa, why?"

Rosa shrugged her shoulders and turned to go back to her room. "Maybe because I can't stand the way you're acting, creeping around the place. It's been two months, Mama, and every time I look at you, you start blubbering, or you're going to every mass. It's a wonder your knees aren't calloused."

Teresa pulled her daughter by the shoulders, her face red with rage. "How do you expect me to behave? You want me to play music so loud I deafen everyone? You want me to throw open the blinds and have a party? My husband, your father is dead! So help me God, what do you want me to do?"

"I don't know. I just don't want anyone else coming here with their prayer books and clasping me by the hand, people I don't know pinching my cheeks as if I were a kid."

"They're being kind, Rosa. They're trying to help us."

"No, they're not. They're just prying. We don't even know them."

"They're from the church."

"But they don't know me; they never knew Papa. He never set foot in church unless you dragged him there. They're just nosy, and you are loving every minute of being the center of attention."

Teresa slapped Rosa so hard she crashed into the wall. She

staggered for a moment, then hurled herself at her mother, fists flying, screaming, "*Leave me alone!*"

"Fine, I'll leave you alone. I won't cook for you, clean for you, wash for you—"

"*You don't have to anyway—*"

"Sure I don't have to, and I don't have to give you money every day to go to college. Sure I'll leave you alone. I won't speak to you until you apologize. May God forgive you, and you'll need his forgiveness for what you said to Father Amberto."

"Why? It was the truth, wasn't it? You think I'm deaf? I heard you two fighting and arguing. I could hear you screaming at each other. He never loved you. He had other women. I know it, everyone knew it. . . ."

Teresa couldn't stop the tears. "Why, Rosa? Why are you saying these things? Since we got home, you've been behaving crazy, I don't know you." Teresa searched for a tissue and blew her nose.

"Oh, don't cry, Mama. Please, I'm sick of the sight of you crying."

"Because you *don't*—"

"Why should I cry? Tell me why? Cry for Emilio? He never loved me; it was all arranged. I'm glad he's dead because I feel used. I was handed over like a piece of meat."

"May God forgive you, you know that's not true, Rosa."

"Yes, it is, and Papa never loved you; they handed you over just like me."

Teresa couldn't listen anymore. She walked into her bedroom and slammed the door behind her. How little her daughter knew, how little she understood. She took out a photograph of herself on her graduation, wearing her cap and gown, younger than Rosa.

Rosa was sitting in front of her dressing table, trimming her bangs with a pair of nail scissors. Small snippets of hair covered the glass top, fell onto her cosmetics, but she snipped and snipped, anything to stop herself thinking, remembering.

"Rosa, can I come in?"

"No."

Teresa hovered in the door. "I want to show you something. It's a photograph of me when I was your age, in my cap and gown."

"I've seen it, Mama. Grandma used to have it on the mantelpiece."

"Look at me, such a stern little face, with such thick glasses."

Rosa gave only a fleeting glance at the photograph, and Teresa continued. "You remember Grandma and Grandpa? I was brought up in that bakery. Papa was always dreaming of going home someday, but Mama never wanted to; she felt that they had done so well here in America. Papa was so proud the day I was accepted in college; he thought by just getting accepted, I was already a qualified lawyer. He told everyone, and they streamed into the bakery with gifts and congratulations. . . ."

Rosa blew at the hair on the dressing table, only half listening. She had few memories of her maternal grandparents, though she never passed a bakery without the smell somehow reminding her of the times she had seen them.

"My father worked in the bakery, Rosa, he didn't own it, and he rented the apartment in the basement. It was dark, airless, and we ran a constant battle against cockroaches. They came in the hundreds as soon as the ovens went off—"

"Why are you telling me this? I've heard it so many times, about how you used to chase them with a broom. . . ."

"Because the man who bought my father the bakery, and bought him the little apartment on the top floor where there weren't any cockroaches, was Don Roberto."

"So what was Don Roberto going to give Papa for marrying me off? Move us out of this dump? Was that the deal? What was I worth, Mama? A new apartment or a bigger slice of the family business? You complained enough that they never treated you like family, like Aunt Sophia! Well, you got even more than you bargained for, didn't you? Now you'll be rich. . . ."

Teresa was too late to stop Rosa from ripping her graduation photograph in two, tossing the scraps aside. She bent down to retrieve them. Then she sprang forward, grabbed her daughter's shoulders, shook her. She shrieked, "You don't know anything, you don't know—"

Rosa dragged herself free and picked up her scissors, jabbing at her mother. The small, sharp blades cut into the back of Teresa's hand. "Why don't you leave me alone?"

Teresa went into the bathroom and ran cold water on her

hand, watching the trickle of blood from the deep cut spread down her fingers.

Rosa appeared, shamefaced, at the door. "Are you okay?"

"Yes."

"You need a Band-Aid?"

"Yes."

Rosa opened the cabinet. Her father's shaving brush, razor, and cologne were where he had left them. She took out the box of adhesive bandages and opened it.

"This size?" She held one up and watched as her mother dried the cut on a towel, then held her hand out. Rosa gently placed the Band-Aid over the cut. "You forgot to take Papa's things out of the cabinet. I'm sorry, Mama, and I'll apologize to Father Amberto next Sunday."

Teresa sat on the edge of the bath. Rosa hesitated before she bent to kiss her mother's head. Teresa slipped her arms around her daughter, resting her face against her. She felt Rosa's body tense, but she tightened her arms around her. "Listen to me, please . . . just listen."

Rosa eased herself away but remained close. Teresa, without looking up, continued. "I never had a boyfriend, you know. All through college. It wasn't for want of trying. I made the excuse that I had to study so hard that I never had the time. My mother was always asking questions, prying, wanting to know if I had 'a young man,' as she called them. She was so scared I'd be left unmarried. Mama was frantic, like there was something wrong with me. Some days when I got home, she would have old women there, ready to introduce me to their sons, grandsons, uncles. . . . The whole neighborhood was intent on finding me a husband, but none of the introductions ever came to anything. My father was still proud, informing every customer that his daughter was a lawyer, though I wasn't. In fact, I never did finish."

Rosa interrupted. "You never finished?"

"No, I always promised myself I would go back and get my law degree, but . . . I had you to think of, and Filippo. He needed me; some of the licenses were so complicated, the export and import paper work was spaghetti to him."

"I thought you were a lawyer."

"You thought wrong. You think you know everything, but you don't."

Teresa took off her glasses and began to clean them on a towel. Rosa noticed the red mark on her mother's nose, the slight rings beneath her eyes—small eyes, watery with tears. The thin, sharp nose and small mouth were so different from her own. She felt moved by her mother's plainness and continued to stare, blushing as Teresa suddenly looked up and gave a weak smile. The smile accentuated the sharp features, stretching the skin over her high cheekbones.

"You look so like him. I see his face every time I look at you. You were conceived on our honeymoon. Did you know that?"

Rosa nodded. She eased the lid of the toilet seat down and sat, elbows on knees, chin cupped in her hands. There was no escape; she had to listen. Teresa continued. "I came home one afternoon, I used to walk in through the bakery and down the back stairs . . . this day Mama was waiting, wearing her best dress. I thought, *Oh, God no, not another suitor . . . not someone else's reject.* 'Quick, quick,' Mama said. 'Go and change, put something pretty on; we have company.' Of course, I refused—in some ways you are very like me—but then Papa rushed up to me, his face bright red. He whispered to me that I had to do my hair, wash my face, he spoke to me as if I were a child, and he repeated, 'We have company, we have company, hurry.' "

"Did you change?" Rosa asked, genuinely interested; this was a part of her mother's life she had not heard about before.

Teresa gave a small laugh. "No, I walked into the best room, the room that was polished and cleaned but rarely used. That was the first time I saw Don Roberto Luciano. Until that moment I wasn't even aware he existed. He was so tall his head seemed to touch the ceiling. He had gray hair, and he wore a dark pin-striped suit with a carnation in his buttonhole. . . . And you know, if I concentrate, I can smell it now—limes; he wore some kind of cologne that smelled of fresh limes. You could smell it in the room hours after he had left. But he stayed only a short while. He was very charming, so elegant, so . . . kind . . . yes, that is the word to describe him. Kind, more attentive to my mother than to me. As he left, he kissed my hand. I knew something was happening, but I hadn't the slightest idea what on earth it could be . . . Papa would not say a word until he was sure Don Roberto was halfway down the street. I don't think my parents ever knew why, but Don Roberto

Luciano had come to meet me, wanting me to marry his son Filippo."

Rosa leaned forward, fascinated. "Go on."

Teresa smiled, pushing her glasses up the bridge of her nose. "I was furious, I was so humiliated. My father seemed furtive, even apologetic, but Mama was beside herself. They had had to go without so much for me to be able to continue my studies, not that I gave that too much thought, I guess I was pretty selfish. I didn't even want to meet Filippo, and we argued and shouted, and Mama cried. My father said he could not insult Don Roberto, but still, I refused. I said I didn't care who he was; I accused them of living in the Dark Ages. My father shouted at me, said I was his daughter, his only daughter, he had not been blessed with a son to provide for him in his old age, he had only a daughter, a selfish daughter who drained him of every cent he earned. . . . He acted in a way I had never seen before, threatening to disown me."

"So what made you change your mind?" asked Rosa.

"Fear. You could feel it, my father was terrified. He was a simple man; he couldn't understand why Don Roberto had come to him in the first place, asking for me, for the daughter they had already begun to think they would never find a husband for. So I agreed to meet him.

"The following day Filippo came around, by himself. He was already waiting in the best room when I arrived home from college. Mama sat with him, and Papa made the introductions. Rosa, it was just so awful, the way he gestured frantically for Mama to leave us alone. I don't know what I had expected, maybe some retard. It was all kind of crazy. . . ."

"Go on."

"I thought he was the most handsome boy I had ever seen, and he was probably even more embarrassed by the situation than I was. I suggested that we go out for a coffee, you know, get out of the house—Mama and Papa were hanging around right outside the door—and he agreed. He took my hand like it was the most natural thing to do, and we walked out. I loved him from the first moment, Rosa. Then I was scared he would turn me down, so scared that I agreed to everything. I agreed to the wedding taking place within the month and agreed to allow the Lucianos to arrange the guest list, the reception, everything. When I met Graziella Luciano, I was even more afraid Filippo would not go through with the wedding. I knew she didn't think I was good enough. She made the mistake of speaking in Sicilian to Filippo; she didn't realize I understood every word. She was tearful, telling him he should wait, he was too young."

"And he was a Luciano."

"That meant nothing to me then. It was only Filippo that I was interested in. I had never had a boyfriend, and suddenly I had the handsomest man I had ever known."

"Did he love you?" Rosa could not help the disbelief in her voice.

"Yes, Rosa, he loved me. I asked him if he was having second thoughts. . . . Part of me was so afraid that he would admit that he was, but he seemed afraid that I had changed my mind, so we got married."

"Why did they choose you? Did you ever find out?"

Teresa stared at the tiled floor. "Don Roberto wanted to find someone steady for Filippo, sensible, and I guess I fitted the bill. He had never left Sicily before he met me, and Don Roberto had decided it was time for him to work in America. . . ."

Teresa suddenly didn't want to talk anymore. She dropped the towel into the laundry basket. "My parents were given the bakery, Rosa, and the apartment, and every day Mama said a Hail Mary for Don Roberto Luciano. She died blessing him, still thanking him. . . ."

"Didn't you ever ask Papa why you?"

Teresa's eyes brimmed with tears. Years later, when Filippo had started playing around, when she knew he no longer loved her, she had asked. All he had said to her was he had married her because it was what his father had wanted. He had said it with such cruelty, such disregard for her feelings, that even now she could not bring herself to tell her daughter.

"Mom? Did you ever find out why?"

"No."

"Maybe he saw you someplace, met you—"

"Yeah, maybe . . ."

Rosa followed her mother into the corridor. "Emilio said

he fell in love with me when he first saw me. You remember
that time at the Villa Rivera last summer, Mom?"

Teresa's head was throbbing; she pressed her fingers to her
temples.

"You think he would have married me anyway? Even if
Grandpa hadn't wanted it? Mom? I mean, he gave your parents
the bakery. Did he ever say what he was going to give you?"

"I've got a headache, Rosa. I need to lie down."

"I need to know. . . . *Mom*, I have to know."

"Does it matter now, Rosa? The boy is dead."

"I know Papa was being squeezed out of the business. Was
Emilio going to take over? Was that why he was going to
marry me?"

Teresa was stunned that Rosa had guessed so much. She
snapped, "Rosa, you talk of things you know nothing about."

"I'll go call Grandma. . . . I'll ask her."

"You won't."

"Why not? You scared I might say something to upset her?
She might cut you out of the will. Are you scared of that—?"

Teresa had taken enough. "Yes, maybe I am. Graziella holds
the reins, and until I get what is due to me, you don't even
speak to her. You are her granddaughter, but she'll cut you out
like *that*." She snapped her fingers. "And that was all he ever
had to do, Rosa, that's all Don Roberto ever had to do to get
people exactly where he wanted them. If it was for his son to
marry me, his nephew to marry you. . . . Grow up, Rosa! He
manipulated everyone, and Graziella was right at his side. You
upset her, and we'll get nothing. Right now that may not be
important to you, but it is to me; it's all I have left."

Rosa shut herself in her bedroom and opened her photograph album. Beneath each one was the name of the person in
her neat, childish print. She tore every picture of Emilio into
shreds. Then she came across an old photo she had forgotten
she had. About to toss it aside, she changed her mind.

"Mom? Mom!" she called.

"I'm in the study," Teresa answered.

Teresa was looking over stacks of papers and documents,
searching through Filippo's desk.

"Mom, who's this?" Rosa interrupted her.

Teresa squinted at the photograph in her daughter's hand. The picture was of the three sons of Roberto Luciano, but Michael Luciano's face had been obliterated by some scribbling. Teresa pointed. "That would have been Michael Luciano, the eldest son."

"Who scribbled over it?"

"Probably your father. That must have been taken . . . twenty-odd years ago, maybe even more. You know this is weird, I got all those old files from the company, the import licenses."

Rosa was still looking at the photograph. "Trying to assess how much we're gonna be worth, huh?"

"I was just interested. I got a bus to the docks. The Luciano warehouses are all boarded up, the gates to the yards covered in barbed wire. . . . *I know I had the files right here.*"

Teresa was banging open the drawers, slamming them shut. Suddenly she sat back. "Someone's been here. There's not one file left with the Luciano name on it, not one letter. Filippo's diaries, his address book, they were all here because I put them on the desk myself."

"You going to call the cops?" asked Rosa.

Teresa shook her head. "What's the point? Nothing of value's been taken."

"Must have been of value to someone. Otherwise they wouldn't have bothered breaking in and taking whatever they took, right?"

"Unless they thought there *might* be something . . . I'll call Sophia."

The ringing of the telephone seemed to be part of Sophia's dream. She struggled awake.

"Sophia? It's Teresa. Did I wake you? I never checked the time."

"That's okay, Teresa. How are you?"

"Broke and waiting. You seen Graziella?"

"No."

"You've not been to see her?"

"No . . . I've had things to do, the new season starts soon, and the sale of last season's dresses. I have to get the stock ready for the boutiques, and I haven't even been near the warehouse—"

Sophia realized she was making one excuse after another for not contacting Graziella. She closed her eyes and sighed; she had done nothing, seemed incapable of doing anything.

"We had a break-in here. . . . Hello? You still there? Can you hear me?"

Sophia closed her eyes. "Yes, I can hear you."

"I said we had a break-in. They took all of Filippo's papers, photographs, some of the files I had from the trucking company and the gasoline—"

Sophia interrupted. "Constantino's desk was cleared out weeks ago. Same thing, just papers."

"Why? You don't think it was Graziella or someone working for that lawyer guy?"

Sophia yawned. "Graziella? Of course not. It could be the police; it could be any number of people. Probably someone who used to work for Don Roberto. It's just a precaution; don't let it worry you."

"Worry? Someone's been inside our apartment."

Sophia threw back the duvet. Naked, she eased her legs over the side of the bed, feeling for her slippers with her bare feet. She held the phone loosely. "Don Roberto had a lot of connections, Teresa, people who don't like anyone outside their circle knowing what they're involved in. They were probably just checking there was nothing incriminating, no names, no unfinished business."

Teresa let the phone fall back onto the hook. "Sophia sounded drunk, slurred, but unlike us, she's not hurting for cash. But then she never did."

"You don't like Sophia, do you?" Rosa asked.

Teresa was still checking the desk for the missing items. She sighed. "Sophia said someone had searched her apartment, and she just seemed to accept it. Well, I don't. I'm having the locks changed."

Rosa perched on the end of the desk. "I wouldn't bother. As soon as we get the money, we can move. I want to live near Central Park."

"You'll have enough, sweetheart, to live wherever you want."

Teresa stared at the old family photograph. The three young

boys all looked so innocent, but the deep scratches obliterating Michael Luciano's face made the snapshot eerie. She traced the deep lines that almost cut through the paper. "It's strange to think, if it weren't for this faceless boy, Don Roberto wouldn't have offered to be a witness for the prosecution. If it weren't for Michael Luciano, they all would still be alive."

Rosa studied her mother's face. Teresa's mouth was drawn into a thin, tight line as she stared at the snapshot. Rosa watched as she tore it into shreds, letting the pieces fall into a wastebasket one by one. . . .

"If we haven't heard by the end of the month, we are going to Sicily, whether Graziella likes it or not. We've waited long enough."

# 6

Graziella rewound the tape. She had played the same section over and over and knew it almost by heart, but today she had a notebook and pen ready to make notes of the names her husband had dictated only weeks ago. The deep voice filled the large book-lined room, and she sat, pen poised. "My firstborn son, Michael, returned from America in the summer of 1963 . . ."

Graziella pressed the fast forward button. Zzzzzzzzzzzzzzz . . . Her husband's voice continued. ". . . and it was Lenny Cavataio, acting under Paul Carolla's instructions, who was waiting for Michael when he returned to Sicily. Lenny Cavataio knew that the heroin he was to sell my son would undoubtedly kill him." Again Graziella wound the tape forward, listened as Roberto Luciano explained how he had traced the heroin and obtained proof that it had been made at Carolla's refineries.

Emanuel's voice began speaking on the tape, asking why, if Luciano had such direct evidence of Paul Carolla's involvement in narcotics, he had never even informed the police. Graziella only half listened as her husband replied that at the time Lenny Cavataio could not be traced.

"Besides," he added, "I am a man who settles my own scores. That is my law, a law within a law."

There was a brief pause on the tape. Then Don Roberto went on. "Nevertheless, I intended to gain enough evidence to convict Paul Carolla if necessary. But it became exceptionally difficult. Witnesses disappeared, and I had to wait a considerable time until my son recovered enough to be questioned. You must understand he was an addict; he was very sick."

Graziella groaned softly. Until she had first heard the tape, she had been unaware of her son's heroin addiction.

Roberto's voice continued. "Two months later my son had made a good recovery. He was well enough for me to bring him home for a visit. But he was still not secure enough in himself to be entirely trustworthy. He needed more time to adjust, to regain his health, mentally and physically."

Graziella couldn't resist the memory of her son, standing beneath her bedroom window with his arms full of flowers, calling up to her "Mama, eh, Mama, I'm home! Mama, I'm well."

Her husband's voice was still without a sign of emotion. "Michael returned to the mountains, staying in a small shepherd's cottage. Four of my men guarded him day and night, only my trusted driver knowing the precariousness of his condition. That was Ettore Callea, who died on the second of August, 1963. There is, I believe, a police file on his assassination. August the second, 1963, was the day I found my son's body. Three of his guards had also died: Marco Baranza, Giulio Nevarro, and Silvio Braganza. They had been shot with a Biretta, but my son had been beaten to death. He had fought to stay alive, fought with his bare hands. His nails were torn out by the roots. A hypodermic syringe, containing enough heroin to kill four men, had been forced into his arm. One guard, the only one to survive, was found with bullet wounds to his chest and groin. Gennaro Baranza was able to describe my son's killers. They were not Sicilian but American. I did not discover their identities until many years later, when Lenny Cavataio made his statement. He knew my son's killers. They had worked for Paul Carolla. . . ."

There was a slight pause on the tape, a rustle of papers. Then Emanuel spoke. "These Americans, I need their names. I will need to question them."

Don Roberto answered, "I'm afraid that will be impossible. Paul Carolla made sure they could never be traced; even their bodies have never been found."

Emanuel asked if it would be possible to question Gennaro Baranza. Luciano replied that Baranza had recently suffered a stroke. His speech was badly impaired, and he had been, since the shooting, wheelchair-bound.

Graziella switched off the tape. The palms of her hands were sweating, leaving an imprint where she had pressed them against the polished surface of the desk. How many lies had her husband told her? Too many even to assimilate. She knew now why the boy brought home in the velvet-lined coffin wore the cotton gloves on his hands, why his face was that of a stranger. He had not been shot, as Graziella had been told. He had died not quickly but fighting for his last breath, clawing at his killers like a pitiful animal.

Graziella's face twisted into part smile, part grimace. She knew she would have to listen to all the tapes.

As Graziella prepared to play the second tape, Adina brought her breakfast tray. She put it down wordlessly and removed the untouched tray from the previous evening. She received only a impatient *grazie* from her mistress, who was wearing the same clothes she'd worn the day before.

The second tape started with a short introduction by Emanuel stating the day and time of the recording. Don Roberto's voice began immediately, saying that he was aware of the obvious repercussions to himself of the information he was about to divulge and that he took complete responsibility. No one else was involved. He made no excuses for his membership in the Mafia but described how, at a meeting of the commission, he had been refused justice for his son's murder. The members had implied that his son's addiction was self-inflicted, that no one but Michael was to blame. They had not dealt with the manner of his death. Paul Carolla's power within the organization was, at that time, reaping vast financial rewards for the members; no one wished to go against him. And no one wanted a vendetta, a war on his own doorstep.

Then Don Roberto mentioned a young don, Antonio Robello, nicknamed The Eagle, and explained how the young man

had approached him, offering his condolences and the help of
his family should the time arise for Luciano to need backing.

"I decided to take the justice I had been refused. I had to
plan with great care; if anyone in the organization were to hear
of my intention, it would cause repercussions within my own
business, my own family."

Graziella felt chilled. All this had occurred when? After
they had buried Michael? When they were still grieving? When?
The tape gave the answer.

"I arranged that in one day, beginning in the early hours
of the fourth of November, 1963, Paul Carolla's refineries, factories, warehouses, and two fishing boats would be systematically destroyed. I had been a bomb disposal expert in the war;
I knew what explosives and timing devices would be required.
Robello was an avid pupil because I offered him, as an incentive, two years' free trading with my companies plus access to
my cargo ships, my docks and warehouses. It was also agreed
that he would inherit Carolla's territory.

"The explosions were to go off at intervals throughout the
day. I knew Carolla was staying in Palermo with his mistress,
and I also knew he had just purchased a new Alfa Romeo. . . .
I wanted Carolla to see, to know he was being wiped out before
the last explosion, the bomb planted in his car that would kill
him. Each device was to be meticulously timed, and I schooled
Robello for two months before the day."

Graziella turned off the tape and thumbed through her diary. The date, November 4, was familiar to her, but she could
not at that moment recall why. She checked her notes at the
front of the diary and discovered that it was the wedding an-
niversary of Filippo and Teresa. . . . The day Don Roberto
had pinpointed for the destruction of Paul Carolla was his own
son's wedding day.

Graziella understood now why Filippo's wedding had been
arranged in such a hurry, why he had chosen that mouse of a
girl Teresa Scorpio. Teresa's family were nothing, dependent
on a small bakery, and had no connection with any of the major
families. She knew why the don himself had overseen the reception, specially invited the handful of guests. She had tried
to persuade Filippo not to rush into a marriage with such a

plain girl, a girl so much older than he, and had been unable to understand why he had even contemplated marrying her. Now she knew: Don Roberto had arranged Filippo's wedding as a cover for his attempt to destroy Paul Carolla. In his desire to avenge one son, he had used another.

Graziella pressed her fingers to her temples. She recalled that the couple Don Roberto had hired to run the villa during their absence resembled the Lucianos so much that no one would even know they had left for New York. She remembered how her husband had laughed about it. She switched the tape on again and felt the hairs on her arms prickle; by coincidence, she heard Don Roberto's laugh again, this time emanating from the tape recorder.

The laughter stopped. His voice was soft, menacing. "A perfect alibi in New York. The couple I had hired to take care of the villa were given my clothes and my wife's clothes to wear, always a hat, pulled down just so. . . . You see, I knew Robello did not trust me. He was too hungry. Foolishly he had already approached some of Carolla's contacts, who, in turn, became suspicious. This I knew, and I intended, should it become necessary, to use the information. So it was imperative that Robello should not discover that I was leaving Palermo. For obvious reasons we had previously arranged that there should be no further contact between us until one month *after* the bombings, after Paul Carolla was dead."

Luciano fell silent. It was a few moments before he spoke again.

"In one day my friend Paul Carolla lost millions, and more than fifteen of his men were arrested."

"How many men died?" asked Emanuel.

Luciano did not reply. He simply continued. "Carolla lost everything but his life. My plan backfired, leaving me in a very vulnerable position. I was, understandably, the most obvious suspect, but I was not even in Palermo. I had a perfect alibi. I was at my son's wedding in New York."

There was another long pause on the tape. Graziella knew it had not been turned off; she could hear the rustle of papers.

"Please continue. I have made a note on the dates and will verify that the police records of the explosions coincide—"

The don interrupted, his voice harsh with controlled anger. "Understand, *amico*, I am not on trial, *capich'*? Be sure, my friend, if I incriminate myself, I am more than aware of it. I am here for one reason only: Paul Carolla. There are many who will be afraid, many, but I have no interest in any other man. I have waited more than twenty years."

Emanuel interrupted hesitantly. "But you must understand my position. If you incriminate yourself, I must make—"

"You make sure, my friend, that there are no repercussions either to myself or to my family, is that clear? Do I make myself clear? Now, do you wish me to continue?"

There was a pause, and the tape clicked. Graziella knew there must have been some kind of agreement between the two men.

Don Roberto's voice was calm and controlled. "Robello failed to assassinate Paul Carolla. I became the main suspect and was accused by Carolla. The outcome of his accusations was that we both were called before the commission. I can give no names, but the commission is made up of a select group of men, top organization men who are voted in by the members to act as jury and judge—"

Emanuel interrupted. "The same men who refused you justice over your son's death?"

"Yes, the same men. I gave them my information about Robello's intentions of taking over Carolla's business, told them that even before the bombing occurred, he had contacted Carolla's people in preparation for the take-over. Robello became the main suspect. On my return to Sicily he tried to extricate himself by making a disastrous attempt to assassinate me."

There was that laugh again, a cold, hard laugh. "Robello's attempt on my life made Carolla offer me his friendship, a truce. Now I will tell you why I have mentioned this entire episode. This was given to me by none other than Paul Carolla, a gift to show his good intentions. The box was delivered to my home with this note."

Graziella could hear something being placed onto Emanuel's desk.

"It is not a bomb, my friend, it is the severed hand of Antonio Robello. You will see, still attached to the finger, his family ring. It resembles a bird's claw, no? His nickname was most apt, no? The remains of Antonio Robello were never discovered, but the note, in Paul Carolla's handwriting, is all the evidence you need."

The tape was switched off and then started again. Emanuel asked, "What was your relationship with Paul Carolla? He offered a truce. Did you take it?"

"On the surface, of course. I had no option, but I was in a stronger position than ever. He had lost millions and owed millions more, but that was not enough. I continued to wait for my opportunity. I swore to avenge my son, no matter how long it took, how many years. You see, my friend, my son is still alive in my heart."

Graziella couldn't listen to any more. She ordered her car and left immediately for the library in the center of Palermo.

Graziella was in the library for three hours, reading newspapers dating back to the time of Filippo and Teresa's wedding. She read about the destruction of Paul Carolla's refineries. The headlines screamed of a Mafia vendetta and the biggest-ever narcotics haul. She also read that twelve men had lost their lives in the series of bombings.

She found the issue that covered the assassination attempt on her husband. Paper after paper named Don Roberto Luciano as a hero, described how he had cooperated with the police, and in one statement after another, Luciano denied all knowledge of a vendetta. Yet again, there was the evidence of her husband's powers of manipulation; the fact that Luciano himself had attempted to defuse the bomb Robello planted in his Mercedes seemed enough, even to Graziella, to connect him with the spate of bombings. Luciano was quoted as saying that he had not even been in Palermo at the time of the previous bombings but at his son's wedding in America. There were letters of thanks to the don from the widows of the police officers killed in the assassination attempt, gratefully accepting his donations. Only one paragraph in each of two papers described the pitiful deaths of two little sisters who had been riding their bicycles past Luciano's Mercedes when the bomb exploded. The grief-stricken parents also thanked Don Luciano for his generosity.

Graziella returned to the Villa Rivera, feeling tainted. Behind the facade of husband and father had been a man she did not know existed. She had never allowed herself to suspect; she had lived surrounded by death and murders.

Graziella looked at her driver, who had worked for her

husband for many years. She leaned forward and tapped his broad shoulder.

"Diego . . . how long did you drive for Don Roberto?"

"For twenty-five years, signora." He adjusted the rearview mirror to see her more clearly.

"Then you must have seen much? Met many people?"

"*Sì*, signora."

"Did you ever meet Gennaro Baranza?'"

"I don't recall his name, signora."

"He was a bodyguard to my son, Michael. Do you remember my son?"

"*Sì*, signora, I remember him well. . . ."

"Eduardo Lorenzi, Niccolò Pecorelli and Giulio Carboni. Did you ever drive these men? See them with my husband?"

He gave a furtive look into the driving mirror. Her blue eyes held his for a moment before he looked back to the road. "I was just a driver, signora, I'm sorry."

They did not speak again until he opened the door for her on their arrival at the villa. The man towered above her, and she looked up into his gnarled, heavily lined face. "For twenty-five years you worked for Don Roberto. Look around you. . . . See? Everyone has gone; there is nothing to be afraid of."

"Signora, I was just one of the drivers, that is all, nothing more."

"But you were his driver on the night of the murders; you were the one to find him."

He made the sign of the cross and bowed his head. Graziella asked him to accompany her into the house, but he refused. She could hardly conceal the anger in her voice.

"I need to talk with someone, I need to ask questions, I need . . . can't you understand? I will pay you, whatever you ask."

He stepped away from her, and she threw up her hands in a gesture of impatience. Turning from him, she walked up the white steps leading to the porch.

His voice made her turn. "I have a family. . . ."

She faced him. "So had I, Diego, so had I."

Graziella phoned Mario Domino, who was greatly relieved to hear her voice. He had tried to reach her for weeks, but she had refused to answer his calls. She had not checked the piles of work he had been diligently overseeing or answered any of his hand-delivered letters.

"Are you well?"

"Yes, Mario. . . . Will you find a man called Gennaro Baranza? I must meet with him as soon as possible."

He felt the chill in her voice. "Graziella? You must meet with me! I have done considerable work on the tax situation, but we must discuss the sales of the companies."

"Another time. I have to go to court. Remember Mario, Gennaro Baranza, he used to work for Don Roberto. It is very important."

"But, Graziella, this must be given precedence over everything else! You must consider—"

"Mario, I leave everything to you."

"You cannot, Graziella. I cannot take the responsibility. Perhaps you should call your daughters-in-law—"

There was a silence on the line.

"Graziella, are you there? Please, this is insanity! I have laid off all the men as you instructed, but don't you understand what you are doing? All Roberto built, everything he spent his life building—"

Her voice was harsh. "I want to speak with Gennaro Baranza. I will call you this evening."

Before Domino could say another word, she had hung up. She was making it impossible for him to negotiate the sales he had set up on many of the companies. Her only instruction to him had been "Get rid of everything, sell everything." She wanted nothing, no part of the Luciano holdings. She wished only for the cash to be accumulated for her daughters-in-law and her granddaughter. Domino had begged her to wait, to get some advice, but she was adamant that nothing must remain. She even instructed him to include the Villa Rivera in the sale price.

Graziella clenched one hand in fury as Adina entered the study. "You may go, Adina, I'll fix myself something to eat later."

"Diego asked me to give you this. He's waiting in the kitchen."

Graziella tore open the cheap white envelope. There was a short note, written on ruled paper.

Dear Signora Luciano,

I am sixty-four years old. I would like to retire, go and live with my son and daughter. I beg you to release me.

Yours with great respect,

D. Caruso

Graziella picked up her checkbook. "He's still waiting, you say?"

"*Sì*, signora."

Graziella wrote out a check and put it in one of her husband's crested manila envelopes. She handed it to Adina.

"Tell Signor Caruso he has nothing to fear. He is free, and I wish him a happy and peaceful retirement."

The following morning Mario Domino set out early to drive to the Villa Rivera in the hope of catching Graziella before she left for the trial. There was only one guard at the wrought-iron gates, and he opened up without even asking Domino's name.

Mario noticed that the gardens were already looking neglected; the hot weather had dried the grass quickly. The swimming pool was a dark, murky green, and decay was sweeping through the orchards. Around the trees, laden with their rotting fruit, the flies swarmed in clouds. The tennis court had begun to sprout weeds; the net hung limply, and a racket that had belonged to Michael lay abandoned on the grass.

The villa was shuttered, every window closed. Domino parked his car behind the Mercedes, which still stood in the driveway, and walked around the back to the kitchen. Adina was hanging out some wash.

They sat in the kitchen. Adina told Mario that Graziella rarely, if ever, ate and most nights never slept.

"She plays the tapes over and over. . . . I hear his voice, like a ghost through the house, and she has taken every photograph down. I don't know what to do, she is making herself ill, she is so thin, so—"

"Has the doctor been to see her recently?"

"No, signor, she sees no one. The phone she will not allow me to answer. . . . And look, see all these letters and cables? She does not even open them. She listens only to the tapes.

Yesterday Diego Caruso left. She has no one to drive her now; she took a taxi into town."

Domino decided he would return that evening with the doctor.

Adina wept, wiping her eyes with the back of her hand. "It is as if she hates the don. All his clothes, everything that belonged to him she has made me give to the missions. . . . Signor, what is on those tapes? What makes her act this way?"

Domino sighed, patting the servant's shoulder. "Perhaps the truth."

Going down the long drive, Domino remembered the day Don Roberto had discovered his wife's visits to his office. At first Domino had tried to deny that they were a regular occurrence, and Don Roberto had snapped that there was nothing that was not reported back to him. Domino had been afraid; this man for whom he had worked all his adult life still terrified him.

"Your wife, Roberto, feels greatly that she is in some way to blame for Michael's death, that you did not allow her to nurse him. If she knew more . . ."

"Understand this, Mario. Graziella is my wife; she is the mother of my sons. You will tell her nothing, nothing, unless I give you permission." Then he had given that charming smile of his. "You may call it jealousy; even after all these years I have not forgotten you were once to be married. I am sorry if I spoke curtly, forgive me. . . . She may come to you once a month. I will give you certain information she may be told, no more, no less."

The spectators were always seated at the trial before the prisoners were brought up from their cells below the court. This was often a long procedure. The cages ranged along one entire wall of the massive courtroom, like a zoo; the bars reached from floor to ceiling, and as many as thirty men at a time were herded inside, in handcuffs and sometimes leg irons. Each cage was locked, and a guard positioned at the door, before the next group of prisoners was led in. In each cage was a microphone that could be turned on if a prisoner requested to speak with the defense counsel.

The lawyers always remained outside the court until all prisoners were locked in. The judge entered last, taking his seat on the high rostrum facing the horseshoe of counsel.

When a prisoner was required to take the stand, he was led by armed guards to the bulletproof glass booth that served as the witness box. Advisers ranged alongside the judge, and there were microphones in front of each man. The courtroom was filled with earsplitting calls for order. When things got out of hand, the judge threatened that the trial would continue without the presence of the prisoners, a maneuver that gained a brief silence.

For Graziella, the prisoners in their cages grew to be a sickening fascination. Had any of these men worked for her husband, carried out the terrible crimes the prosecuting counsel accused them of? How many of these men who had come in chained to each other like animals were linked to the Lucianos?

Carolla's sweating face, his obsession with cleaning his nails, filing and picking at the cuticles, drew her attention. She stared, kept on staring. Had Michael's death, in the end, joined Luciano and Carolla together? If she had known the truth, known the way her son had died, nothing would have stood in her way, no matter what the cost. She could not, like her husband, have waited. Why had he waited? And why, if Carolla was unlikely ever to be freed, had Roberto chosen to be a witness? He must have known the dangers, not only to himself but to his family.

When the trial closed for the day, Carolla had still not taken the stand, had never used the microphone that linked him with the court. He had sat impervious to the proceedings.

Graziella returned to the villa, more determined than ever to uncover the truth. Mario Domino was waiting for her. Adina, as instructed, had shown him into the dining room. The study was always kept locked now; Adina was not even allowed to clean it. It was littered with documents and tapes, and notebooks were stacked on the desk, and Graziella was, in truth, afraid lest anyone find out how much she now knew about the Lucianos.

The dining room was cold. She did not turn on the light, preferring to sit in the shadows. Domino opened his briefcase and took out some files.

"Did you find Gennaro Baranza for me?"

"Yes, he lives with his son in Mondello. They run a small hotel; I have the address and phone number. He is very frail. May I ask why you wish to see him?"

Ignoring the question, she asked if he would like a sherry. Just as he accepted, they heard the buzz of the door intercom.

Mario was slightly flustered. "That may be the doctor. . . . Now please, before you say anything, for me, see him—"

"Please apologize for wasting his time, and, Mario, when I need to see a doctor, I am capable of calling one for myself."

Mario returned to find her flicking through his papers. She looked up, her face paler than ever. "You know, every day at the trial I look at the men in the cages, and I know many of them must have worked for or been known to Don Roberto. I hear of prostitution, blackmail, kidnapping, extortion, murders, and I think of this place, I think of my life. I listen to his voice, and he is a stranger to me. . . . I have lost three sons, but worse, I have lost all respect for him, Mario."

"Then you do him a great injustice."

"Do I? How much of his fortune was built on fear? How many died to make my family worth being murdered for? You want to hear what I have been listening to? Hear him laughing when he describes how he arranged his son's marriage as a cover for murder? Do you want to hear what he did, how he used me, how he used his sons?"

"Throw the tapes away. Don't listen to them."

"I will listen to every one of them. Because even at the end he lied to me. He said he could not rest, could not die in peace without giving Michael the justice he deserved. It was *lies*! He could not die in peace unless he destroyed Paul Carolla. He was not content to have him in prison; that was not enough. Carolla had to *know* that it was Don Roberto Luciano who put him there. Michael had nothing to do with his decision, Mario; it was for himself. He wanted to prove to Carolla that in the end he had beaten him."

"That is not true, Graziella."

"No? How much proof did he need for his courts, for his law? And if my husband had been alive to go to the witness stand, who do you think would have paid the penalty? Paul

Carolla? No! My family, my sons . . . He would have destroyed them anyway. Well, he succeeded, and now I want nothing, nothing to be left. My granddaughter, my sons' wives, none of them must know the truth. I want them to live their lives without fear. I want them free, Mario."

Mario picked up his papers and carefully rearranged them in order, stacking them in his briefcase. He snapped the locks, resting his hands on top.

"As you wish. I will contact you as soon as the transactions have taken place. But understand, you will be giving the very people you despise access to your husband's legitimate companies, companies that werc to have been your sons' inheritances."

"Mario, I know about my sons. Please don't think me that naive. They were part of it, too. I have read enough of your files to understand that much. I also understand how you played Roberto's game. Well, no more lies. I want to go to my grave in peace. Now you must excuse me; it has been a very long day."

Mario looked at her sadly. "I have always loved you. You must know that. I would protect you with my life, but I could not go against his wishes."

"Because you were afraid? Tell me, Mario, were you afraid of him too?"

"What do you mean by that? To whom have you been talking?"

"Diego Caruso. He was afraid even to talk to me."

"What did you ask him?"

She gave a small shrug of her shoulders. His heartbeat quickened, and his indigestion grew ten times worse. He sucked constantly on strong antacids, but the pain would not abate.

Graziella's remark unnerved him. His hands shook as he replied. "Graziella, never, understand me, *never* ask questions of anyone. If you need to know something, then ask me, ask me."

"Who were they, those men? Why did you search this house?"

"For your own protection. I had to make sure there was nothing here, nothing anyone else would need or want—nothing incriminating, do you understand? The men I introduced to you ran certain branches of the Luciano holdings in the States. . . ."

"But you were afraid of them?"

"No, no . . . If it appeared so, then perhaps I am over-tired."

"Mario, have there not been enough lies?"

His heartburn was worse, and he was growing impatient with her. "I was not afraid for myself! On one hand, you tell me to cut all ties with the organization; then, when I do so, you accuse me."

"I am not accusing you."

"Graziella, we are not dealing in small amounts of dollars and lire but in billions! Don't you understand how difficult you have made things for me? I have negotiated with the main families to take over Don Roberto's territories in America—New York, Atlantic City, Chicago, and Los Angeles. But the Sicilian families also want to negotiate. Even though it is against your wishes, I am simply trying to do what I believe is in your best interest. Your demand that I sell everything, whether at a profit or not, has caused nothing but suspicion. I am also trying to transfer all money to a Swiss bank account so that you would not be taxed as you would be if it were paid here in Palermo. You would be losing billions of lire, millions of dollars, in death duties and taxes. . . . And then today one of my clerks—"

Domino had to sit down; he could not get his breath. "I have sixteen men in my offices, all working toward finalizing all the contracts for your daughters and granddaughter. Today, however, we have come across certain discrepancies. . . . One of the buyers, I believe, though I cannot be sure, is acting under orders."

Domino could hardly bring himself to say the name. "I think that Paul Carolla is using fictitious names to purchase the Palermo-based export company, which includes the warehouses, the dock—"

Graziella banged on the table. "How in God's name can this happen? The man is in jail, how can he be negotiating?"

"*He is not*! He is employing men to buy for him, but until I can verify that, until I can trace every one of these buyers . . . Here, see for yourself, see how many contracts, how much work all this entails. Tomorrow I am going to check out as much as I can in Rome."

Domino's harassed face went gray, and Graziella brought him a glass of water, which she held for him while he searched for his indigestion tablets. She watched as he gulped at the water, then slipped her arms around his shoulders.

"Forgive me. I have misused you, tired you, and never said one word of thanks."

He patted her hand. "You know I will do my best; that is all I have ever been able to do. But I am tired, and this—this last. . . ." In a gesture of despair he held up the bundle of notes from his clerks.

Graziella put them back in his case. "If you discover that Paul Carolla is trying to buy so much as a single orange tree, then withhold the sale. There is no hurry; we can wait. . . . Let the ships rot; let the warehouses fall into the water. I would rather be a beggar on the street than sell to Carolla."

Mario smiled at her. "You will never be on the streets. You and your daughters will, I assure you, be well taken care of."

"What will you do, Mario, when it is all over?"

He snapped his briefcase shut. "Retire, live out my old age in blissful ignorance of everything occurring in the world. I have always wanted a garden, did you know that? And I have always lived in an apartment without even a window box."

Arm in arm they walked to his car, surveying the once-beautiful gardens. He laughed. "Perhaps you could hire me; I could come here and take care of that lawn. It is so neglected."

Graziella smiled. "You forget, the villa is to be sold."

"Ah, yes . . . I don't suppose you remember, oh, it was a long time ago. . . . You were standing over there, in front of the groves, and you were wearing a big picture hat and a pair of gardening gloves. 'This is my world,' you said to me. You were so happy, so beautiful, so very beautiful."

She tightened her grip on his arm. "I was happy, Mario, ignorant but happy. My three sons, my husband, this wonderful villa—what more could a woman have wanted?"

"Not me, that was sure." He gave a grunt of a laugh. She opened his car door and stood waiting while he put his briefcase inside, then sat, wanting to go, wanting to stay.

"I made this my world, Mario. I thought it was secure."

He nodded, still recalling that day. The day before Michael had been found murdered.

As if reading his thoughts, she said softly, "I know about Michael, Mario. I know, and I should have been told." She bent and cupped his face in her hands. "I know now that the only innocent was Michael. Roberto used the others, didn't he? Constantino, Filippo?"

Mario agreed sadly. "He was a hard man to refuse, Graziella, yet he was so easy to love. I loved him like a brother, but you were right: I was always afraid of him. No, not always . . . Do you remember when he came back after the war? He was different then; he had changed, he was so vulnerable."

He looked up at her, even now hesitating to tell her the truth. But what was there to fear now? "He wanted out, Graziella, and he tried, but they wouldn't free him. He knew too much, was too valuable."

She stepped back from the car and shut the door. Mario continued. "I'll be in Rome for a few days. If you need me, the office will know where I am. Take care now, and rest."

She waved as he drove away, but her mind was churning over what he had said. It was true, after the war Roberto had been changed. He was very quiet, subdued, with a terrible listlessness to him that she had put down to months spent in the prison camps. As the weeks passed into months and Roberto still made no effort to find work, she had become concerned. The boys had been toddlers then, and the extra rations from her husband's friends—the black-market eggs and chickens that had been delivered throughout the war—had stopped. Sometimes food had become so scarce in the village that she had felt guilty because she had never gone without; there had always been enough bread and sometimes even butter.

Graziella stood in the imposing hall, now filled with antiques and paintings, statues and the finest carpets. How different it had been then. She sat on the stairs and closed her eyes, picturing her husband as a young man, working outside, mending fences, cutting wood for the kitchen fire. The winter had been freezing, but she watched his health return along with his appetite. But the packages had stopped coming.

Graziella put her hands over her ears. She could hear herself, hear the words she had shouted and see the children clustered around her as her voice rose to a screech, demanding that Roberto find food, his children were hungry. It was the first time the Lucianos had been short of food. Where had their supplies come from? She had never asked because she had known it was the black market, just as she'd known when she pressed his white shirt and best suit that he was not going to try to find work in town because there was no work. Sicily was desperately impoverished after the war. . . .

Graziella stood and whispered to the empty, marble hall, "I have always known. . . ."

She paused for a moment by the open carved doors of the dining room. The only sound was the soft ticking of the marble clock. She walked the length of the room, skirting the polished table, the rows of baroque chairs with their plum satin upholstery, passed the priceless paintings, the solid Georgian silver candelabra. . . . She walked beneath the crystal and gold chandelier and continued slowly by the inlaid glass-fronted cabinets filled with ornaments and treasures. Everywhere was lavish opulence.

She sat in her husband's carved chair, her hands clasping the arms, feeling the lions' open mouths with her fingers. "I have always known," she whispered again. There in front of her was the single sheet of notepaper with one line in Mario Domino's meticulous handwriting: "Gennaro Baranza. Hotel Majestic, Mondello."

Adina could not believe it when Graziella burst into the kitchen.

"We are going to Mondello. . . . I need you."

"Mondello?" Adina smiled. She had been born in Mondello but had not been there for many years. "But, signora, you have no driver."

"I know. That is why I need you. You will have the map, and you will direct me. I am driving."

"Oh, no, signora! Please, no, don't drive."

Graziella's driving had been a family joke for years. When she had learned to drive, she had caused so much damage that everyone remembered it. Adina had been tending the vegetable garden when Graziella drove through the wicker fence, backward. Graziella had then given way to the pressure, quite content to be driven.

The single guard on duty had just enough time to open the right-hand gate before the Mercedes screeched past, right over his foot. As he hopped up and down in agony, the car jolted to a halt. He watched fearfully; it seemed to be coming back toward him. . . . With another jolt it stopped, and Graziella leaned out the window.

"No one is allowed into the villa until I return."

"*Sì*, Signora Luciano."

He watched the car weave down the road in a haze of dust, the gears grinding horribly. Graziella, her face set with determination, was at the wheel. Adina sat beside her, clutching her rosary, her eyes tightly closed, but she opened them when she heard Graziella laughing. . . .

"This feels so good, I feel good now, Adina. Now, the map is in the glove compartment."

"*Sì*, signora, but please, don't take your hands off the wheel. I'll find it."

# 7

Sophia hated the smell of the cab. It made her sick to her stomach, and the lurching, erratic driving threw her from side to side.

For the last part of the journey she had to direct the driver along narrow cobbled streets until they reached the open, tall gates to the warehouses, now converted into factories. She could see her garment cutters hanging out the windows, calling to the men at work on the heavy machines in the building opposite. The women would have recognized her yellow Maserati, but they ignored the taxi.

Sophia paid the driver and walked a few steps, swaying slightly. Her head was spinning, and her mouth was dry. She slipped on a pair of dark glasses.

As she left the shadow of the building and emerged into the bright sunlight, she heard a frantic whisper: "It's Signora Luciano!" The women ducked quickly back to their work.

Sophia entered the building by a small side door marked "S&N Designs" and climbed the narrow staircase; she had to clutch the wooden rail to help her up the old, uneven steps.

At the first landing Sophia flattened herself against the wall to allow two workmen to pass, carrying files and artwork. They thanked her politely. Before she could start up the next flight of stairs, two more men came down, carrying armfuls of dresses. She watched from the window as the men loaded everything into an S&N delivery van. Through the van's open doors she could see that there were already two filing cabinets inside.

The last of the stairs up to the top floor were expensively carpeted in a pale peach. She pushed open the freshly painted door with the tasteful gold S&N logo and entered the show-room. The reception area was filled with fresh flowers.

"*Buon giorno*, Signora Luciano."

"*Buon giorno*, Celeste. *Come sta?*"

The young woman appeared flustered. "*Molto bene.*"

"Is Nino here?" asked Sophia.

"*Sì*, signora, shall I call him for you?"

"No, *grazie.*"

Sophia continued through reception and into the outer cor-ridor. She passed her own office and approached her partner's. His door opened, and two more workers came out, carrying plants and file drawers. Nino Fabio flushed when he saw her looking at the men, then returned to his office.

"What's happening?" Sophia wanted to know.

"I've tried to contact you for weeks."

Sophia stood by his empty desk, opened her handbag, and took out a cigarette.

Nino closed the door behind her. "Are you all right?"

Sophia nodded, tossing the match in the wastebasket, then looked around the room. "What's going on?"

"Guess it must be pretty obvious. I'm moving out."

She inhaled, letting the smoke drift from her nostrils. "I can see that. Where are you moving to?"

"Do you want coffee?"

"Yes."

Nino opened the door and called for fresh coffee. He seemed very nervous. "I tried to reach you, to tell you personally. I've had a good offer. So, with this new collection for Milan, I ac-cepted. I've wanted to go for some time now. . . . Well, now I am able to."

"You never mentioned this to me before."

"Things have changed now."

"In what way?"

Nino was fidgeting around the room. "Well, I don't have to explain, do I?"

"Yes, of course, you do. I find the office half stripped, and you tell me you're quitting, just like that. I thought we were partners?"

"I tried to contact you."

She sighed, growing angry. "Well, you must know why I haven't been available."

"Well, of course, I do. I wrote to you. Did you receive my letter, the flowers?"

"Yes."

The receptionist brought two cups of coffee, put them on the desk, and left without a word. Sophia said, "I see everyone is aware of your sudden departure except your partner. You are quitting, just when I need you the most. . . . What were you going to do, clear everything out and then write to me?"

"I *told* you I tried to reach you, Sophia."

"I heard you the first time. How many people are you taking with you?"

"The ones I brought with me."

"I see. . . ." She picked up her coffee, shaking so much that she had to hold it with both hands. "Pretty low, isn't it? Sneaking out the back door?"

"I am not sneaking, Sophia, and if you had spent a little more time here, you would have known that financially we are in trouble anyway. And since—since—"

"Since what?"

Nino coughed, straightened his collar. But he couldn't resist a glance at himself in the gilt-framed mirror. He flicked his bleached blond hair into place.

"Since your husband and—"

"My husband had nothing to do with this business," she snapped, spilling her coffee as she put it back on the saucer.

Nino raised one eyebrow, mincing slightly as he spooned sugar into his coffee. "Maybe he had more to do with it than you were ever aware. Look, Sophia, please, I don't want to go into details—"

"What do you mean, more than I was aware? This is my

business. My husband had nothing to do with it."

Nino put his cup down carefully. Like Sophia's, his hand was shaking.

"All right, maybe you should know a few facts. Your husband, Sophia, was very much a part of this business. You were simply never made aware of it."

Suddenly her knees were trembling. She sat down in Nino's chair so he wouldn't see. Nino took another glimpse of himself in the mirror, then turned to face her. His overpowering cologne was nauseating her.

"The deal, or my deal, was to make sure you never knew—"

She interrupted. "What are you talking about? What deal?"

Nino raised his manicured hands to stop her. "Okay, you may as well know it all. You were an innocent, my love, a married woman with more time than she knew what to do with—"

"Don't tell me about my life, Nino."

"You wanted to open a boutique, wanted to prove something to yourself, right? You also needed a good designer, one with contacts, a good clientele. Remember how you came to me, stole me from Vittorio's? I refused, right? How many times did I refuse? But you had set your heart on having Nino Fabio design for your boutique. Think about it, Sophia: Why would a young designer walk away from a big fashion house to start work with a partner with no credit?"

"Why don't you tell me why, Nino?"

He shrugged. "Money. After I refused, I was paid a visit by your husband. He offered me more, a lot more, Sophia, and he made it difficult for me to turn him down. So I accepted, and from then on, sweetheart, the only way I could have left you was to slit my throat."

Sophia's mind whirled. She could hardly take it all in. Constantino, sweet, kind Constantino?

Nino continued. "Now don't get me wrong, we've had a lot of fun together. But two boutiques and a couple of halfhearted fashion shows a year have hardly helped my career. Your two shops ran at a loss; they were never able to pay for themselves. We have a good clientele—we should have; we've got quality goods, and I am a good designer—but forced to do everything else at the same time—"

Sophia's throat had constricted, and it was a few moments before she could speak. "So . . . my husband paid you on top of what you were earning from the boutiques. Is that what you are saying? He paid you on top of our contract?"

Again Nino sighed. "I also run a lucrative mail-order business." He paused, cocking his head to one side. "You want to see for yourself?"

He led Sophia into the small workroom where eight seamstresses made up the bales of cloth chosen by Sophia. The walls were covered by Nino's designs and notes.

"All these girls worked for how many weeks on that wedding dress for your niece? Now, who do you think was running the boutiques, organizing the stock, while nothing else was being made up? New orders came in left and right and were ignored, right? Eight girls working flat out . . . That costs, Sophia."

Sophia felt dizzy, trying to fight the picture in her mind of little Rosa floating down the stairs of the Villa Rivera in her wedding gown.

They walked out of the building. Two warehouses away Nino opened a door with no sign on it and ushered Sophia ahead of him. The noise of sewing machines was deafening as they walked through to the main workroom. Thirty-two women looked up, then continued their work. Nonplussed, Sophia followed Nino along the narrow aisle as he held up see-through briefs and negligees, hideous brassieres and garter belts, tossing them aside on his way to the back of the room.

They arrived at the open glazed door of an office. Nino turned and waved his hand at the workroom.

"This is what covered the costs of your enterprise, Sophia, all of this. . . . Come on into the office."

A small, balding man in shirt sleeves held up by armbands stumbled to his feet in a cloud of cheap cigar smoke. He looked first at Nino, then at Sophia.

"Silvio, this is Sophia Luciano."

Sophia spent the rest of the morning looking over two sets of accounts, one for her boutiques and the other the lingerie mail-order business. Nino pointed to the figures.

"Hookers and cathouses are the main buyers. We distribute to all the markets, the street traders."

Somehow she kept her control, giving no sign of what this

meant to her, but she felt foolish, inept. She had been proud of owning her own shops, independent of the Lucianos. Yet all the while, without her knowledge, *they* had been running her business, and she had been kept oblivious.

Signor Silvio's body odor was overpowering. "The situation now, Signora Luciano, is that we don't know whether you wish us to continue. We've had no one directing us for six months. Nino Fabio has been overseeing everything here, but as he is leaving, we are not sure who will be responsible for the salaries, the outgoings. . . . We still have orders to fill, but we must bring out a new catalog. We can get better deals, cash transactions, as we have in the past, for photographs, studies, et cetera—"

Sophia stood up and straightened her skirt. "This factory will be closed. Please pay everyone a month's salary."

Silvio paled visibly. He shoved the books and ledgers toward Sophia. "But, signora, this is a very lucrative business. You can see for yourself, there's a big market for these garments, with the kind of woman who dares not buy in a shop. We advertise in sex magazines—"

"The factory is closed."

The sweating Silvio followed Nino and Sophia out of the office, bleating that if he had done anything wrong, if there was a fault in his bookkeeping. . . . He stood in the center of the workroom, among the seamstresses, shouting, "I've got orders; this is good-quality merchandise—"

Sophia turned to see the man's red face as in one hand he held up a bright pink negligee, trimmed with swansdown. In the other hand was a brassiere with holes in the cups for the nipples to show through. She heard herself laughing, an alien, humorless laugh.

Nino poured a large vodka and handed it to Sophia.

"You will never survive without the sweatshop. Your shops have been running at a loss for years. If you want to continue, Silvio's a good, hardworking man. And consider the girls; you'll put them out of work, and hundreds of street traders—"

"Why didn't you ever tell me? Why?"

Nino's face hardened. "Maybe I valued my life."

The neat vodka burned her throat. "Now?"

He gave a shrug. "Now things are obviously different. If you wanted, you could find a buyer easily, but I want out, Sophia. Do you think I wanted to design that cheap shit downstairs?"

She offered him one of the boutiques outright if he would stay, but he refused, saying that boutiques were out of date.

"They will bankrupt you. Get out now, Sophia. Sell the stock. You make good money on the whores' gear, Silvio will take care of things—unless, of course, you don't *need* to keep it going?"

Sophia drained her glass and poured herself another stiff measure. "What about all the designs we worked on?"

"*We?*" Nino's face twisted. "Picking the fabric, my love, is not designing. Face facts, you've been allowed to play at business for years. Now why don't you grow up? I am taking my designs, and I am walking out of the door. If you don't like it, then—"

"Then what, Nino?"

"I've been treated like a piece of meat for too long, Sophia. You can't make me stay; if you try, I'll leak the story of your whores' factory to the press. It'll ruin any chance of your holding on to the clients I brought with me. I doubt if they'll still be interested anyway, not after the things they've read in the papers about the—the—"

She faced him, removing her sunglasses. "Not interested after what, Nino? Not after my entire family has been *murdered*?"

He sighed. "You said it, not me. Look, give me a break. I've been trapped here; now I want out. Is that such a bad thing?"

"There is nothing I can do to stop you."

Suddenly he eased up. "I appreciate it. It's a big chance for me. I will get my own label. We'll have a show in Milan, try for the American market. Sophia, I can never even say that I worked for you, do you understand? I want to go to the States. If it gets out that I was connected with the Lucianos, it could blow any chance of a visa. Your family name and the obvious connection, it's been plastered all over the papers. . . ."

She could feel the tears coming and put her dark glasses back on. "Just go."

He didn't need telling twice. She could hear him outside the office, laughing and joking with Celeste Morvanno. Then there was a strange silence. She wrote a brief note and then buzzed through to Celeste to come to her office.

"Will you type this out, please, and put it on the bulletin board."

Celeste pinned the notice up, and the women gathered around. Sophia was giving them a month's notice with six weeks' pay. The lingerie workroom and showroom would then be closed.

Sophia found later that Nino Fabio had withdrawn all the cash from their business account. He had also removed bales of silk fabrics, racks of evening dresses, and all his designs from the factory. She was to discover that he had removed large amounts of stock from the boutiques as well, forcing her to give those staffs notice. Again she paid them off from her personal account, not caring that she did not have the resources to cover the costs.

Her bankers became alarmed and requested an urgent meeting. Sophia could not even give her apartment as security, because it was part of Constantino's estate. Within two weeks she was millions of lire in the red.

Sophia flew to Sicily and caught a train from Palermo to the small village of Cefalù, where she had left her child in the care of an orphanage.

Having made the decision to find her son, she sat in the small hotel room trying desperately to form some plan of action. She had not registered as Luciano but had used her maiden name of Visconti.

From the tiny high balcony she could see the harbor, the cobbled street where she and her mother had lived, the hotel where she had worked as a maid. Above the rooftops she could see the church spire, but to her consternation, there was a new glass and concrete hotel where the orphanage had been.

Sophia threaded her way among the tombstones, unable to find her mother's grave. Eventually she laid the flowers she had brought beside a small wooden cross that bore no name and whispered a plea for her mother to forgive her.

Walking from the cemetery up the narrow street, she found little that was familiar. Twenty-five years had brought many changes. She evoked curious stares from the locals; the woman in the fine clothes was a stranger to them. She had been a stranger then, too, little Sophia Visconti, the poor girl who had brought her ailing mother to Cefalù in the hope that she would recover her health.

At first it was her beauty that they whispered about, but as the months passed, it became obvious that she was pregnant. Her mother did not live long enough to know of her daughter's disgrace, but she knew of Sophia's love for Don Roberto Luciano's eldest son. She had tried to warn her daughter that it would come to nothing, that a boy from a high-ranking family would not even contemplate marrying her, especially if it ever came out that Sophia herself was illegitimate. Signora Visconti had been relieved when the doctor in Palermo suggested the move to Cefalù; it would give Sophia a chance to forget Michael.

The move had taken nearly all their small savings; the burial six months later had used the rest. Sophia was left penniless, and as her pregnancy neared its term, she found the work at the hotel too much for her. For the last few weeks she lived at the Convent of the Bleeding Heart, where other girls like her worked in the laundry and the bakery until their babies were born.

It was growing dark as she stood outside the convent, looking up at the high roof, the narrow windows. A pale face peered down from one of the upper rooms. She had been there once, frightened and lonely, an outcast.

She turned quickly away and hurried back to the hotel.

In the small dining room a few of the residents whispered together about the beautiful woman with the fine jewels and clothes.

Sophia hardly touched her soup or the fresh fish. She sat staring into space, her hands folded in her lap. She could feel the soft skin, the polished nails, the diamond solitaire ring on hands that had once been red raw from scrubbing floors. She remembered how she had met Michael Luciano at the little coffeehouse where she had worked as a waitress when she was fifteen years old. Of course, she had known who he was; everyone knew the handsome blond boy with the the wonderful smile.

An elderly woman came to remove her unfinished meal, but Sophia was unconscious of the fact. Her past swept over her. She pictured Michael's young face, remembering how he had made love to her in the orchards before leaving for America. He had promised to come back to her, promised to write; but he never had, and she had never seen him again. That one night, that one dreamlike night, he had stripped off her cheap cotton dress and taken her virginity, leaving her with his child. That night had filled her dreams, kept her strong through her mother's death, her pregnancy, and the birth of her son.

Sophia was smiling, her slender hand stroking her neck gently. Michael had given her a little gold heart on a fine gold chain.

"Coffee, signora? Signora?"

Turning, Sophia gave the waitress a sweet smile that brought a dimple to her right cheek.

"*Grazie, grazie . . .*"

The following morning the same waitress noticed that Sophia Visconti still wore black and gave a kindly smile of recognition. The beautiful woman with the madonnalike smile she presumed was, like herself, a widow.

The coolness was as Sophia remembered. The stone walls, the floors, the heavy oak doors had not changed. In a whisper the sister had asked her to wait in the corridor. After a short while she returned.

Sophia followed the sister down a narrow passage. The nun paused at a small bishop's door, where she knocked. Without waiting, she opened the door and ushered Sophia inside.

The mother superior was seated behind a large, ornately carved desk. She wore small, rimless glasses.

"Signora Visconti, please sit down." She watched with interest as Sophia's delicate lace veil was slowly lifted.

"Sister Matilda? Do you remember me? It's Sophia."

They talked of the time when the mother superior had been simply Sister Matilda. There had been many changes since then; sadly the orphanage no longer existed, but there was a new school and a new wing for poor and needy girls like Sophia. It was hard for the mother superior to recall Sophia as a young girl—so many had come and gone—but when Sophia told her the reason for her visit, she remembered very clearly. Sophia wished to trace her son, the child born in the convent.

"I am sorry, but all our adoption records from 1950 up until 1974 were destroyed in a fire, almost thirteen years ago."

"Is there no other record? What about the church register?"

The mother superior apologized; the boy would be impossible to trace. She offered to show Sophia the new buildings, and almost without realizing she had agreed, Sophia followed her.

The sun streamed in through the main doors as the mother superior opened them. She shaded her eyes. "Come, let me show you our new school."

In a trance Sophia followed. She stood and smiled at the rows of little children, and all she could think of was her baby, the little heart-shaped gold locket. . . . During her labor she had caught the locket in her mouth, had bitten on it until her teeth had left small indentations. When she left her baby, she had put the chain and heart around his neck.

She caught the sleeve of the mother superior's gown. "He had a locket, a small gold locket. He used to like me to swing it back and forth and would reach for it with his little hands. . . . I'd swing it for him until he slept—"

"I'm sorry, Sophia. If you recall, you left the baby at the orphanage to enable you to go to work." The mother's eyes glinted behind her eyeglasses, and Sophia could hear the coldness in her voice. "There were many children at the orphanage; their mothers all promised to return. I believe when you left Cefalù, you must have signed papers giving permission, if you did not return for your child, for him to be adopted. Did you sign such documents?"

Sophia nodded. "Is there no one I can speak to, no one who would possibly remember? There must have been more than one set of records. The doctor?"

"He died more than ten years ago, God rest his soul."

Sophia wanted to scream but forced herself to follow the black-clad figure, who was now proudly showing her the gymnasium.

"Our benefactor was a very generous man. All this he do-nated and, of course, the new chapel. We are dependent on charity, as you must be aware."

They walked across the small courtyard and back to the main building for coffee. The mother superior asked calmly if Sophia took cream, sugar. . . .

Sophia stood up. "Sister Flavia, the sister at the orphan-age. I remember when I called to see if my son was still there, I spoke to her; she knew of my baby's adoption. It was Sister Flavia."

The mother superior dabbed at Sophia's spilled coffee with a tissue, then tossed it into the wastebasket. "Why now, So-phia? Why now? You released him, and may God forgive you, but would trying to trace your son now be fair to him? Unless there is a particular reason to find him?"

Sophia's voice broke. "He is my son."

"He was your son when you left him. I know you were just a child yourself, but you made the decision." She folded her white, smooth hands as if in prayer. A gold wedding ring was her only adornment. She glanced at Sophia's wedding finger.

"Please, Mother, I beg you to help me. If I could just speak with Sister Flavia . . ."

"I am afraid that will not be possible. Sister Flavia took a vow of silence more than five years ago. She is with the Sisters of the Holy Spirit. . . . Whatever changes have occurred in your life—"

Sophia had to get out; she couldn't stand the pious wom-an's cold voice another second. "Thank you for your time," she said, searching frantically in her handbag for her checkbook. She wrote a check and handed it over the desk. "Please accept this as a gift."

The mother superior smiled her gratitude as she drew the check closer, trying not to look directly at the amount. But suddenly she stared at the name printed on it.

"Luciano? Sophia Luciano?"

Sophia cursed herself for being so foolish.

"Ah, perhaps I understand."

Sophia was puzzled. The mother superior probably knew of the murders, but . . .

The cold, aloof face broke into a grimace that was meant

to be a smile. "Our benefactor, Sophia, was Don Roberto Luciano."

Sophia tried to speak, but no words, nothing could clear the scream inside her head.

"Are you all right?"

Sophia was given a glass of water. Her teeth felt the cold glass, but she could not swallow. The scream would not stop, and the water trickled down her chin.

The sound of the door opening, of a whispered conversation between the mother superior and whoever was behind the door cut through Sophia's dulled senses. Terrified that she would lose the opportunity to ask what she was so desperate to know, she found her voice.

"Please stay . . . Please, I am all right now."

The mother superior returned to her chair and the door closed.

"Did Don Roberto come to you himself?"

"No, he did not. He sent a representative."

Sophia looked up, directly into the flintlike eyes. They slid away, refusing to meet her gaze.

"Do you recall the name?"

Sophia watched the white hands, one moment relaxed, the next tense. "I believe it was his son."

There was a light tap on the door. Slowly the mother superior rose. There was a swish of her gown on the stone floor and a light creaking of hinges, then again a whispered conversation. When the mother superior returned to her desk, she was carrying a diary. She opened it, flicked through the pages.

Sophia watched as the eyes behind the glasses kept looking up, then returning to page after page of the diary.

*She's frightened*, thought Sophia. *What is she afraid of?*

The mother superior coughed and straightened the spine of the diary. "First a gentleman by the name of Mario Domino came to speak with the then mother superior. He was accompanied by the don's son. They requested to see all the records of the orphanage."

There was strength in Sophia now, and she asked angrily, "Who took my child?"

"Please, Sophia, there were many children. Yours was not the only baby, and it was not until I saw the name that I realized your connection with our benefactor. No child has ever been released to any party without the signed consent of the mother. You must have signed papers pertaining to adoption."

"Did Mario Domino take my baby?"

"Arrangements were made for the child to be adopted. There would have been a record of this event, but as I have told you, our records were lost in a fire."

Sophia rose, leaned over the desk, and snatched the diary. Then she sat back. The page was nearly blank, apart from a formal note of the generous gift made to the convent by Don Roberto Luciano. It was dated two weeks before Sophia's marriage to Constantino Luciano.

Sophia ran across the courtyard, her stomach churning. She didn't turn back, didn't see the pinched face of the mother superior watching her, making the sign of the cross at the stumbling figure. The door closed on the sight of Sophia, her body pressed against the rough stone wall, sobbing to the darkness, "He knew. . . . Oh, God, he always knew. . . ."

Pacing her hotel room, Sophia went over and over in her mind what had happened when she traveled to Palermo after the birth of her son. She had planned the visit for months, saving every penny she could from what she earned washing clothes.

Arriving at the Villa Rivera in her hand-sewn dress and the shoes given to her by the mission, she had been determined to see Michael. If he refused to see her, she would demand to see Don Roberto himself. If Michael would not marry her, he must at least contribute financially to the child's care. She had every intention of returning to the orphanage for her child.

The guard told her to go away, that the house was in mourning, but she had clung to the wrought-iron gates. Pressing her face against the bars, she had shouted that she had to speak to Michael Luciano. The guard finally pushed her from the gate, warning her to stay away, telling her that Michael Luciano was dead and buried.

For hours she had sat at the roadside, unable to move, so dazed that even now she could not recollect what happened next. She was told later that Filippo Luciano had taken a curve too fast in his car and had hit her.

Sophia had woken up in a bed at the Villa Rivera, confused and suffering from a concussion. She had been taken care of by none other than Michael Luciano's mother, Graziella. Sophia had been so terrified and bewildered that she said nothing. At one point she even believed the family intended to kill her.

Sophia rinsed a facecloth, let the water run cold over her hands. Everything that followed was clear; she could remember it all. The Lucianos had cared for her; there had been no danger. Instead, Sophia had unwittingly brought Graziella out of deep mourning.

Graziella's gentle sweetness in caring for a stranger as if she were her own daughter had lulled Sophia into a fantasy that it was all a dream. When Sophia recovered, they had driven her to her cheap motel. They gave her money until she was well enough to work, and she discovered that her room had been paid for. That might have been the end of it, but during her time at the villa she had met Constantino.

She pressed her hands over her face. Constantino had known all along about her baby, had removed him from the orphanage. . . . She could not believe it, would not believe it.

She paced up and down, remembering a long-forgotten moment when Constantino had called to see her at the hotel.

"I wondered if you would care to dine with me one evening."

She had always intended to tell him about the baby and had nearly done so. But the time was never right. . . . Had it not been right because she knew he was falling in love with her? Sophia stared from the window, remembered seeing from her hotel window the guard who had been so cruel, who had pried her hands away from the Villa Rivera gates.

She had hurried down the street, searching for him. Finding him, she had smiled, unsure at first if he knew her or not.

"I am Sophia Visconti, remember? I came to give the family my condolences, but you turned me away, pushed me into the street. Do you remember me? Remember what you said, what you did to me?"

"I am sorry, signorina, I meant no disrespect. I know you have been staying at the villa."

"Don Roberto will not hear of it from me."

She saw the fear in his eyes. Then he gave a small bow.

"I thank you, signorina, for my wife and children. It was a misunderstanding. The family were in—"

She interrupted him, her chin up. "*Sì*, a misunderstanding. The family were in mourning for Michael. I know that now."

Shaking, she had returned to her room but had then congratulated herself. She was sure the man would be too afraid to lose his job to repeat the incident, and she had been right. When Constantino began inviting her to the villa, the man who had turned her away always gave her a deferential bow. She soon realized that Don Roberto employed many men and that the gate guard was too low in the scale to be in close contact with him.

Graziella appeared to encourage the relationship between her son and the "little waif," as she used to call Sophia, but these meetings took place only when Don Roberto was not in residence. When he finally discovered that his son was courting Sophia, all hell broke loose.

Sophia sat down and began to brush her hair, thinking of how she had wanted Constantino, more than she loved him. She had wanted the fine things she had seen at the villa. Michael was dead, but his brother, the shy, stammering Constantino, was desperately in love. Ever since she had tasted their life, she had wanted to be a Luciano.

To attain her ambition, she had abandoned her son, believing that if the don were to find out about the child, he would never accept her. She stared at her reflection in the mirror, continued the slow, rhythmic brushstrokes. She knew the don had made inquiries about her when he found out about Constantino's intention to marry her, but she had believed her secret was safe. Michael's name was not on his child's birth certificate.

She remembered the day she discovered her room at the Palermo hotel had been searched, and that same day Don Roberto had visited her unexpectedly. The don had questioned her, interrogated her about her family and her mother in particular, implying that he knew all about her past.

Sure he had found out about her baby, she had thrown caution to the wind then. She had faced him, eyes blazing, about to tell him that the child was his own son's bastard. But she didn't get the opportunity. The don had cupped her face in those strong hands and told her that she had fire inside her, that he liked it. He had made her sit down and told her casually that even if her mother had never married, she could be proud of her daughter. He was as enamored of her as was his son.

She opened the shutters and walked out onto the balcony, recalling the don's words that day: "Sophia, you must understand, I ask you these questions because I must take care for my son. You love him, no?"

Afraid to speak, of saying something that would change his good mood, she nodded. And he gave his blessing for the wedding. He had approved of an illegitimate seventeen-year-old marrying his elder son.

Her fingers tensed on the balcony railing. In the years that had followed she had become the don's favorite. She had been a good wife to Constantino, had brought the introverted boy out of his shell. The two grandsons she had produced had further ingratiated her with *Papa*.

She knew now that the don had found out about the baby. What he could not know was that his beloved Michael was the child's father. All the lies, Don Roberto's carefully orchestrated cover-up of his precious daughter-in-law's past, was for what reason? Why hadn't he used it to refuse them permission for the marriage? Unless Constantino had discovered the truth himself and, with Mario Domino's assistance, made sure Don Roberto would never know. But then, why would he be named the benefactor?

Sophia gave a strange little laugh. So much had happened, so much had bruised her, battered her, that the laugh was an empty, hollow sound. There was nothing left that could be destroyed. Beneath all the hurt was the sense of betrayal. She felt like a puppet, but who had really pulled the strings? Who was the one person strong enough to have instigated such a Machiavellian plot? Graziella? Sophia was sure that the austere and deeply religious Graziella was innocent; it could only be Don Roberto himself—couldn't it? Yet Constantino had used her business. There was a side to her husband that she had never known. There was no one Sophia could turn to for confirmation or comfort, and the betrayal swamped her, added to the suffocating weight that hung on her.

Returning to her room, she forced herself to bed. The Valium didn't help; it made her feel she should give way to the dragging sensation, take it a step farther and sink into complete oblivion. Her eyelids drooped, and then a burning sensation made her gasp, as if her heart were about to explode. She heaved for breath, because it was not over. At last she had found anger, dredged it up from her belly. She had lost everything because she was a Luciano, but they had not beaten her.

Her son was the only Luciano left alive. Graziella would have to accept him. It was incongruous and tragic, but Michael Luciano's bastard son was the only male left of the line. One person would know the truth, the one person she was sure would help her. If necessary, she would force him. Mario Domino.

# 8

Mario Domino's apartment in the center of Palermo was empty. He was, in fact, in Rome, very close to Sophia's home.

Even at that early hour he was already at work in his room in the Hotel Raphael, sitting at a Louis XIV desk, his papers stacked at his feet and by his elbow. He had opened the windows to the balcony even though his room was air-conditioned. Soon the streets would be thronging with traffic and noise, but now at dawn it was reasonably quiet. His concentration was so deep that when his breakfast was brought in, he jumped from his seat, his heart pounding.

He drank cup after cup of coffee while he worked. On many of the documents he wrote the initials "P. C." with a red felt-tip pen. He had traced the buyers of more than ten of Luciano's subsidiary companies to a bank here in Rome, to a box number and had hired two men to wait for someone to collect. That person was, he discovered later, Enrico Dante, Paul Carolla's partner in a nightclub. The name on the sale contracts, however, was Vittorio Rosales, a name Domino believed was fictitious.

All the information the bank could give him was that enough money was available in the account to cover all the sales.

Domino looked at the photographs of Dante collecting from the box number and paying vast sums of cash into the account of Vittorio Rosales. He was sure Dante was acting for Paul Carolla; that meant Mario had to put all the sales on hold. He sighed; the work seemed endless, was endless. He wanted to return to Palermo, but he had one call left to make. He was not looking forward to it; he knew it would be a long and tedious meeting.

The legal firm that was handling the Luciano business transactions in Rome was being very slow, and Domino wanted to put pressure on it. One of the businesses it handled was Sophia's mail-order lingerie line. The building it occupied was owned by the family, and it was up for sale. There were also two apartment blocks and three gasoline stations.

Domino splashed his face with cold water and patted it dry, staring at his reflection in the bathroom mirror, but what he was seeing was Don Roberto, sitting at his big carved desk, drawing circles on a piece of paper, then holding up his drawing.

"You see, my old friend, the big outer circle is filled with the little companies, like an army. They confuse the enemy and protect the inner circle. That inner circle is really all I care about; it is legitimate and the most powerful. If anything happens to me, the piranhas will be snapping at my heels. They will have to bite through the outer circle, and as they bite, you will have time to ensure that the center stands firm, remains strong for my sons."

Domino sighed. The inner circle was broken, and the massive holdings Luciano had fought to keep, the docks, the warehouses, the ships, all were closed. There was not one son left to take over.

The pain in Domino's chest never seemed to leave him now, and the tablets had no effect. He made a note in his datebook to go for a checkup on his return to Palermo.

Adina brought the tray of lemonade. Her hands were still shaking. Graziella was sitting, perfectly calm, her eyes closed and her face tilted toward the sun. They were at a small roadside café, waiting for the car to be repaired.

They were just outside Mondello and had been waiting for two hours. Across the road the mechanic lay beneath the Mercedes, which had three large dents. They had not had three accidents, just a rather complicated one with a post and a tree.

"This is not as good as yours, Adina," said Graziella, holding up her glass with distaste.

"No, signora. . . . You know, maybe we could get a taxi; perhaps he will be some time."

"No, we have no need to hurry."

Adina sighed. The thought of traveling any farther with Graziella at the wheel was disconcerting. She rarely managed to get out of second gear, and the car tended to jerk. . . . They were only eight miles from Palermo, yet the journey had taken most of the morning.

"Once we pass the bus depot, I know every street; it was just coming here by road—"

"You don't have to apologize, Adina. It was a pleasant drive. I enjoyed it."

Adina's glass rattled on the tray as she put it down, but she said nothing.

"This Hotel Majestic, do you know it, Adina?"

"No, signora, I have not been here since I was a child. I know only my cousin. It is a very popular resort now, not like when I was a girl. It was just a fishing village, but the beach—"

"I know, I know. We used to bring the boys when they were young. Go and ask about the hotel."

Adina crossed the road and held a lengthy conversation with the mechanic. Eventually she returned to Graziella.

"He knows my cousin." Adina sat down and drew her chair closer to the table. "He also knows of Antonio Baranza, the old man's son. They don't like visitors; the old man rarely goes out. Maybe we should talk first to my cousin?"

"As you wish. How long will the car be?"

"Not long. We made a hole in the carburetor. I have directions; it will be no problem. The Majestic is on the far side of the square, not far from my cousin."

An hour later the Mercedes jerked through the square, causing many of the old men, sitting with their beers in the shade, to chortle.

Adina, having said she knew no one, spent much of the journey leaning out of the window addressing what appeared to Graziella to be the whole town. Since the street was too narrow for the car, Adina suggested they park in the square. She would go speak to her cousin and return immediately. It was half an hour before she came back.

Graziella was furious, but Adina paid no attention. She seemed very nervous as they headed out of the square and onto a smaller road on the north side.

"The Majestic is a café, signora. They rent out rooms. They have a few tables in front and a small bar, mostly used by residents. Not many tourists." She asked Graziella to stop a moment. "*Scusi*, signora, but I must ask you to be very careful."

"I am quite capable now, Adina. I know all the gears."

"No, no, signora, it's the Baranza family." She dropped her voice to a hushed, conspiratorial whisper. "They will not speak with you, will not let you see the old man. His son tells everyone he is senile, but my cousin knows the woman who helps in the kitchens. Sometimes she takes the old man for a walk; she pushes his chair along the harbor. There is a small bar, with tables outside. She will take him there this afternoon, and if you are waiting there, she and I will—"

"You know this woman?"

"*Sì*, signora, we were at school together. You must wait. They know who you are, signora."

"Only because you broadcast the news. It doesn't matter. I just want to speak with Gennaro Baranza."

"The Carboni family run this part of town, signora. My cousin's sister works for Alessandrini Carboni. Baranza's son also works for the Carbonis."

"I shall wait, Adina, but not for long."

Gennaro Baranza wore a straw hat, one side looking as if a dog had made a meal of it. He also wore a strange pair of ladies' pink sunglasses perched on his bulbous nose. The rest of him looked shriveled as he hunched in the wheelchair.

The plain-looking woman pushing the chair waved to Adina, who hurried to join her. They talked as they wheeled the old man toward Graziella and parked him in the shade.

Looking at the trembling man in the moth-eaten straw hat,

Graziella felt she had wasted her time. Then she heard his voice, very faintly.

"I wept for your family, signora."

His voice was slurred, and his mouth drooped at one side. He gave a slight shrug of his shoulders and gestured to his mouth. "I had a stroke two years ago. It has not helped."

She whispered, "So you know who I am?"

"Sì, signora, I know. We met, many times. I was only a young man."

"Forgive me, I do not remember."

Again he lifted his shoulders. One of his hands was crippled, but the other plucked at the knitted shawl across his knees. "My son tells people I am senile, but I forget nothing. Perhaps only what has to be forgotten."

"You knew my son Michael?" Graziella asked.

"Sì, I knew him well. He taught me to read and write. We spent six weeks together in the mountains. I loved your son, he was—" he touched his heart with his good hand "—an angel's soul."

They fell silent for a moment. Then Graziella sighed. "I did not know he was addicted to heroin. I discovered this only recently."

"Don Roberto said he would cut out the tongue of any man who told you. You would not be able to push such memories away. They would haunt you, believe me."

"I have only memories, Gennaro, of all my sons. I have lost three sons."

"This I know. I have two, but there used to be four. And my brothers, all gone."

She leaned forward. "Tell me how Michael died. Tell me everything you know."

She could not see his eyes behind the pink sunglasses, but he averted his face, as if he could not bear her to look at him. "I do not remember; my mind sometimes is as dead as my body."

"I do not believe you."

"Believe me, signora, the day your son died, I have every reason to forget, for I was left for dead. Maybe it would have been better if I had died. All that is clear is the pain, pain that is with me day and night."

Even in the shade the heat was overpowering. She offered

to push him a little farther along the harbor.

For all his frailty Gennaro was no lightweight. It was hard for her, but at last they reached the top of the harbor. She turned the chair to face the sea.

Gennaro smiled, cocking his head to one side as he looked over the brilliantly colored fishing boats in the harbor. "Who was King Lear?"

Graziella looked down at the old man. "King Lear? He was a character in a Shakespearean play. Why do you ask?"

He hesitated. "Diego Caruso, you know him?"

"Yes, I know him."

They fell silent for a moment. Then Gennaro began to talk in his croaking voice. "He was with Don Roberto that night. He told me the don carried his son like he was a baby, wrapped in the sheet he had taken from the bed. No one knew what to say to him or what to do for him. Standing in the doorway with his son, he cried out. Caruso told me this. He said it was the worst sound he had ever heard, a single cry, and it reminded him of King Lear. But I never knew what he meant. I still don't."

"He was a mighty king. His favorite daughter died and he carried her in his arms. I think the line is, 'Howl, howl—' "

Gennaro's face puckered into a heavy frown. "A daughter, not a son, eh?"

Graziella turned his chair so he faced her. "They were American, the men who killed my son? All I ask is that you tell me what you know. I would never make you go to court, never force you to be a witness. This is just for me, Gennaro, for me, for Michael's mama. . . ."

He gave a heavy sigh. "They were Americans."

"Did you know their names?"

"No. I was shown many photographs."

"Who showed you?"

"Don Roberto. I recognized their faces, but I did not know their names. But he found them. One by one, he found them."

He gave a hard chuckle. "Don Roberto found every boy from America who had so much as smoked a cigarette with Michael. Not one escaped."

"Did these Americans admit that Paul Carolla ordered the death of my son?"

Gennaro averted his face. She snatched his sunglasses from his face and stepped back in shock. One eye socket was empty, the lid a mass of scar tissue.

His voice was plaintive. "My glasses, signora, please."

She held them away from him. "Lenny Cavataio survived. Do you remember him?"

Gennaro grimaced. "He was the last, the one who knew everything, but he, too, is dead. My glasses, please, signora."

She handed them to him, but he could not manage to replace them. She did it for him, then rested her hand gently on his shoulder. "Forgive me . . . I owe you an explanation. I am trying to understand why, if my husband knew of Paul Carolla's part in my son's murder, why he waited so long. Why did he wait?"

Gennaro stared straight ahead; she had to stoop to hear him. "Don Roberto had two more sons, his family. When he found Lenny Cavataio, only then did he have the evidence, the right to demand justice. But it was too late. Carolla was already in jail."

Graziella bent even closer. "If what you say is true, why did he take Lenny Cavataio's place as a prosecution witness?"

Gennaro looked up into her face. "I don't know, signora, but becoming a witness in Carolla's trial signed his death warrant. He would have had more respect if he had taken a gun and shot Carolla. Perhaps, in the end, he waited too long."

She gripped the arm of the wheelchair as Gennaro tried frantically to turn it.

"Who ordered the deaths of my sons, my grandsons? *Tell me!*"

She could feel his panic. "I know nothing, signora."

Running toward them along the seawall came a small boy. He shouted and waved as he came closer. "Grandpapa! *Grandpapa!*"

Gennaro looked at the child as he jumped down from the wall. The child sensed his grandfather's fear and started to scream, pulling Graziella's hands from the chair.

She pushed him roughly aside. "My husband could have forced you to stand trial; you witnessed the death of my son. You owe him; pay your debt to me. Was it Paul Carolla?"

Adina could hear Graziella's raised voice, the screams of

the child. Panic-stricken, she ran toward them.

"Signora! Signora!"

As frail as Gennaro was, he faced Graziella. His voice rasped as he shouted, "I know nothing, I am nothing! I beg you to stay away from my family."

The Mercedes was swarming with children. They were tugging at the fender mirrors, and the emblem had already disappeared from the hood. Adina flew at them, arms raised.

As they began to pull away in the car, a small Citroën appeared from a side street and blocked their route. The driver was a thick-set man wearing a striped sleeveless shirt and an old cloth cap. He ran from his car, fist raised as if to strike the windshield, and pulled at the door handle. His face red with rage, he screamed and cursed.

Graziella put her foot down hard, and the Mercedes screeched forward, knocking the Citroën sideways. The man yelled after the car, "Stay away from here, *stay away!*"

Gennaro's son's fury dissipated as he watched the Mercedes go. He turned, panting with fear, as his father was wheeled toward him.

"You crazy, foolish old bastard! What did she want? What did she want?"

"Whatever, does it matter? She's a woman, what can she do?"

His son took off his cap and rubbed his head. It was true. What could she do, an old woman?

"So what did she want?"

"Tell me, do you know who King Lear was?"

His son spit at the ground and ordered the woman to take the old man inside, calling after him that from now on that was where he would stay.

Gennaro's body ached from being pushed over the cobblestones; his head sent shooting pains through his eye. But he turned and called out, "You have this hotel, you have money for beer, all from the Lucianos."

"And you are crippled from the Lucianos."

"But I can read, and I can write. . . ."

The old man's chair was hauled up the narrow step and pushed into the hotel lobby. Safely restored to his shuttered room, he heaved his skeletal frame from the chair to the bed and sighed with relief. Tossing his sunglasses aside, he massaged his eye socket with his good hand. A bullet was still lodged in his skull, another in his spine. Many times he had wished he had died that night, the night he had seen the don's car drive up the mountain track. The sentry, high on the mountainside, had shone his flashlight, presuming the don himself had come to visit his son. The passenger wore a similar fedora, the driver was the don's personal bodyguard, Ettore Callea, but as the car drew up outside the cottage, two men had sat up from the backseat, and two machine guns rattled. Two guards, one of them Gennaro's brother, had died instantly. Gennaro had run back toward Michael's bedroom, calling out a warning. He had just reached the door when the bullets tore through his body.

He had been unconscious for perhaps seconds, perhaps minutes, but the men had presumed him dead. In his semiconscious state he had seen them, watched them torture and beat the boy he called Angel Face. There was nothing he could do. He could not even call out. He just lay in his own blood where he had fallen and heard the terrible screams.

After they had left, propping the bullet-ridden body of the don's driver against the gatepost on their way, Gennaro had somehow dragged himself toward Michael. His angel was lying like a broken doll, his face nothing but a bloody mass of skin and bone.

Hours had gone by while his blood drained from his body, the pain so intense he believed he was in hell. Then the lights of a car, voices . . . Don Roberto had wrapped his son in the bloody sheet and carried him like a baby. His howl echoed around the mountains, a terrible sound. It had been Gennaro who had heard it, not Caruso. Why had he lied?

On his return to his apartment Domino found the soup and chicken his housekeeper had left in the refrigerator. He set a small tray and carried it into his bedroom. But he felt too tired to eat, and the burning sensation around his heart was worse than ever. He drank a glass of milk as he sat on the edge of the bed.

He had discovered not only the Carolla connection but banking scams; millions had been fraudulently acquired. On top of all this, there were many discrepancies within his own company; men he had trusted had been systematically siphoning off huge amounts of cash that should have been directed to the Lucianos' Swiss account. Everything was out of control; he felt incapable of handling the situation.

By his bedside were many photographs, all of the Luciano family. Over the years they had become like his own. The one of Graziella on her wedding day he had often touched, lovingly, wondering if she would have been so radiant if he had been at her side instead of Roberto Luciano.

Domino was a very wealthy man; his prized art collection and carefully chosen antiques were his children. He took out his calculator, assessing the possibility of covering some of the losses himself. He had let Graziella down, let down her daughters-in-law and her granddaughter. His fingers flew over the calculator, then froze as his arm went rigid with pain. . . . He could not get his breath, and the pain grew steadily worse. He reached for the telephone, brushed it with his fingertips as it began to ring. The bell was shrill, persistent, but he could not move those extra few inches. . . .

As soon as Sophia returned to Rome, she tried to call Mario Domino. The phone rang and rang; after a long time she hung up and then dialed the Villa Rivera, but no one answered there either. She paced her room, wondering what to do. Eventually she called down to the porter and asked for all her mail to be brought up.

The porter tapped on the door and handed Sophia two days' mail and the morning newspapers. He kept his eyes downcast, appearing eager to be gone.

Sophia closed the door and went into the immaculate living room. Not so much as a single cushion was out of place. There was deathly silence where once there had been so much noise. How many times had she shouted at the boys to keep quiet?

Most of the mail was bills, which she tossed into the wastebasket. She flipped open one of the newspapers; there was a large photograph of Don Roberto Luciano on the front page. It was an old one; his hair was still black, and she could see the resemblance to Constantino.

The headline ran MURDERED MAFIA BOSS ACCUSES FROM THE

GRAVE. She began to read the lead story, which told how the prosecuting counsel at Paul Carolla's trial had caused mayhem in the court by producing the dismembered hand of the murdered Antonio Robello, accusing Carolla of the killing.

Sophia threw the newspaper aside. Others contained even more lurid stories, with drawings of a clawlike, skeletal hand holding a noose. Paper after paper carried Luciano's name; in death he had become the Boss of Bosses. It was more than five months since the murders, yet at every opportunity the press brought up the story. The trial gave the journalists a way to taint the dead, though they continued to be wary of the living.

Sophia was disgusted and threw all the papers into the wastebasket. If she was sickened, it must be torture for Graziella. She felt guilty, knowing she should have tried to phone before now.

There was still no reply from the villa or from Domino's apartment. Sophia had to get out. She was going crazy. She had nowhere to go, just needed some air, but as she left, the paparazzi trailed after her, screeching questions, asking if she had ever met Antonio Robello, the mafioso known as The Eagle. Sophia hid her face with her hands as the cameras flashed, but even when she returned to the apartment block, there was a woman journalist waiting. She smiled sweetly, confusing Sophia. Should she know her?

"Hi, Sophia. . ."

Sophia saw the microphone and ran for the elevator.

"Signora Luciano, you lost your husband and children, our readers would be very interested in your side of the story—"

Sophia banged the gate closed and shut her eyes. Her side of the story? She shouted, to no one, just the cavernous elevator shaft: "Leave me alone!"

Again she tried to contact Graziella and Domino. She shouted at the telephone, demanding an answer, but there was only the ringing tone. In a fit of anger and frustration she threw the phone at the wall.

The small yellow pills drew her like a magnet. At least she would sleep. She could make time pass by sleeping.

No sooner had Graziella returned from Mondello than she received a call from Mario Domino's housekeeper. Now Graziella stood by his deathbed.

He lay with his hands folded on his chest, a rosary twined through the fingers. They were awaiting the arrival of his niece; there had been no one else to contact. With Adina's help, Graziella had removed all the personal photographs of her family, knowing the press would try to bribe the housekeeper; the Lucianos were still front-page material. Graziella had been photographed going into the courthouse, and her picture appeared next day under the heading MAFIA WIDOW WAITS FOR JUSTICE.

The study was full of files, so many that she knew she could not begin to sort them out. Instead, she instructed Domino's law firm to bring them all to the Villa Rivera. She locked the door behind her and walked from room to room with Adina.

She had been in Mario's home on only two or three occasions, and here was a side of him she had never really known: the artistic side of him, the art lover. She had never thought of him as being anything but Mario, their faithful friend. Yet here was such taste, such carefully arranged rooms, but for whom? Who had ever come here to admire his collections? Who had enjoyed searching out the lovingly collected antiques and knick-knacks? She could remember no man or woman who had ever been part of his life except herself.

"It feels like a museum, don't you think, Adina?"

"Sì, signora. I have packed everything away. Have you seen the china cabinets?" They looked at his collection of china, the gold-plated dinner service that no one ever ate off.

"You know, I never realized how rich he was. Somehow he always remained the poor law student to me, and he was so poor, Adina. Well, until he met Roberto."

Domino's niece and cousin stared around the apartment in awe. They had never seen such wealth. But they were to receive none of it; Domino's will left everything he possessed apart from the paintings to his university, to create a scholarship fund in his name. He had detailed every item.

The one thing that was not settled was the ownership of the paintings, which alone were valued at twenty-five billion lire. He had bought them as an investment for Roberto Luciano, but the widows never received them. The works of art were held by the government, pending verification of their rightful ownership; several of the old masters were known to have been stolen. The rest of them would disappear without trace.

The Luciano estate was dwindling fast. Domino had known the extent of the frauds, but his death caused them to escalate out of all proportion.

The documents taken from his apartment were first delivered to Domino's firm. Graziella signed a new power of attorney with the firm, stipulating that everything should be cleared up within the month. She had waited long enough and wished to settle the inheritances without further delay.

Among the papers was a small black diary for the year 1963. One of the entries, written in Domino's meticulous hand, read: "Child removed from Cefalù and taken to the orphanage of the Sacred Heart, Catania."

Domino had chosen the largest city in Sicily, next to Palermo, to ensure that the identity of the baby would never be discovered.

# 9

Luka Carolla strolled through the small town of Erice, wearing monk's robes and leather-thonged sandals. He had a straw bag slung over his shoulder, filled with seeds, wrapped in sacking ready for planting.

He paused a moment at a vegetable stand outside a fly-filled shop and touched the ripe dark plums, then stepped inside. There were cigarettes and candies, jars of herbs, and row upon row of canned food. He asked for a pound of plums and flipped through the rack of newspapers while he waited. A headline caught his eye: MAFIA TRIAL CONTINUES.

Luka busied himself looking at the herbs, but his eyes kept returning to the papers. At the last minute he bought two. He folded them carefully and tucked them in his basket beneath the plums.

The old lady beamed toothlessly. "*Americano?*" she asked. "*Sì, Americano. Grazie.*"

Father Angelo, accompanied by Brothers Thomas and Louis, was encouraged by Guido to survey the vegetable garden. Luka

148

had toiled day and night, obsessively sifting stones in his home-made sieve. Not a pin-size pebble remained. That was part of his punishment; the earth had to be pure.

Guido let the earth trickle through his fingers. "I would not have believed it possible. Look how fine the soil has become; there is not a stone to be seen."

The bamboo canes were neatly stacked; the spades and forks had been cleaned until they shone.

"It's late to plant now, but Luka thinks differently," Guido said, shaking his head. He shaded his eyes to watch Luka in the distance. "I have never seen a boy work so diligently."

Father Angelo smiled, remembering Luka as a child. "He loved this garden so, do you remember, Thomas?"

Brother Thomas breathed in noisily. "How long is he to be with us? He said a few days, but it has been months."

"And you complain? Come, Thomas, look what the boy has accomplished."

They turned as they heard the gate creak open. Luka stood there. Father Angelo smiled a welcome, then leaned on Guido and said, "We were encouraged to see your work. Brother Guido is very impressed. We all are. Is the soil beneath good still?"

"Yes, Father."

Luka's blue eyes were blindingly clear but hard as he looked from one to another. He was angry that they had been walking on his tilled soil. "Will you keep to the grass edge? I have prepared the soil for planting."

He walked past them, heading for his cell, his face tight with fury. He knew it must have been Brother Guido who suggested the visit; he was always snooping around.

Guido had tried hard to make friends with Luka, but Luka had remained silent, either not answering or staring vacantly ahead. So Guido had just watched the boy, seen him working at night, stripped to the waist, digging, sifting, seen how the scars on his back had turned a glistening pale pink. Some nights Guido had seen Luka sleeping in the open by the oak tree or walking along the skyline like a black shadow.

Guido wondered why Luka rarely entered the chapel; he had attended only one mass since his arrival. But when Guido broached the subject with Father Angelo, he was told to leave Luka to his own devices.

"He will come to chapel when he wishes. This is his home, Guido, and I look upon him as my own son. I feel toward him the love of a father for his child. But Luka has many darker— there is a darkness locked inside him that we cannot discuss. Be thankful that he has come to us, pray to God to give him comfort, for that is the reason he is here."

Luka opened the newspapers, turning each page as if he were frightened the walls would hear the rustle of the paper. He read of the prosecution's attack on his father, who maintained that he was innocent of all charges. He read part of the lurid article on the so-called Boss of Bosses, Don Roberto Luciano. He studied the old photograph, the same one that Sophia had tossed in the wastebasket. The hawk nose and black eyes were there, but the man was not as he remembered. This one had black hair; the one he had seen with his sons had been white-haired. . . . If he closed his eyes, he could see them. . . .

Luka's body trembled. Luciano's face made him feel physically sick. He was sweating; his cheeks were red. He tore the articles from the papers, unable to read anymore, folded them frantically, and hid them in his laundry bag. His father had called him crazy. After all Luka had done for him, to call him crazy . . . He had proved he was a professional.

The tap on his door made him spin around. "Yes?"

"It's Father Angelo, Luka. May I speak with you?"

Luka kicked the newspapers beneath the bed and opened the door. The walker inched into the room. Father Angelo held out his hand for Luka to help him sit on the bed.

"Is something wrong?"

"Does there have to be for me to visit you?"

"No, of course not, Father. But I was about to begin work."

"I visit you because you don't come to see me and you do not come to the chapel. One mass, Luka, since you have been here."

"I am sorry, Father, but I must finish the garden. You know yourself it should have been seeded in April. Now we are almost into August."

"When did you last take confession?"

"I have given myself penance, Father."

"You have? And since when have you been father confessor to yourself? I will hear your confession tonight; perhaps tonight you can rest. You have worked hard, too hard. As a boy, Luka, you were the same; if you lied or stole, you always made amends by working. Come to me tonight."

"Very well, Father."

Luka helped Angelo rise and assisted him to the door. There the old man stopped.

"I can maneuver myself now. God bless you. And Luka, remove the newspapers. You know I have never approved of their being brought into the sanctuary. If you wish to read papers, do so when you are outside our walls. This is not a hotel, even though you choose to use it as one."

Luka followed him into the corridor. "Do you want me to go?"

Father Angelo paused and shuffled around to face him. "Far from it. I think you have come here for peace. Perhaps you should think about staying here. In the remaining few years of my life nothing would give me greater pleasure than to see you ordained."

Luka laughed. It was an extraordinary laugh, possibly because it was heard so infrequently. It was infectious, and Father Angelo chortled. "I see the idea amuses you. I always believed you were destined for it, but I must admit I was the only one."

"Is that true, Father?"

"What, that I was the only one? Well, of course, as old Thomas says, you were a devil of a boy."

Luka walked sideways, pressing his back against the wall, keeping pace with Angelo. "You believed I had a vocation?"

"Odd as it may seem, yes. One day, when you triumph over the dark side, you will perhaps see for yourself."

Luka stopped following. As Angelo continued at his slow pace, his voice echoed back: "It is still within you, Luka. I can feel it. . . ."

He looked back. The corridor was empty. Luka's door closed soundlessly behind him.

Luka pressed his back against the door. How could he know? As dear as Father Angelo was to him, he could not know or understand. Tears filled his eyes and spilled down his cheeks, heavy tears. They flowed as he whispered the name of his friend, the poor, misshapen, dependent boy Luka had cared for when he lived at the monastery.

One of the other boys, little Antonio, had witnessed the arrival of Giorgio late one night. Antonio had been the center of attention as he told everyone he had seen the devil, had glimpsed a terrible face and a huge, deformed head with horns.

On learning these rumors, Father Angelo had called all the boys together and told them angrily that far from being a devil, the invalid in their care was a young, very sick boy. They should remember him in their daily prayers, he urged them.

He explained that Giorgio, bedridden since birth, had never experienced even the simplest pleasures. He had been born with hydrocephalus, a malformed spine, and a defective heart. His mother had died giving him birth. His father, unable to cope with him, had paid others to care for him. He had not expected the child to survive infancy, but Giorgio had passed twelve painracked and lonely years, hidden from sight. Now Giorgio was to spend his final days with them.

The wayward and irrepressible Luka had taken dares to sneak to the ground-floor window and peek inside the invalid's room. It was Luka who had started singing "Humpty Dumpty" outside Giorgio's window, encouraging the other boys to follow suit, but he had been caught. As punishment and an exercise in humility, Luka had been forced to help the monks clean the sick boy's cell. For all his bravado, Luka was terrified to confront the "devil."

Luka's delicate, perfectly proportioned face and startling blue eyes were more suited to a girl than a boy; in stark contrast, Giorgio's domed forehead, drooling mouth, and hideously deformed body made him look truly like a gargoyle.

The two boys were left alone, and Luka concentrated on swishing his mop over the stone floor. He didn't look up until he heard the sound of a bee. Then he scanned the room to try to locate it. Both boys watched as the large bee landed on the foot of the bed and crawled closer and closer to Giorgio.

"Well, swat the fucker before it stings me, you asshole."

Luka peered at the bee. "It won't sting. I know about bees. Workers and drones. This is a drone. Its only function is to mate with the queen; it doesn't have a sting. What are you so frightened of? It can't hurt you."

Luka had cupped the bee gently in his hands and carried it to the window. Then he had let out a shriek; it had stung him.

"It's a worker. The bastard stung me!"

Luka had run around the cell, flapping his hand, then had plunged it into the bucket of water. Giorgio had laughed aloud, surprising himself with his glee.

That was their first meeting, and it was the turning point in Luka's young life. The darkness was lifted with Giorgio. For inside the shell of the crippled boy were a vicious wit and a brilliant mind. His intelligence far outstripped that of the other boys at the orphanage, and his extraordinarily worldly knowledge gained from voracious reading encompassed everything from pornography to obscure Jacobean tragedies. It awed and delighted the naive Luka.

Giorgio had had access to a gold mine of books; it seemed he had bottomless accounts in many of the major shops in Palermo. It was the first Luka had seen of "plastic Aladdin's entries," as Giorgio described his credit cards.

Luka sat now in the dark garden, near the tree where the wheelchair he had built for his friend was always placed. The fact that Giorgio was even capable of going outside was a wonder to the brotherhood; Luka had breathed into the sick boy a ferocious will to live. The comical-looking duo were always together, and Giorgio was beside Luka now. Luka was pointing out the neat rows of seeds he had sown.

"Okay, this line will be lettuce; that's beans, potatoes. . . . Come winter, there'll be the fart-inducing cabbages for Brother Thomas, and then there's sprouts. . . . You gotta eat your greens, Giorgio; it's the vitamins. Have to keep your strength up. You are what you put into your body; so far all your strength is in your fucking head. Got to move it around that shriveled trunk."

They had hurled insults at each other as they returned to Giorgio's cell. Luka had lifted the sick boy from his chair onto his cot bed.

"Oh, shut up, turd features. You feed me any more fuckin' greens and I'll puke or get the runs, and you'll have to clean me up. So fuck off, you illiterate shit."

"You fuck off!"

"Cunt!"

"Anus features!"

"At least I've got brains in my head. You've only got turds."

Luka giggled, clutching his knees in the darkness as he remembered. Brother Louis had overheard them, and although Giorgio had seen his approach, Luka— had not. He had continued abusing Giorgio at the top of his voice.

"At least my turds are in the john, not in my bed, asshole."

Giorgio raised his voice. "Good morning, Brother Louis. We were just discussing Latin translations in today's literal terms. You know, the word 'fuck' was first used in the sixteen hundreds. . . . To defecate, to shit—very interesting, don't you think? The Americans use the word 'john,' meaning lavatory; the English use 'toilet,' as derived from the French *toilette*. . . . The lavatorial heel was devised and worn by Louis the Fifteenth of France to disguise his short stature. The red heel could not be detected against the red of the carpet. The heel was shaped like the S bend of a toilet. Now 'john' is used by modern-day prostitutes—"

"Giorgio, please, may God forgive you. These words are appalling. . . . And, Luka, to hear you using language that is from the gutters—"

Again Giorgio piped up, interrupting Louis. "I am so sorry, Brother, have I done something to offend you?"

"Most certainly, and I assure you I will discuss this matter with Father Angelo. He will no doubt punish this outrageous behavior. Luka, please go to your class immediately."

He was again interrupted by Giorgio, his voice even higher. "In discussing this matter, Brother Louis, will you also give him the Latin translations or just the modern terminology? I should hate Father Angelo to misinterpret what Luka and I were discussing, which you inadvertently overheard. Luka cannot in any way be blamed for a conversation you eavesdropped on. My father assured me—"

Luka's mouth dropped open as Giorgio totally flustered poor Brother Louis into apologizing. He hoped Giorgio's father would not be informed that the monks had caused their guest discomfort.

Luka had to clap his hand over his mouth to stop himself from laughing aloud. Giorgio was elated, but the effort had

tired him considerably, though he tried not to show it as Luka
pushed him back into his room.

"You were brilliant! I never heard anything like it. You
got him so mixed up. Giorgio, you are fucking *brilliant*. . . ."
Luka paced up and down, mimicking Giorgio's high-pitched,
haughty voice. "Is your father important? Is he? When you
mentioned him, I thought Louis'd shit himself."

"I just did, so you'd better call him back. He's going to be
in a worse state because he didn't wash me, and if I were to
tell tales to my father, they'd lose out on the monthly check.
One of the reasons they are trying so hard to keep me alive is
that I'm worth so much to them. Dead, the checks stop."

"God, you are so funny. No one in his right mind would
pay to keep someone here! You are the best liar I have ever
met. In fact, I think you're even better than me."

"The best lies, dear boy, are those with an element of truth.
Now, get the wretched man back. I am very uncomfortable,
not to mention stinking."

Picking up the bowl, Luka said that rather than have the
old faggot back he would do it. He removed Giorgio's robe.
That was the first time he saw Giorgio naked.

The wizened legs were no bigger than a three-year-old's,
and the curved spine made the left shoulder humped. Helplessly Giorgio attempted to cover himself, but his head lolled
and slipped from the cushions that propped him up. He wanted
to weep. "Oh, Jesus, why did you do that?" Giorgio began to
shake uncontrollably.

When at last the trembling stopped, Giorgio turned his
head away, unable to look into Luka's eyes. "I stink, I'm sorry."

The only people who had ever seen or touched Giorgio's
body were nurses and doctors, and he felt ashamed that Luka
should be doing this for him.

Luka's eyes blazed with anger; Giorgio's bedsores were raw,
and young as he was, he knew Giorgio had not been properly
attended to. He rummaged in the medicine box and took out
ointment and talcum powder.

"I'll just dab them on, and I'll be as careful as I can so it
doesn't hurt. Now, can you just lean on me? That's it, lean on
me while I do your ass."

Giorgio could smell the institutional carbolic soap on Luka's neck and see the tide line of dirt where he hadn't washed himself. He had never known such a rush of emotion. His face rested on Luka's shoulder, and before he could stop himself, he kissed his friend's neck. It was the first time in his life that he had kissed anyone. In a soft voice he whispered, "I love you, Luka."

Luka held Giorgio gently in his arms and kissed his big, flat face: strange, fluttering, childish kisses. "I've never done this for anybody before, so I guess I love you too, you big, ugly bugger," he grinned. Then he eased a clean nightshirt over the big head and buttoned the front.

Luka wasn't laughing now in the darkness. He sobbed aloud, "You big ugly bugger, you bastard! *Why did you leave me?*"

Giorgio had cheated death for years but had somehow clung on, his death sentence postponed by Luka. Tragically, just as he began to appear physically stronger, his heart condition grew worse. He was barely strong enough to undergo the necessary operation, yet if it were not performed, the doctors said he would die within weeks. When told of the dilemma, Luka had screamed that there was nothing wrong with his friend's heart, and Giorgio shouted back that just as the rest of him was fucked up, so, of course, was his heart.

"What do you mean?"

"It's got a hole in it."

"Can they fix it?"

"What do you think I'm having an operation for, wind? It's all arranged, Luka, and you'll be coming with me. I won't leave you behind, Luka; my father's promised. We'll both go to Rome. It was going to be a surprise."

Luka had cupped his friend's face in his hands, planting frantic kisses of delight on his head and cheeks. But as the date drew closer for them to leave, Giorgio's condition deteriorated rapidly. The doctors were called, and they told Giorgio's father that they doubted the boy would be fit enough to travel, let alone undergo surgery.

They were two children, but one seemed so old, so wise. Giorgio knew by the expression in the doctor's eyes after his last examination that there would be no stay of execution, no operation. He said nothing to Luka, wanting to use the time he had left to prepare his friend for when he was gone. He waited for the bell to signal the end of classes, watched from his window for Luka to come running.

Luka hurtled madly toward the high garden wall, made the insane leap by the skin of his teeth, laughing at his own madness. His strength, his health, his astonishing beauty represented to the sick Giorgio the very essence of life. Giorgio's room was always in shadow, but the brilliance of the blue sky, the bright sunlight entered his cell with Luka.

Luka's exercise books were sent flying across the room with a curse. He was always at the bottom of his class, and Giorgio, on this afternoon, his last afternoon, had wagged a finger, admonishing him. "If you don't read, you won't learn that there is a world beyond this place. It's so big, Luka, and without knowledge it will overpower you. You'll never make anything of yourself."

Laughing, Luka replied that there was no need for him to acquire knowledge; he could always ask Giorgio for it.

This was the moment Giorgio had dreaded. "No, Luka, I won't always be here."

"Bullshit! After Rome you will run with me."

Giorgio patted his bed. "Sit! You lazy slob, sit. I'm going to read to you, Luka, and no, it's not your favorite, Signor Anon."

He was referring to the time when he had asked Luka who his favorite poet was, and Luka had replied in all seriousness that someone called Anon wrote the best stuff. So Signor Anonymous had become one of their many private jokes.

Luka had spent many hours listening to Giorgio reading Byron's *The Bride of Abydos*, *The Corsair*, and *Lara*; they'd even waded through *The Siege of Corinth* and wept together over *Werner*, but the ease and fluency of the beautiful verse were beyond Luka's grasp. He had moaned that the only reason Giorgio read Byron was that the poet had been a cripple, too.

Giorgio opened a thin, leather-bound book, but before he could begin reading Byron's *Don Juan*, Brother Louis tapped on the door and ushered Giorgio's father into the room. His presence meant only one thing: There was less time than Giorgio had hoped.

Luka was asked to leave the room, but he was not concerned as he presumed they were there to finish the arrange-

ments for the long-awaited trip to Rome. Giorgio saw the gleeful
way he scurried out and called after him, "Read Rupert Brooke
tonight!"

To the astonishment and embarrassment of old Brother
Louis, Luka yelled back, "Brooke was a fairy," as he ran down
the corridor so as not to be caught.

Giorgio lay back, gasping for breath. Paying no attention
to his father, he spoke to Brother Louis, "Forgive my incorri-
gible friend. The *Faerie Queene* was written by Edmund Spen-
ser."

Exhausted, he closed his eyes, his white moon face glistening with sweat. He had nothing to say to his father or to the
cloying old Louis with his smell of mold and mothballs and his
clinking rosary. Their presence tired him, and he was too drained
even to talk.

All Giorgio wanted was to be left in peace. He let rip the
longest and loudest fart he could muster, one that he knew Luka
would have applauded, in the hope that its pungency would
make the men leave the room. It did.

Later that afternoon, eager for news, Luka peeked around
Giorgio's door and became concerned at the state of his friend.
The effort of holding out his hand to Luka seemed too much
for him.

Luka held the tiny, soft hand gently in his own, whispering, "What is it?"

"I'm dying, Luka, I'm sorry."

The two boys who had blasphemed against the Virgin Mary,
who had delighted in giving the finger to the figure of the
bleeding Christ on the cross in the monastery chapel now prayed
to them not on their knees but cradled in each other's arms.
Luka's arm lay lightly across his beloved friend's body, his head
so close that he could hear the fragile heart with the hole he
was so sure could be repaired. He gave his word that they would
never be parted; he was sure that because they had prayed so
seriously, God would be kind. He would give them time; they
would always be together. By morning Giorgio was dead.

A month after Giorgio's death his father took Luka to be
educated in America. Luka took with him Giorgio's collected

works of Lord George Gordon Noel Byron, but he never read another line of poetry.

Years later Luka returned to Sicily and saw to it that Carlo Luciano and his little brother, Nunzio, embraced in death. The two sweet, sleeping children would never know the terror of staring, open eyes, of feeling cold, lifeless fingers. They would always be together.

Guido had been wakened by the sound of Luka's high-pitched laugh. He had come to the edge of the courtyard but dared not pass through the gate. He watched for a while, then returned to his cell. At five in the morning he crossed the court-yard again. Luka was still there, now on his hands and knees, pressing down the earth. Guido moved on, toward the kitchens. About to enter, he paused; the lid of one of the garbage cans was only balanced on top, not clamped down. In the heat of the day the flies would gather like clouds. He lifted the lid and discovered torn newspapers, which he took back to his cell.

The missing sections frustrated him, but he pored over the rest of them, then returned them to the can. He could see Luka working, and under the pretext of taking clean sheets for his bed, he went into his cell.

He searched quickly. There were few places to hide anything, and he soon found the missing articles. He scoured them, nervous of being caught, and quickly replaced them. When Luka walked in, he had his hand on the clean sheets, about to strip the bed.

Guido flushed guiltily. "Ah, you are here. . . . I have brought you clean sheets."

"Thank you. I can change the bed myself. I know where the laundry is. There is no need—"

"Oh, but you are a guest. I insist."

He lifted the mattress to pull the sheet free. He did not see the gun case, but Luka did. He moved quickly, gripping Guido's wrist until it hurt. "Please leave my room."

Shaking, Guido stared into Luka's brilliant blue eyes. He could not draw himself away. Slowly Luka released his grip.

Guido rubbed his arm vigorously. "I'm sorry, I did not mean to intrude. Forgive me."

Luka's eyes did not waver from Guido until the door closed

behind him. He waited a few moments. Then in two strides he was by the bed. He threw the mattress aside; he had to find another hiding place, and fast.

The chapel was dark. Luka crept between the familiar worn benches and reached the altar. After looking quickly around, he stepped into the crypt.

The ten-foot-high cross was more than a foot thick. It was held against the wall by two heavy wooden battens. Deftly he climbed up, tucked the gun case into position, and was just sliding back down the cross when the door creaked open. There was a muffled howl and the sound of hasty steps.

Brother Louis ran this way and that, straight into the wall at one point, before he was able to reach the corridor. Arms flapping in panic, he ran, calling for Father Angelo. "Christ has risen. . . ."

Between bouts of hysterical weeping and praying, he insisted that he had seen the figure of Christ at the back of the crypt. No one paid him much attention; these states of his were not uncommon. The last time he had insisted he had seen a circus in the courtyard.

With Louis in such a state, Luka had a perfect excuse for not going to confession. He had been lucky but he believed his luck was running out. Returning to his cell, he pulled out the newspaper articles and knew immediately that they had been touched.

His anger at this discovery turned into disbelief as he read one of the articles, then checked the date. The headline read LEGAL LOOPHOLE CAUSES UPROAR IN COURT.

Emanuel's telephone in Palermo had not stopped ringing for hours. In a state of exhaustion, he gestured for his assistant to answer it while he continued his harassed conversation with two of the prosecution team.

"The judge will surely chuck it out. It's utter madness, insanity. . . ."

Dr. Inzerillo tried to calm Emanuel. "The judge can't. He's got to get the government to agree. They can't pass it, believe me."

"Jesus Christ, how long will it take?"

"As long as the government takes to make the decision. . . ."

Emanuel wanted to weep. Suddenly he leaped to his feet. "Have the press got hold of it? Is it in print?"

Dr. Inzerillo nodded. "You bet, they ran from the courthouse before the defense counsel had stopped speaking. It'll be on the television news. Where are you going?"

"There's someone I have to tell, Luciano's widow."

Graziella had just returned from Mario Domino's funeral. She had therefore not been in the court that afternoon, nor had she read the newspapers.

Emanuel straightened his tie, checked his hair, then drove up the long approach to the Villa Rivera. He felt sick to his stomach.

Graziella offered wine, but Emanuel refused. He seemed unable to sit still; he had taken his pen from his pocket and was tapping it on the polished surface of the dining-room table.

"Signora, I wanted to see you, to tell you personally. . . . Today there was a new development in the court."

He adjusted his tie again and took a deep breath. "I don't know if you are aware of the fact, but here in Italy there is a law stipulating that no man can be held in prison for more than eighteen months without trial. As you know, the court process has been lengthy; hundreds of men have been charged, some separately, some in groups. The law says that it is every prisoner's right to have all his statements and the charges against him read aloud in court before sentences can be handed down. Today the defense counsel demanded that this be done. Do you understand?"

"Sì, I understand. I studied the law before I was married. Do you know about Mario Domino?"

"Please, Signora Luciano, let me finish. Forgive me, but my time is very limited, and I must get back. The majority of the prisoners have been held for a considerable time; for example, Paul Carolla has been in jail for more than sixteen months."

Her voice was hoarse, her eyes frightened as she interrupted. "How long will it take for these statements to be read?"

Emanuel licked his lips. "At a low estimate, more than one and a half years. If the law is upheld, most of the men will have to be freed."

"Paul Carolla?"

"*Sì*, signora, Paul Carolla would be freed."

She sat back in her chair and lifted her hands in a gesture of disbelief. Emanuel continued. "That is why I am here. I wanted to assure you that everything possible is being done. However, the judge does not have the power to dismiss these demands; the matter has to be turned over to the government. It will be up to it to make the final decision. I am sure, signora, very sure, that it will refuse. The trial will continue as if nothing had occurred, until we hear from the judge."

Graziella rose to her feet. Her control was superhuman. "I am well aware of how the government works. . . . Thank you, signor, for having the decency to come and see me personally. As you said, you are very busy, so I do not wish to delay you any longer. . . ."

Adina entered the hall as soon as she heard the bell ring, but Graziella was already ushering Emanuel out. As the door closed behind him, he was still apologizing.

Graziella beckoned to Adina to follow her. "I must contact all my daughters; they must be here. They must return to Palermo immediately." Her face was like a mask. "They are going to free Paul Carolla."

Paul Carolla sat opposite his visitor and talked to him via the telephone.

"I'm gonna walk. They got no fuckin' chance, an' it's all legal. Two more months an' my time is up. Are my guys worth their fuckin' dough? You should have been in court, fuckin' uproar."

Enrico Dante's smile froze on his face. He had been running Carolla's businesses, handling the contracts, the transfer of the money, and siphoning much into his own pockets in the certainty that Carolla would never be freed. He would have a lot of explaining to do.

"Eh, you okay? What's the matter?"

Dante's voice was an octave higher than usual. "Nothin',

Paulie, it's the best news, maybe make up for some of the bad—"

Carolla's face changed; the ratlike eyes hardened. "Everything goin' through okay? You got problems?"

"No, no, everything's on course, just gonna be a bit of delay. The lawyer, the Lucianos' executor, he's dead."

"Who the fuck bumped him off?"

"It was a heart attack. So until the replacement takes over, we can't move. We got deeds but no signatures, an' Domino had agreed prices but nothin's signed and sealed. . . . We got in first, but this'll give the other families time to move in."

"I was first, you mean. I've been buying up Luciano's territory for fuckin' years, an' he never realized. How long before you know?"

"I dunno."

"Well, find out, I want that waterfront, the docks. I'm not interested in all the other crap. Get movin' on it. Up the price if necessary, right? Everythin' else okay?"

"Sure, we got no problems."

"Good . . . Now, listen, what d'ya know about a cop called Pirelli?"

Dante squinted and dabbed at his neck with a handkerchief. "Pirelli? Never heard of him."

"He keeps askin' to see me, wants to question me about that Paluso kid. . . . You know, the jail cleaner's kid that got blown away. How come I'm gettin' more information inside this shithole than you're gettin' outside?"

"I was in Rome."

Carolla stared hard, saw that Dante was uncomfortable. "Well, just as long as you're not spreading my dough around, you'll be okay."

Dante pushed his chair back, but Carolla snapped that he wasn't through yet. "My kid, Luka, he got back to the States?"

"I haven't heard nothin' about him," Dante confessed.

Carolla banged the glass between them with his fist. "Find out. I don't want him anywhere near. I'm gonna walk outta here, hear me? Check it out an' do it fast."

Commissario Joseph Pirelli had reinterviewed every suspect, checked every statement, and all he had come up with so far, after questioning the one witness to the shooting of little Julio Paluso, was that the driver of the unidentified car was possibly young, might have been blond, and was perhaps wearing mirrored sunglasses. That was why the witness hadn't seen his face. . . .

Pirelli had so far not managed to arrange an interview with Carolla, but given the possibility of Carolla's being freed, he had put the pressure on and been rewarded with a six o'clock meeting—along with Carolla's lawyer.

The meeting took place in a guarded room. Carolla was already seated when Pirelli entered.

The inspector briefly acknowledged Dr. Ulliano, Carolla's attorney, who embarked on a small, helpful speech about how his client had already assisted in every way possible in a case that obviously had nothing to do with him whatsoever since he was locked in his cell at the time of the crime.

Pirelli lit a cigarette and tossed the match in the ashtray. "I am fully aware of Signor Carolla's incarceration, but we have important new evidence that could involve Signor Carolla. We now have a good description of the killer."

Pirelli saw the dark eyes harden, the quick glance from Carolla to his attorney. He continued. "You stated that Giuseppe Paluso was cleaning the cell, with the door open. You asked if he would take a message out, is that correct? Knowing it was against the law?"

Carolla pursed his lips. "Look, you got my statement. I admitted I wanted the guy to take out a message—"

"Just the one message, or did you hope Paluso would become a regular carrier?"

Carolla leaned forward. "You read my statement; it's all in my statement. I wanted to get a message to my business associate. That was all."

"And when Paluso refused?"

Carolla laughed and spread his fat hands. "I got uptight, I admit it. I said a few things, maybe made a few threats. You get that way inside."

"So you made a few threats?" Pirelli turned the pages of Carolla's statement, then picked up a notepad. " 'You got family. You got a wife. You got—' Do I need to continue? You admit you made these threats?"

Carolla shrugged and shot another glance at Ulliano. "Like

I said, in the heat of the moment I might have said certain things, but I don't remember."

Pirelli's voice was very soft. "You don't remember. You made a threat against a man's wife, his family, and two days later, two days, his nine-year-old son, nine years old, Signor Carolla, was shot at point-blank range. It blew his head off. Have you seen the photos?"

He pushed the gruesome picture of the murdered child across the table, but Carolla averted his face, turning to Ulliano. "What the fuck is this? Get this guy outta here."

"I say when this interview is over, Signor Carolla, I say, understand? You made a threat, and two days later—"

"I had nothin' to do with that fuckin' kid. You know what it's been like for me in this pigsty? Since that happened, I can't even take a shower without some fucker wants to slit my throat. I can't eat—"

"But you admit it's a coincidence? Now, we have recordings of all your telephone conversations with every visitor. . . . Did you at any time mention this, shall we say, 'problem' you were having with the cleaner?"

Carolla rose to his feet. "I've had enough. This is bullshit. You say you got a witness, a suspect; then you *know* I'm innocent. I got an alibi, one you nor anyone else can do anything about. Go bring in your witness, and go fuck yourself."

With care Pirelli packed away his papers. "Thank you for your time, Signor Carolla. I will need to question you again."

After Carolla had been taken back to his cell, Pirelli stayed in the room. He had gained nothing but a gut feeling that Carolla had ordered the boy's death. He had no recordings of the visits, none existed. But now he would check and double-check every single person who had visited Carolla since the time of his arrest.

Carolla's paranoia increased as alone in his cell, he went over everything Pirelli had said. He clenched his fists and punched at the wall until his knuckles bled, seeing his son's face in the concrete. Then he banged on his cell door. He had to make a phone call.

Teresa was out of breath as she reached her apartment door. The elevator was yet again out of order. No amount of tenants' complaints seemed to get it fixed. Clutching a bag of groceries, she fumbled for her keys, then jammed her elbow against the doorbell.

It rang and rang until finally she dumped the shopping bag on the floor and searched her handbag. The door opened, and Rosa stood there, a towel wrapped around her head.

"Didn't you hear the bell?"

"I was washing my hair."

Teresa kicked the door shut behind her. Rosa made no effort to help her with the shopping bag but went straight back to the bathroom.

Teresa almost missed the cable. She dropped the groceries and ripped the envelope open. "Rosa! Rosa!" She ran down the corridor. "Rosa, it's come, it's here! It's from Graziella, look, look. . . . We've got to go to Palermo, first flight. Jesus Christ!"

Teresa stared, openmouthed. "What have you done? Dear God, what have you done?"

Rosa backed away from her. She had cut her hair, hacked it into jagged pieces, the top so short it was like a crew cut. But worse, it was bright orange; at least, some if it was.

Rosa ran her hand over her hair. "I cut it."

"I can see that! Why?"

Rosa shrugged, keeping well away from her mother. Teresa waved the cable at her. "We are going to Sicily, we've got to get to Palermo, and you *cut your hair*!" She turned and ran back down the corridor.

"Where are you going? Mama?"

"To get you a goddamn wig! If Graziella sees you like that . . . Oh, how could you? How could you do that to me?"

"It's *my* hair, Mama."

"You're *my* daughter! You're Graziella's granddaughter. What's she going to think? You go and pack, right now!"

She slammed out of the apartment. Rosa picked up the cable, which said little: RETURN TO PALERMO URGENT. FIRST PLANE. GRAZIELLA LUCIANO.

Sophia received a phone call in Rome. Graziella sounded distant and would say little except that Sophia must be at the Villa Rivera the next day. She would not discuss anything on the telephone.

\*    \*    \*

Paul Carolla had to wait two and a half hours before the telephone was made available for him to call Enrico Dante. He said little, just that it was imperative that Dante visit him.

Pirelli was staying in a rented apartment in the center of Palermo. The vast rooms were sparsely furnished with heavy baroque antiques. But at least the mosaic-tiled floors were cool to his bare feet.

He padded around the kitchen, making himself a mug of coffee and a sandwich, then carried them to the cavernous dining room and put them on the huge oval table. His gun holster was empty, and the sweat stains on his shirt disgusted him, so he peeled it off and chucked it in a corner. His body was tough and muscular, he looked younger than his forty-one years, but tonight he felt much older. He was tired, his eyes hurt, but he was determined to go through the list of Carolla's visitors over the past sixteen months before getting some sleep. The faster he got on with the Paluso case, the sooner he could return to Milan. His wife had hardly spoken to him since he had canceled their vacation. He had suggested that she go with their son, but she had shouted that the whole point of the damn vacation was for them to be together. He checked his watch; it was after midnight, and he had forgotten to call her, as usual. He'd do it first thing in the morning.

He began working backward; the visitors around the date of the murder were obviously the most important. He would soon discover if the same names recurred over the months.

Luka Carolla stood staring at the neat rows of bamboo canes. His job was finished, but whatever he had hoped to feel at its completion, perhaps relief, had not happened.

He returned to his cell and packed his few possessions, adding the robe and sandals at the last minute. He was ready to leave, but he still had to return to the chapel.

His heart began to pound as he crept along the stone corridor. The fear, the darkness that Father Angelo talked of filled him, weighing him down.

The heavy oak door creaked open, and he winced. But the silence was as heavy as the darkness. He put his bag down, and moved soundlessly up the aisle.

The crypt was lit by a single shaft of moonlight. The Christ figurine on the mighty cross shone; the wounds were deep shadows. Luka moved closer and closer. In the darkness his hair was like a halo, his lean, chiseled features like an angel's. Fear swamped him, making his feet leaden, each step forced, unnatural. He could not, no matter how he tried, move to the cross, climb up as he had done. He could not move. . . .

Brother Guido, watching from his hiding place behind the carved screen to the right of the cross, was almost afraid to breathe. He had been praying when Luka entered and had bent lower until he peered like a thief through the fretwork. The boy's beauty was almost ethereal. He stood with his face slightly tilted, his body straight, poised like a statue, and Guido dared not move.

The sound was very soft, like a moan on a slight intake of breath. Guido realized it was a word; Luka was saying, "No," repeating it as if in terrible pain. Guido could not stand it a moment longer; he stood up.

He could not recall, later, if he actually spoke Luka's name, but the boy's reaction was like an electric shock. He snarled, lips pulled back. His face twisted like a cat's, and he spit, hissed. . . . He began moving backward into the darkness.

Then Luka spoke, and Guido's blood ran cold.

"I know what you are, and I know what you want; but I won't bend over for you, you stinking, fucking faggot."

The door opened and closed. Guido's whole body felt hot, and tears streamed down his face. He threw himself in front of the cross, weeping.

Enrico Dante was thinking how he should go about tracing Luka when the young man sauntered into his office, wearing the mirrored sunglasses, smiling as if he was expected.

"Jesus Christ, what in God's name are you doing in Palermo?"

"I read the papers. They're gonna free him."

"If they find you they won't. You get out on the first plane, understand? They've got a new cop on the Paluso murder, and they say he's got a witness."

"I need money. I've got no money."

Dante fumbled with a set of keys and went to the safe.

"You get out, understand? Your father finds out you're still here he'll go crazy. Here, this is for your ticket and expenses."

"It's not enough."

"You take what you're fucking given and think yourself lucky."

"What if he needs me?"

"He doesn't need you. He wants you as far away from him as possible."

Luka moved around the desk. "You think I'm some dumb bastard, eh? I'm his son, you got that? I'm his son."

Dante wanted to slap his sneering face, but instead, he put another two hundred dollars on the desk. "Grow up, schmuck, we all know about you. You better get one thing clear: If they don't come through an' get Carolla off, he's gonna need somethin' to bargain with, like who did the hit on that kid. So don't play the big hood; you're still wet behind the ears. Take your dough and clear off, an' I mean, clear off . . . *capiche?* You're history."

Luka's expression was like a ten-year-old's. He blinked rapidly so as not to cry.

Dante pressed a button on his intercom and called in one of his men. He nodded to Luka. "See this kid gets on a plane."

Pirelli breezed into his office, and Bruno di Mazzo, his assistant, shot out of his chair. Pirelli was too excited to notice.

"We got a suspect, and he matches the description we got out of our witness. He visited Carolla in jail, twice, wearing mirrored sunglasses. Blond hair, mid-twenties. He had to show his passport at the prison for his visiting rights."

The young officer's jaw dropped, and Pirelli grinned. "Our suspect is Paul Carolla's son."

# 10

Luka sat in the departure lounge with twenty minutes to go before his flight. The flight attendant took up her position to check the passengers through to the plane. He joined the line.

What was there for him in New York? Where would he go? He didn't even know if the old apartment was still available. He still had a few traveler's checks, plus the money Dante had given him, but that wouldn't last long.

There was his father's safety-deposit box, but he discounted that as too difficult. Remembering that safe started him thinking about the one in Dante's office. It had been stuffed with money, most of it, he was sure, belonging to his father. Yet Dante had given him only a paltry few hundred dollars. What if his father meant to cut him off, never see him again?

He turned to check if the goon Dante had sent with him was still there. He had gone.

"Your ticket please," said the attendant. Reacting automatically, Luka almost handed it to her. Then he hesitated, turned, and walked away.

He picked up a cab outside the terminal. On his way back

into Palermo he stopped at a drugstore, then had the cab drop him at a cheap garage, where he rented a beat-up Fiat. He drove into the seedier part of Palermo and booked into a cheap motel. He was still wearing his straw hat and mirrored sunglasses. He picked up the pen to sign his name in the register, then changed his mind and wrote "Johnny Moreno."

The room stank of stale body odor, the sheets were wrinkled, and the floorboards were only partially covered by a threadbare, stained carpet.

He hung his clothes on the bent wire hangers and laid the monk's robe in a drawer. Then he turned to the cracked washbasin. There was no shower or toilet in the room. From the drugstore bag he took two packages of hair dye, read the instructions carefully, and mixed the dye in the plastic tooth mug. Stripped to the waist, he put on the rubber gloves and, with care, applied the dye. Then he sat on the bed to wait the twenty minutes for it to take.

Johnny Moreno had been a driver for his father and a few years older than Luka. He had been killed in a bar brawl. But he was one of the few men who worked for Carolla whom Luka had liked. Johnny had shown Luka how to fire a gun and had taken him to shooting galleries and gunsmiths. Guns had become Luka's obsession, and he bought every firearms magazine he could lay his hands on. Then he started buying guns and built up a veritable arsenal. He also bought a dentist's drill to customize his own bullets.

He had been set on the idea of becoming one of the bodyguards who surrounded his father day and night. Carolla's reaction was to laugh, until he found Luka's hoard of weapons. Then he hit the roof. Luka held no license, and all his guns could be traced. Carolla ordered one of his men to get rid of them.

Luka had begun to haunt the martial arts shops. One of his purchases was a thin-bladed butterfly knife, and he spent hours practicing with it. He sewed a small piece of material into the sleeve of his shirt on which to rest the knife handle. If he jerked his arm up and down quickly, the knife slid out of his jacket sleeve and into his palm. Carolla kept catching him standing in front of the mirror, practicing.

Luka used a human anatomy chart to locate the more vulnerable parts of the body. He pinned it up on his bedroom wall and created little dramas in which he attacked the life-size poster. This sent Carolla into a fury, and he threatened to take the knife away. It caused the first of their terrible arguments.

The rows had become a regular occurrence as Carolla tried, without success, to understand his son. The boy had no friends, was apparently not interested in making any, and showed no natural inclination toward the opposite sex. Women to him were an alien species. But Carolla had neither the time nor the patience to decipher his son's complexes. At this point in his life he was a very worried man, albeit a very rich and successful one.

Both the FBI and the Drug Enforcement Agency were putting the pressure on. The new district attorney was out to get him, and he knew the evidence against him was mounting. To aggravate the situation further, Lenny Cavataio had been traced and taken to Sicily.

Luka had persuaded his father to let him go along when, six months later, Carolla went into hiding. Together they had gone, by way of London and Amsterdam on a roundabout route, to Sicily, traveling on forged documents and fake passports. By the time they arrived in Sicily, warrants were out for Carolla's arrest in the States on narcotics charges.

Lenny Cavataio was being held under armed guard in Palermo. Carolla, arriving in Sicily with the express purpose of silencing him, walked straight into the biggest Mafia roundup in history.

With Luka and his two bodyguards he went on the run as the net began closing in. They fled to the mountains, relying on Carolla's contacts to keep him one jump ahead of the police, and started to make their preparations for a trip to Brazil.

Carolla's attitude to his son changed radically. The boy was calm, thoughtful, and constantly at his side. Carolla was impressed that Luka showed no sign of nerves; on the contrary, he throve on the pressure.

Never before had Luka felt so important, as if he had stepped into a role created for him, that of the professional. Nothing escaped his attention; he watched and listened and, above all, remembered names and faces, especially when he met high-ranking organization men. It was imperative that he never slip up, never overstep the role he played as the son of the most wanted man in Sicily. He had been in training for years, secret, guarded sessions, so had been ready to make his first kill without a single flicker of emotion. He had to prove his worth and expertise to his father.

Unconsciously Luka began to rock backward and forward in tiny, stiff movements as he remembered just how much proof he had given. He had shown how professional he was and had left no clue to his identity. He had learned faster than his father had given him credit for and had made fools of the punks who sneered at him. They, not he, had been caught. They were the amateurs. Now his father would be forced to see just how hard it was going to be to get rid of him.

Luka had been so engrossed in his own thoughts that he had forgotten the time. The hair dye was dripping down his neck. He checked his watch: five minutes to go. He sat staring at himself in the cracked mirror and slowly wiped the trickles of dye from his neck, then looked at the dark brown bloodlike stains on the towel and on his fingers. He ran the cold water and watched the dye run in rivulets in the washbasin. After all he had done, a few hundred dollars was his only payment. His face tightened; his whole body tensed.

Frantically he began to wash his hair, ducking his head under the water, shaking out the shampoo and sending the frothing red dye swirling around the basin.

The shampoo stung his eyes, dripped down his chest. Like a blind man, he fumbled for a towel and covered his head as if he were afraid to see himself. Then he stumbled to the bed, and slowly, as he rubbed his head, he calmed down. Finally he let the soaking wet towel slip away and flopped back onto his pillow. He tentatively lifted first one hand, then the other, holding them in front of his face. They were clean. He inched off the bed and edged around the room until he was close to the mirror, then took a surreptitious look at himself. He turned to the right, to the left, bent his head a fraction. The dye had taken well, and he congratulated himself. He felt cleansed, and Luka Carolla was now, to all intents and purposes, Johnny Moreno.

The day's court session had just finished, but there was still no word on whether or not the charges would be dropped. Carolla's team of lawyers had their hands full as Giuliano

Emanuel's case against their client mounted daily with evidence
of tax evasion, misappropriation of bank funds, blackmail, extortion. And now the accusations of the murders of Michael
Luciano and Antonio Robello. The defense counsel fought for
one statement after another to be stricken from the records, but
the judge consistently overruled them.

But Carolla's spirits were still in good shape, though he
seemed tired when he was led into the visitor's booth that evening.

Dante asked how he was, and he gave a shrug. "I got the
best guys on my side; they could make Mussolini look like the
pope. The package get off all right? You get it out of Sicily?"

Dante nodded and told Carolla that it had left on the four
o'clock plane for New York. His hand, on the communicating
phone, was sweating. "You heard anything yet?"

Carolla shook his head. "It'll take a few days. It's legal, I
gotta be released. . . . Careful what you say. That new guy,
Pirelli, says they're taping these messages." He asked Dante if
there was any news on the Lucianos.

"Nothing yet. I heard the prosecution's got three more
witnesses, lifers willin' to give evidence in exchange for their
sentences being cut, but I got no names. It was just a rumor."

Carolla knew his cell had been searched; personal items
were missing. He shouted for the guard, but no one came. He
stumbled around in the semidark and reached for his lamp, another privilege, but the bulb and batteries had been removed.
He hurled it across the cell. The batteries from his radio had
gone; the television set had disappeared. Notepaper, pens, and
clothes were missing. He shouted himself hoarse, but all he
could hear was the distant echo of the other prisoners and the
clanging of their tin mugs.

For the first time since his arrest Paul Carolla began to
admit to himself that he might never be released.

Graziella knew Paul Carolla could legally be held for only
one month longer, and she fully expected him to be released.
She had spent the entire day watching him in court, and her
rage was now full-blown.

Her body tingled, felt alien to her, but her mind was clear.

She had already dealt with the possibility of being searched. Her daily presence meant that she knew the guards by sight, and they now gave her polite nods of recognition. For the first few weeks she had proffered her bag for inspection, but for the last two sessions they had simply waved her through.

The Luger was in a small velvet bag right at the back of the safe. She felt for it, carefully removed it, and placed it gingerly on top of the wills, stacked on Don Roberto's desk.

Opening the third desk drawer, she took out the cartridges. She knew exactly how to load the gun, even how to fire it. She calculated that she had only one possible chance: the moment they brought out the prisoners. Paul Carolla, handcuffed, was always last in line. He occupied a cage on his own, close to the defense counsel's bench. The procedure was always the same: Before the lawyers took their seats, Carolla would be put in his cage and his leg shackles locked on. Her seat was directly opposite him. She dared not miss.

The kitchen garden had run wild, even though Adina had done her best to keep it cultivated. The strawberry runners caught at the hem of Graziella's skirt as she walked the fifteen paces back from the tree. She held the gun as her husband had taught her, both arms outstretched. He had laughed to see her wince, blinking at the sound, but now she kept her eyes steadily focused on the bark of the tree.

She practiced for fifteen minutes. The greenhouse suffered badly, the fence and the gate were letting the daylight through, but the tree remained unmarked. Tight-lipped with anger, she paced the distance, once more took aim. . . .

"Keep your arm steady. Remember the muzzle of the gun is where the bullet will come from. Hold it steady on the target. Your eyes are the gun." Luciano's voice was like a whispered encouragement in her head. . . . Another fifteen minutes passed, shells littering the ground, before she heard a dull thwack as the bullet found its mark. Elated, she delved into her pocket for the next cartridge.

Enrico Dante turned the shower on and started to strip off his clothes. His trousers were halfway down his legs when he became aware that someone was in his bedroom. He froze, listening, the hair on the back of his neck rising.

The curtains moved. He yanked them apart so hard they almost came off the rail. The window was open; he slammed it shut, trying to remember if he had left it like that. He heard something, listened again, then relaxed; it was the water running. Hissing with relief, he took off his trousers, which he held underneath his chin by the cuffs while he straightened the creases. He opened the wardrobe door and started to scream. . . .

Luka's hand shot out and gripped Dante by the throat, forcing him backward at arm's length. Dante didn't recognize him. His throttled scream gurgled in his throat as he backed helplessly toward his bed. The backs of his knees struck the mattress, and he fell as Luka released his hold.

Luka jerked his arm, and the knife slid into his palm. With one flick he had it open, revealing the razor-sharp blade. He knelt over Dante, held the knife to his throat, and saw Dante's eyes register recognition.

"I guess I missed the plane." He sprang back, clicked the knife closed, and smiled. "I could have slit your throat."

Dante eased himself up onto his elbows. "If Carolla knew you were here . . . You crazy son of a bitch."

Luka opened the knife again. "You gonna tell him?"

Dante shook his head, staring at Luka. With the dyed hair the boy looked crazier than ever. "What do you want?"

"I'm not sure yet. Money maybe."

Dante inched himself further into a sitting position. "Look, I was just following orders, understand? You can't stay here. They'll tie you in with Carolla. They'll make the connection."

"I didn't do anything."

"Okay . . . Whatever you say. You want dough, I'll get it. I don't keep anything here. I got no cash here."

Dante was sitting upright. He moved a fraction toward the bedside table, never taking his eyes off Luka. "We go to my club, and I'll get your cash, okay?"

Luka pursed his lips and nodded, put the knife away.

With relief, Dante said, "Gimme my pants, kid, I'll get dressed."

As Luka turned to reach for the trousers, Dante lurched for the cabinet and dragged frantically at the drawer, where he kept a gun. Luka seemed to fly through the air, landed on Dante, sat astride him, and punched his face.

He twirled his arm, and the knife flew open. This time he pressed it into Dante's neck, the blade so sharp that it drew blood. Luka sprang back, opened the drawer, took out the gun, and tucked it in his trousers.

Dante was blubbering with fear. "Look, it was a mistake, okay? I won't try anything again, please, don't cut me, please—"

He touched his neck and brought his hand away, covered in blood. "Oh, sweet Jesus . . . You're makin' a mistake. I'm tellin' you, if this deal doesn't come off, he's gonna finger you, son or not. He's gonna use you to bargain with the prosecution; he knows you hit that kid. You're gonna need me; you'll never get out of Sicily. They'll have every airport, every station checked. I can get you passports, tickets. . . . *You need me.*"

Dante drove to the Armadillo Club with the gun pressed into his bloodstained collar. They went in by a back entrance and along a corridor. Music was playing so loud that even if Dante had screamed, he doubted he would have been heard.

Once in the office, Luka locked the door and pocketed the key. Dante fumbled with the safe and started taking out bundles of dollars and lire. Luka looked at it.

"Where's the rest of it?"

Dante explained that he had paid the staff that evening, that this was all that was left.

Luka sat on the corner of the desk and tilted his head to one side. "If this deal doesn't come off, how long you reckon he'll be put away for? You think maybe he could be inside for life?"

"Who knows? Look, I can get more cash out of the till."

"Sit down. You think I'm gonna let you walk out to the bar?"

Dante reached for the phone. "Lemme call, I'll call the bar, and they can bring it in. This is all the dough I got in the place, I swear on my life."

Luka suddenly tucked the gun away. "With my father dead, you'd be in a good position, huh? Means the same for me, too."

Dante stared, and Luka smiled. "I'm his son. Everything

he has is mine. Whatever you've got I guess is yours."

Dante said nothing, watching Luka carefully.

Luka sat kicking his heels against the desk. "He's been in-side, what, seventeen months? You've been handling the busi-ness all that time? He never trusted you; he was always sure you were ripping him off. So, if he does get out, where does that leave you?"

Still, Dante didn't reply, but he watched this kid, who was so close to the truth.

Luka continued. "So what I'm saying is either way we both could be hurt, understand? I mean, there's no love lost between us. You said he wanted me out of the way; that's what you said, isn't it?"

Dante nodded.

"If he was dead, we'd both benefit, right?"

Dante found his voice at last. "You'd never get away with it, you'd never—" He shut up fast. What did he care if Luka got away with it or not? If he got caught, with Carolla dead, Dante would be even better off. He changed his tack. "How would you do it?"

Luka pursed his lips. "Maybe in the courtroom, but I'll need your help."

"Look, the law knows I work for him. Do you think they'd even let me in the courthouse? It takes all my time to get visit-ing rights for the jail."

Luka sprang off the table. "I don't mean help with the hit. I work alone. I am a professional, understand? We always work alone."

Dante nodded. "Sure, Luka." He straightened fast as Luka dived toward him.

"No! Not Luka, never call me Luka! I am Johnny Moreno. My name is Johnny Moreno, remember that, okay?"

"Sure, Johnny, I'll remember."

Dante watched as Luka picked up bundles of lire, totally ignoring the dollars. He stuffed the money in his pockets. "Okay, I'll come by tomorrow, tell you what I need."

Luka gave him a wink and walked out. Dante sat trans-fixed, his desk littered with dollars. "Christ, he almost killed me!" The proof, the dark, dried blood on his shirt, was facing him in the mirror.

Dante had no idea what to do. The kid was obviously a maniac, but why should he tell Carolla that Luka was going to attempt to kill him? He had been the bagman for too long; with Carolla dead, he could hold the reins. The kid would get himself either arrested or killed. In the meantime, he'd make no more visits to the prison, would play along with whatever Luka wanted and wait for the outcome.

Sophia Luciano pulled up at the gates of the Villa Rivera. There was no guard. She opened the gates to allow the car through, and then she heard the shots.

She ran back to the car and drove to the house. As she ran up the front steps, two more shots rang out. She shouted for Graziella, pounding on the door, but there was no reply. She ran toward the back of the house as another shot rang out. She screamed Graziella's name.

Graziella's head appeared over the fence. She waved, and Sophia stood panting with fear. "Are you all right? I heard gunshots."

Graziella had tucked the gun out of sight in her robe pocket. "Oh, it's all right. It's the guard. We are having trouble with some wild cats; they are chasing the pigeons. I didn't expect you until this afternoon. Go to the front, and I'll let you in."

Graziella opened the door, kissed her daughter-in-law warmly, and insisted on taking her suitcase.

"Mama, where are the gate guards and Adina? Are you here alone?"

"Oh, no, there's one out back. He'll have frightened the cats away by now."

The villa was dark with all the shutters closed. Sophia followed Graziella into the kitchen. There was a pot of coffee on the stove, and Graziella poured two cups.

"Adina will be back shortly. She is getting some groceries. I have to go to the trial, so you'll be left on your own."

Sophia sipped her coffee and asked when the others were expected. With a shrug, Graziella told her they would arrive sometime that afternoon. She seemed agitated, constantly looking at the big kitchen clock. "They sent a cable to say they were on the way, so we all shall dine together this evening. You don't mind my leaving, do you?"

Sophia shook her head and apologized; she should have called. She could see that Graziella had lost weight and was about to remark on it when Graziella moved to her side and pinched her cheek. "You have lost weight. Adina will fatten you up."

"Is the will final, Mama?"

"I think so, but we have had problems. Poor Mario—"

Sophia interrupted. "I have to speak with him. I'll come into Palermo with you."

"Oh, you don't know? I should have called you, but I have had so much to do. Mario's dead, Sophia."

Sophia dropped her cup. "No . . . No . . ."

Graziella got a dishcloth to clear up the damage. "I'm sorry . . . Sophia, are you all right?"

Sophia was trembling. "No, Mama, he can't be, he can't be . . ."

"He had a heart attack."

Sophia ran from the room. Graziella was about to follow when she heard the tooting of a taxi horn.

Adina had arrived, laden with groceries. The driver had to make four trips to the back door with all the bags. The kitchen table was stacked high.

"Are you going to the trial this morning, signora? If so, I can ask the taxi to wait."

"No, I shall drive. Sophia is here, take her some coffee, she's very upset. I just told her about Mario Domino. I had no idea she was so fond of him."

Adina began unpacking the bags. "Maybe she has had too much death, signora."

Graziella nodded. "Maybe."

"The taxi can wait. Signora, please, for me, take the taxi."

"No, I am taking the other car."

"The Rolls-Royce, signora? Oh, no, please, why not the Mercedes?"

"It's out of gas."

Adina hurried to the waiting taxi driver and paid his fare, then went around to the back of the house. She passed the stables and the greenhouse and saw all the shattered glass. Then she opened the garage doors. The Mercedes was in terrible condition, the front bumper mangled, both fenders dented and scraped. She searched for the keys to the dusty Corniche. Unable to find them, she returned to the house, stepping over jagged pieces of glass.

Graziella was in her room changing when Adina called to ask what had happened to the greenhouse during the night. Graziella told her that a cat had been chasing a bird, nothing to worry about. Adina shook her head and brewed some fresh coffee for Sophia.

She paused on her way upstairs with the coffee and watched from the window as the Corniche made its way down the drive. She winced as it glanced against the gate, which was open wide enough to let a truck through.

Adina tapped on Sophia's door, then eased it open. Sophia was sitting on the bed, holding her head in her hands.

"May I speak with you, Signora Sophia? She is driving the Rolls-Royce, the don's car; she is unsafe, I am so worried. She must not drive, she has no license, and she doesn't know how to reverse. We went to Mondello, no more than nine miles, it was terrible. We hit a tree and a post, we could have been killed—signora? You must stop her, please."

Sophia had not taken in a word. "What do you think has happened to Mario Domino's papers, his personal papers? Would they still be in his apartment?"

"I don't know, signora. There are boxes and boxes of documents from his firm in the study. We have only one man, and he comes and goes as he pleases; we have no driver, no gardeners. . . . She needs someone here; she should not have been alone. Every day she goes to the trials. It is all she thinks of."

Sophia rose slowly to her feet. "We'll all be here now, Adina. The others are arriving sometime today."

Sophia tried the study door. It was locked, so she went into the living room. She stood in the center of the room, looking around.

Adina followed, wringing her hands. "All the photographs, you see, she has taken them away."

"Open the shutters, Adina, and take the dust covers off. This place feels like a tomb."

Adina began to pull at the white cloths, talking all the while, telling Sophia it was too much for her to care for. With her arms full of sheets she paused at the dining-room doors.

Sophia said, almost to herself, "I needed to speak to Mario Domino."

"I am sorry, signora."

Sophia gave a soft laugh, almost a cry. "So am I. You'll never know how sorry I am. Nobody will." She gave Adina a sweet, gentle smile, and the dimple, a tiny shadow, appeared in her right cheek. "I'll help you get the rooms ready."

"Oh, no, signora, please . . ."

"*Please*, Adina, I need to do something."

Dante handed the student's identity card, in the name of Johnny Moreno, to Luka. It had been simple to acquire.

Luka looked it over, then tapped it against his cheek. "This should help me get into the trial. I'll see you later, but I want a passport in the same name. Can you get me one?"

It would take a little longer, but Dante agreed. Luka paused at the half-open door. "I'll also need a weapon, but I won't know what until I've been to the trial."

As soon as Luka left, Dante called his man Dario and told him to stick to Luka's heels, but to keep his distance. Luka must not suspect.

Luka stood in line, waiting for the guards to search the spectators as they slowly filed into the courthouse. The line was long, and Luka had paid a man halfway along to allow him to take his place. He would have to be much earlier next time if he wanted a good seat, close enough to the cages. But for now the farther away from Carolla, the better. Even with his hair dyed, there was a chance his father would recognize him.

It was the same procedure morning and afternoon; always Paul Carolla was the last prisoner brought in. Luka had noticed the delay before Carolla was brought up the steps from the cells below, noted the delay while the cage door was opened.

Carolla stared around the court. He appeared confident, even waving and talking to the other prisoners.

The guards stepped back to allow Carolla to enter the cage. For just a few moments no one was near him.

Luka asked the man sitting next to him if he had been to many of the sessions, and he nodded. Luka asked if it was always the same routine, and again the man nodded, jerking his head toward Carolla. "That arrogant bastard always does that. He behaves as if this were some kind of theater. If he's on the stand, you'll see one hell of a performance."

Luka sat down in his seat, paying no attention to the proceedings, sizing up the best possible position for the next day. He noticed the elderly woman dressed all in black and concentrated on her for a few moments, then let his eyes drift down the aisle. The end seat, that was the best one. He spent the rest of the afternoon deciding exactly what weapon he would need and how to get it into court. He had no further conversation with the man next to him.

Graziella did not have to wait in line; her seat was reserved. She had sat in the same seat since the opening of the trial and continued to pay highly for the privilege.

She was holding a crucifix. Her hands rested on her handbag, in which she had brought a large stone. The guard had not searched it.

She twisted her crucifix, her eyes constantly straying to the hunched figure of Carolla. She found a strange satisfaction in knowing there was so little time left; she would kill him the next morning.

Pirelli had received a fax from the States. Paul Carolla had married one Eva Gamberno in New York on April 19, 1955, but there was no record of a child. Eva Carolla had died in May 1959, yet the prison records stated that Paul's son Giorgio Carolla had visited him in January and in February 1987. The records stated that he had produced a passport for identification, but it did not give its number.

Pirelli's second fax drew a blank; there was no record of Giorgio Carolla's existence; he was not an American citizen. The third yielded a glimmer of light; Eva Carolla was buried in Sicily. Pirelli consulted the records for 1959.

Sure enough, there was Carolla's wife. But there was still no record of a child. So who had visited Paul Carolla, using a false passport? Who had received the order from Paul Carolla to murder the Paluso child?

Pirelli demanded another meeting with Carolla, only to be told by his chief that Carolla would be on the stand for the entire day and probably the following day, too. His evenings were taken up with his lawyers, that was his right, and unless Pirelli had some new evidence involving Carolla directly, he would not be given permission to question him.

Pirelli snapped that he had evidence that someone had used a false passport to gain access to Carolla just two days before the Paluso child was killed. He had to know who that someone was. He presented his proof that Giorgio Carolla did not exist. He was finally granted leave to see Carolla after the court session the next day.

Disgruntled, he returned to his office to find his assistant sitting in his chair again. But this time he did not jump up; he held out a piece of paper.

"Have a look at this. It's unbelievable. I was in C-four when it came through; that's how we got the copy. It's a ballistics report. You know the Luciano children were shot, two of them. . . . Look at the description of the bullets."

Pirelli snatched the paper; his eyes flew over the page; then he let it drop. "Holy shit, what the fuck is going on in this place? Who's on the Luciano case?"

Detective Sergeant Francesco Ancora looked up from the latest football results when Pirelli walked in, waving the ballistics report.

"Have you seen this? The same gun that killed the Paluso kid was used on the Luciano children."

Ancora laid the paper down carefully. "They *think* it was; it's not a hundred percent. They're still doing tests; they got only fragments from your boy."

Pirelli snorted. "Fuck that, look at the similarities, the grooves. You got the blowup photos?"

Ancora tossed him a folder and watched as Pirelli read the reports and checked the photographs of the minute chips of the bullets.

"Why weren't these sent to me earlier? How long have you had them?"

"They came in yesterday. They're still working on it. They figure the bullets were customized with a diamond drill, probably a dentist's. Holes are bored in the tops to make them explode on entry. All they've got is one millimeter from—"

"How much do you want, for chrissakes? A flag flying over your head? I don't believe this. . . ."

"Got a suspect?"

Pirelli tossed the file back on the desk. "I'm not sure, not a hundred percent. When I am, I'll let you know."

The glass in the door threatened to crack as he slammed it behind him. Ancora leaped from his seat and yanked the door open.

"Pirelli, hey, Pirelli! I don't like your attitude. You got a problem, you know that? I'm working my butt off."

Pirelli kept walking but called out, "Yeah, it looks like it, your ass is hanging over your chair."

He entered his office, and the door banged behind him.

Dante's heart pounded. He hadn't heard Luka enter his office. "You move like a cat."

Luka smiled, liking the description, and sat down in his usual place on the edge of the desk.

"I'm gonna do the hit tomorrow. Main problem is getting the gun into the courthouse, but I think I've found a way around it. That is, if you can get me what I want."

Dante spread his fat hands. "You name it, I got contacts. Just tell me what you need."

Luka beamed. "This is it. . . ."

Dante stared at the single sheet of paper, then looked up. "How the fuck am I gonna get hold of that?"

Luka smirked. "There's one in the museum, and there's one in a case at the Villa Palagonia. I've seen it on display. It'll need a lot of adjustments, but we've got all night."

The Villa Palagonia was an outrageous Gothic house on the outskirts of Palermo. It had been built by an eccentric, deformed nobleman, and the high walls were topped by strange dwarflike figures in stone, standing like sentries.

Luka pointed up to one of the figures. "That remind you of someone?"

Dante shrugged, more intent on listening to one of the tourist guides, who was explaining to Dante's man, Dario Biaze, that no one was allowed in; viewing times were four and six, the villa was closed.

"The statue looks like my father," Luka laughed.

Dario Biaze returned to the car, bending to talk to Dante. "Place is shut up, there're alarms, but give it a couple of hours, and we can get in. . . ."

Luka settled back in the seat and closed his eyes. "Well, I guess we just wait. Drive around, don't want the guide getting suspicious."

As the car passed the villa, one of the stone dwarfs seemed to leer down at them. It did, as Luka said, resemble Paul Carolla.

# 11

Teresa let the curtain fall back into place. "Here's Mama now. I can see the Rolls coming down the hill."

Sophia took a cigarette from a solid gold case and lit it with a gold Dunhill lighter. Her movements were unhurried and casual, yet she chain-smoked, stubbing out each cigarette only halfway through.

"Can I get anyone a drink?"

Teresa looked at her watch. It was not five o'clock, and she murmured that it was too early for her.

"Do you want anything, Rosa?"

Rosa shook her head and continued finishing *The New York Times* crossword puzzle. Her legs were crossed, and her right foot tapped annoyingly against the chair. She was wearing jeans, a T-shirt, and sneakers.

Sophia rose from the sofa and stretched, catlike, yawning, then walked across to pull the bell beside the door. She rang, leaned against the door, and turned her attention to Rosa.

"How's college, Rosa?"

"I left. . . . What's five letters, 'Almost with warmth but no affection'?"

187

Teresa stood up. "Tepid . . ." She couldn't bear to look at her daughter. The new haircut had caused considerable interest, if not amazement.

There was a bang and a sound of scraping metal outside. Teresa looked through the curtains again. "My God, the car's hit the gatepost—I don't believe it, Graziella is driving. She's driving the car."

Sophia smiled. "You'd better believe it, and never accept a lift. You should see what she's done to the armored Mercedes."

"Why isn't there a driver? There's not even a man at the gate, and it's obvious no one's been tending the garden. The pool's covered by millions of wasps. It's disgraceful. How could she let the place go?"

They heard Adina opening the front door, the two sets of footsteps on the marble floor.

The three women looked expectantly at the double doors. They heard Graziella's voice, then footsteps going up the stairs.

Sophia went into the hall to call after her mother-in-law. When she returned, she lit another cigarette.

"Mama's tired. She'll see us at dinner, eight o'clock. . . . And she would like us to dress."

"Who else is coming? Mario Domino, is he coming?"

"No, Teresa, he's dead. Didn't you know? He died a week or so ago."

Teresa took off her glasses. "Nobody told me. Why didn't Mama tell me?"

Sophia's head began to throb. "She didn't tell me either. Does it really matter?"

Teresa pursed her lips angrily. "Well, he was supposed to be seeing to Papa's will. I just thought I should have been informed."

"Well, now you are, and if you'll excuse me, I'm going to take a shower."

Teresa watched as Sophia left the room. Rosa gave her mother a hooded look. "Why don't you take a rest, Mama? I'll be up in a minute."

Left alone, Rosa tried to concentrate on her crossword puzzle, but she wasn't that interested in it. She tossed the paper aside and looked over at the piano. It was strange to see it without any photographs on display. Suddenly she didn't like the feel of the room or being alone. She went upstairs.

Rosa looked at her mother. "Aunt Sophia's very noticeable, isn't she? I mean—I don't know what I mean, just that she's kind of magnetic."

"If you say so."

"Don't you think so?"

"I notice she isn't short of money. That diamond she's wearing must be worth thousands. . . ."

"You really don't like her, do you, Mama?"

"Not particularly. I don't think she'd put herself out for anyone. And I always felt there was more to her than she admitted. How come she knew about Domino and we didn't? Do you think she's been seeing Graziella and not letting on? You are her only grandchild. . . . Out of all of us, you are the only one who can carry on the line. If you were to have a son—"

Rosa snapped coldly, "I'm not likely to before dinner, Mama, so don't even think about it."

"Well, if you insist on wearing those awful jeans, you won't find anyone decent. Be a good girl and dress up tonight. Let Grandma see how pretty you are, will you?"

"God, you are so old-fashioned! But if it means we get more dough, I'll wear a lampshade on my head, okay?"

Teresa banged her pillow and turned her back on her daughter. Sometimes she could throttle her, she was so infuriating.

The lights in Carolla's cell were already out. The loss of his many privileges had continued, and it did not bode well. No matter how much money he offered, it was now refused. Did they all know something he didn't?

There was a loud banging on his cell door, and the peephole cover slid back. A guard peered through. "You've got an interview with Commissario Pirelli before court. Be dressed by seven."

Carolla hit the cell door with the flat of his hand. "I wanna talk to my lawyer. I won't talk to that bastard again unless my lawyer's with me. . . . *Hey, come back, scum.*"

He leaned his back against the door, thinking. He would

have to make a statement before he saw Pirelli again. It was the only way out.

The table could easily seat fourteen, and the four places set at one end looked cluttered compared with the long stretch of starched white cloth at the other.

The table glittered as if for a banquet. The heavy silverware, each piece monogrammed with a large *L*, was highly polished, and the fine bone china dinner service, Graziella's wedding gift from her husband, shone as if it, too, had been polished. There were five cut crystal glasses grouped around each setting, and an eight-branch candelabrum in the center. Decanters of red and white wine were placed within reach.

The three women were waiting for Graziella to appear. Sophia wore a full-length black silk gown with long sleeves, the tight skirt and bodice beautifully tailored. Diamond earrings and a diamond ring were her only jewelry. Her hair was pulled back from her face into her usual severe knot. She looked stunningly beautiful; the black Valentino gown enhanced her creamy complexion and dark, slanting eyes.

Teresa had made a great effort, but her black crepe dress with a V neck was ill-fitting and old-fashioned. The long sleeves were too wide for her slim arms, and the whole dress seemed several sizes too large. She wore three rows of pearls and pearl stud earrings, and her hair was pinned up at the sides in combs.

Rosa wore a simple black dress in a shiny satin material. One glance told Sophia exactly where it had been bought. It was cheap, but somehow Rosa's prettiness made it acceptable. She wore no jewelry, and her hair, springing up in uneven tufts, made her seem much younger than her twenty years. Her eye makeup was unnecessarily heavy for her large brown eyes and emphasized the fact that she wore no foundation or lipstick.

Graziella entered like a duchess. Her weight loss made her appear taller, more austere, and reminded them of how beautiful she must have been in her youth. Adina seated her before the women could make up their minds whether or not to stand. The wine was poured, and Graziella lifted her glass in a toast.

"To you all: Thank you for coming, and God bless you."

Graziella hardly touched her wine, but the other women toasted her and drank. The conversation was very stilted, each complimenting the others on their various styles while Adina served thick lobster bisque and hot rolls. They began to eat.

The furnace gave the room terrific heat. The loud clanging of the gunsmith smelting and reshaping the firing chamber made the waiting men wince. Luka watched every stage, asking eager questions. He even put on a huge protective mask so he could stand close to the man as he filed the metal.

The old man, nearing eighty, was a master craftsman, painfully slow and methodical. He took great pride in his work, holding it up for inspection at each stage. The bullets would have to be made, of course; the weapon was so old that none of the ammunition he had in stock would be suitable.

Luka inspected the drills and turned to Dante. "You want your teeth done while we wait?"

Dante looked at his watch. "How much longer?"

"Four or five hours," said the old man, and Dante swore.

"I am a professional, signor. I have to remake the firing pin, and then there will be adjustments. It's the length of the barrel, that's the problem."

"Just do what you have to, signor." Luka patted the man's shoulder encouragingly, then walked casually over to Dante. "When he's finished, maybe it's best he's not around."

Dante snorted, shaking his head. His voice was very low. "He's eighty years old, he won't talk, believe me."

Luka's eyes glittered. "I, too, am a professional, signor, and he's a fucking witness."

Luka turned back to the old man, whistling with admiration at his work.

Graziella waited until Adina had set down the coffee tray and left the room. She did not want to discuss the will until she was sure they would not be interrupted. She herself served the coffee from its silver pot.

"Two days ago there was a new development at court. The defense lawyers requested that the entire testimony of the accused be read aloud to the prisoners. If the government does not give the judge the power to deny them this right, then the prisoners will walk free."

Sophia refused sugar, passing it across to Rosa, all her attention on her mother-in-law.

"You mean he'll be freed?"

"Yes, Sophia, I mean exactly that. The justice we had hoped for will be nonexistent. Paul Carolla will be free."

Teresa said sharply, "But isn't he also wanted for drug dealing in the States? This trial isn't just front-page headlines in Palermo; it's worldwide."

"The judge will have to get the government to overthrow the law, and you and I know how many in our precious government will be too afraid to do anything. . . . But that will be dealt with. First, I must apologize for this long delay. Now you're here, I think you will find much work has been done. I gave Mario the power of attorney."

Graziella opened a file, began picking out pages. "And at his suggestion we began to liquidate all the assets. As you are aware, because of my sons' deaths, I alone inherit the entire estate. The reason for the delay has been the joining of the three wills—"

Teresa sipped her wine. "About six months, Mama."

Graziella looked at Teresa coldly. "Mario Domino assumed that you would not want to handle the companies yourselves but would prefer to have the money. So we arranged that I would divide it equally among you."

Teresa interrupted her mother-in-law. "Wait a minute, Mama, liquidate all the assets? Are you serious? I mean, there was surely not enough time to arrange sales, auctions. . . . How much work did Domino do before he died?"

Graziella ignored Teresa and turned to Sophia. "Constantino, as you know, ran the export companies. Mario was in the middle of negotiations shortly before he died, and he accepted an offer below the original asking price, but from a good and reliable source. I have decided that as you, Sophia, were Constantino's wife, this should be handled by you, and I have therefore organized all those contracts for you to look over while you are here."

Teresa was at it again, not liking what she was hearing. "Does that include Filippo's company in New York, Mama?" But she received no reply as Graziella turned over pages in her file and passed a number of papers to Sophia.

As Teresa was about to interrupt again, Sophia looked up and waved her hand for silence. "Mama, these don't make any sense. These are warehouses?"

Teresa leaned forward. "Surely, Mama, Domino cannot have begun negotiations without conferring with us? Filippo's business depended upon the cargoes, and the company is at a standstill in New York. Who has been overseeing the trade during the past months? I tried to get into the offices myself, but they've changed the locks, so who has been handling that? Domino?"

"I left everything to Domino. He had great difficulty with the tax people. They said we owed death duties amounting to—" Graziella was flustered as she searched the file.

"Mama, is that Domino's file?" asked Teresa. She was sweating as she realized Graziella's total lack of understanding of the business. "Mama, why don't you let me sort through it all? I can go through them tonight. That used to be my job. I'll at least be able to get them into—"

Graziella almost shouted "*No!* I want none of you involved in this. It must be sold. I want everything sold, nothing that can cause you trouble."

Teresa was trying to control her temper. "But, Mama, who is taking care of the legal side?"

"Mario Domino."

Sophia took her mother-in-law's hand. "Mama, Domino is dead. Now, why don't you let Teresa have a look at all this? Then we can discuss it tomorrow. Right now you can't say I have this and Teresa has that because we don't know what we have."

Teresa spoke up for herself. "Mama, I don't know Sophia's situation, but the past six months have been very tough for me and for Rosa. Filippo left nothing but debts—"

Graziella responded with pride, "No, that is not true! No Luciano ever has debts, this I know."

"You didn't know, Mama, but you do now because I am telling you. I paid off what I could, but right now they are probably taking our apartment. I need to know what actual money I am going to see, you know, hard cash. Because I, more than anyone else, know exactly what the turnover for the New York side was."

"You know nothing, you don't know, Teresa. . . . No, you don't."

"*Yes, I do!*" Teresa was shouting now. "Because I saw the contracts, all the licenses! I am taking these files, all of them, into the study. I am going to go through them, now, tonight, okay? When I've got a better idea of what's going on, why don't we talk about it? Anyone against this?"

Sophia put her hand on the top of the file and gave Teresa a warning look. "Is it all right, Mama, for Teresa to do this?" Graziella nodded, but Sophia could see a muscle twitching at the side of her mother-in-law's mouth. The atmosphere in the dining room was electric.

Teresa read the first page of the file, which listed part of Don Roberto's liquid assets. "Oh, my God, I don't believe it. I don't believe what I am reading. . . . Rosa, there's forty million dollars!"

Sophia saw the look on Graziella's face. As Teresa continued to read the papers, the two left the room.

Sophia followed Graziella across the hall and waited while she unlocked the study door. There were file boxes everywhere, and the desk was littered with folders and loose papers.

"Oh, my God, Mama, what's all this?"

Graziella shrugged helplessly. "After Mario's death, his firm took over. When I knew you were all arriving, I told them I wanted everything returned to me, including anything that wasn't complete. Some of these boxes contain Mario's own papers from his desk. It was impossible for me to go through everything."

Sophia just stood looking at the boxes. Graziella searched the top of the desk and then handed Sophia a sheaf of telexes. "I don't understand this. . . ."

Sophia lit a cigarette, inhaled deeply, and began to read the telexes. Eventually she looked up.

"Mama, I don't understand these either. . . ."

"And there's more." Graziella handed Sophia a folder bulging with loose papers.

Sophia and Graziella did not return for almost half an hour, but Teresa appeared not to notice the time or the fact that Sophia needed a brandy before she sat down at the table.

Teresa squinted up at her, pushing her glasses along the bridge of her nose. "There's forty million dollars in a Swiss account, lump sums that appear to be cash. Mama, do you have the account numbers because as far as I can calculate, there should be even more? It's unbelievable!"

Sophia sighed and took another sip of brandy. "Teresa, just listen to me, calm down. As far as I can make out, there's enough for us to live comfortably, if not in luxury."

Teresa laughed. "Oh, come on, what is comfort to you may be outright luxury to me and Rosa. There's forty million—"

"Just listen, Teresa. Where's Rosa?"

Rosa appeared at the door with a cup of coffee. "Here. Maybe we should have some champagne?"

Sophia gestured toward a chair. "Sit down, Rosa. There's nothing to celebrate. The main liquid assets have been swallowed up by taxes, and according to Domino, there's been a massive misappropriation of money by men connected with his own firm, high-ranking, trusted men who once worked for Papa—"

Teresa half smiled. "Well, with cash you can expect fingers in tills. I mean, what sums are you talking about? Five, fifteen thousand?"

Sophia lit a cigarette with visibly shaking hands. "There's no trace of the Swiss bank account. There are yards and yards of telexes. Domino was trying to—"

Teresa interrupted, looking dazed. "Wait . . . wait . . . The company, is that still ours? Oh, Jesus Christ, I am trying to take all this in. . . . Are you saying—Oh, this is unbelievable. Tell me again, say what you said to me again."

Graziella took over, calmer now. "The main company, Teresa, the import-export section, is dormant and has been since Don Roberto died. All the workers were paid off."

Teresa was on her feet. "Jesus Christ, I don't believe this!"

Rosa seemed to be in a world of her own, staring into space. Teresa put her head in her hands as Graziella continued. "Everything is up for sale: the warehouses, the factories, the docks, and the ships."

"Where are the ships? I mean, are they just sitting in the dock?"

Graziella's face tightened with anger, and she ignored the question. "The section of the dock we own outright will be auctioned, but because of the delay—"

"What caused this delay? Are you telling me there are warehouses full of cargoes just sitting there rotting? Who decided to pay the men off, for God's sake?"

"I did," replied Graziella. "Please allow me to continue without interruption, Teresa. We have had to pay heavy fines and duties on shipments that were not delivered. There were thefts, the men were robbing us blind, we had to—"

"Well, what could you expect if nobody was in charge? This is—Don't you realize we should have been here months ago? Where are the records of the death duties? I mean, what sums are we talking about? Thousands? Millions?"

Graziella sipped her water and put the glass down. "I have already put the villa up for sale, all the land and orchards, the groves. The offers are substantial, and as I have told Sophia, there will be more than enough for you to return to your homes."

Teresa's voice was hoarse from trying to control herself. "Sophia, what did you mean by 'misappropriated'? Is that just a nice way of saying we have been ripped off, everything stolen from us while we sat over in the States *waiting like idiots*?"

Graziella slapped the table with the flat of her hand. "Mario Domino did everything humanly possible. He and his company worked with the lawyers in America. He had to fight to—"

Teresa sprang to her feet. "He was an old man. What in God's name did he know? Jesus Christ, Mama, on one sheet of paper there's forty million in *cash*! Where the hell has it gone? You want me to believe this bullshit about misappropriation? It's *theft*! What I want to know is who in Domino's company is handling our affairs now? And how long has he been dead?"

Sophia looked questioningly at Graziella. "How long is it? A week? Ten days?"

Graziella fiddled with her beads. "Eight days. He was dead when I returned from Mondello."

Teresa looked from Sophia to Graziella. "Are you telling me that this happened in *eight days*? Who had access to our money, money that belonged by right to me, to my daughter, your granddaughter? Oh, Jesus God, I can't believe this! Do you think I want to go home and live, how did you say— in *comfort*? After what we have been through, comfort is not enough. . . ."

Sophia held Graziella's hand. "Mama remembers, many weeks ago, Domino had three visitors. They came from America. Right now she can't recall their names, but Domino entrusted much of the estate to them."

"Who, Mama? What are their names?" Teresa sounded hysterical.

Graziella released her hand from Sophia's grasp and stood up. "Forgive me, at this moment I cannot recall. The most important thing to us is that we will have justice. Don Roberto was an honorable man. . . . We will have the justice he wanted. It is not over. I brought you here because—"

Teresa hurled the papers from the desk. "Damned right it's not over, but let me tell you, Mama, I don't give a goddamn about his honor! He should never have done what he did, and you should never have allowed this to happen. *I don't care about justice*, do you hear me? All I care about is *me* and my daughter. And I care about the years I slaved in the background for the Luciano family, that's what I care about. To be left with nothing . . ."

She gritted her teeth, determined not to cry. Her face twisted with anger. "You think that is justice, Mama? I am forty-six years old. All I had was my inheritance, that was all I had, and you have thrown it away. *Screw your fucking justice . . .*"

The slap was so hard it sent Teresa reeling, but she leaped forward and gripped Graziella's wrist. "That's the second time! Never, never hit me again! What gives you the right? *What right do you have to slap my face?*"

Graziella jerked her wrist free. "Because I am now head of the family. You will never speak to me like a fishwife, and you will never again swear in this house, is that clear, Teresa? I have every right to do what I wish, behave as I wish. This is my house, my home. You insult my husband's memory, you insult yourself, you should be ashamed, you have no pride, no honor—"

The room fell silent. Graziella stared from one daughter to the next.

It was Sophia who answered her, her dark eyes glittering. But there was no hysteria in her voice; it was low, husky.

"I don't think, Mama, that we are concerned right now with honor. The fortunes, the money you sneer at our desperation for, would have eased the loss, the emptiness. Papa put his faith in justice; well, I hope he turns in his grave when Paul Carolla walks free from the court. Papa's death wasn't honorable, Mama. It was a tragic, sickening murder, but he had lived a long life, unlike my babies. I have lost too much by being a Luciano and would, if you offered me the chance to live my life again, walk away from this house, walk away from being what I am now, one of the Luciano widows. Our men were killed so there could be no retaliation. With the men gone we are nothing. . . . You may be content with the crumbs they throw to you, Mama, but don't ask me to be. I have too much pride, maybe too much honor. Good night."

She left the room and Teresa followed, closing the door quietly behind her. Graziella bowed her head. She had almost forgotten that Rosa was in the room, she had been so quiet. She looked up, surprised, when she heard the young woman's voice.

"Grandmama, can I ask you something?"

Graziella nodded, picking up one piece of meaningless paper after another.

"Grandma, did you and Grandpa arrange my marriage, like you did Mama's?"

The last thing Graziella could think of was arranged marriages. She felt so exhausted that she held out her hand.

"Rosa, help me to my room."

Rosa moved away, not wanting to touch her. Graziella let her hand fall. She sighed and walked out and up the stairs, knowing Rosa was following.

As they entered her bedroom, she sat heavily on the bed, patted the bedspread nervously.

"Let me tell you something, Rosa. Filippo loved your mama. I know, because he told me so. Just as your Emilio loved you and asked Papa for permission to marry you. He needed no encouragement. He loved you, Rosa. Don't you think he did?"

Graziella wanted to weep. She was becoming an adept liar. But was there any harm?

Rosa tossed her head and began to swing the door back and forth, irritatingly. "You shouldn't have slapped Mama. You don't know things. It's been very hard for her even when Papa was alive. He had mistresses; she was never happy—"

"It's been hard for all of us, child."

"But it's different for you. You're old."

"Yes, but it's not over yet. Now, good night, I'm tired."

Rosa left the room without kissing her grandmother, and

Graziella felt truly alone. She had not expected such anger, such desperation from her daughters-in-law. They had no notion of what she had been through, of how much she still had to do to avenge the murders.

She wrote a brief note, giving Sophia charge of everything. No matter what she had said, Sophia was still her favorite. Then she took from her dressing-table drawer the photographs she had collected from around the villa and arranged them on every available surface. Surrounded by her dead family, she prayed to God to give her strength.

Teresa had waited until Rosa was sleeping before she crept down to the study. The door was open; she was determined to see for herself what had happened to her inheritance.

Sophia saw the light beneath the door hours later, when unable to sleep, she crept down the stairs. She peeked around the door.

Teresa was elbow-deep in papers, and the entire study was strewn with documents and files. "I could do with some help," she acknowledged. "It'll take days to get things sorted out. They've got invoices in with the payments. I can't even tell how many men we've still got on the payroll."

"I'd say help is putting it mildly. We need an army of secretaries."

Teresa rested her hand on a neat stack of papers. "I think the fewer people who have access to our so-called inheritance, the better. I'll do it, all of it, if necessary. These are Papa's shares; they alone are worth"—she picked up a notebook and flicked through her notes, then gave a wry smile—"at least ten million dollars, but right now, according to the brokers, would be a bad time to sell. They all have been reverted to Graziella's name; at least Domino got that settled. All she has to do is sign them over to us, and we sell when the time is right. Don Roberto was certainly no organization man at the end. That's why he poured his bulk cash into shares, so it couldn't be traced. Maybe he was trying to free us. He almost succeeded. From what I've discovered, it looks like he was trying to liquidate everything. He just didn't get it done soon enough. . . ."

She flicked through another file, while Sophia watched. Teresa squinted through her glasses and tapped the folder. "This is an offer to buy the tile factory, dated May 1985. . . . Now, here . . ." She searched the desk and picked up another sheet of closely typed letterhead paper. "Here's the same company's offer to Mario Domino, nearly two years later, for less than the original price, and by your elbow you've got all the factory's sales ledgers and export orders. For two years the business expanded, so how come they offer less? Domino was stalling. There's writing all over the contracts. Two of them were bids that came in *before* Papa died, when Papa wanted to sell everything off, right? But Domino turned the offers down. Then, after Domino's death, the lawyers just carried on, but look at this. . . . All these are offers from a man called Vittorio Rosales, and the only address I can find for him is a box number in Rome."

She pointed to the contract so that Sophia could see. "Can you read what Domino's written in the top right-hand corner? Here, where it's underlined. What do you think it says?"

Sophia took the contract and held it under the desk lamp. "I think it's Parolla. . . ."

"I think it's 'P. Carolla.' Rosales could be a front for Paul Carolla."

"What? Are you serious?"

Teresa was shaking with tension. "If I'm right, it means Carolla had good reason to order the murders of our men. He stood to gain the entire Luciano organization if there was no heir left. If we can prove he is Vittorio Rosales . . ."

"How can we do that?"

Teresa held up one contract. "We do it by checking out the only address we have, a box number in Rome. But we have to do it fast because all these documents are ready for exchange. Tomorrow we revoke the power of attorney to give us more time. Carolla is going to be free in less than a month, but if we can prove this, we can have him arrested again. . . ."

Sophia nodded, then patted the stack of documents nearest to her. "How much do you think it's all worth?"

Teresa shrugged. "Minus the shares, I would say the company could be worth ten million, maybe fifteen million dollars. But we won't get that or anywhere near it if these contracts go through. We've got to get them back, put a realistic price on them. But I'm beginning to feel better, and I'd say we can live in a lot more than just comfort."

Sophia sorted through one of Domino's crates. "Teresa, are there any more boxes with Domino's personal papers in them?"

"There's one in the corner, mostly junk, old diaries, and four more behind me."

Sophia saw the stack of calendar books right on top of the crate. Her heart was beating rapidly as she shuffled through them: 1980, 1979, 1976 . . .

"I've made a note of Rosales's box number for you, Sophia," Teresa said.

Sophia's hand was shaking. She had found it, a small diary bound in black leather, dated 1963. She stood up, slipping it into her pocket. "Yes, I—I'll leave tonight."

"Well, there's no need to rush."

Sophia was already on her way to the door. "The sooner, the better. Just write down everything you want me to find out, while I go get ready." Her hand was on the doorknob; she couldn't wait to read the diary in privacy.

Teresa stood up. "You must be careful. Is there anyone who can help you? I mean, we don't know anything about this guy, and if he does work for Carolla—"

Sophia turned, her eyes blazing. "If I discover that Paul Carolla gave the order to kill my babies, then I hope he is freed because I'll kill him myself."

Domino had made no detailed entries in his diaries, just lists of figures and occasional initials. Sophia licked her finger to help turn the pages, looking for the date of her marriage.

There it was, just a single line: "S & C wedding." She turned to the next page. How long was it after the wedding that she had called the orphanage? She jumped as Teresa knocked and peered around the door.

"This is the box number in Rome for Vittorio Rosales. Sorry, did I startle you?"

"Yes, yes, you did. Good night, and thank you. I'll return as soon as I know anything."

She almost pushed Teresa from the room, then locked the door after her and snatched up the diary. She couldn't suppress a half moan when she found the entry.

\*     \*     \*

Graziella heard the front door close. By the time she reached her window Sophia was driving away from the villa, moving very fast. She let the curtain fall back into place. So Sophia had left her. She picked up the note she had written to her favorite daughter-in-law and tore it into shreds.

At eight o'clock the next morning, Graziella left the villa. She was wearing her black crepe de chine dress, a lightweight black coat, and her widow's veil, and she carried a large black leather clutch bag. In her black-gloved hand she held her rosary.

Luka Carolla, a small bundle under his arm, left his hotel at eight-fifteen. He walked to the public rest room and changed into his monk's robe. After carefully folding his own clothes, he wrapped them in brown paper and hid them on top of the toilet tank. He stepped down from the toilet seat and picked up his cane.

As he walked along the street, he began limping. He turned down a side street and through an alley that brought him out onto the square, facing the Unigaro jail and courthouse. It was now nine o'clock; the court session would begin at ten.

Dante received the phone call at nine-thirty. He was told exactly what Luka had done.

"Turned into a fuckin' monk? You kiddin' me? Did he get into the courthouse?"

Dario, calling from a phone booth in sight of the courthouse, said Luka was in the visitors' line. Dante told him to keep watching and to call as soon as he knew Luka was in his seat.

Dante put the phone down and went to the bathroom, rubbing the stubble on his chin. He and Luka had spent most of the night working on the weapon and a further two hours of practice out in the woods, Luka firing over and over at one small mark in the chosen tree. When the tree was splattered with bullets, he had loaded one of the specials he had drilled. This time, when he fired, the trunk of the tree seemed to explode. Dante had been stunned, but Luka had laughed.

Dante lathered the soap, spread it around his chin, and

picked up his razor. His hand was shaking; the kid, Carolla's son, was a freak, and a dangerous one. Could he get away with a courtroom murder?

Pirelli knew something was up the moment he stopped his car in the courtyard outside headquarters. Ancora was waiting for him with news that the chief wanted to see him. Pirelli charged up the wide stone steps.

The chief took Pirelli to one side. "You'll have to forgo your interrogation of Carolla until after today's session. The government has refused the defense request to read out the statements. None of them will be freed, and Carolla's on the stand again this morning. But his counsel doesn't want him to know."

Pirelli nodded, keeping his anger in check. The chief patted his shoulder. "This could be the lever to get him to talk. They've agreed to let you see him right after today's adjournment. They need something to bargain with; Emanuel is going to throw the book at him today."

Graziella's heart was pounding as she made her way slowly to her seat. She was one of the first to be allowed into the courtroom that morning.

Luka propped his cane against the wall as the guards ran their hands down his body. They would not meet his gaze; they were embarrassed to be searching a father from the Holy Mission. Luka had leaned against a guard as he reached for his cane, then asked in a throaty, watery voice if it would be possible to have an aisle seat at the far side because his leg gave him pain if he could not stretch it out.

He was shown to an end seat four rows in front of Graziella. She sat staring straight ahead, her face hidden by her veil. As Luka eased his body into his seat, he placed the cane against the seat in front of him.

Paul Carolla was five feet nine inches tall, and Luka knew he had to raise the tip of the cane, which now pointed to the empty cell at the end of the line, Paul Carolla's cage.

Graziella opened her handbag, purposely dropping her rosary. She did not have long; the seat beside her was vacant for now, but the court was filling up and someone might sit there at any time. She had chosen an aisle seat today. When the time came, she would step into the aisle and shoot from there.

She bent down as if to retrieve her rosary, opened her handbag, and took out the gun. She rested it beneath her bag as she sat back in her seat. The gun felt cold. Her fingers searched for the safety catch.

After eighteen months the prisoners in the cells below the court were accustomed to the routine. The guards opened each cell as the occupant's name was called out, and the handcuffed prisoner was linked to the others by leg irons.

Dr. Ulliano's clerk argued with the guards that he had to speak with his client. It was against the rules, so there was considerable shouting and much gesticulation, but at last he was given permission to make his way along the narrow corridor to the last cell. The noise of the prisoners was deafening.

Carolla stood with his face pressed desperately against the bars. At last he saw the clerk making his way with difficulty toward him. Twice the red-faced young man was stopped by guards, but he eventually pushed his way to Carolla's door.

"You got any news for me?" Carolla demanded. "There're rumors flying around down here."

The clerk shook his head. He was under strict instruction not to tell.

"You would be the first to hear, Signor Carolla. You know this is irregular. If you continue to abuse the privileges you have been granted, they will not allow me to see you as fre- quently. . . ."

The clerk was pushed roughly aside as two prisoners started arguing with a guard. Carolla reached between the bars and caught the young man's sleeve.

"Wait, wait . . ."

"Signor, they are leading everyone into court. Unless you have something of the utmost urgency . . ."

"Closer, come closer. . . ."

Carolla drew the clerk nearer to the bars. "About what Dr. Ulliano said, I got a name, but I want your word you will use it only if we don't get the injunction—"

"Signor, please."

Carolla was sweating with fear, terrified that the other prisoners would overhear. He lowered his voice so much that the clerk had to press his face against the bars to hear him.

"A name?"

"He said if I could give you a name, someone who might have been responsible for the Paluso kid . . ."

The line of prisoners was moving out as cell after cell was emptied. The shouting and the noise of the roll call made it almost impossible for the clerk to catch what Carolla was saying.

Carolla grabbed the young man's hand through the bars. "You trace my son, trace Luka Carolla. . . ."

The clerk could hardly believe his ears. Was he naming his own son? It was too late to ask again as the guards ordered him to leave. They were opening the cell next door.

Carolla was weeping.

In the robing room the clerk joined the rest of the lawyers. He took Dr. Ulliano aside and helped him into his robe, saying, "He's come up with a name, after our talk last night. He's come up with a name for the Paluso boy."

"What, are you serious? Can you trust him?"

"He's named his son, Luka Carolla."

"*What?*"

"That's what he said. What do you want me to do about it?"

The guards were calling the lawyers to stand by for the beginning of the session. Ulliano began gathering his things together.

"Get over to police headquarters, get Commissario Pirelli to see me during my lunch break, but don't say why until I've spoken to him."

Ulliano approached the prosecution counsel and gestured for Emanuel to come to his side. "Lunchtime, can you give me a few moments? I might have something to—"

Emanuel turned, his face pinched. "Too late to make any bargains now. You had your chance. I'm going to crucify him today, and you know it."

He strode out, heading the group proceeding through the underground passage to the courthouse. As he edged his way to the back of the courtroom, Ulliano's clerk was already run-

ning toward police headquarters. Unable to get a seat, Pirelli
stood up at the back of the crowded courtroom.

Luka twisted the handle of his stick gun. Now the safety
catch was off, and his finger was on the trigger within the handle of the cane. They were filling the next to last cage. His
hands were steady as he waited.

Graziella's hand was sweating. She felt for the safety catch
on the Luger and released it.

The guards were locking the cage next to Carolla's. She
turned her head to look at the prisoners' entrance just as the
signal was given to lead Carolla into the court.

As always, he was hemmed in by guards to his front and
sides. As he shuffled toward his cage, there were catcalls from
the other prisoners. Many of the men cheered, and some tried
to touch him.

Carolla, his head slightly down, looked to neither right nor
left. But as he reached his cage, he stepped aside to allow it to
be slid open and glared around the court. And that was the
moment.

The door began to slide back. One guard stepped aside,
the other moved to Carolla's left, and he was completely clear.
He turned his head, and his small eyes flickered.

Graziella rose to her feet, sending her handbag clattering
to the floor.

Luka's hand never wavered.

Both guns fired together as if the split-second timing had
been rehearsed. Carolla was hit in the face, the impact blowing
his skull apart.

Graziella's bullet went wide, hitting the cage bars and
splintering the wall, but it was she, rather than Luka, who drew
the attention of the courtroom. Screams and scuffles broke out
as guards ran toward her. Spectators rose from their seats, hysterical, and Luka turned like the rest of them to see what was
happening.

Pirelli couldn't see what was going on. All he knew was
that a gun had been fired and Carolla was hit. He began pushing his way down the aisle, holding up his ID card.

It was pandemonium. People tried to run from the court

while the guards grabbed Graziella. Within seconds she was overpowered and the gun taken from her. Above the screams and shouts the guards tried to call for order.

The prisoners screamed and clanked their chains while Luka carefully steered himself closer and closer to the exit. The guards asked the spectators to remain quiet, stay in their seats, it was all over. . . .

Dante didn't recognize the garbled, hysterical voice on the telephone for a moment. When he did, he had to sit down. Dario Biaze had lost Luka in the pandemonium, but the police had arrested a woman, an old woman. *She* had shot Carolla.

Dante asked if Carolla was dead and was assured that the man's head had been blown off.

"Go back to Luka's hotel and check if he's there. Then get back to me. I'll be at the club."

Luka made his way back to the public rest room and changed his clothes. By the time he returned to his rented room his whole body was shaking with exhilaration. Sweat dripped from his hair and glistened on his body as he stripped. He ran water into the small washbowl and stuck his head beneath the tap. When he swung his head back, the water was dark red.

His pupils were two black dots in his face. Slowly he dried his face, checking the growth of his hair. He had to use a more permanent dye.

And he had to make contact with Dante. He stood for a moment like a statue, wrapped in his own reflection, as if unable to move. His brain would not function; Dante would have to wait. He was too tired; he had to sleep.

Luka took out the little gold heart and swung it by its chain above his head until his eyelids drooped and he fell into a deep, dreamless sleep.

# 12

Sophia had waited an hour outside the orphanage in Catania before it opened, then a further half hour before the father who ran it was able to see her. When she explained her reason for being there, he excused himself, explaining that he could not help her personally as he had been at the orphanage for only ten years. He returned with an elderly sister, who carried a file with dates and lists of names.

Sophia watched tensely as the file was opened; page after page was turned, the nun showing the open pages to the priest. He leaned over the desk, reading, his face furrowed. He did not look at Sophia but asked the sister if there was any further information. She shook her head and gave Sophia a forlorn look.

"Was my son brought here? Please tell me, please . . ."

The nun looked at the priest, who drew his chair over to Sophia and sat next to her. His voice was caring, soft, and made Sophia tremble. Something was terribly wrong.

"We have a record of your son for the first five years of his life, the years he was with us."

Sophia leaned forward. "Was he adopted? Can you give me names? I beg you."

The priest nodded to the sister, and she pressed both hands flat on the desk, as if needing the contact to enable her to speak.

"I recall your child, even though it was a very long time ago. He was perhaps four, almost five, when I came here. We used to take the children on picnics after Sunday school. There was a fair, run by Gypsies. The children did not have money to go on many of the attractions, but some of the fair people were very kind and gave them free rides. . . . Your child, he was very wayward, irrepressible, and he was angry when we had to leave and ran back to the fairground. We brought him back, and he was reprimanded; but at some point on the return walk to the orphanage we believe he ran back again. His absence was not noted at first; there were fifteen children. . . . We returned to try to find him, and when it became dark, the police were contacted. We did everything possible; the fair was forced to remain for an extra week as the police continued their investigation. . . ."

Sophia was unable to speak. The father turned the file around so Sophia could read for herself the many letters, the press clippings. She stared blankly at the pages.

When she finally spoke, her voice was almost inaudible. "Is he dead?"

"We don't know. No body was ever found; he just disappeared. As you can see, we tried everything humanly possible to find him. The police searched for months."

"Did they suspect that the Gypsies took him?"

"Obviously, but the child was blond and blue-eyed, very easily recognized among the dark-skinned Gypsies. The police kept in touch with them when they moved on, but they never found him."

Sophia made as if to rise; but her legs gave way, and she pitched forward in a faint. They carried her to a small leather sofa and gave her sweet tea when she revived.

She was shivering with cold, but she could not cry. She could not assimilate what they had told her; it was too unreal. The sister sat with her and held her hand. Sophia's long red nails cut into the elderly woman's hand. The nun made no effort to release herself.

"You have been very kind. I thank you," Sophia said eventually. She had very little money on her and did not dare write a check, so she slipped her diamond ring from her finger. "When

I left my baby—I shall always bear the guilt of my sins—when I left him, he wore a small gold heart on a chain. Did— When he was brought here, did he still wear it?"

The sister thought for a moment, touching the crucifix at her own neck. "Yes, yes, I remember. . . . He used to move it like so before he slept." She lifted the cross and dangled it, letting it swing back and forth.

Sophia broke into heartrending sobs. The sister knelt and prayed, her hands clasped, but Sophia could not bring herself to join her; prayers could not help her. Instead, she whispered that she must leave and waited for the sister to rise.

"Please accept this. It is worth a considerable amount. It is all I have."

Sophia drove out of Catania, cocooned in her own misery. She had made no effort to trace the owner of the box number; nothing could have been farther from her mind. In a daze she headed back to Palermo, almost letting the car run out of gas.

She pulled in at a filling station and found herself listening to the attendant's radio blaring pop music. It was followed by a news flash: Paul Carolla had been shot dead during the morning's court session. The impact of the announcement cut through her dulled senses, and she sat, electrified, hearing that an elderly woman had been arrested and charged with the murder.

The television set in the kitchen was on; a newscaster was giving a rundown of the latest headlines. Teresa paused at the mention of Paul Carolla and turned up the sound.

A moment later Rosa came in. Teresa, shock on her face, turned to her daughter. "Oh, my God, I think Mama's shot Paul Carolla."

Commissario Pirelli spooned sugar into his coffee. It was cold. He was staring at the papers on his desk while trying to take in the morning's events. The excitement he'd felt with the lead to Luka Carolla seemed almost unimportant against the murder of Paul Carolla.

There was a tap on the door. Without looking up, he called, "Come in," expecting it to be his assistant, Bruno. When he finally looked up, he rose quickly to his feet.

"My apologies, signora, you wish to speak to me?"

Sophia Luciano hesitated in the doorway, and Pirelli walked around to the front of his desk. He ran his hands through his hair, thick, wiry hair that stood up, out of control. "May I help you?"

She came a little farther into the room. "I was not sure whom I should speak with. My name is Sophia Luciano."

Her deep, husky tones made the hair on the back of his neck rise. She was the most beautiful creature he had ever seen.

He swallowed and gestured toward a chair, which he then pulled out for her.

"You must be here about Signora Luciano, but I'm afraid I'm not handling the— Er, please sit down, signora. I can find out where she is, and then I'll take you to see her."

He offered coffee, but she refused, sitting with her head slightly bowed. "I heard it on the news. I came straight here. I wasn't sure where I should go. . . ."

The feeling of loss, the terrible emptiness in her demeanor overwhelmed him, and he had an urge to take her in his arms. He was trying to remember which Luciano she was. Was she the mother of the two little boys? He excused himself and left the office.

He let out his breath as if he had been holding it the entire time he was with her. He hurried along the corridor and straight into the red-faced Ancora.

"Commissario, Luka Carolla was booked onto a flight two days ago, but he never got on the plane. There was a seat reserved in his name—"

"In the name of Luka, not Giorgio?"

"Yep, so it means he's still here, in Sicily, unless he has another passport or took off from Rome. I'm checking there."

Pirelli nodded, then caught Ancora's arm. "Which one of the Luciano widows was the mother of the two children?"

Ancora paused, chewing his lip as he tried to remember. "Sophia Luciano, married to Constantino."

"She's in my office. I'll take her down to the old lady. Who's got her, do you know?"

Ancora told him that Graziella was with the Mincelli team on the top floor, then bustled off to his own office.

Sophia was sitting in exactly the same position. Pirelli closed the door. "You will be able to see her in a few moments. All the statements have been taken, and . . . I doubt very much if she will be held."

Sophia's dark eyes were so frightened that he busied himself with the pens and pencils on his desk.

"But she killed Paul Carolla?"

"No . . . She tried, but she did not kill him. There was another gun fired at the same time. I have no details yet, and perhaps I shouldn't have told you."

"Someone else shot him?"

"It appears so. . . . I am sorry. When I take you to her, you will obviously learn more."

She nodded and whispered her thanks. He offered her a cigarette, but she refused, then opened her handbag and took out her own cigarette case. She clicked it open.

"I smoke only these, they are very expensive and difficult to find, and I pretend to myself that it helps me not to smoke so much. Would you care for one?"

Pirelli had already put his own Marlboro in his mouth, and he nearly cut his lip on the filter in his haste to remove it. "No, *grazie.*" He fumbled for a light, and she beat him to it, holding up her gold lighter. Her cigarettes were a strong Turkish blend. She exhaled and let the smoke drift into a haze around her head.

"Did you see her?" she asked.

He loved the sound of her throaty voice. "No, I did not see her, but I believe she is greatly shocked. The officer said he was not sure whether it is from her attempt to kill Carolla or from learning that her gun did not kill him." He quickly wiped the smile off his face.

"Have they arrested anyone else?"

Pirelli shook his head. "Not to my knowledge."

She searched for an ashtray, and he moved quickly to place one near her. She stubbed out the half-smoked cigarette and stood up. He had not realized how tall she was, almost his height, and his eyes flickered down to her high-heeled shoes as he noticed her perfect legs.

"You have been very kind to me. May I see her now?"

After making a brief phone call, he went to the door. She moved toward him, seeming to sway slightly, and he reached out to clasp her elbow. For a moment she leaned against him.

"Are you all right? Would you like a glass of water?"

"No, *grazie*, no . . ."

She followed him up to the next floor and was introduced to the detective in charge. Pirelli waited while she asked what would happen to Graziella, then walked slowly away. He didn't want to leave her. . . .

He overheard the officer's reply: "She'll be charged with attempted murder and possession of a dangerous weapon, but with mitigating circumstances. She will have to stand trial, but I doubt if Signora Luciano will be imprisoned. You can come into my office while we sort it all out. Then she's free to go."

Pirelli entered his own office to find Ancora on his phone. He gestured for Pirelli to come to his side and wrote on a notepad, "Eva Carolla had a son . . . born in Rome. Giorgio Carolla . . . He's older than we thought, twenty-eight. Born 1959."

After a moment he put the phone down. "She died in childbirth. They're getting all the particulars sent over. Joe? Joe, did you hear what I said?"

Pirelli nodded. They were getting closer, he could feel it, but all he could think about was Sophia Luciano. The phone on his desk rang again, and Ancora answered, then held it out to Pirelli. "It's your wife."

Pirelli made a face and took the call. Ancora listened as Pirelli tried to explain why the case was taking so long, and yes, he hoped to have it cleared up shortly. . . . He interrupted her to ask about their son, but as she talked, he could only picture Sophia and her two little boys. He closed his eyes, remembering her musky perfume, then forced himself to concentrate on whether his own son should take extra violin classes or not.

"I thought it was the guitar? . . . Oh, that was last term? . . . Well, do whatever you think best. . . . Yes, I'll see you this weekend."

He hung up and stretched, walking to the window and peering through the blinds to the street below. Sophia Luciano was helping her mother-in-law into a Mercedes 280SL.

Ancora returned while Pirelli was still watching. "Glad one of us is on the ball. I've just had words with Carolla's attorney. What a supercilious bastard he is! Seems more concerned with losing his fees than his client . . . Joe?"

Pirelli turned. "I call that one hell of a lady."

Ancora shrugged. "If my grandmother had started taking potshots at people, I don't know if I'd call her that. I'd put her in a home where she couldn't do any damage."

Pirelli didn't correct Ancora, who was now thumbing through a train timetable.

"You ever been to Erice? There's a monastery there. According to Ulliano, Giorgio, alias Luka, or whatever his name is, was staying there. Want to check it out?"

"Monastery? Are you serious?"

Ancora nodded. "I guess his son was for real. When Carolla gave his name to Ulliano's clerk, he was crying his eyes out."

Pirelli stuffed his hands in his pockets and wandered around the office. "They got any suspects for the shooting this morning?"

"None. They're still scraping Carolla's brains off the floor. It'll be a while yet. They've got to check every single person who was in the courtroom. You were there, weren't you?"

"I was at the back. I couldn't see anything. Then, when the shots were fired, it was chaos." He opened the file drawer and flicked through the files. In theory he was still heading only the Paluso murder, but he had retained the files on the Luciano children. He slid the drawer slowly back in. "Who's taken over the main Luciano case?"

"My old chief, Mincelli. Poor bastard, he's got the Carolla shooting as well. Guy's going nuts, but this'll take precedence. Joe . . . a word of advice: Stay out of the Luciano business if you want to go back to Milan. You'd be here for—Joe?" But Pirelli had already left.

Sophia drove Graziella home, waited with her while the doctor gave her a sedative, and sat beside her until she slept. Graziella had held Sophia's hand like a child, crying with relief that it was Sophia who had come for her. She had thought her favorite daughter-in-law had gone away.

The act of madness touched her daughters-in-law, along with their guilt that neither of them had accompanied her to the trial. They arranged legal representation for Graziella, Teresa handling everything.

When they had exhausted the subject of the shooting, the shock dispersed and left them subdued and listless. They ate dinner in silence, until Teresa brought up the point that now that Graziella seemed safe, their main objective was to settle the family business. Sophia apologized for not being able to discover anything in Rome, giving the excuse that no sooner had she arrived than she heard the news and so returned.

Teresa flipped her notebook open. "Well, as it turned out, it would have been a wasted effort anyway because old Mario had already done the investigating. I found these photographs, don't know who took them, but on the back someone's written, 'Enrico Dante, alias Vittorio Rosales.' Dante works for Paul Carolla and has been doing the buying for him. He's the one who's waiting to exchange contracts. Mario obviously got on to it and refused to complete the deal. Now is our chance to get the contracts back."

She showed Sophia several columns of figures. "In this first column is what we might make from the sale of everything I've been able to verify as legally ours. The second is what we might be able to get back, with a little help. A couple are U.S.-based, trucking companies, et cetera. The third column is what I can see as a long-term prospect. That is, if we run the Luciano business ourselves."

Sophia paid little attention to the figures. "Do you think we'd be allowed to do this?"

"Whether or not we would be allowed is nobody's business but ours. I know enough about it, on the import side anyway. When Filippo was alive, I used to run—"

Sophia threw up her hands in a gesture of impatience. "And Papa was alive, and Constantino . . . You were protected, Teresa, you never ran anything. So maybe you did a few figures, juggled a few contracts. You're living in some kind of fantasy world. Papa wanted us to have the cash and get out. This is what Mama wants, what Mario Domino was trying to get for us—out, Teresa! And that is what we will do. We sell all of it, lock, stock, and barrel."

"But you don't understand. The companies are worth three times that amount. Dante, or Paul Carolla, was ripping us off. I agree to sell, if that is what you want, but not to Dante, not at the price he's offering. If he is prepared to pay us a fair price, then maybe we can discuss it, but until we know what we own, there's no point arguing about who's doing what, okay?"

Too tired to argue, Sophia shrugged and gave in.

"What do you say, Rosa?" Teresa asked.

Rosa, bored and only half listening, leaned on her elbows. "I'll go along. Sooner we leave here, the better."

Teresa picked up her notebook. "Then it's agreed. I don't think it's necessary to tell Graziella about any of this. Let her rest. You stay with her, Rosa."

"Where are you going, Mama?"

"Dante's club, might as well do it right away. Sophia, you'd better come with me."

Sophia rose to her feet, muttering under her breath, "Do I have a choice?"

Dante had closed his club, paid off the staff, and was moving as fast as was humanly possible.

When Dario Biaze returned, Dante knew the gunsmith had been taken care of. That left only Luka; then Dante would be safe.

"I'm getting out," he told Dario. "I'll come back when the heat's off. I suggest you do the same. There's a club up in Trapani; you take your wife and kids." He stacked the lire on the desk, and the big, broken hands of the ex-boxer couldn't grab at them fast enough. Dante reached down to stop him.

"Wait . . . You'll get ten times this, but I want Luka taken care of. Neither of us can trust him; he's crazy. How many kids do you know could kill their own father?"

The big hands didn't move. The watery eyes blinked; then Dario nodded.

Dante slowly lifted his hands away, saw Dario hesitate. . . . He put another bundle of money down. "Ten times . . ."

Dante waited until he heard the heavy, plodding footsteps pause at the front door, waited until it banged shut, then got a black satchel and started loading it with money, making two more trips to the safe. The gun went in last. Dario Biaze would never reach Tapani; he knew too much. When he came to collect his payoff, Dante would kill him. This one he had to do himself.

He carried the bag into the dark area of the bar and put it

down near the till. Then he returned to his office and worked for almost an hour.

Satisfied, he went back to the stocktaking in the bar. He paid little attention to the rattling of the door chain at the fire exit, believing it was a customer who didn't realize the club was closed. Then his mind raced; no customer would try to come in the back way. . . .

The door rattled again, and he stood poised, listening. Finally he made his way through the curtained archway toward the fire exit to see who was there.

He called out that the club was closed. There was silence, and he listened, then took a heavy bunch of keys from his pocket and unfastened the padlock, pushing the doors open slightly. He stepped out and looked up and down the back alley. He could see no one. As he was about to relock the doors, he heard a noise, this time inside the club, in the bar.

"Dario? Is that you?"

Dante moved slowly backward, standing half hidden behind the curtains, and peered through the gloom. There was only the working light behind the bar. . . .

"Dario?" He squinted, screwing his eyes up to see more clearly. He looked over the tables, the stacked chairs, and moved farther into the room, almost to the edge of the dance floor.

"Hi, okay if I help myself?"

Luka appeared from behind the bar. He was holding a glass of orange juice, raised slightly as if in a toast. "You see the news on the television?"

Dante's heart stopped for a moment. "How did you get in? Dario with you?"

Luka sat on a high stool and sipped his juice. He was wearing a shirt, no jacket, and it was obvious he wasn't carrying a gun. "No, came through the front door; it was open."

Dante swore under his breath; that fool Dario hadn't shut it properly. He kept a frozen smile on his face.

Luka dug into his pocket and brought out a bullet, holding it between his thumb and forefinger. "Here, you want a keepsake? We made two, just in case, but . . . Is he taken care of? The gunsmith?"

Dante poured himself a brandy. "Yeah, Dario—It's done." He took a gulp of brandy. "I've closed the place, gonna lie low until the heat dies down. I've been stuffing a bag with some dough for you."

"That's thoughtful, but where's the heat, man? They don't have a fucking clue; they've got nothing. . . ."

Dante had inched farther behind the bar as he talked. He had to get to the bag, to the gun; it was propped up beside the till. Luka's wide eyes looked at Dante, then at the bag.

"How much did ya put in there for me?"

Dante put his glass down. "A few thousand dollars, could be more. Should last you awhile, and later we can get down to sorting through the rest." He bent down for the bag, his back to Luka. "You want to count it?" His hand was in the bag, feeling for the gun. The touch of the cold metal gave him confidence. He smiled, looked up, and froze. Through the mirror, Luka could see every move he made.

Luka quickly shifted his glass to his left hand, flicked his arm up a fraction and down again until he felt the knife slide down his arm. He cupped it in the palm of his hand. They stared at each other. Then Luka smiled warmly. "I guess I can trust you. What's a few thousand dollars between friends?"

As Luka said the word "friends," Dante fired, through the bag, through a wad of dollars. The glass of orange juice slipped from Luka's fingers and rolled onto the floor, intact. Luka didn't even feel the bullet smash into his shoulder, he was moving so fast. The knife sliced into Dante's stomach, ripped through the muscle, the blade so fine and sharp it was like a razor.

The gun was still in Dante's hand inside the torn bag. He tried to hit Luka with the bag, but Luka dragged it away from him. Dante began howling and gibbering, clutching his stomach, blood streaming between his fingers. He made a desperate effort to get clear of the bar, knocking bottles to the floor.

As agile and fast as the cat Dante had once called him, Luka wrenched the bag open, took out the gun, then swung up and over the bar. He faced the terrified man and fired twice, aiming once at Dante's throat and again into his heart. The big man wouldn't go down; the impact of the bullets at such close range threw him backward into the rows of glasses, but he was still standing. Luka was about to fire again when, in slow motion, Dante died on his feet. He gurgled as his lungs filled with blood. It oozed from his mouth as he crashed backward and finally lay still.

Luka stared at himself in the splintered mirror. He was fascinated to see his shoulder covered in blood, spreading over his shirt, dripping down his arm. . . . He had been hit, and only then did the burning pain cut through his brain like a scream.

The bullet was lodged deep in his left shoulder blade. Part of his shirtfront was covered with bits of the bag and dollar bills. He knew he had to get out, and fast; three shots had been fired, and someone must have heard. He hurried to a table to collect his own bag and carried it back to the bar. The pain was now so fierce that he felt dizzy; it was useless trying to salvage any of the cash Dante had stalled him with. Instead, he went to the office and kicked open the door. He put the bag on the desk and went to the safe.

The door was wide open. . . . He was just about to start filling his bag when he heard the chains on the fire exit door rattle. . . .

Luka staggered and dropped the bag. He turned toward the bar and heard the door rattle again. Then a woman's voice called, "Is anyone there?" He switched off the one light behind the bar and picked up the gun. Again he stumbled.

Another woman's voice: "It's open, Teresa, it's open. . . . It's all right, there're lights on, somebody's in there. . . ."

Sophia pushed the door farther open, then peered into the dark corridor. "Is anyone here? Hello . . . Anyone here?"

Luka entered the cloakroom, leaving the door open no more than a crack, and stared out. Sophia appeared in the doorway from the main room, Teresa behind her.

They peered around in the gloom. Then Teresa whispered, "You see an office? Maybe there's someone in the office. Hello?"

Teresa made her way to a door marked "Private." She knocked and waited, then swung the door open wide. Sophia remained standing on the dance floor.

From his vantage point behind the door, Luka could see Sophia clearly. He gritted his teeth, wishing the women would get the hell out of there. The pain was beginning to burn, and the blood dripped down his hand. He was losing a lot, and fast.

Sophia looked around, puzzled that the doors should be unlocked, wondering why there was every sign that somebody was there yet there was no one. Something on the bar gleamed where it caught the light, and she walked toward it. It was Luka's bullet, and she was just reaching for it when Teresa called from the office doorway.

Her voice was full of excitement. "Sophia, I found them! The safe was open. There are papers on the company, the warehouses. . . . Everything's here. Without these he's got no proof of anything."

Teresa went back to the office, and Sophia turned away from the bar. She was only a few feet from Dante's body, and her foot struck Dante's bag. She bent down and picked it up, then stood up quickly. Her hand was stained and sticky, but in the darkness she couldn't tell what it was.

"Sophia, come in here. Hurry!" Teresa called from the office. The safe door was wide open, and she was eagerly removing file after file. "Holy Mother of God, you should see what some of these are. . . . Look at this!"

Sophia said quickly, "Just take our contracts, Teresa, nothing else. And hurry." She picked up Luka's bag and handed it to Teresa. "Here, put everything in this."

Teresa brought out stacks of lire and dollars.

"Take the contracts and nothing more. You leave the money. *Leave it.* Let's get out of here."

Sophia went around behind the bar. Now she could see all the broken glass. She inched forward, the glass crackling beneath her feet. Then she screamed.

Teresa ran to the dance floor. Sophia, still behind the bar, was backing away and pointing in horror. "He's dead! He's dead! Oh, my God . . ."

Teresa leaned over the bar and then turned away. The sight of the body made her sick to her stomach. Sophia tried to pull her away.

"We've got to get out of here."

Teresa stepped back. "Do you think I don't know that? Who is it? Did you see who it was?"

"No . . . Come on, please let's go, please," said Sophia, almost weeping with fear.

Teresa glared, told Sophia to pull herself together, and walked around the bar to look down at the body. "Is this Dante? Sophia?"

"I don't know. How do I know? I've never even met him."

After a moment's hesitation Teresa rolled the body over and slipped her hand into the back pocket of the corpse's trousers. She flipped open his wallet. "It's Dante." She touched his hand. "And he's still warm. This must have just happened. What do you think we should do? I mean, do we call the police, or what?"

Carrying Luka's bag, which she had stuffed to bursting with papers, Teresa slithered on the wet blood, and her high heels gave way beneath her. She screamed, and panic-stricken, the two women turned and ran for it.

As soon as Teresa and Sophia arrived home, they shut themselves in the study. Teresa began tipping the files from the bag they had picked up in the club. There were stacks and stacks of papers and, to Sophia's fury, bundles of banknotes.

"I told you not to take any money."

"I didn't mean to. I just swept everything into the bag. I swear I didn't mean to take the money. . . . It's not much; it was an accident." She tipped out the rest of the contents of the bag, Luka's bag. The separated parts of his cane gun clattered out; the heavy top section slipped off the desk and fell on her foot. She swore in agony.

Sophia turned over the strange horse's head on the short piece of cane. She checked the handles of the bag; they were covered in blood.

Teresa saw them too. She touched the bag. "Look at the handles of the bag. Give it to me, Sophia. It's blood. Is this his bag?"

Sophia's voice rose. "I don't know. How would I know whose bag it is?"

Teresa paced up and down. "What if this bag belongs to someone else, someone who shot Dante? He was still warm when I touched him. What if it happened just before we got there? What if we disturbed the killer?"

Sophia couldn't get her breath. She gasped, "Oh, God, we should have gone to the police."

Teresa shouted, "Don't you understand? Don't you see that if we disturbed the killer, he could still have been there? Could also have seen us? He would have seen us taking the papers from the office."

Sophia's nerves were in shreds. "Don't shout, you want to wake Mama?"

Teresa seemed frozen; she stood staring into space.

"Are you okay?" asked Sophia. She watched as Teresa turned slowly around, her eyes searching the room. "Teresa, what's the matter?"

"Where's my handbag?"

"What?"

"My handbag, where is it? Did you bring it back with you?"

"Do you mean from the club? I didn't even see it. Did you take it?"

"Oh, my God, please, God, don't say I left it there."

They searched the car, they searched the study, and Teresa became more and more panic-stricken. When Sophia tried to calm her, she became hysterical.

"Don't you understand? Are you stupid? If whoever shot Dante was still there, and he finds my handbag, he not only saw us but now knows exactly who we are."

Sophia snapped back, "Don't blame me. It's *your* handbag. *You left it, not me.*"

"Okay, okay, I'm sorry . . . But we'll have to go back. Give me the bag we brought from there, and I'll replace it."

"Why don't we call the police? Teresa, please."

Sophia was still trying to persuade Teresa to call the police while they drove back to the Armadillo Club, but Teresa wouldn't hear of it. They parked a little distance away and turned off the lights.

"We'll just watch the place for a while, see if anyone comes or goes. If it's all quiet, I'll go back in. You wait outside, and if anyone looks like he's going into the Club, give three blasts on the car horn."

Luka Carolla was in trouble. He had managed to get himself back to his own rented room, but he could not stanch his wound. He had torn up a sheet to make a bandage, but the blood was seeping through that.

The bullet had to come out, and the wound needed cleaning; but he could not go to a hospital. There would be questions. He was aware that the gun he had used to kill his father

was in the bag the women had taken. All he had was Teresa
Luciano's bag. The contents were now spread across his bed.

Sophia watched Teresa hurry across the road and disappear into the alleyway beside the club. Sophia turned the radio
on while she waited, then off. She waited, waited. . . .

Suddenly there was pandemonium. A police car with siren
screaming, followed by an ambulance, drove into the street.
They slowed down, right outside the main entrance to the club.
Sophia pressed the car horn once, twice, three times. *Dear God,*
she thought, *will she hear me?*

The police car turned down the narrow alley. The ambulance was too wide, so two men jumped from the back and
followed the police on foot. A group of kids began running this
way and that, some from the alley and some toward the blinking police lights. Sophia pressed the horn again, once, twice,
then switched the engine on and blew the horn a third time.

Teresa ran from the front entrance of the Armadillo Club,
carrying a bag. It was all Sophia needed to see; she reversed
fast, and Teresa got in.

"Didn't you hear me? Didn't you see the police?"

"Drive, drive! Get out of here."

"Did you find it?"

"No. Put your foot down, don't go so slowly."

"You want to get us picked up for speeding? Why did you
bring that bag out again?"

Teresa hugged the leather carryall. Luka's bag. "I realized
it's got my prints all over it. I thought it was safer to bring it.
I'm praying I was wrong. Maybe I didn't leave my handbag
after all. I should have looked in the bedroom."

"Oh, thanks! Now you tell me. . . ."

But Teresa knew she hadn't left it at the villa. She fell
silent, trying to remember the contents. Perhaps she could call
the police, as Sophia suggested, without saying they had been
at the club, and report the theft of a handbag.

As they let themselves in, Rosa rushed to greet them,
pointing to the dining room and gesturing them to silence. Teresa paid no attention, thinking she was referring to Graziella.
She entered the study and shut the door.

Rosa gripped Sophia's wrist. "There's a man in there, in

the dining room. I didn't know what to do. He's weird; he says Mama knows what it's about."

Teresa, white-faced, came out of the study, her eyes on stalks. She locked the door. "Rosa, go to bed. Get up the stairs *now!*"

"But, Mama, who is he? He's in there, just walked in when I opened the door."

"What?"

Sophia found her voice. "There's someone in the dining room. He told Rosa it's something to do with you."

Teresa almost screamed, "Rosa, do as I say! Just go to bed, *now!*"

She watched until Rosa reached the top of the stairs and was out of sight, then whispered, "Well, why don't we go in and find out what he wants?"

Luka was sitting in the don's chair, a balloon glass of brandy in front of him. He was very pale, and blood still seeped from the wound through the makeshift dressing. His right hand, with Dante's gun in it, rested on the bandage. Close to him on the table was Teresa's handbag.

He half rose to greet them, but the pain was so bad he sat back instantly. "Allow me to introduce myself; I am Johnny Moreno. Which of you is Teresa Luciano?"

"I am."

"This, I believe, belongs to you."

Teresa stared at him. "What do you want?"

"I have a bullet in my left shoulder. I need the wound treated. It must be obvious to you why I can't go to the hospital. You'll have to take care of me."

"What makes you think that we'll agree?" asked Teresa.

"Because you were at the club. I'll make a deal with you. I'll take the cash you stole and walk out of your lives as soon as I am fit. The papers you can keep. I have no interest in them."

"What's to stop us calling the police right away?"

"If you wanted their involvement, you would already have called."

"Did you kill him?"

"In self-defense." He looked directly at Teresa. "The money you stole from Dante he owed to me but was not prepared to pay. It is a very simple arrangement, ladies. Now, do you agree or not?"

Sophia shook her head. "We didn't mean to take any money. You can have what we took, but you cannot stay here."

Luka looked pointedly at Teresa, and she hesitated, then eased open the door. She looked out to see if the coast was clear. "Put him in the small room at the top of the house. I don't want Mama to know he is here. I'll get some disinfectant and hot water."

Angry, Sophia turned to her. "Are you agreeing to this?"

"Why not? It seems we all need each other right now, unless you want to discuss this evening's mess with the police. I don't think they would be too cooperative, especially after the Graziella episode. . . . He gets the cash, we get the documents. . . . It's a deal, Mr.?"

"Moreno, Johnny Moreno."

Luka relaxed, sure he had made the right decision.

The police found a corpse in the parking lot at the rear of the Armadillo Club. The body was identified as Dario Biaze, ex-boxer, doorman, and bodyguard to Enrico Dante. The bloody footprints led the police from the lot to the back entrance of the Armadillo. The doors were open.

It was clear that Dario's throat had been cut near the club fire exit and that somehow, bleeding badly, he had staggered down the alley to the parking lot.

The club looked as if it had been ransacked, so robbery was considered the first motive. The double murder was in Mincelli's territory, and the harassed man was dragged out of his bed to deal with it.

Commissario Joe Pirelli was having a beer with his detective sergeant less than three blocks away. They intended to drive past the scene of the crime, but Ancora pulled up.

"The Armadillo's part owned by Paul Carolla," he said.

Without another word they got out of the car, crossed the road, and entered the club. Patrol cars were lined up along the sidewalk and an ambulance was standing by.

As the two men entered, Detective Mincelli called Pirelli over to look at Dante's body, then yelled at him to step around the cordoned areas. Mincelli put his arm around Pirelli's shoulder.

"You're trying to trace Paul Carolla's son, right? Well, I'm doing you a big favor. I know this is in my territory, but this guy worked for Carolla, and the other stiff in the parking lot was his bodyguard. Could be a link." He raised his right eyebrow, clowning, wanting this investigation no more than Pirelli did.

Pirelli looked at him. "Thanks for the tip. I'll keep it in mind. Maybe I'll come down to your office in the morning to see what you've come up with. But don't let me keep you. Looks like you'll be here all night."

Pirelli winked to Ancora as they left, murmuring to him to stick around and see if there was anything useful for their case.

Pirelli wondered if in fact, there was a connection, but he couldn't fathom what it could be. He punched his pillow and tried to switch his mind off by conjuring up the face of Sophia Luciano. He could see her, standing hesitantly at his office door. He turned onto his back, feeling like a schoolboy with a crush. He laughed aloud at the thought and told himself he'd better wrap the case up fast and get back to his wife in Milan, at least for a weekend.

# 13

Luka was shown up to the small bedroom at the top of the house. It had been a maid's room and contained only a single bed, a wardrobe, and a chest of drawers. There was a small handmade rug beside the bed.

Sophia brought a pair of pajamas from Michael's room and handed them to Luka. He waited, and it was a moment before she realized he wanted her to leave him to undress. While Teresa looked for clean bed linen in the laundry room, Sophia busied herself boiling water and fetching bandages and antiseptic.

Alone, Luka kicked off his shoes and took off his trousers. The pain was so intense that he had to sit on the bed to undo his shirt. He felt the wound drag as he pulled it off. The bandages had stuck to the caked blood. He gritted his teeth. "Oh, sweet Jesus."

Teresa found him sprawled across the bed, but he still held the gun in his right hand.

"I have to make up the bed. Can you stand?"

Luka leaned against the wardrobe while Teresa prepared the bed. Sophia entered with a bowl of hot water.

"We'll need more," said Teresa, taking the bowl. Sophia went back down the stairs without a word.

When the bed was ready, Teresa gestured to Luka to lie down. She dipped a cloth into the hot water.

"You'd better take that chain off, I'll have to disinfect the whole shoulder."

Luka removed the gold chain with the small gold heart and tucked it beneath his pillow, watching Teresa as she moved back and forth.

She checked his bandages and said, "I'll have to soak them until they come away easily, I don't want to rip the wound."

Sophia was creeping up the stairs carrying a bottle of brandy and a tumbler. "Is this what your mother wants?" she whispered to Rosa.

Rosa whispered back, "She says he's got the gun under his pillow. Maybe if we give him enough of that, he'll pass out, and then we can take it."

Sophia passed her the brandy. "I am having nothing to do with this. I still say we should go to the police."

She stopped as she heard Luka moan, and Teresa came to the bedroom door. "I'll need some help. The bullet's still in him, and I don't know if I'm doing the right thing or not. He's lost so much blood, and he's in agony."

Sophia snapped, "Why don't we stop all this nonsense and call a doctor? If he's still losing blood, he could die. Then what would we do?"

"He's not going to die," Teresa said sharply. "I just want him fit and out of here as soon as possible. Now will you help me? We need fine tweezers to get the bullet out."

Luka lay with his eyes closed, his wound streaming blood. The room was heavy with the smell of antiseptic and steam from the bowls of hot water on the chest of drawers.

Sophia picked up the tweezers and joined Teresa at the bedside. She leaned over the bed. "Mr. Moreno? I've brought some brandy. Maybe it would better if you had a few drinks. This is going to be very painful, and we have nothing to stop the pain."

He shook his head, and Teresa switched on the gooseneck lamp, directing the light into the gaping wound. "Can you see the bullet, Sophia?"

Sophia nodded. The skin around the wound was red and swelling fast. The bullet was deep. She leaned closer. "Are you all right?"

Luka nodded, gritting his teeth. Sophia poured the antiseptic all over his shoulder, then looked at Teresa. "Okay, I'm going to have a try."

Teresa looked away as Sophia began probing the wound. Luka winced, and tears rolled down his cheeks.

Sophia could not clamp the ends of the tweezers around the bullet; they were too narrow. After two attempts she gave up. Luka gave a long, shuddering sigh.

Sophia washed the tweezers and stretched them as far as she could. "I'll have another try. At least he won't feel it now; he's out cold."

Luka did not stir when she slipped her hand beneath the pillow and brought out the gun.

"Steady the light," said Sophia. "Okay, you ready?"

She worked for fifteen minutes and finally eased the bullet out. She dropped it into a bowl. Teresa worked to stanch the wound as the blood drenched Sophia and the sheet. Then she bent to feel for the pulse in Luka's neck.

She freaked. "Jesus, Mary, Holy Mother of God, I can't feel anything. . . . I can't find his pulse. . . . Sophia, there's no pulse."

Sophia pushed her aside and touched Luka's neck. Even she had difficulty finding a pulse because it was so faint. Blood still oozed from the wound.

"It needs stitches; it'll never heal open like this. Get me a needle and cotton, anything. Go on, hurry."

An hour later the bleeding had been stemmed and Sophia had stitched Luka's wound with white cotton. She poured more antiseptic over it and then carefully wrapped heavy pieces of lint around his shoulder. Finally she made a sling and folded his arm across his chest, so tightly that he could not move and break the stitches open.

Luka rested against Sophia for a moment. She smoothed his hair back from his sweating white face. "I think he's started a fever. We'll take turns sitting with him. I'll take the first shift. You get a few hours' sleep and take over. Where's Rosa?"

"I sent her to bed. I'll wake her when it's her turn." Teresa inched open the door, afraid to make any noise, and whispered,

"If we can get him to eat, we can keep him drugged. I've got a few sleeping pills. We can break them up and put them in his food."

When she had gone, Sophia fetched ice cubes and more hot water. She sat beside Luka, alternating hot and cold compresses on his head. Occasionally he moaned softly, but he did not return to consciousness.

Three hours passed. The fever was worse, and his pulse was even weaker. When Teresa came up to do her shift, Sophia was loath to leave but was so tired she needed rest.

"What time is it?"

Teresa squinted at her watch. "Almost five."

Sophia sighed. "You'd better wake me if his condition deteriorates."

Sophia's mind was in turmoil, and she could not sleep. She had used up most of her supply of Valium, so she crept down into Graziella's room and searched her dressing table.

"Is that you, Sophia?"

"Yes, Mama. Go back to sleep, I'm just looking for those tablets. Remember the ones you gave me. Are there any left? I can't sleep."

She returned to her room with almost full bottles of Valium and Seconal. Her hands shook as she tipped out the tiny yellow pills. She even swallowed a sleeping tablet to make sure she would sleep. She was so drugged that Teresa had to shake her awake. The young man, she said, was shivering. One moment he seemed cold, and the next he was sweating. He looked terrible, and she was scared.

Sophia hurried upstairs. Luka's body was burning up with fever, yet he was dripping with cold sweat. She ran downstairs to get her duvet and tucked it around him. Finally, the shivering subsided, and he seemed to grow calmer. She pulled up a chair to sit by him.

"Father . . . Father . . . Father . . ." Luka's voice was less than a whisper; his words were almost unintelligible. Sophia bathed his head, and his face twisted with pain. Then his eyes opened wide. He recoiled from her, not knowing who she was, pushing her hand away. He felt as if he were buried in soft clouds. Then his body filled with pain, and the clouds began suffocating him. He couldn't breathe. . . . He pushed the duvet from his racking pain. He was hot, burning hot.

Sophia rinsed the cloth in ice water and held it gently to his neck, his chest, and his right shoulder. The bandages were still clean; the bleeding had stopped. His body relaxed at last, and he slept.

Rosa slipped into the room. "Mama said I should take over. How is he?"

"I think he's doing fine. The fever broke, and now he's sleeping. As soon as he wakes, his bandages must be checked, just to see that the wound is clean. We must keep it clean. It was already showing slight signs of infection. I wish we had some antibiotics."

Rosa approached the bed and looked down at Luka. "He's very handsome, isn't he?"

"What?" Sophia was winding the bandages to be washed so they could use them again.

"How old do you think he is, Aunt Sophia?"

"Oh, I don't know, and to be honest with you, I think the less we find out about him, the better."

"What's his name? He's American, isn't he?"

Sophia crossed the room to pick up Luka's clothes. "Moreno, Johnny Moreno. Sounds like some kind of ballad, doesn't it?" She checked the pockets of his bloodstained jacket and trousers; they were empty. "He has nice clothes, very expensive labels, and all American. He sounds American. Maybe he is American."

"His shoes are Italian," said Rosa, holding up a Gucci loafer, "and very expensive."

Sophia picked up his gold Gucci watch and put it down again. It was still only eight-thirty in the morning. "Call me if the fever starts again. I'm going to take a bath."

Even though he had hardly slept the night before, Pirelli was in his office at eight, and he didn't even give Ancora time to take his coat off.

He began, "Main suspect for the Carolla hit, you're not going to believe it. . . . They've been checking out every person in the courtroom, a few of them not interviewed as yet." He listed a few names, then waved a printout, smiling. "This is the one. Listen to this: 'Brother Guido.' Our boy's last known address was a monastery, right?"

Ancora threw his hands up. "What are we waiting for?"

"Hang on, there's even more. The man who was sitting in front of the monk came forward last night. They've found traces of wadding on his coat, which was laid over the back of the seat, in front of the monk."

On the train journey the two men went over what they now knew of the case. Paul Carolla had obviously taken his son to the United States, illegally, as there was no record of him in America. The boy had subsequently changed his name to Luka. He was the chief suspect not only for the murder of the Paluso child but, since the same weapon had been used on the Luciano children, probably for their double murder as well. His last known address was the Monastery of the Holy Mission; the main suspect so far for the murder of Paul Carolla was a monk, Brother Guido.

The long uphill walk from the station took its toll on the overweight Ancora. Pirelli had to wait for his sweating, red-faced companion to join him.

They were shown into an anteroom beside the main gate of the monastery. The bells were ringing, the echo thudding through the small, bare room. It contained only a wooden bench, a table, and a bookcase.

Pirelli's mouth was dry. Ancora was still panting, his shirt wringing wet with perspiration, though the room felt chilly. They waited for more than fifteen minutes before a monk approached them and introduced himself as Brother Guido, gesturing for them to be seated on the bench. He drew up the chair and sat at the table.

They showed him their ID cards and asked him if he had been in Palermo at all in the past few days. He said he had not. He seemed very nervous, twisting a rosary around his fingers and blushing when asked if he could verify his statement. He assured them that he could as he had not left the monastery at all and had many witnesses to prove it.

Watching him carefully, Pirelli told him he was investigating the whereabouts of Luka Carolla. Guido flushed deeply. Pirelli went on to say that Paul Carolla, the said Luka's father, had been shot.

Guido's hands trembled as he whispered that he was aware that Carolla had been shot. He was able to tell them that Luka Carolla had been staying at the monastery up until the week before the killing, but he could give no information on his present whereabouts.

"Did you ever hear Luka referred to as Giorgio, or was he always called Luka?"

"Always. I never heard the name Giorgio mentioned."

"Is there anyone here who would know more about him?"

Guido nodded but told them it would not be possible to talk to Father Angelo now because he was giving the last rites to a dying monk, Brother Louis. All he could tell them was that Luka had been raised at the monastery before going to America with his father. He had returned recently and had stayed for nearly six months. He gave a detailed description, adding that Luka was very strong physically and had done a great amount of work in the garden.

Pirelli asked when it would be convenient to interview Father Angelo and was told that was in the hands of the Lord. Pressed by Pirelli, he eventually said it could be two or three days. The only other person who might be able to help was Brother Thomas, but he wasn't available either. Pirelli asked if he could borrow a monk's robe, to be returned on his next visit.

As they were about to leave, Pirelli asked Guido if Luka had brought much luggage. He described the leather carryall. Then he hesitated a moment before he said, "When he first arrived, he had a case, a small, flat leather case. I remember it because I offered to carry it into his cell, but he refused."

"What size?"

Guido demonstrated with his hands an object about twelve inches long.

"Did you see him leave?"

Again there was the deep flush as Guido shook his head. "I am afraid not. You could see his cell if you wish."

They inspected the small, bare room, and Pirelli asked if it had been cleaned recently. Guido told him he had washed and swept the room himself directly after Luka's departure. They were shown the gardens, where the new seeds were sprouting. "He turned all this soil single-handed. I have never seen anyone work so diligently. Do you wish to speak to him in connection with the killing of his father? Perhaps he does not know?"

Pirelli said he doubted it; every paper had been full of the news. He looked around; the place seemed desolate, not a soul in sight. "I will need to speak with Father . . . Angelo, you said? It is of the utmost importance. And please tell the others that I will return in two days, if they can be of any help." He paused, then said, "I don't suppose there is a photograph?"

Guido shook his head and apologized. They did not, to his knowledge, have one in the monastery.

The two men were silent on the train back to Palermo. Pirelli said, "I think he was holding something back, but until we get to the old father, someone who knows more about Luka Carolla, there's no point. . . ."

The monk's robe was shown to the guard, who was positive that the man in the court that day was wearing an identical one. He also remembered he wore leather sandals.

There were further developments concerning the weapon used to kill Carolla. The guard who had searched Luka described the cane as best he could, recalling that it had a brass head, some sort of animal, but he couldn't quite remember.

Pirelli mulled over the possibility of the gun's being a customized special. They knew from Guido's description that Luka Carolla had carried what appeared to be a gun case. Bruno was instructed to check out all the gunsmiths. Luka had been in Erice directly before the assassination; it was possible that the gun had been purchased locally.

Pirelli paid a call on Mincelli to see if he had anything new and was greeted with a stream of furious abuse.

"You wanna work on this with me, then say so. I sent three men up to that monastery for fucking nothing! You knew, because you'd already been there, that some old boy's croaking and they won't speak to anyone. . . . You wasted my time, Pirelli, and right now I don't have the time to waste."

"And I do? Look, all I want is to get the hell out of here an' back to Milan."

Mincelli sighed. "Not as simple as that an' you know it, not if we've got the same suspect. What do you think? Is this Carolla character our man?"

"I don't know. He could be."

"There's another possibility: that the Luciano women hired the guy. They'd have the connections."

Pirelli was incredulous. "You serious?"

"They're all the same; they close their eyes, see only what they want to see. And then, when one of them gets shot, they scream blue murder—"

"The whole family was wiped out."

Mincelli shrugged. "Read the papers, Joe. That old boy, Don Roberto, must have wiped out more than a few families in his time. Anyway, I'm trying to get a trace on the weapon, sort out the corpses at the Armadillo Club. . . ."

"Okay. I'm getting the gunsmiths checked out, and anything we get I'll pass straight on to you. And I'll save you a journey; I'll go see the Lucianos."

Mincelli cocked his head to one side. "Fine, that old lady might know something about Carolla's kid. Old Roberto Luciano and Carolla knew each other for forty years. . . ."

As soon as Pirelli left, Mincelli scuttled in to see the chief and suggested that since their investigations had the same suspect, Pirelli should be given the entire Luciano case. Mincelli would then be left with the Carolla killing and the nightclub investigation.

The chief put a call into Milan, requesting that they retain Pirelli for as long as necessary. Mincelli was greatly relieved; the race to find Luka Carolla was on, and he reckoned that with his desk clear, he would get to him first. Then he could take off for a skiing holiday, leaving the rest in Pirelli's lap.

It was almost eight-thirty in the morning. Teresa was in the study. Sophia, showered and changed, popped her head around the door.

"Have you had breakfast?"

The doorbell rang, and Teresa peeked through the blinds. She let them snap closed. "It's the carabinieri."

Commissario Pirelli was shown into the dining room by Adina while Teresa tried to calm Sophia.

"It's probably about Mama. Go sit with him, offer him coffee, anything, but give me a chance to warn Rosa. And Sophia, don't say anything about last night, promise me?"

Sophia gestured for Pirelli to follow her into the dining room. Apologizing for the darkness, she opened the shutter slightly. The light cascaded around her, and she blinked, put her hand over her eyes.

"Is it cold out?"

"No, very pleasant, fresh. I always like the cold, sunny September days."

She stared at him as if she hadn't understood what he had said.

"How is Signora Luciano?"

Sophia sat as far away from him as possible, right at the end of the table. "She is well, very tired. It is good that we are all here for her."

She was wearing a dark maroon cashmere dress that draped her figure softly, and he noted she wore no jewelry. She was no longer wearing the red nail polish; her nails were very pale.

Sophia was desperately hoping the others would hurry and join them; she hated the way he was scrutinizing her.

"That is a very nice painting."

She turned to stare at the large oil, a puzzled expression on her face. "You like it?"

He looked properly at the painting; it was dreadful, a group of men slaughtering a pig. "No. I don't know why I said that."

"It's a pig being slaughtered."

"Yes, I see that now."

He stood up as Teresa entered with Rosa behind her. He shook hands with each of them.

Sophia, Teresa, and Rosa sat at the long polished table like schoolchildren, their hands clasped neatly in front of them. He tried to put them at their ease, smiling and assuring them he had not come to arrest Signora Luciano, but they remained silent. He refused coffee but asked their permission to smoke. Sophia accepted a cigarette from him. As he leaned across the table to light it for her, Teresa and Rosa could see that her hand was shaking. Uneasy looks passed between them.

"Have you run out of your Turkish cigarettes?" Pirelli inquired.

Sophia inhaled the smoke. "Yes, I must get some. Thank you."

"I know a good tobacconist. I'll have some sent to you."

"That won't be necessary."

He opened his briefcase and took out a small notebook,

then searched his pockets and brought out a fountain pen. "I apologize for calling on you unexpectedly and at such an hour, but I wondered if you would mind answering a few questions."

He hesitated, looking around, and Teresa placed a heavy crystal ashtray in front of him. He thanked her and continued. "I will not detain you long. Allow me to give you some good news."

He told them that the judge had overthrown the defense counsel's pleas for the defendants' statements to be read in court and that sentences on the accused would be heard next week.

"So Paul Carolla would not have been freed?" asked Teresa.

"No . . . As a matter of fact, it is concerning Paul Carolla that I am here. We are trying to trace a man we wish to interview. His name is Luka Carolla."

He looked at each of them in turn, but there was no reaction. He went on. "Have you ever heard of him? Possibly even met him? He is Paul Carolla's son."

Sophia shook her head and seemed to look to Teresa for permission before she spoke. "I never met Paul Carolla. This man . . . Luka? Is he suspected of the murder of my children?"

Pirelli gave her a concerned look and chose his words carefully. "I am afraid that investigation is not the reason I am here. This is an entirely different matter. At this moment we simply wish to interview Luka Carolla. So far we have been unable to trace him."

He paused, and they looked directly at him, waiting expectantly.

"Carolla's son had apparently been visiting a monastery. It was the only address the lawyers had for him, but unfortunately he has left."

The women froze as Graziella walked into the room, and Pirelli rose to his feet. He kissed her hand and gestured for her to be seated, drawing out a chair next to his own.

"Are you arresting me?"

"No, no, signora, it is a very informal call. It's just that we have the name of a possible suspect in the Paluso child's killing."

Graziella listened as he told her of the search for Luka Carolla, asking if she had ever seen him or knew of his whereabouts. She told him she was not even aware that Carolla had a son.

Pirelli replied that the police had only just discovered Luka Carolla's existence themselves when Paul Carolla had suggested that his son be questioned.

Teresa leaned forward. "You mean, Paul Carolla implicated his own son?"

Pirelli nodded and tapped the edge of his notebook with his pen. "I think at the time Carolla would have implicated his own mother had she been alive. The case was going against him; the tragic murders of your family, the death of the Paluso child, and the mounting accusations in the press placed him under enormous pressure in the jail."

Sophia's cigarette ash dropped on the table, and she brushed it away. Graziella asked if Pirelli had any knowledge of who had killed Carolla.

"I am not on that investigation, signora, but I believe they are making headway."

"So they make headway in finding the killer of the man who murdered my children, but there seems to be no one continuing our investigation. Why have we not been visited before, kept abreast of what is happening?"

"As I have said, Signora Luciano, I am not—"

"Yes, you are not involved . . . Who is? I do not believe the carabinieri know anything. This trial will end, but still the murderers walk free, just as it has always been. . . ."

Pirelli saw the hatred in her eyes, washed-out blue eyes like chips of ice. He looked at the still faces of the women and bowed his head. "I believe that the man who shot Carolla was a professional. Ballistic reports have suggested that the gun was special, a custom-made single-shot gun, possibly disguised as a walking cane. The killer carried it undetected into the courthouse. Perhaps he was hired by one of the families that suspected Carolla was cracking under the strain. It was even suggested that the Luciano family—"

"Ah, now we have it. You are not here to question us about this Paluso murder. The reason is you think we are involved; you believe we had something to do with the man who murdered Paul Carolla."

Graziella pushed her chair back and stood up. She was

shaking, her whole body trembled, and the others rose from the table almost in unison. Teresa put a protective arm around Graziella's shoulders; the old woman was, for a moment, unable to speak.

Her chest heaved, but she pushed Teresa's arm away and turned to face Pirelli, who rose slowly to his feet. "My daughters had no knowledge of my attempt to kill Paul Carolla. This I have said in my statement. No one assisted me, no one knew of my intentions, and I swear before God and the Holy Virgin that it is the only criminal act I have ever committed in my life—"

Pirelli interrupted her. "Please, Signora Luciano, I had no intention of—"

Teresa could not keep quiet. She looked at him with contempt. "No intention of what, Commissario? Why don't you actually ask us, ask us if we hired an assassin to kill Carolla? Do you think if we had even considered it, we would have let Mama go into that courtroom? What do you take us for? What kind of people do you think we are?"

Pirelli stared hard, then reached for his raincoat. "You must realize, these questions are bound to be asked. Whoever killed Paul Carolla escaped because of the hysteria surrounding Signora Luciano's attempt. I had no intention of insulting you, and I apologize; but I am investigating the death of a nine-year-old child."

Sophia stepped forward then. "And my children? They don't concern you, do they?"

Pirelli faced them. "I am pursuing this investigation to the best of my ability. . . . Thank you for your time."

Pirelli put his hand out to shake Graziella's, but she turned and walked toward the door. She paused and said, "My daughters will show you out, Commissario."

Teresa picked up his notebook and glanced at it. The doodle on the page was a picture of a walking cane. She closed the book and held it out to him.

"There was one more thing I wanted to ask you," said Pirelli.

The women stood side by side, waiting. Pirelli flipped his notebook open and turned a few pages, then snapped it shut and said questioningly, "Enrico Dante?"

Teresa pressed her hand into the small of Sophia's back.

Pirelli continued. "He was an associate of Paul Carolla. Does his name mean anything to you?"

Teresa shook her head. "I have never heard of him."

He looked at each of them, then strode into the hall. Teresa opened the front door, and he walked out without another word.

As the door closed behind him, he went slowly down the steps. He paused for a moment, then continued along the gravel drive. He had left his car outside the gates. He stopped suddenly and turned back to look at the sprawling villa, the gardens, the groves. . . . The hood of a dark blue car, a Fiat similar to his own and in no better condition, was just protruding through the bushes. He gave it no more than a cursory glance. His mind was elsewhere, because he knew that what Sophia had said was right. The Luciano murders were, to him, on a par with the hundreds of Mafia vendetta murders that occurred all the time. At least their dog-eat-dog methods cleared some of the filth from the streets.

Back at headquarters, Pirelli opened the file cabinet and flicked through it. He withdrew the file with the photograph of Sophia Luciano's children. After removing everything from his bulletin board, he pinned the photo up.

"So it's true, you're taking on the Lucianos?"

Pirelli gave Ancora a puzzled look. "How do you know? I've only just thought about it."

Ancora shrugged. "Well, the rumor is that Mincelli's off the case, you're on it. Milan's given the go-ahead for you to stay. I thought it was just a rumor. I mean, I know you want to get home."

Pirelli smiled, shaking his head. "The little bastard, he must have worked overtime, an' you know what? I'm gonna make him sorry for the day he went behind my back."

Ancora placed two reports on the desk. "Young Bruno's done some good work. We think, though we're not sure, that the weapon was a shooting cane, made in the early eighteenth century. The top part is a horse's head, and it comes apart in three pieces."

Pirelli snatched the paper. "What are you talking about?"

"The weapon used to kill Carolla."

"You've found it?"

Ancora shook his head. "No, but here's a report of a theft from the Villa Palagonia. It was broken into, and the only thing stolen was this old shooting cane."

Pirelli read the report of the stolen gun. "It hadn't been fired for sixty, seventy years. If this is the one, someone must have worked his butt off."

Ancora nodded. "Stolen the night before Carolla was shot. We've got Bruno checking out all the gunsmiths capable of carrying out that kind of work."

Pirelli was leaving, fast. At the door he turned. "Get that over to Mincelli's crowd; get them to do the legwork. You get over to the Villa Palagonia, take the composite of Luka Carolla, see if he was there."

He paused, frowning. "Also get some ID from records, those two corpses at the Armadillo Club. Take their mug shots with you and see if anyone recognizes them and . . . start checking out car rental firms, garages, see if our boy rented a car."

Ancora sighed. He wondered what Pirelli himself was going to be doing.

He was faxing the police in the States, requesting a check on schools, colleges, etc., in the area of Paul Carolla's last known address. Perhaps someone could come up with a recent photo.

Graziella, dressed in mourning, found Sophia lying on her bed. She had obviously been crying, and Graziella kissed her gently. "I am going to the mausoleum. Will you join me?"

Sophia shook her head. "No, Mama, I have a headache. Maybe Rosa will go with you."

"I would like you to accompany me."

Tears trickled down Sophia's cheeks, but she made no sound of weeping. Graziella went to the window and opened the shutters a crack. The sunlight streamed in, and Sophia put her hands across her face.

Graziella's voice was firm. "They do not care about your babies, Sophia. That Pirelli was only interested in Carolla. Well, I thank God for his killer. At least he gave us justice, may God forgive me. I would like you to come, and I will wait downstairs for you."

Graziella paused a moment by the bedside table and looked

at the bottle of tablets. It was open, and some of the small yellow pills were lying loose on the tabletop. She said nothing.

Graziella and Sophia stood side by side at the mausoleum gate. Red paint had been scrawled over the walls: "*Mafioso finito* . . . Bastards . . ."

The two women went to the taps and filled cans of water to try to wash the paint off the walls. Sophia searched for a stone, dipped it in the water, and started scrubbing at the paint, rubbing so hard that she could feel her fingers getting raw, but she couldn't stop.

Graziella's voice calling her name over and over eventually made her stop. "It's all right, my love, see? See, it's all gone now; it's clean. Come inside, let us go inside."

Sophia struggled against Graziella, twisting away from her. "No, no, don't make me go inside, Mama, please. . . ."

Confused by Sophia's hysteria, Graziella released her hold, and entered alone. Sophia clung to the railings. Her mouth was dry, she couldn't swallow, and she began to search her pockets frantically. She needed something to calm her, she needed— needed . . .

An old man appeared, carrying a bucket and scrubbing brush. "Signora Luciano, I didn't want you to see this. I don't know when it happened. I care for these graves as if they were my own family."

Sophia could not speak. She turned to the gates as Graziella reappeared. The old man kissed her hand, near to tears himself. She drew her veil down over her face and thanked him, then held her hand out to Sophia. The caretaker bowed, apologizing again and promising to guard the tomb with his life.

He was still apologizing as they walked slowly along the white-pebbled lanes, past the tombs, and eventually to the main path.

Sophia slipped her hand into the crook of Graziella's arm. "Mama, I want to tell you something. Michael—"

Graziella gripped Sophia's hand tightly, squeezing her fingers. "You know what Rosa said to me the other night? She said, 'Grandma, it's different for you, because you are old.' Well, Sophia, let me tell you, I feel the pain now as sharply for Michael as for your babies. I think, *What a terrible waste.* I have outlived my sons, my husband, my grandsons; everything I produced has died, and the only thing I have to remind me that they lived is my pain. It no longer makes me weep; it no longer brings tears; it is just proof of what I had, of what I lost, my family."

Graziella wiped her dry eyes, then sighed. "All we have is little Rosa."

Pirelli rubbed his eyes, which were red-rimmed from reading the Luciano files, and answered the telephone as Bruno brought in a single sheet of typed paper. He held his hand out for it as he listened to the caller; there was no record of a Luka Carolla leaving Sicily or Rome in the last three months. "What's this?"

"From Enrico Dante's place, found on the floor of his office. Whoever robbed the place made a good job of it, but that was left or dropped. Looks like a list of properties. The ones underlined all belong to the Luciano family, and Enrico Dante worked for Carolla. They also found this; it'd been dropped beside the bar."

Pirelli took the bullet and turned it over in his hand, rubbing the point. "Looks like it's been drilled."

"Yes, but it also matches the bullet fragments taken out of Paul Carolla. This one hasn't been fired."

Pirelli sucked in his breath. "Anything on the prints of that glass they found?"

"No one who's got a record. Could have been a customer, but the orange juice it contained was spilled all over the floor. . . . Oh, yeah, there was something else, don't know if it's of any interest. There was a clear print, in the blood around the bar, of a woman's high-heeled shoe."

Pirelli held the bullet, rubbing his finger over the minute drilled rings, then shot to his feet. "Get this back to the lab; get them to check the fragments of bullets from the Luciano children, see if the grooves match these. I want to know if the same drill was used."

Bruno paused. "Christ Almighty, you think it's the same guy?"

"It's a possibility, and it looks like we've got some kind of contract killer who likes to leave his calling card."

"What do you want me to do about that list?"

"Leave it with me. Oh, and get me the train timetables. I'm going back to that monastery to see if we can get anything more on this Luka character."

"You think he's the bastard?"

"I don't know, but I want him found."

Luka stared at Sophia, dull-eyed, as she spooned the soup into his mouth. He managed only three mouthfuls before he slumped back against the pillow.

Teresa opened the door and whispered, "You'd better come down to the study; there's something I want to show you. Leave him, come on."

Sophia put her finger to her lips to indicate that he was sleeping and followed. Teresa closed the door and locked it.

Luka waited a moment before he slowly eased himself into a sitting position, gritting his teeth against the pain burning in his shoulder. He inched the bedclothes away from him and slowly swung his legs over the side of the bed. He could not stand and flopped back against the pillows.

"Shut the door after you," said Teresa, and Sophia kicked it closed.

"He took only a couple of mouthfuls," said Sophia. "Rosa crushed up two Seconal and sprinkled them over the top. . . . Did you hear me?"

Teresa opened the desk drawer. "Yes, yes . . . This was in his bag, Moreno's bag. The one we brought the papers in from the club? Now, watch."

She picked up the first part of the cane, the section with the horse's head, then slotted the second piece into position. "It's a single-bullet gun, see? The horse's head is where you fix the bullet, safety catch is the ear, and you fire it by pulling the head back. . . . Acts as a trigger. Moreno is the killer, Sophia; he has to be. It's almost exactly the weapon Commissario Pirelli described, isn't it?"

Sophia had to sit down. "What are we going to do?"

"Keep it. As soon as he's well, he's out. We pay him off, just as we agreed."

"What? Are you mad? If this gun is his, he's murdered two men, Teresa. We have to get Pirelli back here, and if you don't, then I will."

"You can't."

"It won't just be me; it'll be all of us. We are harboring a killer; we're withholding evidence."

"But with Carolla dead, with Dante dead, we all are going to benefit. We'll just pay him off as soon as he's well."

"Pay him off with what? The few hundred dollars that were in that bag? Do you think he'll be satisfied with that? He could blackmail us. Think of the hold he has over us! If we keep him here, we are as guilty as he is. We have to call the police."

"Fine, you want to call Pirelli? Go ahead, explain why you never told him about Moreno when he was here. You were at the club; you knew that he had to have shot Dante. If he also shot Carolla, then we should give him a goddamn medal! Call Pirelli, go on. Get me arrested while you're at it."

Teresa's eyes frightened Sophia, because beneath all the bravado there was something else; she could sense it.

"What have you done?"

Teresa was almost in tears. "I did it for us." She took her glasses off and rested her head in her hands. "I did it for us."

"What?"

Teresa fumbled with the dial of the safe and swung the door open. It was stacked with bundles of bank notes, dollars, and lire in thick bundles.

"I took all the money from Dante's safe when I searched for my purse. That was why I brought the bag back. It's all used notes; it can't be traced."

Too shocked to speak, Sophia stared first at the cash, then at Teresa's frightened face.

"We had no cash, Sophia, we need this money, and who's to say it's not ours anyway? He can't blackmail us because we could have him arrested."

"How much is there?"

At least Sophia was not shouting. Teresa felt more confident. "Enough to start clearing up the docks and warehouses. Enough to prepare everything to sell. We can't get a good price with everything the way it is, run-down. We need this money to put the buildings in order, pay workers to clear the filth, the rotting cargoes. I've been making lists of everything that has to be done, estimating the costs, and—"

Sophia interrupted. "I don't want any part of it, Teresa. I can hardly believe what you've done. . . . How do you think Mama and Rosa will feel?"

"Why tell them? They don't have to know, especially Mama. She's got to go before the magistrates. She needs us all here; she needs you."

Sophia shook her head. "Don't try that tactic, Teresa. You stole that money, and it's on your head."

"Fine, it's on my head, I'll handle it. I'll make sure we all get what's due to us, and that is all I care about, Sophia. This is family business."

Sophia leaned over the desk and spit, "The family is in the graveyard, Teresa. Just leave me out of it, and get rid of that boy upstairs, or so help me God, I will call the police."

It was after midnight, and Rosa sat reading by Luka's bed. She checked the time, then felt his forehead, relieved that his temperature had gone down.

Her bookmark slipped from between the pages, and she knelt to retrieve it. As she straightened up, she saw something glittering beneath the bed.

The small gold heart dangling on the fine gold chain was covered in dust; she blew it clean, then dropped it into a small glass bowl on the chest of drawers.

# 14

Luka had been at the villa for two days, sleeping most of the time and eating little. On the third day he was feeling strong enough to want to bathe.

Teresa was surprised and a little afraid when she discovered his room empty.

"Where is he?" she whispered to Rosa.

Rosa had changed Luka's bed, piling the dirty linen on the floor. "He's taking a bath."

"Go tell him to get out, and hurry. Your grandmother thinks it's you in the bathroom. Go on, quickly. I'll finish the bed."

Rosa picked up the small heart and chain from the chest of drawers. "I found this under his bed. I don't know if it's his or maybe was left by a maid. See, it's a little heart—"

Teresa took it from her. "Go along. I'll help him back to bed."

Luka opened the bathroom door, wearing a terry-cloth robe that had once belonged to Roberto Luciano. It swamped his slender frame, making him look even more boyish. He was weak

247

from the effort of bathing and drying himself, and he clung to
the door handle for support.

When Teresa reached the landing, she found Rosa still
hovering with her arms full of laundry. Keeping her voice low,
she ordered her daughter, "Go downstairs, and put that in the
machine yourself. Don't let Adina see it."

Luka moved slowly and cautiously along the landing, sup-
porting himself on the wall. By the time he reached his door he
was exhausted.

Teresa offered to help him, but he recoiled from her, so
she stepped aside as he entered the small room. She had opened
a window, and Luka sat on the freshly made bed. He lifted the
pillow and searched beneath it.

"I have the gun, Mr. Moreno."

He turned to her with a puzzled expression, then touched
his neck. "My chain, my gold chain . . ."

"Is this it? Rosa found it; she thought it might have belonged to a maid."

"No, it's mine."

She watched as he twisted the chain around his fingers,
nervously. She asked, "How are you feeling?"

"Much better. My shoulder doesn't hurt so much now."

"How long do you think you need to stay here?"

"Until I feel strong enough to leave."

"We had Commissario Pirelli here asking questions. . . .
He knows nothing, but we know you killed Dante. Did you
kill Paul Carolla?"

Luka gazed at her innocently. "Who?"

"Paul Carolla. He was shot during his trial."

Luka lay back and closed his eyes. He could feel her looking at him. This one was different from the others. This one
had cold eyes, and he didn't like her.

Teresa moved closer to the bed. "The police think there is
a connection between the two murders. If you did kill Carolla,
we will never give you away. I think we might even congratu-
late you."

He opened his eyes and turned to face her. His voice was
soft. "I did not kill this man. I have never heard of him."

She gave a humorless, twisted smile. "I think you did. I
have not only the gun from under your pillow, but the other

one, too, the one that looks like a walking cane. It was in the bag we brought from Dante's club—"

She was caught by the expression in his strange ice-blue eyes. "What bag? I don't have a bag. You must be mistaken."

Teresa raised her eyebrows and smiled. "No? Don't lie to us, Mr. Moreno." She left the room and closed the door behind her.

As he heard the key turn in the lock, his body curled into a fetal position. The gold chain was wrapped so tightly around his knuckles that it broke the skin. "Please, don't lock me in. . . . Please don't."

Teresa stood on the landing outside, the key in her hand, and listened to the muffled sobs. She began to walk slowly down the stairs. Could they be wrong about him? She shook her head.

As she came to Sophia's room, she tapped on the door. Sophia called her in. She was lying on her bed, the room in darkness.

"I want to talk to you and Rosa downstairs," Teresa whispered.

Sophia didn't answer; she was listening to the faint sound of weeping. "What's that? Can you hear it? Is it Moreno?"

Keeping her voice low, Teresa said, "Yes . . . Oh, God, do you think Mama can hear?" She stepped out on the landing, looked upward, listening. The muffled sobs were like those of a child. She was about to go upstairs when the weeping stopped. She listened for a moment longer, then rejoined Sophia.

"It's okay, he's stopped. You know, I think I was wrong about him. Maybe he shot Dante in self-defense, but well, I doubt if he'd have the guts to kill Carolla. Seems like a wimp to me . . . And I suspect it *was* Dante's bag, not Moreno's. After all, it was his club. If it's true, it should ease your conscience about harboring a mass murderer, Sophia? Did you hear what I said?"

Sophia sighed and nodded. "Let me wash up. I'll meet you downstairs, Teresa."

In the silence they heard it again, very faint but clear: the eerie sound of weeping, like a child's.

Teresa sat behind the desk with a stack of printed posters in front of her. Rosa had pulled her chair close to the desk, and

Sophia was sitting slightly to one side, looking over one of the handwritten posters.

"They go up on every wall, in the docks, the warehouses, in the streets," Teresa said. "I want every man who ever worked for Don Roberto to read them. I'll pull every string I know to get these men back working for us. We do it together, all of us, and we use any tactic we can, even make them feel so guilty they will at least give us—"

She was interrupted by Graziella, who walked slowly and sedately into the room, carrying a vase of fresh flowers. As she put it down on the desk, she picked up one of the posters, read it very slowly, then pursed her lips.

"These men all work with other families; it will cause trouble. Not just for them but for you, all of you. Hasn't there been enough death in this family without asking for more?"

Teresa was growing impatient. "They owe us, Mama. For years Don Roberto gave them employment."

Graziella surprised them then with the cold, hard edge in her voice. "But he is dead, Teresa. You are not head of this family. I am, and I refuse to let this theatrical gesture continue."

"We need you with us, Mama, would like you with us. If you refuse, that is your prerogative, but we are going ahead whether you like it or not."

The stench of warehouses full of rotten oranges left in their cargo boxes was like an open sewer. Rats scurried across dank floors. The cargo boats rusted in their dry docks. Rows of trucks, their tires slashed and canvas tops ripped, stood abandoned, their paintwork blistered by the sun. Engines had been stolen; almost every removable part was gone. The wanton neglect was heartbreaking.

The once-flourishing tile factory was shuttered, thick dust from the tiles covering even the offices. Windows were shattered, and the place had been broken into so many times there was hardly a room left intact.

The women were silent, but their sight-seeing tour was not over. They drove out to the massive canning factory, towering above the desolate yards, then to the groves themselves. Now they were witness to mile upon mile of dying trees, orange, lemon, and olive, their fruit rotting, fly-infested and stinking. The sprinklers had rusted, the irrigation canals were filled with dead fruit, and the flies hummed in thick clouds above the trees. Graffiti could be seen, written in the dust and painted across the walls: "*Mafioso finito. Bastardo Luciano . . .*"

Teresa's face was set, rigid with determination, while she strode from one nightmarish scene to another, making notes and murmuring to herself as Graziella trailed after her.

When they returned to the villa, Rosa slipped upstairs to unlock Luka's room and check his bandages. The others remained in subdued silence in the study. Teresa flicked open her notebook.

"First we will need men to clean, remove the garbage, check the trucks to determine what we can use, what we have left."

Sophia brushed the dust from her skirt. "It's not a house, Teresa. You can't just get a crew of people in with mops and buckets."

Ignoring her, Teresa continued. "The trees need to be pruned, cut back almost to their roots, and the sprinklers started. They'll not harvest for at least a couple of seasons."

Sophia flung her hands up. "A couple of seasons? And in the meantime, what do we do? After we clean up the docks, the warehouses, the ships, what happens then? We have no product. It's madness, as Mama said; we'll never be able to start again."

Teresa snapped, "We're not! We are simply preparing to sell. I have a list of all the export companies in Palermo; we will approach them. Then we decide either to sell, depending on the price offered, or to lease space. We have export licenses, we have the space for goods in New York, the warehouses Filippo ran, we have a delivery and trucking company, we have the Luciano name—and that is worth a lot more than we have been offered to date. Now does it make sense? I am trying to put together the best possible package for a deal, and to make those who have already made offers up their price. In other words, I am doing exactly what I would do if I were trying to sell an apartment for the highest price possible."

No one argued; no one said another word. Teresa sat smugly behind the desk. "All you have to do is exactly what I have planned. I have someone waiting to distribute the posters."

You came in your hundreds to bury the man you de-
servedly called *Il Papa;* to weep with his women, cry
for his sons, and pray for his grandchildren. Signora
Luciano asks you who knew Don Roberto Luciano to
show your respects one last time, for the men he employed, for the women he provided for, for the children who grew to manhood safe under his protection;
to show his women the love he gave freely to you.

> Signed:  Graziella Luciano
> Sophia Luciano
> Teresa Luciano
> Rosa Luciano

On the designated day Teresa drove the white Rolls-Royce.
The meeting was called for two o'clock in the afternoon. As
instructed, they all wore mourning, but only Graziella wore a
thin black veil over her iron gray hair. The gleaming white car
and the black-clad women made a touching spectacle for the
press.

They stood on the small raised platform in a line, facing
the crowd. No one could remain unaffected by them; they had
the same air of calm they had borne at the funeral.

When Teresa stepped forward, she was greeted by a respectful silence. She thanked everyone for coming and offered
a short prayer. Then she lifted her voice.

"You are standing in the Luciano warehouse. I have no
need to point out to you the neglect, just as I am sure I have
no need to tell you of the sad condition of my father's companies, now empty and unproductive. At some time all of you
here benefited from Don Roberto's generosity, from his kindness, his love and understanding. He gave you work; he gave
you protection; he gave of himself freely and unstintingly for
many years. He never turned people away if they needed
his help."

Cameras flashed as she paused to let the message sink in.
The press had turned out in force.

Teresa continued. "We now need your help to get started.
We do not ask for your charity or for your hard-earned lire; we
ask of you your time, for each of you here to give us a few
hours of your time. . . ."

She explained how workers were needed to clean up and sweep the floors, mechanics to repair the trucks, glaziers to repair the windows. She explained that for the widows to get the price that the buildings were worth, they would need to be put into working condition. She told them of the loss of Roberto Luciano's fortune, that they were destitute.

Teresa explained that the tile factory would be their headquarters, and those willing to give their time and expertise should put their names and trades into a big voting box as they left the warehouse.

The newspapers published Teresa's speech and in a few instances gave reporters an opportunity to deny the rumors about Don Roberto Luciano during the trial. But they also spawned more spurious, defamatory stories of Luciano's past and his Mafia connections.

Pirelli was the only passenger in the small train compartment, heading once again for Erice. He opened his briefcase and sifted through Ancora's reports.

The gunsmith suspected of reworking the antique gun had been found dead, suffocated beneath bales of straw in his workshop, the type used for firing practice. They had found numerous drills for customizing bullets, and there had been further developments in tracing the gun itself. When inquiries had been made at the Villa Palagonia, the tour guide had identified the deceased Dario Biaze and Enrico Dante as the men he had spoken to the day the gun had been stolen, but he could not identify the third man, who had remained practically hidden in the backseat of the car.

Pirelli reached into his briefcase and brought out his notebook, flicked through it until he came to his scrawled notes on the interview with the guard from the courthouse. He described the priest, the suspected killer of Paul Carolla, as having thick, reddish dark hair. He had been unable to make a positive identification from the police composite picture.

The last part of the report was a copy of the forensic findings on the fingerprints taken from the bullet and the orange juice glass at the Armadillo Club. There was a thumbprint, but so far they had been unable to match it with any on record.

Pirelli closed the folder, picked up an old newspaper from the floor, tossed it onto the seat opposite, and rested his feet on it. His right heel covered the black-and-white photograph on the front page, but the article on the Luciano women that accompanied it caught his eye. He picked it up and was surprised to see that the widows had virtually asked for charity. The train pulled into Erice before he could finish reading.

The sheets from Luka's room were still in the dryer, and Sophia busied herself unloading it. As she folded one of the pillowcases, she noticed stains on it. She threw it into the wastebasket, presuming the dark brown marks to be blood. It was not until she went in to check on the sleeping Luka later that evening that she noticed his hair was very much lighter than it had been. She leaned over him for a closer look and was startled when Rosa walked in.

Rosa looked at her suspiciously. "What are you doing?"

Sophia put her finger to her lips. Luka was still asleep. "Come and see, here. . . . Look at his hair. It's dyed. He's blond, see?"

Rosa leaned over to look, then agreed. She whispered, "Why has he dyed his hair?"

Sophia did not reply. After they left the room quietly and locked the door behind them, Luka opened his eyes. He was able to get out of the bed with ease now, and he began to walk up and down the room. He had heard them talking and stared at himself in the mirror; the roots were beginning to show blond, and he swore softly to himself. His time was running out; he had to leave. He began to stretch the fingers of his left hand. The pain still lingered, but he slowly took off the bandages and began to exercise. . . .

Pirelli was sweating from the long walk up to the monastery, even though there was a cold wind blowing. Brother Guido welcomed him and showed him to the little room near the gates. Father Angelo would be with him shortly, he said, and Brother Thomas was also coming to speak to him.

The small bookcase beneath the crucifix caught his eye. For something to do, he took out one of the worn leather-bound prayer books and traced the embossed gold cross with his fin-

ger. He was about to replace it when one of the other books
fell to the floor. It opened at the first page, and he saw the
inscription inside: "Giorgio Carolla, 1973 . . ."

Brother Thomas shuffled into the room, carrying a brown
manila envelope that looked dog-eared and well used. "I wondered when you would return, Commissario. I did not get the
chance to speak with you last time you were here. Please, shall
we be seated? I am Brother Thomas. You wish to discuss Luka?
Luka Carolla?"

Pirelli sat down. The old man's robes had a heavy, musty
smell, and the brother himself looked as though he could do
with a bath. His fingernails were black, and his feet, encased
in thonged sandals, were filthy. But he was eager to talk. He
busied himself taking papers from the envelope and stacking
them in front of him, then put his hands over them and gave a
sly smile, rocking backward and forward.

The old man's eyes were like peas, small and muddy green;
they were sly eyes. His whole manner was furtive; he looked
constantly at the closed door, lowering his voice secretively and
sucking breath noisily between his gums. "I knew he was bad,
a liar. He stole a chicken leg once, you know. . . ."

Pirelli listened to the old man's rambling tale about a theft
committed by Luka in the orphanage. He was very patient, and
when they heard the slow footsteps approaching, Thomas pressed
the worn envelope into Pirelli's hand, saying he was not to
mention it.

Father Angelo moved painfully slowly, and Guido helped
him to the chair. Pirelli was getting more depressed by the minute. Brother Thomas had proved incoherent, and he was sure
this elderly man would be even worse.

"You may leave us, Guido."

Pirelli sat back. The voice, though wavery, was direct; the
old man's eyes were clear and bright. As the heavy oak door
closed behind Guido, Father Angelo folded his hands.

"So, you wish to know about our son Luka. Is that correct?"

"Yes, Father, it is of the utmost importance."

Father Angelo nodded, lifting his hand slightly. "Perhaps
I should begin at the very beginning, yes? When he first arrived
here?"

"If you wouldn't mind, I think the more I know of him, the better."

Father Angelo smiled, shaking his head. "I don't think anyone ever really knew Luka. Not all of him at least. There was always a hidden side, a terrible, terrible dark side, that all the years he was with us I was never able to release. I collected him from the Holy Nazareth Hospital, where the juvenile courts had sent him for treatment. It was 1968 . . . July."

"I'm sorry to interrupt, Father, but didn't Paul Carolla bring him to you?"

"No, no, it was much later, many years later that I received the letter from Signor Carolla. His son, Giorgio, was dying, and Signor Carolla begged that we give him sanctuary. He was a highly intelligent child but was unable to walk because of a terrible birth malformation. He also suffered from a heart condition and had been confined to a bed all his life."

Again Pirelli interrupted to clarify. "So Luka was not Carolla's blood son?"

Father Angelo shook his head. "No, no, they were very different boys, Commissario, but both had suffered. Luka was not brought here until he was five, perhaps six years old. He was arrested along with a group of street boys who were attempting to rob a warehouse. Luka was an orphan, and because he was too young to be sent to an institution, I was requested by the authorities to bring him here. He had spent considerable time in the hospital. He had appalling injuries for a child so young, injuries, I was told, that had to have been inflicted over a number of years. His back was a mass of deep lacerations; his arm was broken; his pelvis at one time had been cracked; he even had a fractured skull. He was, Commissario"—Father Angelo chose his next words carefully—"a tragedy. What misery the child had lived through I was never able to ascertain, but such anguish touched my soul. I insisted that we try our utmost to give him peace. We didn't find it easy; he was a thief, a liar, and he turned most of the other children against him. He was always fighting, yet he had the face of an angel. . . . At one point we were doubtful that we could restrain him, but God moves in unexpected ways. In Luka's case his salvation came in the tragic guise of a boy so sickly, so heartbreakingly malformed that the other children called him a gargoyle, a devil incarnate. This child was Paul Carolla's son, Giorgio."

Pirelli sat very still, listening intently.

The priest's gentle voice continued. "Luka had committed some misdemeanor in our monastery, and as a punishment he was to clean the rooms. One of those rooms was that of the dying boy, Giorgio Carolla. What occurred, Commissario, was nothing less than a miracle. Luka embraced the invalid, cared for him as a mother would her child. They became inseparable. This poor boy who had never walked, never joined in the simple pastimes of other children recovered to such an extent that it was indeed miraculous. Luka washed him, fed him, dressed him, and in the carpenter's shop made him a wheelchair of sorts so the child could sit outside. Within two years of his joining us, Giorgio was fit and well enough to take part in the daily classes. His intellect was far above the other children's, and he was an inspiration. . . . We had no further trouble with Luka; he had found a family; the sick boy became everything to him."

Taking a linen handkerchief out of his robe, Angelo wiped his eyes. Pirelli remained silent.

"But Giorgio only seemed well. The added strain was making his poor heart fight to keep up. We knew he could not survive." Father Angelo's hands were shaking as he tried to pour himself a glass of water. Pirelli rose and poured it for him.

"In January 1974, Giorgio required an emergency heart operation. He contacted his father, insisting that if he were to go to Rome for the operation, he would agree only if Luka could accompany him. It was, you understand, doubtful from the very beginning that the operation would be successful, but without it there was no hope at all. The travel arrangements were made, and Giorgio's physician came to prepare him for the journey. It had been a matter of days, perhaps a week, but in that time the boy's condition had deteriorated rapidly. Sadly the operation was no longer a possibility. Instead of Paul Carolla's arriving to take his son to Rome, he came to wait for his inevitable death."

Father Angelo pressed the tips of his fingers together, his head bowed. "During the sick boy's time here, time spent mostly with Luka, he had changed radically. I believe for the first time he wanted to live, had someone to live for. And Luka, oh, how Luka had changed! I cannot impress on you the goodness that flowed from this our most wayward boy. He was born with an angelic face; during his metamorphosis, for that is the only way I can describe it, he became an angel. He doted on the sickly boy and would, I believe, have died for him. We knew time was against the child. The day his father came to stay, Giorgio seemed somewhat recovered. He accepted the news that there would be no operation; I believe he made a joke. He was such a joker. You must understand, if any one of us had realized how close to death he actually was, we would never have left him alone."

Father Angelo stared silently at the blank wall. Many times he had relived the terrible winter morning, hearing the cry that echoed around the cloisters, and now he could not stop the tears. "It was forbidden—" He swallowed, unable to continue until he had a sip of water. "It was forbidden for the children to leave their dormitories after nine, but somehow Luka had crept out, past the father on duty. Giorgio died in Luka's arms, Commissario. Many times I have comforted the grieving, but never, never have I witnessed such depth of grief. Luka stood by Giorgio's window; he clung to the sill, his body rigid, his shirtfront soaked with tears that streamed endlessly down his cheeks. He would not come away from the window, and in the condensation on the glass he had scrawled—"

Father Angelo's voice dropped to a whisper as he told Pirelli that Giorgio's room had always been kept warm by special oil heaters his father had bought, and in the condensation that resulted, Luka had scrawled Giorgio's name over and over again, frantic scribblings, as if by repeating his beloved friend's name, Luka could recall him to life.

"I tried to pry his cold hands from the window ledge; his knuckles were white with the effort of holding on. He spit and kicked out at anyone who tried to move him. It broke my heart, Commissario. He would not let anyone touch him or hold him. He shrank from any contact.

"Signor Carolla was deeply touched by the boy's reaction; he asked if he might speak with him. When he came out of Giorgio's room, Luka was holding his hand. Signor Carolla adopted Luka shortly afterward and took him to live in America."

Father Angelo made no mention of his own anguish at how

Luka had behaved to him after Giorgio's death. The expression
on the boy's face, the hard glint to his eyes, had been identical
to the closed, unforgiving look he had worn the day Father
Angelo had brought him to the orphanage, as if the years of
loving care had counted for nothing, had never existed.

Pirelli waited, watching Father Angelo's bowed head, then
said gently, "Please continue, Father."

"I received a number of letters. I have brought them for
you to read if you wish. I signed the adoption papers, releasing
him from our care. I believed it was for the best. I believed
Luka would have a great opportunity." The tears trickled down
his face. "I did not see him again until his return this year."

Again he reached for the glass of water, taking small sips.
"Would it be possible for you to tell me why you are so interested in my son Luka? Do you believe he has committed some
crime?"

Pirelli coughed and licked his lips. "Yes, Father, I believe
so."

"Then I am to blame. I should never have let him go. At
that time I had no knowledge of what Paul Carolla—of what he
became. I thought it only for the best. Please, you must excuse
me, I—"

His frail body shook as he wept. Pirelli was at a loss to
comfort him. How could he even begin to tell this kindly old
man what Luka Carolla had become? He rose to his feet.

"I think that is all I need to know. I don't wish to distress
you further."

"He came back to me; he came back here for help. I know
that now. You see, as a boy, whenever he had done wrong, he
would attempt to make up for it by working. Painting, digging,
anything . . . He came here and worked very hard for six
months, and I knew, I knew something was terribly wrong."

Pirelli rang the bell by the door for someone to escort Father Angelo away, but Father Angelo was not finished.

"There is something more I must tell you. That darkness
in Luka . . . He had been sexually abused as a child. Do you
understand what I am saying?"

Guido overheard the last few words as he entered the room.
Father Angelo acknowledged his presence but persisted.
"Whatever happened to him made him terrified of small spaces,

of being locked in. He would become hysterical, violent even, and for the first few years he was here we were unable to get him to enter the chapel. He had a terror of the chapel and would become physically sick if we attempted to take him there for prayers. . . . Gradually this phobia subsided, and he would, though not frequently, go to mass. I believe that whatever sins were committed against Luka were within the confines of a holy place. May God forgive me, but that is what I believe."

Guido, flushing deeply, would not meet Pirelli's eyes. He fussed with the walker.

Almost as an afterthought, Pirelli asked, "Did you speak with Luka before he left, Father?"

The old man shook his head. "No . . . No, I did not. Brother Guido was the last one of us to see him. Our poor deceased Brother Louis was in a very nervous state. He once believed we had a circus in the courtyard and more recently that Christ has arisen in the chapel. He died shortly afterward. Perhaps he did in truth see Our Lord embracing him."

He inched toward the door, then paused, with his back to Pirelli. "Luka did not even bid me good-bye. . . . Have a safe return journey, Commissario."

"One moment, Brother Guido . . . Could you spare me a few minutes after you have seen to Father Angelo?"

As he waited for Guido to return, Pirelli felt drained and cold. The dampness of the room, coupled with the overpowering sadness of Father Angelo, made him long to breathe fresh, clean air—either that or smoke a cigarette! But he could hear Brother Guido approaching.

The young monk's nervousness was very apparent. Pirelli noted the tension in his hands as they plucked at his robe.

"You were the last to see Luka. Why did you never mention this before?"

"I did not think it was important."

"It might be. Brother Guido, I believe Luka Carolla is a very dangerous man. I am sure he has killed at least one child, and he possibly murdered his father, Paul Carolla."

Guido gasped. His eyes blinked rapidly, and he slumped into the chair, putting his hands over his face as he spoke. "The night Luka left, I was in the chapel, close to the crypt. I was kneeling in prayer, and he didn't see me."

Pirelli rested his hand on the monk's shoulder, encouraging him to continue.

"I saw him enter and put down his bag, the small leather bag I told you of. He moved up the aisle; I was about to call out, say something to let him know I was there—"

"But you didn't?"

Guido shook his head. "He stood so still, facing the cross, and . . . his face, it was like watching a statue. I have never seen such stillness, such—"

His shoulders trembled. Pirelli could feel it through the rough robe. Guido was whispering, "Such exquisite beauty. His face was like a carving, like Christ Himself." He crossed himself quickly.

Pirelli released his hold and moved away. "What happened then?" He repeated his question, this time more sharply. "What happened?"

"I stood up, revealing my presence, and he reacted like a wild animal. He hissed . . . a terrible hissing sound, and backed away down the aisle into the darkness, until I could no longer see him. He then said something blasphemous; I beg you not to ask me to repeat it. I heard the doors open, and he was gone."

"Taking only the small bag? You didn't see the other case you described?"

Guido sobbed, "No . . ."

Pirelli made the sign of the cross before following Guido up the stone steps to the crypt. He edged around the massive wooden cross and looked up. At first he saw nothing, but then Guido switched on his flashlight.

Pirelli walked into the ballistics section of the forensic laboratory. He handed over the gun case he had taken from the monastery. "I want this checked out now, and I want the rifling matched against the bullets used in the Luciano children's murder and the Paluso murder, and I want it done by tonight."

The technician moaned, but he carried the case to a long trestle table where three men were working. Pirelli followed.

"Did you come up with anything from the gunsmith's?"

The assistant paused. "The report's with Inspector Mincelli."

"Give me a rundown."

"Well, as far as I can remember, it's all in the report."

"I heard you the first time," Pirelli snapped.

The assistant took a file from a cabinet. "The unused cartridge found in the Armadillo Club was the same type used to blow Carolla's head off. The fragments taken from the corpse had the same drilled grooves as the unused bullet, and we verified that they had been made with a drill found at the gunsmith's. Similar grooves, also made by the same type of drill but not the same one, were found on the bullet fragments taken from the Luciano and Paluso children."

Pirelli interrupted. "Got any idea of the type of gun used in the kids' murders? Could the bullets have been fired from a forty-four magnum? I brought one in. It's loaded, two bullets in the chamber."

The assistant slammed the filing cabinet shut. "Look, we are working overtime down here. There're more fragments of bullets around here than you've had hot dinners. If the gun you brought in is the one, then, when we've checked it out, I'll let you know. It's not our job to make guesses."

Pirelli gave the assistant a hard look and turned to walk out. The man called after him, "What about prints from the weapon you brought in? You want it checked for prints?"

Pirelli hesitated, then gave a tight nod. He had been so eager to bring his find in that he had forgotten. "Yeah, no one's touched it."

"Except you, right? You must have handled it to find out it was still loaded?"

Pirelli flushed. "Yeah . . . You've got my prints, so you can eliminate them, and . . . you're doing a great job."

The assistant muttered an obscenity under his breath as Pirelli walked out.

Pirelli was irritated to find Ancora using his typewriter again. "Don't you have an office of your own?"

Ancora grinned. "Not anymore. It's a shoe box at the end of the corridor. Had a good day?"

"Yep, and it's not over. Take a look at this. . . . An old

brother at the monastery gave it to me, very furtively. There's a photograph of Luka at twelve, maybe thirteen. Get it blown up, may help. And he's got very distinctive blond hair all right, almost albino, blue eyes, about five-ten and a half to eleven. According to Brother Guido, he's pretty strong."

Ancora looked at the photo and wrinkled his nose. "Jesus Christ, is this a kid, the one in the wheelchair?"

"Yep, that's Paul Carolla's son, Giorgio."

Ancora's mouth fell open. Pirelli nodded at the photo. "Luka was adopted by Carolla when he was twelve or thirteen. No one's too sure of his exact age; they've got no birth certificate. But Carolla adopted him, took him to America after that poor, malformed creature died." Suddenly he picked up the phone and dialed records. "It's Pirelli. Do you think you could trace the records of a kid arrested in July 1968?"

The voice at the other end of the phone laughed and told him, humorously, to fuck off.

"I'm serious. All I've got is that he was blond, named Luka. I've got no surname, but he was in a bad way, brought in with a bunch of kids working the waterfront. He needed hospital treatment. Would have been about five or six years old."

"You got an arresting officer?"

"Nope, but the hospital was the Nazareth."

"Oh, come on, Pirelli, that burned down ten years ago."

"I know, but do what you can." Pirelli hung up and swiveled his chair. Only then did he notice the memos in his in tray. He picked them up, read them carefully, and leaned back, closing his eyes.

"Sweet Jesus . . ."

Ancora looked over. "That came in this morning. It's from the Luciano file. Must have come loose."

Pirelli shook his head. "I don't believe this! It says the chef from the San Lorenzo, the restaurant where the Lucianos were all poisoned, was shot, according to ballistics, with a Heckler and Koch. The other . . . How old is this? When was this report done?"

Ancora shrugged. "Must be months back. What, eight, nine months old?"

Pirelli turned over the page. "Second waiter was shot in the back of the head. Weapon, a forty-four magnum."

"They found the bodyguard stuffed down a well, but he'd been cracked over the head. There was no trace of the extra staff, the dishwasher, but they think he must have been a plant, you know, to get them into the place. There were three, possibly four men on the hit, judging by the footprints around the well. Joe—Joe, you listening?"

Pirelli was standing poised, his mouth open. "You're not gonna believe this . . . I just brought in a weapon from the monastery, and it's Luka Carolla's, and it's a forty-four—magnum."

It was Ancora's turn to gape. "You're kidding?"

"No fucking way . . . Get back to the labs; they've given no details of the bullets in this report. Find out if they were marked, you know, with drills, like the others."

Ancora got on the phone as Pirelli started to pace the office. He was sweating. The Paluso boy, the two Luciano children, Paul Carolla, the restaurant staff—had their killer left his calling card on all these murders, the telltale scratches on the bullets? Could the same man have been responsible for the poisonings of Roberto Luciano and his sons?

"Hey, man, take it easy. . . . Take it easy, this is crazy," Pirelli said aloud.

"That's the first sign, talking to yourself." Ancora was getting no reply. He dialed again.

Pirelli pointed to the wall where the photographs were displayed. "I want pictures of all the Lucianos up there and of everyone else murdered at the restaurant. I want Paul Carolla up there. . . . I want to see all their faces. Because I think they were all, and I mean all, killed by the same man."

"What are you, crazy?"

"No, I'm not, but I think their killer must be."

He got up and crossed the room to stand directly in front of the Luciano children's photo. "Look at the way he's positioned those two babies—shot them and then turned them to face each other, put their arms around each other as if they were sleeping."

The two men stared at the pitiful Carlo and Nunzio. Then they looked at the tragic Paluso boy, lying beside his bicycle in the gutter, his face a mass of blood, the back of his scalp blown away. The ice cream he had been holding had melted and mingled with his blood on the pavement.

Pirelli chewed his lips. "The Luciano children were killed at what time? Nine, nine-fifteen, yes?"

"They weren't discovered until eleven o'clock, I think. Lemme check . . ."

Pirelli rubbed his hair until it stood on end. "The Luciano men were not discovered until after eleven, but their bodies were still warm. . . . The chef, the staff, you got a time on them?"

Ancora's hands flew over the files, slammed one drawer shut, and opened another. He took out a file and thumbed through it, turning page after page. Impatiently Pirelli snatched the file and dropped it; the papers scattered on the floor. He swore, got down on his knees, and scrabbled around until he triumphantly held aloft the page he wanted.

"Now, let's see . . ." He got to his feet and threw his hands in the air. "There's no time; this report's only half finished. What the fuck have those guys been doing? Get me Mincelli on the phone. . . . Never mind, I'll go up."

About to slam out of the office, Pirelli paused. "Did you read about the Luciano women? What do you think is going on?"

Ancora shrugged. "The docks are swarming with men, clearing the warehouses. They must have some big shot behind them, smells like trouble to me."

Pirelli nodded. "Yeah, that's what I thought."

"That's the problem with this city: We can see trouble coming, but we're all too busy to do anything about it. Those women should watch out for themselves; something's going down. . . . You want a word of advice? Don't get involved; we've got enough going on. You start looking for—"

Pirelli had already left. Ancora sighed, turning to look at the bulletin board, then glanced back at the confusion of paper covering the desk. Pirelli was very good at unearthing evidence, but it was always up to Ancora to check it out. Still, he had to admit that he and Pirelli had moved things forward at a gallop. But Ancora had the uncomfortable feeling that the horse was out of control.

# 15

For eight weeks work went on around the clock. The canning factory was cleared and swept, the machinery put back into running order, and the tile factory, offices and warehouses, were made ready for occupation. The delivery trucks and even the typewriters were repaired.

Teresa worked herself to near exhaustion, driving a heavy truck from one location to the next, overseeing the workers and paying out the cash—always cash—and it was Teresa who ordered supplies, organized the painters and glaziers.

Rosa and Sophia worked well as a team. They were in charge of the twenty women cleaners and the army of men who were doing the heavy clearing, ferrying them from one place to the next. The women needed careful handling because they fought among themselves, argued about who should do which tasks, and complained if they thought they were doing men's work.

Rosa began to enjoy driving a pickup truck, wearing an old pair of overalls and a cloth cap, while Sophia spent her time hiring industrial cleaning machines and mechanical diggers, because along with the general cleanup they needed to uproot dead trees and remove tons of rotting fruit from the orchards. The sprinklers were repaired in readiness for the next season.

The three women worked from five in the morning until the last light of the evening. On occasion, when the factory's generators were restored, they stayed until after ten. They would arrive home at different times, baths would be run, food eaten. Then they would collapse into their beds exhausted, too tired to argue. They used a rotation system for taking care of their so-called houseguest, and he had been warned not to attempt to leave his room or to be discovered by Graziella.

Graziella shopped and cooked, helped wash their work clothes, and took their lunches to them in the factory. She enjoyed feeling a part of it all but knew not to meddle because Teresa's temper would make her own rise. Rather than stir up trouble, she kept herself busy.

One afternoon she returned home earlier than usual. Adina was at the market, and the house, she presumed, was empty. She decided to take a nap and was about to lie down when she heard a creak. A little afraid, she listened, then crept to her door. Someone was moving slowly down the stairs from the top floor. She inched her door open.

Luka had not heard Graziella return. As he made his way down the stairs, he checked each room, familiarizing himself with the layout. He passed Rosa and Teresa's room with its two single beds. Sophia's room had been left with the curtains drawn; he saw the pill bottles, the unmade bed.

He continued along the landing and was almost caught; Graziella was just going into her bedroom. He moved quickly into the nearest room, wincing as the door creaked badly. The room was obviously unoccupied; he left the door ajar and peeked out, listening. All was silent. He looked around at the small, neat bedroom with the sports equipment, the guitar with loose strings, the old posters on the wall.

He was just about to leave when he heard Graziella calling for Adina. He saw her pass along the landing and lean over the banister.

"Adina? Are you home?"

Through the gap he saw Graziella turn and stare toward him, at the partly open door. He had no idea that it was unusual, that he was in Michael's room and that Michael's door was always closed.

Slowly Graziella crossed the landing and pushed the door wider, wider. . . . There was no hiding place. He was caught, trapped, in the center of the room. But the scream he had expected didn't come. Instead, she stared at him and continued walking into the room.

"Who are you?" she whispered. "Who are you?"

"Don't be afraid," he stuttered. "I won't harm you. They know about me, I work for them, don't be afraid. . . . They said I could stay here, do you understand me?" Luka had spoken in English and was afraid she had not understood.

"Teresa? Did she say you could have this room?"

"No, no . . . Upstairs. I had a fall—see, I've injured my shoulder."

"But you're American?"

"Didn't they tell you about me?"

She was staring at him, moving closer and closer. "No, nobody told me. How did you get in?"

"They gave me a key."

"They should have told me; you gave me a fright. What is your name?"

"Johnny."

"You are in my son's room."

She came closer, staring into his face, then looked at his shoulder. "Did you break your collarbone?"

He put his hand across his chest. "I guess so, kinda wrenched it when I fell—fell onto a rusty nail."

"You want me to take a look?"

"No, they've done it up for me. . . . But I'm hungry."

She nodded and gestured for him to leave the room, closed the door behind them. "What part of America are you from?"

"New York."

When Adina arrived home and let herself into the kitchen, she was surprised to discover Graziella sitting with a strange boy, each enjoying a large dish of pasta.

But when Teresa returned, hours later, there was a different Graziella waiting, an irate one who didn't even wait for her to take her coat off.

"I want to talk, Teresa. I don't mind your using Papa's study as your own, but when you want someone to stay, you ask me. You don't let strangers come to this house without my permission, you understand? You don't know where he came from, who he knows, and you never let anyone have a key."

Teresa was so stunned she was hardly able to follow Graziella's meaning. "Wait, wait, Mama, what are you talking about?"

"You know, Teresa, the boy, the American student. I found him in Michael's room. Nobody goes in there, nobody."

"Shit, where is he now?"

"In the kitchen, helping Adina wash up. First I wanted to talk to you. You want to apologize now?"

"I, uh, I'm sorry, Mama. I'll go and talk to him."

"You do that. If you think he should stay until he's better, then we'll talk it over, but he's never to have a key to this house."

That night Teresa announced to the rest of them that Johnny Moreno, an American student, had been hurt in an accident at the factory and was staying with them until he recovered. Sophia waited until she was alone with Teresa before asking just how long their guest intended staying.

"Until he's fit to leave."

"He looks fit enough to me. I don't like his hanging around Mama while we are working."

"You just don't like him."

"And you do? Teresa, for God's sake, get rid of him. He makes my skin crawl. Pay him off, but get him out."

"He needs a few more days, okay?"

Sophia looked hard at Teresa as she stubbed out her cigarette. "For now, Teresa, but not for much longer."

The workers applauded as the freshly painted sign, LUCIANO EXPORT COMPANY, was hauled into place. It was hard to believe that the dockland warehouses were the same ones that so recently had resembled rat-infested sewers. They had been painted, the doors repaired, and the cavernous interiors swept and washed clean.

A navy blue Alfa Romeo was parked near the main warehouse, beside the white boundary markings. Its two occupants looked on all the activity with as much interest as Sophia. One

of the men was using a camera with a telephoto lens, and as
Sophia turned, shading her eyes against the sun, the camera
clicked rapidly, bringing her face closer and closer.

That afternoon the two men also took photographs of the
olive groves, the vineyards, and the tile factory, then drove to
the headquarters of the Corleone family in the mountains, where
the photos, still wet from the processing, were displayed to il-
lustrate that the Luciano family was back in business. The
question was, Who was injecting the cash to get things started
again?

Luka was wearing a robe over a shirt that Rosa had left
out for him. He watched as Graziella slowly entered the room,
smiling and carrying a tray.

"I have been baking fresh bread. Can you smell it?"

She put the tray down and drew up a chair for him. She
gestured for him to eat. "Now you are *my* guest, so eat, build
up your strength."

Luka found it disconcerting to eat with Graziella watching
his every mouthful, but her warmth and smile eventually helped
him relax while she chattered. "Teresa said that she would see
to your meals, but they are out all day." She pointed to the
apple pie. "That was my son's favorite," she said, then folded
her hands in her lap.

He said in Sicilian, "It is delicious, very good."

"You are not Sicilian?"

"No, American, but I have often been to Sicily."

"You speak it well. What work do you do?"

"Engineering. I was just traveling around."

"You are wearing my son's shirt."

"Do you mind?"

"No, I like it. . . . Will you explain something to me if I
ask you?"

"Sure."

"Teresa is going to sell space, you know, in our warehouses, our storage bays. Do you think that is good business?"

"Depends if it is needed. If there is already enough space
to go around, enough storage, then people won't buy. If there
isn't, they'll most certainly go for it. Supply and demand are
really all the selling knowledge you need."

She leaned forward and patted his knee. "You sound like my husband. . . . Eat, eat . . ."

As Teresa opened the front door, she heard Graziella on the stairs and looked up. Alarmed, she called, "Mama, what are you doing?"

Graziella gave Luka a mischievous smile and hurried down to Teresa. "I've been having a rest. Now I am coming downstairs. Is that all right?"

Teresa tossed her coat onto a hall chair. "The sign is up; it looks wonderful."

Rosa bounded in and caught her grandmother in her arms. "You would be so proud, Grandma; it's in bright red and gold letters, 'Luciano Export Company.' "

Throughout dinner Teresa talked to Sophia about how they should dress for their "sales pitch." She wanted the Luciano women to wear the most elegant and expensive clothes. Sophia was sure that she could get dresses for them from her warehouses, and besides, a trip to Rome would do them all good.

Teresa pursed her lips. "I don't think we all can go, but you could take our sizes and bring everything back, couldn't you? I trust your taste."

Rosa pouted. "Oh, come on, Mama, we all could go just for one day. It'd be fun."

Sophia was running her fork along the tablecloth, leaving small tracks. She had hardly touched her food. "What about accessories? Do we have enough money for those, too, Teresa? Shoes, handbags . . . where will the money come from to buy them?"

Teresa caught the edge in her voice. "Oh, come on, Sophia, you can't kid us that you are that broke. Can't you get some of your contacts to give us things for free?"

"I have about a twenty-thousand-dollar overdraft, Teresa. On my business account I am close to three hundred thousand in the red. Yes, sure, I can run to a few thousand more to dress us all. Why not? I was just wondering if there was any cash in the house. Perhaps you have some we could use."

Coldly Teresa tilted her head toward Graziella as an indication to Sophia to stay quiet. Graziella cleared the dishes and carried them into the kitchen. As soon as she had left the room, the atmosphere, already tense, became icy.

Teresa pushed back her chair, threw her napkin down. "In the future watch what you say in front of Mama, and for goodness' sake, stop running that damned fork up and down; it's getting on my nerves."

Carefully Sophia laid the fork down. Rosa glanced at her mother, then asked, "Where's all the cash coming from to pay the workers?"

Teresa snapped, "We have not had to pay a single lira to a single person. They're giving us their time for nothing."

Sophia joined in. "Teresa, why don't you tell us where it's really coming from, clear the air? We're not stupid, we've all seen the cash going out, and it's a lot. So where did it come from, Teresa?"

With a glare at Sophia, Teresa replied bitterly that she knew damned well where it came from.

"Yes," said Sophia, "I know, but why don't you tell your daughter?"

Teresa shrugged. "All right . . . I took the money from the safe at the club. I had to get things started."

Rosa stared at her mother, shaking her head. "What money? What are you talking about?"

Sophia waited, but Teresa said nothing. "Tell her! Okay, I'll tell her. The money, Rosa, came from Enrico Dante's safe. The night we went to find our contracts, we found the safe open, and it was stacked with money."

Rosa looked at Teresa, back to Sophia. "How much?"

Teresa sighed. "Let's just say it was a lot. You can see where it all went. It's not as if I took it for myself. I did it for all of us."

"Fine, but we pay off Moreno tonight and get him out of here," said Sophia, pursing her lips. "Agreed? Do you agree?"

"I have no intention of paying off Mr. Moreno. He should count himself lucky we saved his life."

Sophia picked up her fork again. "What are you going to do with him?"

"Nobody knows he's here, so he is not likely to start calling the police, is he?"

Sophia banged the fork down. "Teresa, for God's sake, tell Rosa about the gun."

"What gun?" Rosa demanded of Sophia. "The one from under his pillow?"

"No, the other one. Tell her, Teresa, and stop treating her like a child."

"She is a child."

"Mama, what is going on between you two?"

Sophia looked ready to explode. "Teresa, Rosa has a right to know! She's working alongside us; she is part of the whole setup. Now either you tell her everything or I will."

"Mama?"

While Rosa looked expectantly at her mother, Sophia got up and walked out, slamming the door behind her. Teresa sighed, then, without looking at Rosa, said quickly, "I didn't tell you everything, I wanted to protect you, but in the bag I brought back from Dante's club, the one belonging to Moreno, was another weapon, like a walking cane. It fires a single bullet, Rosa."

Just then Sophia walked back into the dining room and placed the three parts of the cane on the table. "Pirelli said that they believed Paul Carolla was killed by a specialist gun, possibly disguised as a walking cane. Well, what's this?"

"Holy shit!" Rosa's comment drew a frown from Teresa. "Why haven't you said anything about this before?"

Sophia slotted the horse's head into position. "Because your mother didn't want me to. But now Moreno is well enough to leave, and I want to get rid of him, pay him off."

"We can't. I spent the last of the cash today."

Sophia was sweating. She ran her hands through her hair. "Well, then, we have no alternative, do we, Teresa? We have only his word that the gun is not his, only his word that he shot Dante in self-defense. If we go to Pirelli, explain the circumstances—"

Teresa interrupted. "Sophia, you leave Mr. Moreno to me. You go to Rome."

Sophia walked to the door. "Fine, I'll go, but don't expect me to come back."

Teresa's eyes narrowed. "That's what this is really all about, isn't it, Sophia? You want out? Well, it's your decision. You do exactly what you want, just so long as we can trust you. Can we trust you, Sophia?"

Sophia felt sick. Her voice was hardly audible as she said,

"You can trust me, Teresa. I hope for your sake you can also trust Signor Moreno."

As Sophia left the room, Teresa turned to see her daughter staring at her. She caught Rosa's hand, gripped it tightly. "Everything I am doing is for you, Rosa."

"Are you, Mama? It doesn't look that way."

"What do you mean by that?"

"You've changed."

"Go to bed, Rosa, before you say something you'll be sorry for. I loved your father, and I miss him every waking hour; but life goes on. I intend to make it go on the best way I know how."

"And you don't care how or what you do, is that it?"

"If you want to side with Sophia, we'd better get the air cleared now. What do you want, Rosa? You want to go to the police?"

"I don't know. . . . Good night, Mama."

Left alone, Teresa remained sitting in Don Roberto's chair at the head of the table. Her hands caressed the carved wooden lions on the arms. Then, slowly, she rose and walked from the dining room into the marble hallway.

Graziella was in the hall, carrying a hot drink for herself.

"Can I speak to you, Mama?" Teresa said.

They went into the study. Teresa chose her words carefully. "You said that we could have your jewelry if we needed it. I'm afraid, Mama, I do. We are almost ready to sell, and we've run out of cash. I want to do the job properly, and—"

Graziella opened the safe, took out a large leather-bound box, and unlocked the lid. Together they examined the splendid jewels: the diamond pin worn by Luciano, the brooches, the rings. . . . Teresa picked out the long strand of perfect pearls. Graziella relocked the case carefully and put it back in the safe.

"All you have to do is ask me, everything I have is yours— well, Rosa's. Perhaps this is not the time, but her future must be discussed. We must find a suitable man for her to marry; she is an attractive girl."

"As you say, Mama. But are these real? How much do you think they are worth?"

She held the pearls under the desk lamp. They were large

and appeared perfectly matched. Graziella flushed, not liking to see her pearls inspected like that.

"My husband paid twenty-five thousand dollars for them in 1950. They must be worth considerably more now."

Teresa felt the barbed sweetness and had the grace to blush. "Thank you, Mama, they will be put to good use. I'm sorry I had to ask."

"That is perfectly all right. I doubt if I would have the occasion to wear them, unless for Rosa's wedding. The family needs an heir, a man."

Teresa received a light kiss, but she could not rid herself of the feeling she always had: She was not good enough, and never had been, for the Lucianos.

Teresa knocked softly and waited. Luka opened the door, then stepped aside.

Unsure how to begin, she sat in the chair he offered her. Then: "Tomorrow we will be going to Rome, returning in the evening. I would like you to have left by the time we return; that is twenty-four hours before we deliver the guns to Commissario Pirelli."

This was the woman Luka didn't like. He felt as if she were staring into his head with her hard, unfeeling eyes.

"What about my money? We had a deal?"

"Sophia believes you killed Paul Carolla. She wants us to hand you over to the carabinieri."

"I have never met this Paul Carolla. You tell me you have my bag, a gun, but that is my word against yours. I went to Dante's club, he tried to kill me, and I shot him in self-defense."

She hesitated for a moment, then said, "You speak fluent Sicilian, and to judge from your clothes, you are not a student. Did someone hire you to kill Dante?" She fetched the Bible from the dressing table and held it out. "Swear on the Holy Bible that what you say to me is the truth."

He placed his hand over the gold cross etched into the black leather cover. "I swear. I was to give Dante a packet of heroin. He was to pay me three million. He received the heroin, but when it was time to pay me, he tried to kill me."

Teresa put the Bible down and took from her pocket a slim

leather case. "The pearls are worth more than we owe you or what I took from the safe. You can have them now and leave by morning or wait until I get back from Rome with the cash. Here, look at them. . . . They belong to my mother-in-law."

Luka took the double row of large pearls in his hands. He had not the slightest knowledge of their worth. He handed them back. "I want the cash."

"When you leave this house, I don't want ever to see you or hear from you again, is that clear? You'll have your money, all right?"

Sophia could not sleep. She tossed and turned, got up, and searched for her pills. The bottle was empty, so she threw it away and searched her bedside drawer for Valium. There were only a few tablets left; she could feel herself breaking into a cold sweat; the more she thought about it, the more desperate she became.

She dressed and crept down the stairs. The clock on the landing chimed ten-thirty. All she could think of were the long hours stretching ahead. She went into the study, drummed her fingers on the desk, wondering if it was too late to call. Then she picked up the phone and asked the operator to find the number of Don Roberto's physician; she was sure he would see her.

Sophia drove out of the villa without putting her lights on until she was clear of the gates. Teresa was the only one who heard the car, but by the time she had run down to the front door there was no hope of stopping Sophia. Panic-stricken, she went into the study, deciding to work until she returned, if she returned. She poured herself a stiff brandy. Sophia wouldn't go to the police, would she?

The doctor himself answered the door wearing a smoking jacket. His face registered such concern that Sophia said immediately, "I am sorry I called you so late. I should have left it until tomorrow. . . ."

"Are you ill?"

"No, no, _grazie_. It is my mother-in-law. She has great trouble sleeping, and tonight she seems more restless than ever.

I wonder if you could give me something to help her sleep, a prescription I can take to an all-night pharmacy, Seconal? I think you prescribed some before. . . ."

He began to write out the prescription, then paused and looked at Sophia. "How have you been?"

"Oh, I'm fine . . . and could you also give me some Valium, for my sister-in-law? She is very tense, you heard about the court incident? I think she said ten milligrams is her usual. . . . She meant to bring some from New York, but she forgot."

He nodded, about to say something, then continued writing. It seemed to take forever, but eventually he tore the slip of paper off the pad and handed it to her. "Tell her not to make this a regular practice; they can be addictive. But I can understand the strain you all must be under, especially after—"

Sophia couldn't wait to get out. "Yes, it has been . . . a difficult time for us all, and I thank you again for your care and understanding that night. Graziella sends you her best wishes."

Sophia took two Valium and replaced the cap. She leaned back in the driver's seat and closed her eyes; just knowing she had the Valium calmed her. A tap on the window made her heart feel as if it would explode.

"Signora? It's me. I'm sorry to make you jump. I was sitting in the bar across the road."

Sophia pushed a button, and the window slid down. "Commissario Pirelli, how are you? I'm sorry I didn't recognize you. . . . I have just been to the drugstore for my mother-in-law."

"Would you join me for a drink?"

"Thank you, no, I must take her medicine back."

"Please, just one small drink, or a coffee? There have been a few developments, and I'd like to keep you informed. I was going to come by tomorrow."

Sophia hesitated. She knew she would be in Rome the following day and didn't want Pirelli to find Graziella alone in the house with Moreno.

Pirelli smiled. "It'll take no more than a few minutes, and I hate drinking alone."

The bar was seedy, so Pirelli suggested they walk a block

to another. About halfway, Sophia paused at a café with tables still outside.

"Why don't we sit outside? I would prefer a cappuccino."

"Won't you be cold?"

Sophia shook her head; she was wearing her mink coat. He drew out a chair for her and signaled for the waiter.

"A pastry?"

She smiled and shook her head, and the waiter took the order for two coffees plus a brandy for Pirelli. He was feeling the chill in the night air.

Sophia opened her cigarette case, and Pirelli smiled. "You have replenished your stock, I see." She didn't seem to understand. "The Turkish cigarettes?"

She remembered and tilted her head back as he struck a match for her. Keeping it alight while he took out a Marlboro, he burned his fingers. She flicked open her lighter with a soft, low laugh, and he gave her a boyish grin, putting his elbow in a dark, congealed mess of spilled coffee. He wiped it off with a paper napkin.

"I'm afraid this is probably not what you are used to. My apologies."

Again that delightful laugh.

"The bar is nicer, if you would prefer . . ."

"This is fine, Commissario, really."

The waiter brought their coffee, shivering as the night was getting really cold. Sophia snuggled into her fur coat. She was beginning to feel lightheaded. . . . She raised a hand and called the waiter back.

"I've changed my mind. I would like a brandy."

Pirelli promptly handed her his, and she sipped it, feeling it warm inside her. He offered sugar, and she shook her head. He put two spoonfuls into his own coffee and stirred it.

"You said there were some new developments, Commissario?"

He tilted his head. "Joe, please . . ." He coughed and fingered his tie. "Yes . . . They are connected to your case, specifically to your children." He wanted to reach for her hand when he saw the way the sadness swept over her face. She turned away, her perfect profile motionless.

"I think we found the gun today."

"Do you know who it belongs to?"

"Not as yet, but it won't take long. It was a forty-four magnum, and we have a strong lead on the killer. We think the same man also killed Paul Carolla." He had said more than he had intended, but he went on. "We believe it is Luka Carolla, Paul Carolla's son, signora, and any day now we will arrest him."

Sophia turned to face him. What he was saying was that the American boy hiding in the villa could not have killed Carolla. Moreno had, after all, been telling them the truth. . . . She relaxed slightly and sipped the brandy.

"So you have been able to trace him? When you came to the house, you were trying to find him."

Pirelli pursed his lips, careful now. "We can trace anyone, find anyone, especially now with all the computer equipment. Data are easier to pass from country to country, town to town; fingerprints can be faxed in seconds."

He had changed the subject purposely, wondering if she would still ask after Luka Carolla, but she had a frown on her face. "You mean, you can trace, for example, a child who has been missing for years? Does all this computerization help with that?"

Pirelli thought for a moment, then nodded. "I guess so. . . . What it actually does is give more people access to information. The computers themselves cannot do the tracing; they provide the shortcuts. You pump in data, everything you know, about your lost child, for example, send it to Rome, and it can be dispersed all over Italy, over the world if necessary. That would have taken years in the old days, but now . . . a few hours."

"And does everyone have access to these computers?"

"No, no . . . But if, say, we take this lost child again, if it becomes an investigation, then, of course, we can use all the facilities open to us. . . ."

Sophia nodded, then looked at him. "You have coffee on your top lip."

He raised his eyebrows and wiped his mouth. "Clear?"

She nodded, stubbing out her cigarette, deep in thought. Pirelli tried to lift her mood. He laughed. "It's not as bad as spinach caught between the teeth. You know that feeling when you get home and find one tooth black with spinach? What always amazes me is why nobody ever tells you. . . . I mean, everyone must have noticed but said nothing. . . ."

Sophia giggled, and he leaned over toward her. "You have the most infectious, wonderful laugh. . . . Will you have another brandy?"

She agreed, saying that afterward she really must go.

The waiter was just bringing their bill, and they sent him back for more brandy. Pirelli was racking his brains for something witty and original to say. Sophia was feeling the effects of the Valium and the brandy, enjoying the sensation of not caring.

She realized he had asked her a question and looked at him. "I'm sorry, did you say something?"

"Nothing that is worth repeating; you were miles away."

She tilted her head—it was a habit she had—and her eyes were sparkling. She leaned forward on her elbow. "You know, when I was about fifteen, I used to work in a café like this one, cleaning the tables and washing dishes."

"You did?"

She laughed, letting her coat fall open as if she didn't feel the night air. Her cheeks were flushed; he didn't think anyone could be so beautiful. . . . She crooked her finger for him to come closer, and he could smell her perfume, a light scent of fresh flowers.

"One of my earliest memories is of my mother. . . . Have you ever heard of a Toni perm? They used to call them that after the war, Toni?"

He nodded, though he had no idea what she was talking about; he just loved the sound of her husky voice, loved the fact that she had beckoned him closer. With both elbows on the table he was close enough to see her flawless skin, her perfect white teeth. His mind was working overtime, wondering how he could make the move to kiss her. He had never wanted to hold a woman so much in his entire life.

She was saying, "My mama was so desperate to have her hair permed; she had long, dark, straight hair, like mine."

"How long is your hair?"

"Oh . . ." She gestured with her hand almost to her hip and continued talking, but he was seeing her naked, with her long hair splayed across a pillow. . . . She wore it in such a severe style, drawn back from her face, but he liked that. He sighed; he liked everything about this woman. He realized she was still talking.

"So they agreed, and she was in there for hours and hours. I was only about six or seven. She came out with all these curls, and she looked so pretty, so happy, but then she strapped this board around her, you know, a sandwich board? She was advertising the hair salon. I had to give out the leaflets to the passersby while she strode up and down the street, up and down. . . ."

He smiled. "She must have wanted that permanent very badly."

His heart was thudding in his chest as two tears, two absolutely perfect pear-shaped tears, rolled down her cheeks. "Yes, she did. I don't think she felt any humiliation. I did. As young as I was, I felt it so deeply. I was so ashamed for her, you understand?"

Pirelli nodded, and she continued. "Well, I stuffed these terrible little pamphlets into every refuse bin I could see. All the time men were jeering at her, women pointing and snickering. 'Mama,' I said, 'Take it off, please, people are laughing, look,' and she answered, 'Yes, I know, but I have got the best perm in Sicily for nothing.' But it wasn't. I paid for it; she paid for it."

She sat back, turning her face away. "I have no idea why I told you that. Maybe so you would understand that I have not always had wealth, not always eaten in the finest restaurants. We were very poor. My mama had nothing, not even a husband. . . ."

"And you used to wait on tables?"

"Yes . . . it was a roadside café." She breathed in deeply, staring ahead for a moment before she looked back to him. "I must be very boring, and I must go."

Pirelli jumped to his feet and went into the café to pay the bill. She waited for him outside; he could see her with her back to the brightly lit window. On a sudden frivolous impulse, he pointed to the vase of flowers on the counter and delved into his pocket. "How much?"

Highly embarrassed, Pirelli presented the flowers to Sophia, realizing only as he did so that they were plastic. "Well, I have managed to make an utter fool of myself."

She held them in her arms, smiling. "No, I am touched. They will keep forever. . . . Thank you."

He walked her to her car and remonstrated with her for not locking it, but she pointed out that he had been with her and so was partly to blame. He opened the door for her.

"Would you have dinner with me, Sophia? May I call you Sophia?"

"I'm going to Rome. . . ."

"Forever?"

"No, but I don't know how long I will be gone."

"Will you be there for Christmas?"

She was very close to him, bending to get into the car, and she straightened. "Christmas?" Her large, dark eyes lowered, and he could see her thick, dark lashes.

*She uses no makeup*, he thought. Then he heard her whisper, "Oh, God, it will be Christmastime soon. . . ."

Her eyes were like a frightened child's as the grief engulfed her. At first he couldn't see what had distressed her to such an extent.

Her voice was a soft, pleading moan. "My babies . . . my babies . . ."

Suddenly he understood. Christmas would be a nightmare for her, with all the tinsel and bustle. It was for children, and Sophia's were gone. He hardly realized he had taken her in his arms. He was holding her tightly, saying over and over that it would be all right, it would be all right, he was there. . . . She clung to him, the soft fur feeling like silk against his cheek.

He never knew how it happened, but suddenly he was kissing her, to comfort her. His lips had found hers. . . . She turned her face away, pressing her cheek into his coat. His body was on fire; he had never experienced such passion or tenderness. She remained in his arms for an eternity; then he gradually felt her draw away.

He helped her into the car and tucked her coat in. "Will you have dinner with me?"

She searched for the car keys, without replying.

"I'll come to Rome, to Turkey, wherever you want."

She put the keys in the ignition and started the car. When

she turned to him, it was as if she were a stranger. He was desperate to keep her with him a few moments longer.

"I read today that you and your sister-in-law are starting up the business again. You must promise me to take care, great care, and if you ever need me . . . Look, let me give you my card; this is my direct line, any hour of the day or night. And this is my home phone number."

He was talking fast, scribbling his number on the card. He handed it to her through the window, and her hand felt icy to his touch. She didn't look at the card but slipped it into her pocket.

"You have been very kind, but I think it best if we forget this ever happened. Good night."

She drove off fast, and he stood like a lost soul, completely devastated. Around his feet were the plastic flowers.

Sophia entered the house soundlessly and had crept to the foot of the stairs when Teresa came out of the study.

"Where in God's name have you been?"

"Out. I needed some air."

"You've been gone hours; it's half past two in the morning."

Sophia paused on the staircase, looking down at Teresa. "You are not my jailer. If I want to go out for some air, then I will."

"No, you won't."

Sophia snapped, "What did you say?"

"I said from now on you tell me where you are going, is that understood?"

Sophia kept her voice low, but the anger was all there. "Just who do you think you're talking to? What right have you to speak to me as if I were a child?"

"Right now, every right. Where did you go?"

"I went for a drive, and this you will really love, I had a brandy—no, two brandies—with Commissario Pirelli. You want to make something of that?"

"Did you tell him anything?"

Sophia threw her coat off. "I was sitting in my car, and he came up and asked me if I would like a drink because he had some information. He was going to come here tomorrow, so rather than have him in the house with your precious Moreno, I agreed to have a drink. They have the gun that killed my babies. They also believe that whoever killed my sons also shot Paul Carolla; it's the same man, the one he was asking about when he first came here. Paul Carolla's own son, Luka. . . . And they are about to make an arrest, which leaves that creature upstairs in the clear."

Teresa sighed with relief. "You think he was telling you the truth?"

"Why would he lie? Here, he gave me this card; call him for yourself. We all are going to Rome tomorrow, and thanks to what he told me, I, for one, will feel a lot better about leaving Moreno here with Mama."

"And you never mentioned Moreno?"

"I did not mention Moreno, I said not a word about the gun, I said nothing. . . . Now, would it be all right if I went to bed? I'm tired; it's been a long day."

"I'll come to Rome with you tomorrow."

Sophia was on the stairs. She didn't even turn. "Fine, what do you want me to do, applaud? Good night."

A few minutes later Teresa crept carefully into her own bedroom. Rosa was fast asleep, lying on her belly, her arms splayed out. Teresa climbed into bed and pulled the duvet around her. But she couldn't sleep; the arguments and disagreements were getting harder to handle. Perhaps the trip would help them get on a better footing. At least Johnny Moreno had turned out to be just what he had told them; it meant he would be easier to get rid of. As soon as she sold the pearls, she would pay him off. A few more days, and they would be ready to sell everything; a few more days, she told herself, and it would all be over.

# 16

Pirelli had lit a fire under the overworked and harassed Inspector Giulio Mincelli. Accusations were flying about inadequate reports and loss of evidence. Pirelli's eyebrows, famed for telegraphing his moods, were permanently in a single line: danger zone.

He had no verification of the exact times of the Luciano deaths, so he could not ascertain if a killer could have been in both places, the Villa Rivera and the San Lorenzo restaurant. But the major and most frustrating of all his problems was that there was still no trace of the only suspect to date, Luka Carolla.

The gun Luka had left at the monastery was definitely the one used to kill both the Luciano children and the Paluso child, but there was no confirmation of its use at the restaurant. However, with the evidence that was mounting against him, the hunt for Luka had to be stepped up.

The morning paper ran yet another article accusing the police of doing nothing to find the killer of the jail cleaner's son. The Palermo chief walked in unannounced, carrying the paper.

"You read this?" He tossed the newspaper on the table, took his horn-rimmed glasses from their case, and looked over the many photographs pinned on the wall. "That the wall of death everyone's talking about?"

Pirelli shrugged, waited for the chief to spew out whatever he had come in for. The chief continued. "You serious about this Luka Carolla character? You really think it's feasible that he's involved in every one of these?"

Pirelli nodded. "I think he's psychotic, very dangerous, kills indiscriminately. We know he was not alone at the San Lorenzo, but I'm certain he was involved. And we have the weapon, his weapon, the magnum."

The shiny-suited figure remained firmly planted in front of the bulletin board. "A few officers are getting pissed off about your using the forensic and ballistics teams at all hours, giving them no time for any other cases. There's a backlog building up. . . . You've got Ancora, the young what's 'is name, Bruno di Mazzo, and now Mincelli and his men working alongside you. That's more than ten men. How long is this going to go on for? If you know your suspect, haul him in."

"I'm trying. Believe me, I'm trying. We just can't get a trace on him."

"I gathered that, so I've called a press conference this afternoon. We'll have to give them something, and you must have enough to—"

"We've got the warrants, but we can't find the bastard."

"You need that boy picked up fast. So we'll get all the help we can and try to flush him out."

Pirelli was getting uptight. "Every uniformed man's got the composite, every hotel, hospital, we've had men—"

"I know, I know how many men, Joe, and you've found no trace. So we'll pull out all the stops and try to flush him out. That includes the prisons; see if there's anyone inside who can help, and we'll make a deal. This city is a sewer, Joe, and it's getting clogged up. You can't have much more time; I'm sorry, but I need my men back."

"You canceled all leaves?"

"I did, and it's not gone down well. You wanted to go back to Milan for the weekend? Get your wife to come here; we can't afford the time."

"Okay," said Pirelli, "but I'm still not sure about the press."

"You're not sure, Joe, if he's even still in Sicily, right? We're going to the press."

"I hear you. It would help me if you could put pressure on in the States; someone somewhere must have a recent photograph of him. He lived there for more than ten years."

"I'll see what I can do. Look, I don't want this to sound like I'm running you down. Far from it. You're doing one hell of a job, and I wish you could be here permanently; but the sole reason we were able to get you was that we were short of men, and you're taking up even more of them. The security for the trial, which, in case you are not aware, is still going strong, is using all the extra men I shipped in. I know the Paluso case is connected to all the others, and I know why you need everyone, but as I said, the gutters are overflowing. We have to move on."

Pirelli had begun making notes for the press conference when Bruno rushed in.

"This was on Mincelli's desk, came in three days ago. I don't know what the hell is going on with him. It's from the St. Sebastian Hospital, the medical report on Giorgio Carolla. As soon as I got it, I went over to main records. There's a passport application in Giorgio Carolla's name, dated January 25, 1974, plus a copy of his birth certificate. I checked back; when the application went in, Giorgio Carolla was already dead. But now we've got a passport number; the U.S. must be able to track him down. Reason we got no trace of Luka Carolla is he was never registered. And we're out by several years; Giorgio was older than Luka. Giorgio was born in 1959, Luka in '62 or '63. All Carolla did when he adopted Luka and so far there's no legal documentation of that either, was to use his dead son's papers."

Pirelli beamed. The intercom light flicked on for his call, but he didn't notice it. "Okay, let's start over again. Get back to New York; tell them we're out by maybe three or four years. Now they've got to be able to give us something, school—Christ, kid had to go to school, didn't he? Get them to check all the schools around Carolla's known addresses. We've got to trace someone who knows him, maybe get a more recent photograph."

Pirelli finally noticed the flashing light on the intercom and

picked up the call. There was more good news. After weeks of
inquiries, Pirelli's friend had come up with a radiologist from
the old Holy Nazareth Hospital who remembered a child being
brought into the X-ray department, one fitting the description
of the boy now known as Luka Carolla.

Pirelli left the office early to meet the radiologist. As he
waited for the elderly Signora Brunelli in the small, neat apartment, he wondered if this was a waste of time. What good
would anything he learned be to him in the present situation?
He lit a cigarette and searched for an ashtray; he finally dropped
the match into a dolphin-shaped bowl.

Signora Brunelli walked painfully slowly into the room.
After he had helped her sit down, she asked why he was so
interested in a patient she had seen more than fifteen years ago.
With total honesty he told her that he didn't really know; it
was just that anything he could find out about the young man
he was trying to trace might, in the long run, help his investigation.

Signora Brunelli stared at the faded photograph of the or-
phans that Brother Thomas had given him. Her hands shook
as she took out a magnifying glass and studied the picture
for a considerable time, moving the glass from one face to the
next.

"The boy ringed with red, the blond child—I am sure he
is the one I X-rayed."

Pirelli nodded as he took the photograph back. "It was, as
you so rightly said, a long time ago. You must have had
hundreds, if not thousands, of patients. Do you remember
them all?"

"No, no, of course not, but sometimes children stay in
your mind longer, particularly children in that little boy's condition. Also, and possibly the reason I recall him, is that he had
swallowed a . . ." She pursed her lips as she tried to remember, then nodded her head. "Yes, it was some kind of locket.
They had tried to take it from him, and he had swallowed it.
It showed up clearly on the X ray. We were worried that it
might cause a stoppage of his bowels, but there was no need to
operate."

"What condition was he in?"

Again she pursed her lips. "It was a long time ago. . . . I

had to do a number of X rays. . . . Skull, he had a fractured skull, the type of injury caused by consistent . . ." She demonstrated a motion like a karate blow. "I also remember his shoulder, his left shoulder, was dislocated, and the arm broken. You know, a child's bones are very supple, but there were complications because his injuries had been left unattended for so long a time."

"You have an exceptional memory, signora."

"Thank you. It is just that this child was so pitiful. He had been sexually abused, tormented, I would say. It was horrifying, he was not more than five or six years old, and his body was skeleton thin, covered with scars and bruises." She shook her head. Even now, all these years later, the memory disgusted her, upset her.

Pirelli remained silent for a moment before asking if she had spoken to the boy. She looked at him in surprise.

"Oh, no, Commissario Pirelli. The child was dumb. I may be wrong, of course, but I am sure the boy was a mute."

It was an incredible coincidence. As Pirelli drove back to headquarters, the engine of his Fiat began to make strange noises. He kept on driving but used the back streets in case he broke down. The car chugged and chuffed, and smoke began pouring out of the engine.

He stopped and lifted the hood, then realized that not fifteen yards away down the back street was a small repair and car rental shop.

Pirelli wandered across to a mechanic who was working under an old Fiat. Showing his ID, he asked if the mechanic could drop everything and fix his car for him. The man turned out to be the owner, and as he slid from underneath the car, he asked Pirelli if there was any word on his own car.

Pirelli, puzzled, looked at him. The owner persisted. "It's been five days. Haven't you traced it yet?"

Pirelli shook his head. "I'm not with traffic. What's the problem? Stolen, was it?"

"Yeah, five days late back from rental. I sent in a report, but I've heard nothing. American, and he's not at the address he put down."

In the hope of getting his car fixed quickly, Pirelli promised to pass the papers to the right department. Then he saw the name.

The driving license particulars were in a neat, clear print. The car had been rented by Luka Carolla.

Through the window Adina watched the car pause yet again. Three times it had cruised past the villa gates. This time it turned into the drive.

A young man wearing dark glasses and a navy blue suit stepped from the Alfa Romeo, walked casually up the steps to the porch, and rang the bell. Then he pressed his face against the stained glass, trying to see into the hall.

"Who is it, Adina?" Graziella made her way slowly down the stairs.

"Shall I answer, signora?"

"Yes, yes, quickly."

Graziella turned to look up the stairs. Luka remained on the first landing, peering over the banister.

The man leaned against the doorframe and smiled at Graziella. "Signora Luciano, allow me to introduce myself. I am Giuseppe Rocco. My father was a great friend of Don Roberto. May I come in? Thank you, thank you . . ."

Graziella could not recall the young man's father, but she gestured for him to follow her into the living room. She offered sherry, coffee, or tea, but he refused. He sat in the center of the sofa and placed his expensive leather briefcase on the floor beside his highly polished black shoes. His eyes, behind the dark glasses, roamed everywhere while his lips continued to smile.

"Sadly, my father died more than two years ago. I now work for the Corleones; I handle their real estate business. May I give you my card, Signora Luciano?"

Graziella gazed at the neat white card, then tapped it against her hand. "If you have come to discuss business, then you must speak with my daughter-in-law. Are you interested in leasing the factory? Is that why you're here?"

"Pardon?"

Graziella blushed. She was uncertain of Teresa's plans, so she quickly changed the subject. "Are you sure I cannot offer you tea? Some lemonade? I made it myself."

"Thank you, a lemonade would be most refreshing."

Left alone, Rocco was like an eel, slithering around the room, picking things up, turning over papers. Then he walked out into the hall.

The stairs creaked. Luka winced and slipped into the nearest room. Rocco almost caught him; he knew someone had been on the stairs, and he paused, listening. Rocco moved quickly to the study and had the audacity to try to enter, but the door was locked. Again he listened intently at the foot of the stairs, then walked into the kitchen.

Graziella was startled by his sudden appearance. "You've met Adina, my housekeeper, Signor?" She handed him the lemonade, unable to recall his name.

"Giuseppe Rocco." He smiled and sipped the lemonade. "This is very nice, refreshing." He stared at Adina, then back to Graziella. "Is your daughter-in-law at home?"

"Teresa is at the tile factory. If you would like to leave a message, I will make sure she receives it."

Rocco smiled and put his half-finished lemonade on the wooden table. "What time is she expected home, Signora Luciano?"

"Maybe five o'clock, maybe later. She is very busy."

"Then perhaps you would tell her that I called and that I would like to talk with her as soon as possible. My clients are the purchasers of the villa, and they would like to discuss immediate occupancy. Thank you for seeing me and for that delicious lemonade."

He removed his glasses. His eyes were strangely unfocused, with deep red pressure marks around the sockets. He replaced the glasses quickly, and with a small bow and a slight click of his polished heels, he saw himself out.

After watching Rocco drive slowly away from the villa, Luka turned from the bedroom window and noticed the big bed with the wooden posts, draped in a dust cover. He recognized it as the room where the two little boys had been murdered. His body tensed, the adrenaline pumping through him, making him as alert as a cat. He moved quickly and silently upstairs to his own room, his breath hissing through clenched teeth.

He unbuttoned his shirt and eased the bandage from his shoulder. The scab was larger than the bullet hole, but the swelling had subsided, leaving only a dark bruise over most of his shoulder. He flexed his muscles and felt the stiffness of his fingers. The shoulder had bothered him since it was broken when he was a child. Now it felt as if small grains of sand were grinding together, but it was healed well enough to leave the bandage off.

He searched the room for a small pair of scissors. Then, watching his actions in the mirror, he began, clumsily, to cut the stitches. Suddenly he whirled, scissors raised in a reflex gesture of protection, but he dropped his arms immediately when he saw that it was Graziella who had entered the room.

Her arms were full of clothes. "I'm sorry. I didn't mean to startle you. These are for you. They were Michael's."

She put the clothes on the bed and turned to him. A drop of blood trickled down his arm from where he had cut the first stitch, and she hurried to him with motherly concern.

Luka sat at the kitchen table while Graziella and Adina fussed with hot water and antiseptic. Adina cut the stitches, using a razor-sharp kitchen knife, then pulled the thread away with tweezers. He clenched his teeth as he felt each stitch go, and tears smarted in his eyes. Finally he felt a pad with cool disinfectant cream placed on the wound, and Adina cut strips of adhesive to hold it in place.

When he was bandaged, Graziella cupped his face in her hands and gently kissed his forehead. "What a brave boy you are. It's all over now."

Slowly Luka lifted his arms, slipped them around her, and rested his head against her breasts. Her hand stroked his hair with feather-light touches, and his grip tightened. He had never felt so safe, so protected, in his entire life.

Graziella's hand patted Luka's bare back, and she froze. Her fingers traced the scars; she released him to look at his back.

"My God, your back, what happened? Look, Adina, the scars . . . Mother of God, Johnny, who did this to you?"

Adina gasped at the sight, the deep scars crisscrossed in weals, rough where they ran together in ridges, leaving deep, stretched white lines.

Luka backed away, grabbing his shirt. "It was nothing—"

"Nothing? I have never seen such scars. What happened? How did you injure yourself like that?"

Luka tried to put his shirt on but needed Graziella's help.

She kissed him again. "It hurts you to remember, yes?" She began to button his shirt for him.

He nodded; then, feeling safer with his shirt on, he lied. "It was a water-skiing accident. I fell off and got caught in the propeller of the speedboat."

"Oh, you poor boy. You are lucky to be alive, no?"

"I guess so . . . yes, I guess so."

Graziella nodded her sympathy, then smiled. "You know, your hair looks like—Have you seen Rosa's hair? She cut it herself."

He smiled, and Graziella tutted. "You young people, when you've got something God gave you, you want to ruin it. Now, sit down, and let Adina give you a haircut."

Luka ran his fingers through his hair and gave a boyish laugh. Adina opened a drawer and brought out a pair of scissors and an old tablecloth. Graziella pulled out a chair.

"Come on, sit down, we'll make you look handsome; we'll cut off that color."

Luka asked Adina, "You know how to cut hair?"

"Oh, sì, Signor Johnny, I have a sister who is a hairdresser, and I taught her everything she knows. Sit . . . See my hair? I cut my hair."

Adina's hair was what could only be described as a basin cut.

Graziella gave him a wink. "I'll make sure she cuts it good. I'll watch, tell her what to do. I'll get Don Roberto's clippers from the bedroom."

Graziella was not gone more than a few minutes, but when she came back, she gasped. Adina had chopped off all the dye, leaving small sprouts of blond hair sticking up. "Adina, what have you done?"

"Cut the dye off, like you told me to."

Luka looked up, bits of hair covering his face and shoulders. "She's fast, I'll give her that."

The two old women fussed and argued while Luka sat passively, not even complaining when Adina cut his neck as she shaved it. Then they stood back to review their handiwork.

Graziella blew the hair from his eyes. "I don't think you will like it, but when it grows a bit, you will. . . ."

The three trooped into the hall, and Luka stood in front of the big mirror. There was no sign of any hair dye; in fact, there was very little sign of hair at all. Adina had given him what was virtually a crew cut, a very short, slightly lopsided crew cut.

"What do you think?"

Luka tipped his head slightly, then smiled a beautiful, slow smile. His pale blue eyes twinkled. "I think I look like I just got out of prison."

Graziella put her hands to her cheeks. She looked so upset that he bent and kissed her. She reached out and touched his hair.

"My son Michael was as blond as you. For a moment you had such a look of him, don't you think, Adina?"

Adina was busily trimming bits off her own hair. She turned, scissors in hand.

"Signora, would you like me to trim your hair?"

Graziella ran into the kitchen, squealing like a girl. "No, heaven forbid! One prisoner is enough!"

Adina caught Luka's arm and whispered, "If the signora asks you to go for a drive, refuse. She is crazy in the car; she has no license." She nodded, her lips pursed, and followed Graziella into the kitchen.

Luka giggled, stared at himself, then hurried after them, not wanting to leave them, wanting to feel their warmth, their affection.

He stood, smiling, in the doorway while they argued about which one was going to make his lunch. He went up and put his arms around Graziella from behind.

"We will sit in the garden, yes, Johnny?"

Adina hurried to get Graziella an old coat and brought another for Luka. "It's cold; you don't want to catch a cold. . . ."

He put the coat on and followed Graziella, then turned back to say, "I like my haircut, Adina; it's a very good, professional cut. Short, yes, but with great style."

Luka and Graziella sat side by side on the swing chair in the garden, both wrapped in their heavy coats. The ground was covered in white frost. Adina opened the kitchen window and heard them talking.

"I was just thinking, soon it will be Christmas." Graziella sighed.

"You like Christmas?"

Her eyes filled with tears. "I used to, with all my family around me. Now . . . what a terribly empty day it will be. No sons, no grandchildren . . . You see that big tree?" She pointed to a big elm. "That was where we would hang the lights, and Papa, when the boys were young, would creep out and hang their stockings in the tree. And on Christmas morning, oh, how they would run, shouting, calling up at our window that Santa Claus had come. . . . My grandchildren, too . . . This Christmas there will be no one waiting for Santa to come."

Luka took her hand gently in his and held it to his lips. "Don't cry, please don't cry."

From the kitchen Adina saw the gesture and smiled.

The women's first priority on reaching Rome was to sort through Sophia's stack of mail. Teresa needed no more evidence that her sister-in-law was in even worse financial trouble than she had stated.

They toured the workrooms, which lay as dormant as the Lucianos' warehouses in Palermo. Bales of cloth stood where they had been delivered. The machines were covered in dust.

Teresa carried with her the papers on the sale of the warehouse and asked Sophia about the other business Domino had cited. Sophia hesitated, then shrugged; why not let her see everything? She checked the drawer of the reception desk and found the keys.

"Follow me. I had no idea this place existed until my so-called partner showed it to me. It was apparently very lucrative, so it shows how hopeless I must have been as a businesswoman."

They crossed the yard to another small door. Rosa pointed to some men watching from the building opposite and snickered at their wolf whistles. Teresa turned sharply, looking from Rosa to the workmen.

"Rosa, don't encourage them."

Sophia smiled. "She's young. Besides, she looks very pretty."

"She is also still in mourning. Rosa, don't look."

Rosa gave Sophia a tiny wink and lowered her head modestly.

Sophia tried one key after another before she found the right one. Teresa was almost breathing down her neck.

"So this wasn't connected with your boutiques?"

"Well, in a way. They used my business as a cover. This is a cheap mail-order business. . . . You'll see what I mean when I show you the stock."

"And you never knew anything about it?"

Sophia sighed. "No, Teresa, I have just said I didn't know anything about it. I had no idea."

"I don't understand."

Sophia paused on the stairs and looked down at her. "Because they didn't want me to. I believed I was doing everything on my own, all separate from the Lucianos, making my own money, when in truth I was doing nothing. Don Roberto financed me, via Constantino. It was very simple. I used their accountants, their business managers. My boutiques were a cover; they lost money. But they used them, used me."

"And you never suspected?"

Sophia opened the door into the sweatshop. "No, I never suspected."

She was astonished when Teresa suddenly put an arm around her. "Bastards, huh? You must have felt sick."

"I think 'betrayed' is more the word. My husband used me. Papa, too. What does it matter? I failed. They treated me as if I were a child, and the boutiques my toys."

She led them into the cavernous empty room. It had been stripped of all the machines, and Sophia gave a humorless laugh. "There were about thirty girls working on machines in here. As you can see, when I paid them off, they took everything they could lay their hands on. Either them or the disgusting manager."

"Your so-called partner must have had a hand in this," Teresa said. "Those machines were worth a fortune."

Sophia agreed. "I guess he felt he could do exactly as he wanted. There was no one to be afraid of anymore."

There was still some discarded stock left, some hanging out of the boxes. Rosa picked up a pair of frilly panties. "Oh,

I love these, and look at this nightie! Oh, Sophia, they're gorgeous."

Sophia looked at Teresa, and they burst out laughing. "Rosa, they are disgusting, cheap crap. Look at the colors, and it's all nylon. Still, take what you want."

"You serious? Oh, thanks!"

While Teresa and Sophia looked around the building, Rosa delved into the boxes with relish.

The luxurious apartment was the first thing Teresa suggested should be sold. The cash released by the sale could be used to start Sophia's company functioning again.

Among the bills and letters were several orders, two of them from major department stores wishing to restock on specific lines and requesting details of S&N's new-season show. The orders in themselves were not enough to salvage the business, but they gave Sophia confidence. So did Teresa's enthusiasm, which was fueled by Rosa. She assured Sophia that her taste was perfect and that the range was "mega" because it catered to all ages. Sophia laughed; they knew so little, understood even less about her business, and their presumption that she designed everything on the rows of hangers amused her. They didn't notice the designer labels, possibly because they could not believe the price tags—and those were the wholesale prices!

They raided the stock rooms, sorting through hundreds of garments and laughing like children let loose in a toy shop. Like everything else, the stock would be swallowed up by the bankruptcy, so with Sophia's permission Rosa and Teresa took as much as they could carry. They returned to the apartment for their own private fashion show.

Teresa had surprised Sophia with her choices; they all were brilliant colors, swathed silks, and brocaded velvets, sequined and frilled, and most in the wrong size. Teresa's disappointment was pathetically childlike when she tried to squash herself into a size 12 although she was closer to a 16. Rosa had grabbed gowns that were far too sophisticated, again with lavish embroidery and beading. Sophia praised and made suggestions, treading very carefully, but when she brought Teresa a plain black velvet gown by Valentino, it was viewed with scorn.

"My God, it's awful, like an old bag would wear! It'd maybe

suit Graziella, but I was thinking of something more . . . rich-looking, you know, maybe with sequins. . . ."

Sophia nodded, then looked at Teresa with a professional eye and brought out a gown by Gianfranco Ferré.

"Maybe this is more you. It was actually ordered by Princess Loredanna, but she never collected it. In dollars it'd cost about five thousand."

"What! Five thousand?"

The price tag attracted Teresa more than the garment itself, and she couldn't wait to get into it. "Oh, she must be my size."

"Yes, she is very slender, and the dress complements rather than—"

"I see what you mean. Hey, Rosa, what do you think? This would cost five thousand dollars in New York."

Rosa was wandering around in a *Gone with the Wind* green shot silk gown with a hooped skirt and enormous puffed sleeves, decorated with dark green velvet ribbons.

Teresa squinted. "Oh, Rosa, that is worth dying for! Sophia, what would that dress set us back if she were to buy it?"

Sophia shrugged. "It's a very popular English line, quite reasonable, maybe a few hundred—"

"Oh, a few hundred! In that case, *get it off*!" shrieked Teresa, and Rosa made a face, having rather fancied herself as Scarlett O'Hara.

Sophia brought out a velvet dress with tiny ribbon straps and a full skirt, but the layered petticoats were trimmed with sequins that glittered when the skirt swayed. "I don't know if you like this, Rosa, but I designed it myself. I just never saw it modeled. Would you try it on just for me?"

Teresa surveyed herself in the mirror. "Oh, she won't wear that, hates frills. Sophia, what do you think I should do about my hair? And is there anything you can do with Rosa's?" She turned as Rosa stepped into the frilled black velvet and cocked her head to one side, impressed. "Oh . . . oh, Rosa, that is . . . Is that expensive, Sophia?"

Sophia nodded. It was a perfect fit, and she fussed with the skirt until it hung right. Standing behind Rosa, she looked in the mirror and sighed. "You have to be young to wear those tiny straps, and you have such beautiful shoulders. . . ."

Rosa said only, "Yeah, it's okay," but she couldn't resist a spin and danced around the room.

Sophia looked at them both, knowing that with a few touches they would be walking advertisements for her designs. She picked up the phone.

"How about having our hair done, facials, really go to town? Yes? Shall I call?"

Teresa hunched her shoulders, more girlish than ever, and Rosa nodded, then suddenly leaned over and kissed Sophia. It felt so good, the impulsive show of affection brought tears to Sophia's eyes.

Then they descended on the beauty parlor. There were not enough hours in one day. They agreed to spend another day in Rome. While Rosa went shopping, Teresa and Sophia spent the remainder of the afternoon with the accountants and lawyers. It was finally decided that Sophia should let the bankruptcy go through, then start up again under another name.

They put the apartment with all its contents on the market, and by the time they met Rosa, they were laughing excitedly at how well the meetings had gone. With so many of Nino's designs still in her possession, Sophia would not even need, initially, to go to the expense of acquiring a designer for Luciano, her new label.

It was after six in the evening. Teresa, her hair set in rollers, looked up from Sophia's scrapbook. It was filled with newspaper clippings covering her fashion shows, magazine articles featuring Sophia discussing women's wear, interviews with Nino Fabio plus many of his designs, and photographs of the two of them at social functions. They all were pasted in and neatly labeled.

"I had no idea you were so productive, Sophia. Quite a celebrity. Did you have a PR company arrange all these articles?"

Sophia nodded. "Nino hired them. I guess if the truth be known, I didn't really do all that much. I was very decorative; it was lovely to have access to such beautiful clothes. I hired good people, Nino especially. He did most of the work, all the designs. I just made the suggestions."

"Yeah? Well, don't put yourself down! Rosa and I know

just how good your suggestions are. . . . I mean, I'd have put money on it that Rosa would never have looked at that dress, but when it's on! You can tell it costs, looks beautiful. Good thing you still have his designs. I like his work—I should! It costs enough, and he certainly cost you."

"May I ask you something, Teresa? Why, after you've had your hair done, are you wearing rollers?" Sophia was trying not to stare.

"Well, I've got straight hair, and Rosa said it was dropping, so she put them in. Don't you think she should have?"

Sophia shrugged.

Teresa continued, "Do you like the color? I would never have gone this blond, but Rosa said it suited me. What do you think?"

Sophia smiled and was truthful. "It makes you look a lot younger."

Rosa called out, "You ready? Remember that gear from the sweatshop? Get ready for this . . . Ta-raaaa!"

She entered the room, grinning sheepishly at first, and sashayed across the room like a model on a catwalk, letting her robe slide to the floor. She wore a black nylon lace half-cup bra, her young breasts spilling out, and a pair of disgusting panties with holes in the rear through which her round pink buttocks protruded.

Teresa sat with her mouth open, in a state of shock. Rosa pouted, then sprawled full length on the sofa, sucking her thumb.

"Rosa! Rosa, *get them off this minute!*"

Humming "The Stripper," Rosa began to peel one stocking off, slowly.

Teresa leaped to her feet. "Rosa, what would your father say if he could see you?"

"Mama, he loved it. All men love it! It turns them on, doesn't it, Aunt Sophia?" She hooked the stocking over her toe and catapulted it across the room, to land at Teresa's feet.

"That is enough!"

Rosa giggled and picked up her robe. "You are such a prude, Mama. Don't you know women get a kick out of wearing these things under straitlaced suits and shirts?"

Teresa stood over her, hands on hips. "They do not! No decent woman would be seen dead in those panties. You know what they are for? Sophia, tell her what kind of women wear these things—sluts, prostitutes. . . . Tell her, Sophia."

Sophia was biting her lip, trying not to laugh. Teresa pointed majestically to the door for Rosa to leave. As she went, she wiggled her bottom. . . . Teresa screeched, but she surprised Sophia because she wasn't angry. When she turned around, she was grinning from ear to ear.

"What am I going to do with that girl, huh? I tell you, we've got to find her a husband fast. She knows too much, and it's not good for her. When I was her age . . ."

She hesitated and gave a little shrug. "I tell you, Sophia, when I was her age, they couldn't even say I had a great personality, you know. I was no beauty, and sometimes I look at her and I don't know how I did it. But her papa, he was handsome, the one with the Luciano looks and not much else. My daughter got lucky, she took after him. I say a Hail Mary every night for that. I grew up scrimping and saving every dime. I was dressed from thrift shops, and I used to think all clothes smelled of mothballs; I thought that was how they were made. I was never young, Sophia; I was born looking middle-aged, and now I am. My mama said once, 'I'm old, I'm fifty,' and my father said, 'No, you're not old, that's still young.' And she said, 'It's middle-aged, Lenny. How many people you know live to be a hundred?' "

Without a word Sophia got up and went to her room. She came back carrying a large box and calling for Rosa.

"These are samples for a line I thought about starting, but they proved too expensive. They are silk, all hand-embroidered. Provençal lace . . . And there're all sizes, so take your pick. Maybe no one else sees them, but you know you are wearing them, makes you feel good. Go ahead, take what you want."

She paused at the door, their oohs and aahs delighting her, bringing memories of the first time Constantino had given her silk underwear. She had always worn the finest ever since but had almost forgotten her reaction that first time. Seeing them now, she remembered.

Teresa was holding up a silk chiffon underslip. She sounded breathless, and there were two bright pink spots on her cheeks. "Could I have this?"

Sophia smiled. "Sure, take whatever you want. I am going to take a bath."

As she left the room, Teresa sighed. Rosa looked at her mother and said softly, "I am beginning to feel better, Mama, like things are not so dark anymore . . . Mama?"

"She's right, Rosa, these are really special. I mean, wearing this kind of thing makes you feel like a lady, you know, precious."

Later that evening the women stood together, admiring themselves in their new finery, ready to end the evening with a sumptuous dinner at the Sans Souci restaurant.

The uniformed chauffeur of the hired Mercedes raised his eyes in admiration, bowing to each of them as she stepped into the car. Rosa wore her new dress that she said swirled with tiny stars, and Teresa wore the wonderful sleek Ferre. Sophia herself wore a swirling taffeta gown with a vast frilled wrap, designed by Nino Fabio. They all were different in style, but they had one thing in common: All the gowns were black.

The Sans Souci was located just off the Via Veneto. The small bar was dimly lit but shimmered with mirrors and wonderful tapestries. As the three women entered, the maître d' hurried to greet them. He bowed and kissed Sophia's hand.

"Signora Luciano, we have missed you greatly. You have your usual table."

As if they were royalty, he ushered them to the central table. Waiters scurried to draw their chairs out for them, and the other diners turned and stared. The whispers flew around that they were the Luciano widows.

Even the women had to acknowledge Sophia's beauty, with her blue-black hair coiled like a snake at her neck. She slipped her black silk cape off, revealing slim shoulders that were a fragile contrast with her dark, strong eyes.

Under the pretext of reading the menu she glanced around the room. She had dressed many of the women diners, yet not one of them acknowledged her.

A group of laughing people arrived, and for a moment attention was drawn away from the center table. Then the buzz of whispers began again at a feverish pitch.

Sophia leaned close to Teresa. "The group that just arrived, the small man leading them is Nino, my designer. Don't turn your head. . . ."

Nino stared, then ignored Sophia, although he came within feet of her as he led his party to a table near the wall. After he was seated, however, he could not help looking at her. He knew she was bankrupt, everyone in the fashion world knew it, and he had presumed she was out of business. He still feared some sort of retaliation for his betrayal of her.

One of his guests squeezed his hand to get his attention and demanded to know who the occupants of the center table were.

Nino swiveled around to face the widows squarely and flipped his napkin in their direction. "Sophia Luciano . . . God knows who the others are—perhaps a schoolteacher and a virgin."

The general laughter that followed was obviously directed at the Luciano women, but the widows sat like royalty, apparently impervious. They continued their meal, talking quietly, but each of them was aware of the attention. Finally, Sophia could stand it no longer. She rose from the table. Teresa put out a hand to restrain her, but she was too late.

Sophia moved between the tables as if mesmerized, then came to a standstill at Nino Fabio's table. Nino, flustered, introduced Sophia to his companions. She leaned toward him slightly, placing her hand on his neck as if feeling his pulse.

Nino sat back, his face white, his own hand at his throat as he felt her cold fingers. It would take him a long time to forget her tiny whisper: "So, Nino, you are still alive. . . ."

As Sophia returned to her own table, Nino stared after her, his face pinched and terrified, his right hand still pressed to the pulse at the side of his neck.

Rosa leaned over to ask what on earth Sophia had said to Nino. Sophia just smiled and lifted her champagne glass in a toast. "To our future."

The following morning *La Repubblica* carried a photograph of the three elegant women with the caption "Bella Mafia, remnants of the once-powerful Luciano family."

The photograph, at first greeted with amusement, somehow left a nasty taste. The accompanying article went over well-worn ground about the murders and the family connections. Teresa tore the offending paper to shreds and tossed it in the trash can. She still had to find a buyer for Graziella's pearls, so with the excuse of checking out some of the Luciano subsidiary companies she left Sophia and Rosa together.

Sophia arranged with a real estate agent for the apartment to be sold with contents and began to clear out her personal belongings for storage. Rosa helped for a while but grew bored and took herself off for some more shopping.

At noon Teresa returned, the pearls sold. She was ready to leave for Palermo, but she had to wait a further three hours for Rosa to return, laden with suitcases in which to carry her new clothes back to the villa. They spent two more hours sorting through Sophia's stock, this time selecting day clothes as well as evening wear. They also found some accessories left over from the fashion shows.

By midafternoon Rosa and Teresa were ready to leave, but Sophia received a call to say someone was interested in seeing the apartment. She decided to stay on alone and to take the opportunity to call on Nino Fabio.

It was late evening when Teresa and Rosa arrived at the Villa Rivera, and Graziella was already in bed. Teresa checked on Luka; the key had been removed from his door. She stood looking at him, but he lay with his eyes closed, as if sleeping. She stared around the room, then back to the bed, but decided against waking him when she heard Rosa talking to her grandmother.

As soon as Luka heard the door close, he threw aside the bedclothes and got out of bed. He was stronger now and knew he would have no excuse to stay. Teresa would be ready to pay him off.

The next morning Teresa showered and dressed and hurried directly to Luka's room. The door stood ajar; the bed was empty. She rushed down to the breakfast room; to her consternation she found Luka sitting at the table.

He gave her a small smile of recognition and continued to butter his toast. He was wearing an open-necked shirt, and his hair had been cut. In front of him was a notepad, and he was explaining to Graziella his layout for a kitchen garden. Graziella welcomed Teresa and called Adina for a fresh pot of coffee, then returned her attention to the drawings.

Rosa was munching on a bowl of cereal. She looked up at Teresa and beamed. "Good morning, Mama. You sleep well? Did you wear your silk nightgown from Sophia?"

Teresa raised an eyebrow at Luka, and Rosa pulled a face as if she had no idea why he had joined them.

Graziella suddenly pointed to Teresa's head. "Your hair, what have you done to it?"

"It's dyed, Mama," said Teresa frostily. She turned to speak to Luka, but Graziella interrupted.

"I can see that. I don't understand why you can't just be natural, especially at your age."

"All of us, Mama, are not blessed with your natural beauty. Some of us need a little assistance, me more than others."

Luka cocked his head to one side and smiled. "It suits you."

Teresa saw the familiar way he patted Graziella's hand as she said, "Well, if you say so, but Rosa's hair looks better without that dye. Do you see what we did to Johnny's hair? Adina cut it."

Teresa nodded. "I noticed, Mama."

Graziella pulled a face at Luka. She asked, "Has Sophia had her hair dyed?"

"No, Mama, Sophia is still dark. She'll be back as soon as she's arranged to sell her apartment. She's meeting some people about selling the warehouse and reopening her boutiques."

"Oh, we had a visitor. He left you this." Graziella handed over Rocco's calling card. "He wanted to speak with you, about business. I said you were at the tile factory. I didn't like to tell him you were away. Papa never allowed outsiders to know our movements; it's safest. Besides, I didn't like him. Nor did Adina. Maybe we should think about hiring someone to take care of the gates, so we know who is going in and out. Do you agree?"

Teresa murmured her agreement and read the card. "This'll be about the sale of the villa. I told you Domino had agreed to it. I doubt if we can get out of it, unless you particularly want to stay. It's too large just for you."

Graziella blinked and looked down at her cup. The thought

of being left here alone hurt her more than she could have imagined.

Teresa left the room without looking at Luka but asked him to go with her to the study.

Rosa began to clear the table, carrying the dishes out to the kitchen. Graziella remained at the table. Rosa returned and began to fold the tablecloth.

"Is Sophia coming back, Rosa?"

"Yes, of course. There is so much to be done, you know, but I'm looking forward to going home."

"I shall miss you."

"But why? You'll be with us. We won't let you go; we need you. And besides, we're your family. When everything's settled, we'll have money, we'll buy a big apartment. I know you don't like what Mama is doing, but it's for the best, for our future. Mama's doing this for all of us, you must know that. All you've got to do is tell her she looks good blond! Okay?"

Graziella held her arms wide, and Rosa went to her, hugged her tight. "I love you, Grandma. Don't be scared; we won't leave you alone."

"There's your money, Mr. Moreno. Want to count it?"

Teresa tossed the envelope on the desk. Luka slipped it into his back pocket. He hesitated, then said quietly, "Rocco works for the Corleone family."

"Thank you, Mr. Moreno. What time will you leave?"

Luka's voice was soft, persuasive. "Signora Luciano, please take care. One kilo of heroin will make a million dollars. The people who want your space, your trading name, will be junk dealers, and when they learn that you intend shopping around for the highest offer, the only valid contract will be the one to protect your life. The Corleones have sent their representative, Giuseppe Rocco, to see you personally. They have already bought this villa; there is no one who dares argue with them. They can offer you, Signora Luciano, any price they choose, and you would be wise to take it."

Teresa was unnerved by his knowledge of what she was trying to do. "Did you go through *all* our private papers, Mr. Moreno?"

Now he looked up, stared directly at her. His eyes, a moment ago so pale, were now a brilliant blue, but totally expressionless. Then a small, tantalizing, cherubic smile moved on his lips.

The sound of the doorbell interrupted them. Teresa crossed quickly to the window, but he was ahead of her. He lifted the blind, then let it snap back into place.

As Giuseppe Rocco was being ushered into the study, Luka hurried across the hall, through the kitchen and into the garden. He could see Rocco's waiting car, the bodyguard leaning casually against the porch, cleaning his nails.

Rosa could see how much of the overgrown garden had been cleared. She smiled at him. "You certainly did a lot of work while we were away."

He stuffed his hands deep in his pants pockets and kept his distance from her. Rosa moved closer. "When are you going?" she asked.

"Today, maybe this afternoon."

For a moment she looked disappointed. Then she stuck her arms out like a tightrope walker and balanced along the edge of the small ditch he had dug in preparation for seeds. But he was paying no attention, for he had spotted the nose of the rented car he had hidden in the bushes. He had forgotten he had left it there. His body tensed, and he cursed himself.

Luka knew he had to get rid of the car, and fast. He was so wrapped up in his thoughts about it that when Rosa innocently reached out to touch the gold heart at his neck, he reacted instinctively, twisting her roughly away from him. Her head crashed against the fence, and her face puckered with fear.

He berated himself for his foolishness, but she smiled and said it was all right. He took her hand away from her reddening cheek, concerned at first, but then he found himself fascinated by her soft, fresh skin. Her arms slipped around his waist, pulling him toward her. He offered no resistance, just bent his head and kissed her. It was a soft kiss, childish, passionless.

Graziella appeared at the kitchen door, wearing an overcoat and carrying a trowel. Luka waved as if the embrace had never occurred. He turned back to Rosa.

"I am going to clear the kitchen garden." He blinked against the bright winter sun and shaded his face.

Rosa was struck by the vivid color of Luka's eyes, and she

smiled. "You have the bluest eyes I have ever seen."

He turned away from her, hearing his beloved Giorgio's voice: "You've got the bluest eyes, Luka. Come here, let me see. . . . No, don't look away. Let me see your eyes. . . ."

Rosa watched the strange sadness moving across his face as he whispered, "Your eyes are like soft blue flowers. . . ."

She laughed. "Mine? No, mine are brown. What flowers are mine?"

He cocked his head; she could not know that he was hearing Giorgio. "Forget-me-nots."

"What are they?"

He had never played this kind of bantering game before. He stepped closer, lifting his hand to touch her cheek, exactly as Giorgio had done. "You know why they are called forget-me-nots, Rosa?"

She shook her head, and he moved closer. "Once, long ago, Rosa, a young man fell in love with a beautiful lady, and on the bank of a river she saw these small blue flowers. It was dangerous, but because she said she liked them and because they matched the color of her eyes, he climbed down to pick her a flower. The closer he went to the river, the steeper the bank became. He reached out his hand like so . . ."

He bent forward, leaning farther and farther. "He caught a single flower. Then he fell, tumbled into the wild waters. As he was swept away he held up his hand, with the little blue flower, and called out, 'Forget me not!' " He half fell forward, then stumbled and turned back to smile at her.

"Is that a true story?"

He nodded.

"What happened to him?" she asked.

"He was swept away in the water. He drowned."

"You're putting me on."

Luka laughed. "No, it's a true story. Giorgio told me." He sprang away from her then, knowing he had made a mistake.

"Who's Giorgio?"

Luka backed away, and she could feel his sadness, hear it in his soft, whispered reply: "My brother."

He turned and headed toward the kitchen.

Teresa saw him approach the kitchen and was about to call to him when she saw Rosa, who had followed him.

"Rosa, take your grandmother into town to get the groceries. I've got some paper work to see to, and I want to call Sophia. We'll go over to the factory this afternoon."

Rosa helped Graziella down the front steps. As soon as they were gone, Teresa gestured for Luka to follow her into the study. When she spoke, her voice was strained, edgy.

"Rocco laughed at my proposition. The Corleones want us to finalize the sale of the villa. They will cover our debts and pay what they feel is a substantial amount to ensure that the Luciano women live in comfort—comfort, not luxury. But what they are offering is an insult. I have until this evening, when Rocco returns, to make up my mind. The amount decreases with every day that I do not agree to their terms."

She started twisting her wedding ring around. Finally she looked directly at Luka. "He said that no other family would oppose them, that I had no alternative but to accept their offer. I want to fight them, Mr. Moreno. If need be, I'll go to the government."

"They *are* the government. Take whatever they offer."

Her hands were shaking, and she was close to tears as she poured herself a brandy, but when she faced him again, the fear was gone.

"There was an offer sent to Mario Domino from a man called Michele Barzini. It's ten times the Corleones' offer. Have you ever heard of him?"

Luka's eyes narrowed, and he nodded. "Barzini's a middleman, you know, a negotiator. He works out of New York, but I don't know which family he is affiliated with."

Teresa began to pace the study. "But if we all travel to New York, we can get to him? If necessary, ask for his protection? Then, if he agrees to buy us out, on whoever's behalf, they can handle the situation here. All I want is our rightful inheritance. We haven't come this far to be cheated, robbed, after all we have done."

Luka remained impassive. Teresa continued, wringing her hands nervously. "We will need someone to protect us, someone we can trust. You know everything there is to know about our situation, and I know enough about you to have you charged with murder. As an incentive, we will pay you first the money from the pearls and then, when we go to New York and the deal is done, five percent more of everything we make. Then you are free to do as you wish."

Luka did not reply. She opened a drawer, took out the gun Luka had taken from Dante's nightclub, and laid it on the desk.

"Do we have a deal, Mr. Moreno?" Her eyes were bright, alert, her body tense and waiting.

She was surprised by his gentleness, even more by the light, childish kiss he gave her cheek. "We have a deal, Signora Luciano. You will not regret it, I give you my word. I will do anything to repay all of you for your kindness. You can trust me. . . ."

Luka hummed to himself as he made his way back to his room. He let himself in and lay on the bed, then sat up as he remembered the newspaper. Quickly he retrieved it from beneath the mattress. He had taken it before Graziella had awakened.

There on the front page was the story: POLICE STEP UP HUNT FOR SUSPECT LUKA CAROLLA. The paper reran the accounts of the Paluso killing, the Lucianos, and the shooting of Paul Carolla.

As Luka skimmed the article, he found nothing that even hinted at any knowledge of his whereabouts. What really worried him was the picture of him and the description. He held the picture beside his face, examining them both in the mirror, convincing himself that no one would recognize him with his new haircut. The face in the picture had long blond hair, but the description was good, including the height. The age was wrong, they thought he was much older, but he didn't like the suggestion that he could be taken for an American.

He tore the paper into scraps, beginning to wonder just how safe he was at the villa. Had the others seen the article? He paced up and down the room, thinking about the car at the gate. It was not well enough hidden; he had to get rid of it. If, as Graziella had suggested, they were to get a guard, he'd spot it immediately. Luka opened the high window and climbed out.

# 17

Commissario Pirelli now had details of Luka Carolla's driver's license, which had been faxed to the States, and a description of his car. A flood of telephone calls was still coming in from the public.

The press conference had paid off faster than they had anticipated; one of the calls had come from the owner of the motel where Luka had stayed.

Police headquarters seemed to be buzzing. The police now had verification from forensic that the prints on the orange juice glass and the unused bullet at the Armadillo Club matched those on the gun found at the monastery.

Ancora had to sit down. "Jesus, this is getting out of hand. If we keep at it, we'll close every unsolved murder for the last ten years. This means that fucking Luka Carolla was at Dante's that night, could even have killed him."

Pirelli was on his way out when the phone rang. Ancora reached over the desk and snatched it up, then signaled to Pirelli to stay.

"Okay, we'll get someone there. . . . Yeah, don't let anyone touch it." He put the phone down. "We've got the car he rented. It's on the outskirts of Palermo, driven into a field. The guy knows it wasn't there last night, so it must have been dumped in the last few hours. Means our man is still here."

Pirelli punched the air with his fists. "Now we're moving! Get that car towed in as fast as possible. I'll be at the hotel."

By the time Pirelli and his men arrived at the small hotel the room was already being stripped. Everything that could be removed was taken to the forensic laboratories. They had a long, arduous task ahead of them because the room had been rented to three occupants since Luka's stay.

The owner of the hotel, sweating with nerves, was driven to headquarters, where he was questioned for more than three hours. He had little information to give, having seen Luka Carolla only twice: once when he signed in and once when they had passed each other in the hallway. But Pirelli now had his most valuable lead: Luka's signature in the register as "J. Moreno."

Nevertheless, another piece of information confused and delayed the issue. Luka, alias Moreno, the hotel owner assured the police, was not blond but dark-haired.

Pirelli sighed. "You're sure?"

The man nodded. "He was dark. When he signed in, I couldn't see his face too good; he wore a straw hat and sunglasses."

"Describe them?"

"Well, the hat was kinda brownish and—"

"No, no, the glasses. What sort were they?"

The man shrugged. "Sunglasses, you know, the kind with mirrors in them; you can see your own face, but you can't see their eyes."

"So, let's go to the second time you saw him. . . ."

The man thought hard. Then: "It was the same day they shot that guy at the trial. I was going up the stairs, about seven-thirty, maybe later, in the morning. He passed this close." He spread his hands about a foot apart, then continued. "So I got a clear look at him. He didn't have those sunglasses on or the hat. He was carrying some kind of parcel, and he didn't reply when I said good morning. He just walked on, so I just looked over the banister, watched him leave. I thought, *Rude bastard.* . . . His hair was real dark, almost black."

Pirelli nodded and leaned forward. "But you saw the composite, and here, take a look, the man's obviously very blond, so why did you call us?"

The man shook his head and shrugged. "The face . . . the eyes more'n anything else. I remember them; they were blue, you know, those real pale blue eyes. . . ."

Pirelli watched as Bruno ushered the man out. There was nothing he could do but wait to see what forensic came up with on the hotel.

Ancora barged in. "You wanna see the Fiat? It was set on fire, but the guys are working on it. We got lucky; fire centered on the engine and the seats, but on the driver's door it looks like bloodstains. Can't tell as yet."

A fax came through from the States; Luka Carolla's driver's license was a fake. With time on his hands, Pirelli went in search of Mincelli and found him standing in his office having a screaming match with someone on the other end of the phone. Seeing Pirelli, he slammed the phone down.

"You really landed me in the shit. That was the oily bastard from C-eleven. They've got some big burglary on, and we've got virtually every man down in the labs, elbow deep."

Pirelli sat down and started picking up Mincelli's pens. "So, you checked out the times of death of the Lucianos and whether it was possible for someone to be in both places that night?"

"Yep. The two Luciano kids were killed nine to nine-thirty, the men not until ten-thirty. If your man was driving, he could do it easily . . . and here, this will make your day."

The ballistics report now verified that the magnum had killed one of the victims, the waiter at the restaurant. The other victim, the chef, had been shot with a gun of a different caliber.

Pirelli whistled. "This guy has taken out more people than the Ripper. It's unbelievable."

Ancora and Pirelli moved down the wide stone staircase and out into the yard behind headquarters. The pens for suspect vehicles were on the other side. They stepped over the cordon surrounding the Fiat.

"They've got prints from the glove compartment, thumb

and forefinger," Ancora announced. "The rest, they think, was wiped out in the fire. The blood group is type O, Rh negative, and there was quite a lot of it. The blood group is common; but I asked if there was enough blood to think our man was badly injured, and they said possibly. You know they never take a chance."

Pirelli walked around the car. "Let's go up to the labs, see if they've got an ID on the fingerprints."

Pirelli breathed down the lab technician's neck as he laid the fingerprints on the slide, then mounted it in the microscope. He looked up and nodded. "Looks like the same prints taken from the glass and the bullet. See for yourself. . . ."

Pirelli squinted into the eyepiece. "Now we need only one thing." He moved the glass aside. "The owner of these babies."

Sophia Luciano arrived back at the villa earlier than expected and went in search of Teresa. She found her in the study, with Luka.

Sophia stood in the doorway and addressed herself to Luka. "Do you mind leaving us? I need to talk to Teresa."

Luka left quickly, giving Sophia a smile, which was ignored. But as he passed her, she caught his arm. "Your hair . . ."

He ran the flat of his hand over the crew cut. "Graziella and Adina cut my dye off. . . . You like it?"

Sophia raised an eyebrow. "Graziella?" She turned to Teresa. "He's making himself very much at home here, isn't he?" She turned back to Luka. "Close the door, please."

As he shut the door, Sophia sat down. "What's been going on?"

Teresa was a little edgy. "A lot . . . Everything go all right in Rome? I wasn't expecting you so soon."

"Obviously."

"What's that supposed to mean?"

"I thought we'd agreed to pay him off? And here he is, sitting chatting away. Graziella cutting his hair. Next thing we know he'll be eating with us. He's no good. You have to get rid of him. You promised."

"We may need him."

"Oh, come on, Teresa, need him?"

"Did you arrange to sell your apartment?"

"Yes, at least that was simple enough. It's on the market. But Nino Fabio refused to see me. Then I received this by hand from his lawyers about an hour later. He wants his designs returned, all of them that are still in my possession."

Teresa read the lawyer's letter. "He wants his chunk of flesh, doesn't he? Not satisfied with ripping you off for years, he's trying to block you from starting up again. Did you find out if he was the one who stole the machines?"

"How could I? He wouldn't even see me. He wouldn't have dared treat me like this when Constantino was alive."

Teresa settled her glasses on her nose. "Listen, we have more important things to discuss. We seem to have really sent some shock waves through the families. They think there must be someone behind us, you know, overseeing all the work and so on, perhaps even financing us, and they—"

Teresa chewed her lip, trying to hedge around the subject.

"Come on, what's going on, Teresa?"

She got up and went to stand by the shutters. "The one thing Domino had virtually settled was the sale of the villa and the orchards. We were offered a good price, Graziella signed the agreement, and Domino banked the deposit. Where in God's name that's gone to I don't know. I can't trace it, just as there are huge sums of cash I can't trace. . . . It was supposedly all put into a Swiss account, but so far I haven't found it."

Back at the desk she handed Sophia a card. "That's Giuseppe Rocco, the card says real estate, it's a joke. He's a front man for the Corleone family, and they, Sophia, are the ones who have bought the Villa Rivera."

Sophia scanned the card. "So? Does it matter who we sell to? You said yourself it's a good price; that, added to the sales of all the various companies . . . Are we going to put them all under one contract? There're so many different sections, the warehouses, factory, docks, ships. Are we going for a complete sellout?"

Teresa sat down and took off her glasses. "That was my intention, to sell the lot. Just as it is their intention to buy us out lock, stock, and barrel. But that figure is all we get, Sophia. You see, their price for the villa, they insist, includes all rights to everything, warehouses, properties, everything you've just mentioned. And every day we do not accept their deal, the money goes down. They want possession as of five days from today."

Sophia stood up. "They can't do this."

"But they can, Sophia. And to make sure, they are cutting out every other possible buyer, seeing to it that no one stands against them. If we refuse, down goes the money, and they will let the company disintegrate."

Sophia stared at her sister-in-law blankly.

"It means, Sophia, all the work, all the money we took from Dante's club were a waste of time."

"They can't do this. Look, why don't I call Pirelli and ask him to help us?"

"Do you want to put Mama in danger? Rosa? We need someone to protect us, someone who knows the way the families work. So I've hired Johnny—"

"Oh, no, no way . . ."

"Just listen! We can trust him because he has to trust us. One call to your precious Pirelli, and Johnny'll be arrested for Dante's murder. Besides, he's already agreed, and he's been more than helpful in setting it up."

Sophia folded her arms. "So you've already made up your mind whether I like it or not."

"You can back out. I've not even discussed it fully with the others because it *is* dangerous."

"Oh, yes? As dangerous as going against their offer?"

"Not if we work it right. We should be out of the country by the time what we've done becomes known."

"Did Moreno suggest this?"

"No, I put it to him, to see what he thought. The only way it's going to work is if we can stall them, somehow hold them off while we get ourselves ready to leave Palermo. We leave with all the contracts, every legal right to the entire Luciano holdings, still in our possession. We get to New York, and we sell to a guy called Michele Barzini, who's already made a reasonable offer to Mario Domino. This way we are clear of Sicily, and they won't want to get involved in a fight with the States. Even if they did, we wouldn't be part of it."

White-faced, Sophia said, "Dear God, Teresa, if they found out, wouldn't they send someone over to the States? They'd get us, wherever we were. . . ."

"I know, and I've thought of that. We agree to sell only if they give us protection. If we are approached, we tell the Corleone family that we had no option, that Barzini threatened us. We have to play the innocent widows, incapable of dealing with the situation. That's how they think of us, so we play it to the hilt. Johnny thinks the only way we could possibly get away with it is to make sure the Corleones believe we are acting completely alone, have no idea what we are doing, have no one behind us."

"But, Teresa, we *are* alone, for God's sake."

"Except for Johnny. He'll look out for us until we get away."

Sophia's laugh was humorless. "One kid to protect four of us, Teresa?"

Teresa shouted, "So what do you suggest? Have you got any better ideas? Or do you just want us to accept the offer and get out? Haven't you been cheated enough? Used and betrayed enough? I have, and I won't take any more, Rosa won't—"

"You have to include Graziella."

"Of course, we can't do this without her. So, shall we call them both in and go through it?"

Sophia nodded. "I guess so. . . ."

"I'll call them."

Sophia was still standing by the shutters when Rosa and Graziella came into the study. Teresa shut the door firmly behind them and returned, hesitantly, to sit behind the don's desk. She was slightly irritated that Sophia remained apart from them.

Graziella and Rosa sat, like two schoolgirls, on the chairs in front of the desk.

"Have you two been arguing?" asked Rosa.

"Tell them, Teresa, and get it over with." Sophia faced the room now, arms folded.

Luka had not been included in the meeting, but he listened at the door. There was a long silence; then he heard Teresa. She spoke quietly, and he had to press his head to the door to hear clearly.

"We had an offer for a buyout of the entire Luciano holdings, from an American, a man who, I am told, is a negotiator for a number of American families. Michele Barzini—do you know him, Mama? Have you ever heard the name?"

Graziella shook her head. "Maybe I met him with Papa,

but I met so many business associates. I remember a time, we used to stay—"

"Not now, Mama, this is important. You see, he has made a good offer, one that is acceptable, if not as much as we hoped for, and twenty times as good as the Corleones' offer. Their offer, which I believed was only for the villa, was for the entire company; they are insisting on a complete buyout. The contract for the sale of the villa, which we all have agreed is fair, has gone through, but it does not state anywhere that it includes all the Luciano holdings. But they have given us an ultimatum: Sell them everything, and for every day we hold out the price goes down. They will, I am assured, block any other family or company attempting to buy the business."

"Can they do this? I know we agreed to sell the villa. Mario Domino handled it, I know—"

"Mama, whether they can or can't is immaterial. They insist, and we are powerless to stop them. If we try, from here in Palermo, they will hold off any other offer. No one in Sicily will oppose them. Our only chance is in America; we sell to the Americans, to this man Barzini."

Sophia moved closer to the desk. "If we do this, we all are in danger."

Teresa turned on her. "Let me tell them, or are you taking over?"

Sophia snapped, "I am not taking over, for God's sake, but get to the point."

"That is what I'm trying to do, but Mama and Rosa have a right to know everything. . . ."

Graziella leaned forward. "If we decide not to sell the villa, we pay back the money already paid by the Corleones, yes?"

"We can't do that, Mama; it's gone too far. We sell them the villa, as agreed, but then we have to stall them, long enough for us to get out of Italy and to New York. We have five days to do this; we have to leave without their having the slightest notion of our intentions. We leave Italy and go straight to Barzini. We ask for protection from his families, and we sell to the Americans."

Graziella pursed her lips. "Is he to be trusted?"

"His offer is good, and I have called to see if it still stands. He has agreed to meet me, so, yes, Mama, I think he is to be trusted."

Graziella folded her hands. "How much would we receive from this man Barzini?"

Teresa took a deep breath. "I'd ask for twenty million, but I would accept eighteen, possibly a little less."

"Dollars or lire?" asked Rosa.

Teresa snapped, "Dollars, Rosa, don't be so dumb. That'll be a good split for all of us." She was growing impatient. She looked at Sophia, but her sister-in-law had returned to her stand by the window.

Graziella spoke up again. She was very calm. "Teresa, don't make us hurry. We must think this through, as Sophia said—"

"Mama, we don't have much time. We have to arrange our flights, leave here, travel to Rome. . . . We have a lot to organize, and only five days."

"I know. But what was Barzini's original offer?"

Teresa sighed and looked over the desk. "It was made just after the murders. Mario Domino seemed to think it was not enough. He made a memo to—"

Graziella interrupted. "How much?"

"Twenty-four million . . . dollars."

"So why ask for less? Ask for more than his original offer. We must not appear to be desperate in any way. We can negotiate when we are in New York."

Sophia turned slowly and stared at Graziella, hardly believing what she heard. Teresa moved fast, suddenly aware that Graziella was not opposed to her plan.

"Okay, do you want to put it to the vote? The more time we waste, the less we have left. So, if you all agree?"

Graziella held up her hand. "No, no, wait. You understand everything, Rosa?"

"She understands, Mama. You understand, don't you, Rosa?"

"No. I mean, what would we get if we just let the sale go through to the Corleones?"

Teresa sighed. "Okay, if we just sell the villa and everything else to them, we get about one million dollars between us. Then, from the smaller businesses, the ones they have no interest in, Sophia's warehouse, a shoe shop, a gas station, and some candy shops—"

"How much?" demanded Graziella.

"Maybe we'd clear two million, possibly two and a half."

Rosa looked at Graziella, then at her mother. "Okay . . .
I say we go for it."

Graziella opened the safe. "Yes, I agree. And I think I
have something that will help us. The less anyone knows about
when and how we leave, the better."

They watched her take out a brown envelope. "These are
passports, for me, for anyone. All in different names. Papa and
I used them when we went to America."

Teresa smiled and held out her hand for them. "Thank
you, Mama!"

Graziella's cheeks flushed. "We are together. That is all
that is important; we are together."

Sophia sighed. "Yes, Mama, we are together, but this is
not a game. It is very dangerous; we are going directly against
a very powerful family—"

Graziella's eyes flashed. "I know the dangers, Sophia. I
lived with them all my life. I played no part in them; I wanted
no part. I stood by and watched, but no more. We have been
cheated, we have been lied to, and now they try to force us to
accept the crumbs they throw to us like whores in the street.
We are not worthy of respect, of honor. Not one of these people, these so-called powerful families, came and gave us their
justice. And if we went to the courts to beg for help now, we
would not be given it. They have destroyed the Luciano name.
No one gave Don Roberto justice for Michael; no one gave any
of us justice. We are treated like the guilty, but we have committed no crime except that of loving. My sons, your husbands,
Rosa's husband-to-be, my grandsons died. For what? Are we
such nothings that we have no rights? Why not take what is
ours, fight for what I almost lost for you? And if it's dangerous,
we'll take care of each other!"

Sophia turned to Teresa. "Call Giuseppe Rocco. Stall him,
ask for more time. Say we've got lots of last-minute packing to
do."

Graziella nodded her approval. "And tell them to meet with
us here, in the villa. Tell them to give Graziella Luciano the
courtesy of calling on her. They should come to us!"

Rosa jumped up. "Mama, why not say we are delayed because we need to find a new, smaller home in Palermo, an
apartment? Then they won't be suspicious."

Teresa smiled. "Okay, okay, but be quiet; let's hear what they say."

Rocco returned Teresa's call almost immediately. He said that Don Camilla of the Corleone family had agreed to meet with the widows, along with his advisers, at the Villa Rivera in three days.

The women had three days to organize the getaway. They were united now; there was no argument, no bickering. They packed everything Graziella wished to keep, and decided to use trusted men from the factory, old men, to take the crates away for storage. The evenings were spent going over every detail with Luka Carolla.

Luka was satisfied with the passport Enrico Dante had obtained for him in the name of Johnny Moreno since none of the newspapers had mentioned his alias. He was confident it was safe to travel with the women. He was unaware that police at every airport in Sicily and on the mainland were on the alert for someone using that name. The police computers carried a detailed description, and all the men had received the composite picture. Even if the Luciano women got away, Luka was sure to be arrested.

A major hitch developed at the last moment. Graziella received a summons to appear in court on the charge of attempting to murder Paul Carolla. Her lawyer said there was no way around it; she would have to appear, which might necessitate her traveling back to Sicily. After a hurried discussion they decided, as a precaution, that they all would leave the villa but that Graziella and Sophia would stay in Rome. They would give away their plane tickets at the airport, rather than exchange them.

Teresa suggested to Luka that he go with Graziella and Sophia in case of any trouble. He hesitated, wanting to leave Italy more than they could have imagined, but in the end he agreed. Graziella would travel back to Palermo for the hearing, then fly directly with Sophia and Luka to New York.

When she was alone with Sophia, Teresa told her to ask her friend Pirelli for protection until they left Sicily.

*     *     *

Lisa Pirelli walked from room to room, complaining of the dust, the musty smell of the Palermo apartment. Then, while Pirelli opened his son's jigsaw puzzle, she slipped her arms around his neck. "Are you pleased to see us?"

He kissed her affectionately. "You'll see just how pleased tonight. . . ." She giggled provocatively. "Are you going to be here for Christmas, Joe?"

He shrugged. "I hope not. We should wrap it up before then."

"I've read about the Carolla boy."

He sighed. "You and thousands of others, but we still can't trace him. He must have good contacts; somebody must be shielding him."

Lisa wrinkled her nose. "You wouldn't think they would, knowing what he did."

He gave her a glum smile. "You never can understand people, my dearest, particularly in Palermo. The place is a sewer."

His son rode his bike into the dining room and piped up, "See, I need a bigger bike. . . . And by Christmas I'll be even taller."

Pirelli gave him a wink and tapped his nose. "We'll see how many inches you can grow in three weeks. No promises, though."

He could see Sophia, hear her voice: "My babies, my babies . . ." He put his arms around his son, hugging him tightly.

Lisa shouted from the kitchen that everything was ancient, she had never seen such an old gas stove. Pirelli heard the gas pop and ran to see if she was all right. She turned with the box of matches in her hand.

"Are you okay?"

"Yes, minus an eyebrow. Have you cooked anything on this since you've been here?"

"No."

"I didn't think so. Never mind, I'll get it sorted out."

He put his arms around her, kissed her cheek. "I know you will, and I'm sorry about the vacation. Maybe at Christmas we can go skiing."

They held each other, and she looked into his eyes. "You seem tired. Why don't you lie down? And I'll come in and further exhaust you." He laughed, loosening his tie.

But as they reached the old iron bedstead, the phone rang. He pulled a face.

"Don't answer it, let it ring." She pulled him toward the bed, but he picked up the phone.

It was Ancora, who apologized, but he had a good fish on the hook, a con doing life who knew Luka Carolla and wanted to make a deal.

Pirelli sighed. "Can't you handle it?"

"Sure I can, just thought you'd like to be in on it. The guy is called Tony Sidona, used to work for Carolla. He was picked up as an accessory to the Lenny Cavataio murder."

Lisa was kissing Pirelli's neck now, undoing his shirt.

"I'll be there, wait for me," he said.

As soon as she heard the words, she flopped back, arms outstretched. "I don't believe it, I come for a weekend, I'm only here two minutes, and he's going out!"

He kissed her, grinning. "But I'll be back." As he reached the door, he turned again. "I love you. See you later, okay?"

Tony Sidona would talk only after it was agreed that the government would review his case, and he insisted on having it in writing, with his lawyer present. Pirelli, tired, wanting to get back to his wife, agreed to everything.

"Okay, let's hear what you have to say, and make it quick."

"You won't back down?" Sidona demanded.

"We've agreed to have your case reviewed. You know what that means: You'll get an early parole. So let's go."

"And nothin' I say will be used against me?"

"No," Pirelli growled, getting really angry. Ancora saw the eyebrows meet and wondered what had put him into such a foul mood. Then he remembered that Lisa had arrived.

Sidona received a brief nod from his lawyer. He began, "Okay, Carolla came to Palermo with me an' another guy. We both had worked for him in New York. His kid, this Luka you're looking for, nobody liked. He was a pain in the ass, real weird. He used to hang around the apartment, get in everyone's way; he was always hanging around."

Pirelli offered Sidona a cigarette, which he accepted but stuck behind his ear. "Did you ever see Carolla mistreat his son?"

"You must be kidding. He shelled out dough to the kid like peanuts, never asked what he was spendin' it on. Gave him a Porsche just before we came out here, two-hundred-and-fifty-thousand-dollar Porsche."

"You know the registration number?"

Sidona shook his head. "Carolla used to try everything to off-load his kid, get him some kinda work. He wasn't heavy in the brains department, got kicked out of every school."

Sidona spent ten minutes trying to remember the names of the schools, until at last Pirelli got one that he could check. He still needed a recent photograph of Luka Carolla.

Sidona continued. "Put him in a pizza parlor, kid was a fiasco. Tried him in a few gambling joints, you know, runnin' the bets. Fucked up." He rubbed his head. "There was one time I saw him lay into Luka. He found a cupboardful of weapons, a fuckin' arsenal in there. Carolla went apeshit; they were traceable. Stupid bastard had bought them over the counter, Jesus only knows where. We hadda chuck 'em."

Pirelli stubbed out his cigarette and lit another. "Did he have any drills, dentist's drills?"

"I dunno, but Carolla beat the shit out of him over that arsenal. Then the kid gets this knife, a martial arts knife, you know, a butterfly thing? Every time you looked at him the kid was flicking it open, made some kind of sling in his sleeve. I didn't think he could use it, looked more like it was some kinda circus act, opening and shutting it, sliding it down his arm into the palm of his hand, and the blade was like a fucking razor. He had Band-Aids all over his fingers where he cut himself."

Sidona asked for a glass of water and took another cigarette from Pirelli, which he put behind his other ear. "Carolla has to get out of New York, right? He's got the FBI houndin' him; they're buggin' his car, his apartment. He's got a few families hasslin' over some booty that was supposed to be divided up and funneled into some business; that was fucked up. So between them and the FBI pushing to have him cited for racketeering and narcotics trafficking, plus there's this other bunch callin' themselves the Organized Crime Strike Force breathin' down his neck over his business in Brooklyn, any way he looked at it he was in shit up to his armpits. So he hadda get out, you know, go under cover. So there's me an' this other guy all set to go with him, but he's dragging this kid along, too. We couldn't say nothin', but Luka starts acting up like he's gettin' one hell of a kick runnin' from one country to the next, playin' it like a game like one of the TV programs he's always watchin'. Talk about aggravation, I mean, he's coming on like gangbusters. But Paulie takes it, kinda liked the way the kid was always looking out for him."

Pirelli interrupted to ask, "Do you think Luka cared for his father?"

"Oh, yeah, I guess so. Maybe more like he was always wanting to prove himself. See, nobody ever got a thank-you or a kiss-my-ass from Paulie. He was a real bastard. We go to London and Amsterdam, then to Sicily, an' all hell breaks loose and we'd walked right into it. Lenny Cavataio was talking his head off, pointin' the finger at Carolla about some stiff he'd knocked out more than a decade ago. I never seen Carolla scared, but he sure as hell didn't like this Lenny talking. He was like a madman, frothing at the mouth about what he was gonna do to him, but he couldn't move. He was wanted, warrants flying around like confetti. He was holed up in this barn of a place in the mountains."

Sidona leaned forward and tapped Pirelli's arm. "I later found out that the stiff was something to do with Don Roberto Luciano. You know the guy? You know who I'm talking about?"

Pirelli nodded. "I know him."

Sidona sat back, waving his hands around. "You don't fuck around with the old guys, know what I mean? They keep a vendetta going for fucking centuries over an insult, you know? So, it wasn't really Lenny getting at Carolla, but Luciano. I mean, it was the don's son, right? An' I know if Carolla hadn't had his head shot off in the court, he'd have had it done by Luciano, right?"

Sidona gulped his water and wiped his mouth on the back of his hand. "We got a lot of assistance from the families, right? I mean, he was paying out millions to get out of the country, he was heading for Brazil."

Pirelli put in, "Did he have tickets for Brazil? Passports?"

"No, we were waiting for them to arrive. Meanwhile, witnesses were coming out of the woodwork, and Carolla was being hunted by Christ knows how many cops. So Carolla decides that before he goes to Brazil, Lenny has to be shut up, you follow me? That way he reckons he'll get Luciano off his back. So me an' this other guy go back down the mountain, on foot, gonna get to Palermo by train. We couldn't believe it; he sends his kid with us, says he might be useful because he looks like an American, talks like one. I lived in New York for twenty years, but I still sound like a Sicilian, know what I mean? But this kid don't have no accent, and he's got the freaky blond hair. Christ only knows who his mother was because he certainly didn't take after Paulie Carolla."

Pirelli looked at his watch and gestured for Sidona to continue.

"So, now we got Luka around our necks, and he's a fuckin' nightmare. Questions, questions . . . Jesus Christ, he never stopped talking. We discover that Lenny's holed up in this supposed safe house, hotel, or whatever, and he's got two guards day and night. I mean, no fuckin' way could we blast our way in. They got one guy inside the room, one outside."

Sidona looked at his lawyer. "You sure I'm okay sayin' all this?"

Pirelli said, "We made a deal, go on."

"Well, I can't get in the hotel, right? One look at me an' I'm gonna cause suspicion. Same goes for my partner."

"This partner, he got a name?"

Sidona considered for a moment. "I don't know his name, understand me?"

Pirelli sat back. "Okay, go on. Can't blame me for trying."

"Well, the kid walks straight in, all American innocence. He's a student, gets a room. Second floor, balcony. So we climb in that way. Now all we gotta do is make it to the next floor and to Cavataio. Fucking kid does it again, he walks out of the elevator, we're in it behind him, and we put it on hold. Luka walks up, asks if he's on the fifth floor, dangles his key. My partner takes the guard out, kicks open the door, one guard, three of us, right? Fuckin' guy backed off so fast he didn't even try to protect Lenny. Dropped his shooter as soon as he saw we meant business, yelped that he had two kids and a fuckin' white rabbit—you know the score. My partner saw to the guard, then hit Lenny Cavataio. One bullet, here . . ." He indicated his right ear, and his voice dropped. "He was dead, we could have walked out, no? But the next minute Luka's pulled Cavataio's trousers down. I said what the fuck? He said, 'Gettin' a small present for my father.' He cut his testicles off, I'm not kidding, just swiped them off with his fucking knife.' He shook his head from side to side.

Pirelli stubbed out his cigarette. "Then what?"

"Well, he still wasn't satisfied with just that; he had to show whoever found the body that no one talked against his father. . . . He slashed out Cavataio's tongue. There was all this blood, me an' my partner standin' there wantin' to get the fuck out of it, but he wouldn't leave, he was like crazy. . . . He's got these eyes, eyes that go really pale, you know, freak's eyes. We both turned and walked out, left him in there. We got as far as the elevator, and the two relief guys walked straight into us. I made it to the next street before they picked me up, and I was in the fuckin' patrol car, sittin' in the car when I saw him. He must have got some clean clothes, maybe Lenny's, I dunno. He was standin' with the crowd outside the hotel, lookin' on like he was just a spectator."

"And after, did you ever hear from him again?"

"No. I heard they picked Carolla up three days later, but his son wasn't with him. You think I'm sorry? If it wasn't for him, I wouldn't be in this shithole."

Pirelli said, "So you were in jail when they brought Carolla in?"

"Yeah, that's right. And if he was mad about Cavataio givin' evidence, you should have seen the guy go stark, ravin' mad when he was told about Luciano taking his fuckin' place."

"You know if Carolla ordered the deaths of the Luciano family?"

Sidona pulled a face. "Come on, Carolla was a made guy, lotta contacts, but he wasn't that important. That was a God almighty hit."

"Who would you say organized it?"

Sidona became shifty and tucked his hands beneath his chair. "I dunno . . ."

"Two little boys shot, an entire family wiped out."

"Look, I made a deal to tell you about Luka Carolla, that's all, no more."

Pirelli remained silent, staring at the tip of his scuffed shoe.

Sidona wriggled uncomfortably, looked at his lawyer, back to Pirelli.

"I don't know any names, but if Don Roberto had been allowed to take the stand, it was like breakin' up the system, understand? He was old, respected, a lot of power. . . . I figure maybe the U.S. had a hand in it; nobody could afford to let him talk, he knew too much. Could have hurt too many people, so they used him as an example to warn off anyone else."

"Which U.S. family do you think could have played a part in it?"

"Oh, shit, I dunno. I swear on my mother's life, I dunno."

"Would Luka Carolla know these American people? I mean, could he have been involved in any part of it?"

Sidona ran his hands through his hair. "He met a lot of family over here, must have had the contacts in the States; he was Carolla's son."

Pirelli leaned forward and gripped Sidona's knee tightly. His voice was a low whisper, hardly audible to Ancora or the lawyer.

"One name, give me one name you think might know something about the Luciano murders."

Sidona was scared, they could smell it. He leaned forward as if to speak, then sat back. Pirelli held his knee tighter, leaned closer. Sidona licked his lips and finally leaned forward, close to Pirelli's face, whispered, "Michele Barzini, maybe."

Pirelli smiled, patted Sidona's knee, gave him a small wink. He had no idea who Barzini was, but he would find out.

He smiled and lighting another cigarette, suggested Sidona go back to the beginning.

Ancora sighed, checked his watch. It looked as if Pirelli was going to be a long, long time.

Pirelli did not get through until three o'clock in the morning. Even then he returned to headquarters. He faxed the United States to check the schools Sidona had remembered. He repeated over and over that they needed a recent photograph, urgently. He also asked for any information on Michele Barzini.

Ancora yawned for the tenth time. "Can we call it a night,

Commissario? I don't know about you, but I am dead on my feet."

Pirelli put an arm around Ancora's shoulder as they headed for the parking lot. "You know, we've got enough evidence to put him away for the rest of his life."

Ancora nodded, opened his car door. "What's sick about it is, we find him, any lawyer's going to plead insanity. In the end, how can you say that's justice for what he's done? They had it right in the old days, hanged, drawn, and quartered. For this creature I'd do it personally."

Pirelli slammed the car door. "Yep, but first you have to find him."

Ancora started the engine and wound the window down. "You'd better get home. See you in the morning, okay?"

Pirelli moved over to his own car. He was tired. Perhaps that was why he felt so depressed.

As he drove out of the lot and into the square, the workmen were already hauling the twenty-foot Christmas tree into position. Christmas? He heard her soft, pleading voice: "My babies . . . my babies . . ."

# 18

Luka and Teresa were awaiting the arrival of the Corleone men. Luka was carrying a pair of binoculars, hoping to recognize the men from a distance.

The Luciano widows were about to deal with the advisers to Don Luciano Leggio, the infamous *capo di tutti capi* and the most feared man in Sicily. Leggio had slaughtered his way to the top of the Corleone family in a bloodbath that Sicily would never forget. Before he was even twenty-three, he had filled his private cemetery in the wilds of Rocca Busambra with countless skeletons.

Under Leggio's supervision, the city of Palermo had issued more than four thousand building permits in the space of four years. Four out of every five went to four front men: a bricklayer, a charcoal vendor, a manual laborer, and a work site guard. These men, all of them illiterate, were authorized to build almost anything anywhere on behalf of "unnamed parties," the Corleones.

And now, with Don Roberto Luciano dead, they believed nothing could stand in their way.

At the dot of two o'clock a black Mercedes-Benz turned in at the driveway, followed by a Jaguar. Teresa hurried to the door and called to the women that their visitors were about to arrive.

Luka studied the men in the cars. "You've got one of the *consiglieri*, don't know the other guy with him. They've got two bodyguards. Yeah, they're carrying . . . Oh, yeah, nice one! They've got the new twenty-two. I can see one tucked into the guy's belt. It's a real assassin's weapon; with the silencer it's almost soundless."

Teresa's nerves were already on edge. "Who's this *consigliere?* Do you know him?"

"Well, you're not important enough to get the top men or Leggio's underboss even. The *consigliere* is the counselor, like a lawyer, oversees all the contracts."

"Can we trust him?"

"Yeah, they've just sent him to deal. His name is Carmine something or other. They always move around with armed bodyguards. . . . Rocco's in the Jag, alone. I'll get up to the roof to see if they've got anyone on foot. You'd better go downstairs to greet them."

Teresa was shaking with nerves. The women, as Luka had warned, were stepping into a snake pit more dangerous than they could have dreamed.

The two cars stopped in front of the villa. The men in the Mercedes remained seated until Rocco got out and opened the door for them. The *consigliere* and his companion looked like respectable bankers, white-haired, in dark suits, somber ties, and whiter-than-white shirts.

Luka eased open the window of the bedroom above the porch and crawled on his belly toward the edge of the roof.

"Stay with the cars?" an incredulous voice asked below.

Luka peered over as Rocco turned away, hands on hips. "Stay with the cars? Me?"

"Yeah, you . . ."

"How long do you want me to wait? I've got business to see to. I've got a property deal goin' down. You want a carhop, get one of the guys to do it."

No one replied, and the four men disappeared under the porch. Rocco stared after them, his face tight with anger. He called, "I can't wait long. I don't want to lose this deal—"

Luka heard the doorbell ringing and pulled back, afraid Rocco would spot him.

Adina ushered the men toward the dining room. The two bodyguards remained in the hallway, standing like sentries, arms folded, as Adina came out and went to the study door and tapped.

"Signora, your guests are here."

Adina returned to the kitchen, head down, afraid even to look in the direction of the bodyguards.

The women filed in, led by Graziella, who took her husband's position at the head of the table. She alone was veiled; the others, bejeweled and sophisticated, formed a line beside her to greet their visitors. Graziella's hands were shaking as she tried desperately to remember all her instructions. Teresa gave her a brief nod to begin.

"Please allow me to present my daughters . . . Sophia Luciano, widow of Constantino, mother of Nunzio and Carlo . . . Teresa Luciano, widow of Filippo. Her daughter Rosa, who lost Emilio Luciano, her fiancé. I am Don Roberto Luciano's widow, Graziella Rosanna di Carlo Luciano."

Unexpectedly Graziella continued. "I am sorry that Don Camilla could not be present himself. He must be unwell. Please give him our condolences. And you are?"

Teresa was impressed. Graziella was majestic. When the two men introduced themselves, she stretched out her hand to be kissed. Then Teresa seated them around the table and took over the meeting. She spoke deferentially, her head slightly bowed.

"Signore, I thank you for coming. For all of us, I would like to say how very much we appreciate Don Camilla's most generous offer. We will vacate the villa by the end of this month and hope that our request for an extra three weeks will not inconvenience Don Camilla. We are unable to leave before because the apartment we have purchased here in Palermo is being refurbished. We wish the Corleones well. May they have a full and happy life here at the Villa Rivera."

"*Grazie*, signora, *grazie* . . ."

*    *    *

Luka was about to climb back into the house when Rocco's car phone rang. Luka inched back to listen.

Rocco snapped instructions into the phone, said he would be there as soon as he could. He then wandered toward the fence by the kitchen garden, looked around, and walked back to his car. He got in, started the engine, and reversed the Jaguar toward the lane that led to the rear of the house.

Luka climbed back into the house and moved quickly down to the first-floor landing. He pulled up short when he saw the two bodyguards in the hall. There was no way past them without being seen, so he backtracked to the floor above, to Teresa's room, which overlooked the garages. Rocco was just climbing out of his car. Luka was not sure what to do; if Rocco entered the garage, he would see the packing cases and the women's luggage in the cars, ready for their departure. Yet at this very moment the women were pretending that they were going to remain at the villa for another three weeks.

Teresa smiled as she passed over the deeds to the villa, and both men nodded and smiled in return, presuming that she was agreeing to the completion of the sale of the entire Luciano holdings. Their faces fell as Teresa said, "We also take this opportunity to refuse our dear friend Don Camilla's offer for the Luciano companies. We will leave all the financial arrangements for the sale of the villa and its contents to our lawyers, who have worked so well on our behalf during this tragic time. If you wish to speak with them, they await your instructions."

"Signora, did you understand Don Camilla's offer?"

"Oh, yes," Teresa answered. "Signor Rocco made it most clear, but after discussing it with the lawyers and with Don Scarpattio and Don Goya, whose families run the north side of the docks and so were exceptionally interested in our waterfront sections, we were persuaded by Don Emilio Dario and Don Bartolli that they, too, would be prepared to purchase sections, and all four families might perhaps form a group buyout. This would give each family access to our waterfront and bays, plus our cargo vessels at present in dry dock, and, of course, we would agree to sell the cold storage and the warehouses with the package. Since the factories are not at present productive, they, too, would make valuable storage areas. As for the vineyards and groves, though they are sadly destroyed by drought and neglect, we have been assured they could be productive again in two years.

"According to our lawyers, the contract for the sale of the villa does not include these properties. You must understand, we are just four women who have no interest in the complexities of the business and have simply placed everything in the hands of our lawyers. Considering the subsequent offers from America, you will understand our confusion and accept our apologies for the delay. Until we are told by our legal representative to accept Don Camilla's offer, we must sadly decline at this stage to sign any documents. Thank you again, and please give our most respectful good wishes to Don Camilla. We hope he will pay us a visit before we leave. If you wish to discuss the matter again, we will be here. I would also like to take this opportunity to thank your associate Giuseppe Rocco, who was kind enough to suggest that we approach the other families. As I have said, we are dependent on the advice of others, having no business experience ourselves, and appreciate all the help and kindness that has been shown to us."

Teresa stepped away from the table and held out her hand to assist Graziella. Both men rose quickly as the women left the room, just as they had entered, together.

Rocco cupped his hands around his face and peered through the Rolls-Royce window, puzzled. He squeezed past the crates and went to the trunk of the car, opened it, and looked at all the suitcases. He read the label on one. Then, leaving the trunk open, he went farther toward the back of the garage and bent over a packing case. He read the neatly written shipping labels, with the date clearly visible.

He squeezed among the crates again, lifting his jacket so as not to snag it. Suddenly the heavy, electrically operated garage doors moved back into place. . . .

"Hey, what is this? What's going on?"

He had no cause for alarm; he didn't even attempt to run the last few feet toward the closing doors. Only when the stinking heavy blanket covered him did he start fighting, trying to free himself and reach his gun. He lost his balance, fell against one of the crates, and rolled to one side, frantic to get the blanket off his face.

The first blow hit the side of his head and dazed him, but he managed to stagger to his feet and pull the blanket off his head. The next blow thudded into his scalp. Still conscious, he sank slowly to his knees and moaned. The third blow, the shovel coming down blade first, almost decapitated him.

Luka panted, wheezing from the effort. The pain in his shoulder was excruciating; he was afraid he had reopened the freshly healed wound. He put the shovel down and bent over Rocco, knowing without checking his pulse that he was dead.

Adina closed the door behind the Corleone representatives, who paused only a moment when they realized that Rocco's car was missing, then drove off hurriedly. Rocco would have a lot to answer for when he turned up, especially for suggesting other people the women might sell to.

The men were silent, completely controlled; the minor setback would simply be dealt with. The widows would be forced to agree to the offer; it was no longer negotiable. But it never had been; that was just Don Camilla being courteous, a show of respect for the women. Now they would find out that they had been very foolish to abuse that respect.

A short time later the women were ready to leave and were doing a last-minute check on the rooms. Adina was tearful and hardly able to assimilate the directions Teresa gave her, over and over again. Between sniffs she stuttered the instructions: The lawyer was to be contacted and given the thick white envelope from the table; the keys were to be left at the real estate office of Giuseppe Rocco.

As Teresa pressed the button to operate the garage doors, she noticed Rocco's car parked outside. She paid little attention, just waited for the door to swing up and over.

She stepped forward and froze. Her shriek was so long in beginning that Luka had time to reach her side. He put his hand over her mouth.

"Shut up, Teresa, shut up! If I take my hand away, will you keep quiet?"

She nodded as best she could.

"Yes? I'm taking my hand away. . . ."

He removed his hand, and she whimpered with fear. She tried to move away; but he gripped her hand tightly, and she howled, kicked out at him, trying desperately to leave the garage. He pushed her roughly to one side and pressed the button to close the door.

She was so terrified that her teeth chattered in her head. He slapped her face, hard. "Listen to me, you have to keep quiet. I don't want Graziella frightened."

She pressed her back against the garage door. "Oh, God, let me out, please let me out."

Luka was covered in blood: his hands, his shirt, even his shoes and trousers.

Teresa turned away from the shrouded body, sick with revulsion.

"I had to do it," Luka explained. "He was opening the suitcases; he knew we were leaving. But they don't know he came back here. They drove off—"

"What—what are you going to do with him?"

Luka held up a filthy old blanket, the one he had used to throw over Rocco's head. "I'll wrap him in this. Help me, hurry, get me some rope or string to tie the ends."

The body looked like a mummy, bound at the neck and ankles. "Put him in the trunk of his car. After you leave, I'll drive it someplace and dump it."

Luka told Teresa to open the doors and made her help carry the body out to the Jaguar.

"I did what I had to do," he insisted. "There's no need for the others to know about it. Especially Graziella. If Rocco had reported back what he saw here, you'd never have got away and—maybe it'll work out for the best."

"What do you mean?"

"Well, they're not going to think a mere bunch of women did it, are they?"

Teresa's head nodded, but she was rigid with fear.

"Go into the house," he whispered.

Teresa backed away, never taking her eyes from Luka. She stammered, "What—what will you d-do with him?"

"I'll take care of everything. Now hurry, get back to the house."

Suddenly Teresa turned and ran toward a low wall. Hunching her shoulders, bending almost double, she began to retch.

Luka moved toward her. She raised her hands pleadingly.

"No, please, don't . . . Stay away from me, please."

She ran back to the house then and said nothing of what had occurred. Two hours later she left the villa with Rosa, without seeing Luka again.

The Luciano trucks had taken all the crates, and they were still on schedule. Luka had burned his clothes in a bonfire in the garden, together with the blanket he'd removed from the body. Graziella didn't think his behavior strange inasmuch as there was a lot of paper work to be burned, all the private letters and papers from the don's office and the boxes of papers from the lawyers.

At six in the evening the fire still blazed. Sophia watched from the bedroom window. Luka was, she supposed, being useful, but they were running late; they should have left. She went out into the garden and called him.

"Are you ready to leave, Johnny? It's after six."

He asked for another half hour; he still had to get rid of Rocco's body and the car, without their knowledge. He waited until they were sitting in the kitchen, having coffee. He was dirty from the bonfire, and he smiled at Graziella.

"Okay, I'll just have a shower and change. Can I raid the wardrobes again?"

Graziella nodded. "Take whatever you want; it's being left here anyway. That goes for you too, Adina. As soon as we go, you bring your family here, let them take whatever they want."

Adina broke down, sobbing.

Luka climbed out the back window, shinnied down the drainpipe, and ran to Rocco's car. He clashed the gears badly and swore, hoping the women hadn't heard. He ran the car down the drive quietly, without lights.

He could not take the car any great distance since he had to get back to the villa, so he drove by the back streets to a multistory parking garage on the outskirts of Palermo. He tossed the ticket away and parked the car on the fifth floor. Just as he was getting out, the car phone rang. He was startled at first, then smiled and picked it up.

The voice was distorted at first because of the concrete building. "Giuseppe, is that you?"

"*Sì.*"

"Where the fuck have you been? Hello? I dunno why you use this make, you never get a good line. I told you to get one same's I got. . . . Rocco? You there?"

"*Sì* . . . I've got to leave town for a few days."

"You kiddin' me?"

Luka laughed, then raised his voice to a singsong: "I'm kidding."

The voice went silent. Then after a moment the man said, "Who the fuck is this?"

"Leave the Luciano women alone, pass it around. They are protected, understand? Rocco's dead."

Luka had only just torn his clothes off, throwing them across the room, and stepped under the shower when Sophia knocked on the door. He turned the shower off.

Sophia didn't wait for him to answer; she just walked in. "Do you know what time it is? If we don't leave now, we'll miss the last ferry."

Luka wrapped a big bath towel around him. "I'm sorry, I'll get my clothes on."

"What have you been doing in there?"

Luka shrugged. "It takes me such a long time to dress and undress, my shoulder is still very painful."

The dressing on his wound was fresh, but the wound was bleeding; a small dot of blood had seeped through.

She picked up his shirt. "I'll get you a fresh one."

By the time she returned Luka had put his trousers on. She held the shirt out for him, and he slipped his right arm in, turning his back to Sophia as he did so. She stepped back.

"My God, your back! I never noticed the scars before."

Luka went back to the bathroom, buttoning his shirt. "I fell into a combine harvester when I was a kid. Gimme two minutes, and I'll be down."

Sophia was already leaving. "I'll bring the car around to the front."

Graziella was sitting in the front passenger seat. Sophia was impatient to leave. Luka finally appeared, kissed Adina, and hugged her, promising to take care of Graziella.

Sophia snapped, "Would you just get in the car?"

"You want me to drive?"

"No, I'm driving. You can take over later. Is your shoulder all right?"

Graziella offered to drive, and Sophia jumped into the car quickly. "No, Mama, that won't be necessary."

Adina crumpled her sodden handkerchief. She had been well provided for and would return to Mondello to live out her old age in peace. But what was to happen to her beloved mistress?

"*Arrivederciiiii*, Signora Graziella, *arrivederciiii!*"

Graziella turned and gave her a small wave. "Good-bye, Adina."

Sophia turned the car and headed slowly down the driveway. Adina waved frantically. "Write to me, take care . . . God bless you . . ."

Luka turned around in the backseat, put his fingers to his lips, and blew her a kiss. He could not see her face, did not hear her cry as the car disappeared through the gates.

The last time Adina had seen Michael Luciano alive was the day the don had driven him back to the mountain hideout. As the Mercedes moved off down the drive, Michael had turned, lifted his fingers to his lips, and blown his mother a kiss. Adina had seen it. Now, more than twenty years later, a boy with a face like an angel, a boy so similar in looks to Michael that he could have been his ghost, had given an identical farewell kiss. Adina felt chilled to her soul; it was, she was sure, a bad omen.

It was two weeks before Christmas, and there was still no trace of Luka Carolla. STILL AT LARGE was now the headline, but many papers didn't want to give it front-page coverage any longer because it was the festive season, and a scandal had just broken involving two prominent society figures.

Commissario Joseph Pirelli was now in receipt of a photograph sent from the United States. It had been taken at the last school Luka was known to have attended, when he was fifteen years old. With the photograph was a rundown of his known associates, his educational prowess, and a brief note from the principal. He had been a poor student with below-average marks and was absent more often than present. He was a loner, moody and prone to rages that caused his dismissal from several classes.

After the midterm break he had simply never come back. In the opinion of the education authorities he was a disturbing influence and required psychiatric treatment.

Pirelli called a refresher meeting in his office of everyone involved in the case. He stood in front of his notorious "wall of death," where the photographs of Luka's many victims were pinned up. Pointing to the photos, he began quietly. "I am sure, I would stake my career on it, that one man is responsible for all these murders. My problem is not proving that I'm right, but finding the bastard. You all know what lengths we've gone to, and so far nothing. But if we find Luka Carolla, it will end this investigation."

Pirelli lit another cigarette from the one he was smoking and, in a low, tired voice, repeated what he had been told by Signora Brunelli. That, coupled with his discussions with the police psychiatrist, made him certain that they were looking for a psychopath who felt nothing whether his victims were nine years old or ninety. Again and again he pointed to the photos of the children.

Inhaling deeply and letting smoke drift from his nose, he looked from man to man. "He's clever as hell, and my guess is that he works alone. His signature, so to speak, is the marking of his bullets. You can see what evidence we have so far, but what I can't figure out is what triggers him. Is it money? Or hate? Or just blood? I don't know. I don't even know if he's hired by a family. I am sure he killed his adoptive father, Paul Carolla. He was the monk, so he's good at disguising himself, and he may have more than one alias by now."

Pirelli paused, sucking at his cigarette. "I have talked to a good inside man. He knows the families. He wouldn't say whether or not the Luciano assassinations had been ordered from the top. I have one name which he tied in somehow; Michele Barzini, a big wheel in New York, acts as a negotiator between families. As yet we have found no connection between Barzini and Luka Carolla, and when I pressed my informant about the possibility of Carolla being used for a hit directed from New York, he doubted it. But Luka Carolla was brought up around Carolla himself, so he must know a lot of made guys. Maybe somewhere along the line he was subcontracted. Okay, that's it, thanks for coming in."

Pirelli had just tipped his overflowing ashtray into the wastebasket when his phone rang. His face lit up as he listened. Then he smiled broadly and turned to Ancora. "We got our break. Security guards at Rome Airport are holding a guy; he's got a ticket in the name of Moreno, Johnny Moreno."

Teresa and Rosa's plane had already taken off. They didn't even see the young student arrested. The guards took him out of the departure lounge, and he was held in the airport customs area to await the arrival of Commissario Joseph Pirelli.

The two remaining first-class tickets the women had handed out, Graziella's and Sophia's, had been given to two hitchhikers, who could not believe their good fortune. They had changed them for tickets to Los Angeles.

Sophia, Graziella, and Luka had arrived safely in Rome and were already installed in Sophia's apartment.

Pirelli took one look at the student in custody and knew he was not Luka Carolla, not Johnny Moreno. He banged out of the room, leaving the poor boy so terrified that he broke down, weeping. Pirelli kicked at the wall, and his foot went through the partition. A terrible coughing fit forced him to sit down, and he hacked and spluttered into his handkerchief.

In Rome Graziella was preparing for bed when Luka passed her door on his way to the children's room, where he was sleeping. He stopped and watched her brushing her hair. The long braids she usually wore coiled in a bun were now loose. She placed the silver-backed brush on the dressing table and picked up a worn black Bible. She had not noticed him and he moved on, soundlessly. By the time he had washed and brushed his teeth, Graziella's light was out, although her door was still slightly ajar.

Sophia jumped. She had not heard Luka enter the kitchen. "I couldn't sleep. Do you want a drink?" she asked.

He shook his head no and sat down opposite her. On the table were a glass of whiskey and a small pill bottle. He bent his head to read the label, but she picked up the bottle and slipped it into her pocket.

"Do you mind me sitting with you?" he asked.

She shook her head and shrugged slightly. The ashtray was full of half-smoked cigarette ends, and he watched as she picked it up and emptied it into a garbage can.

"Rosa was telling me you're having a lot of trouble with a designer, is that right?"

She sighed and rinsed the ashtray under the tap. Her hair, now loose, reached almost to her waist, like Graziella's. It was dark and silky, and he wanted to touch it; but he didn't move. Sophia dried the ashtray with a paper towel and brought it back to the table.

"Maybe I can sleep now. . . ."

"You haven't finished your drink."

She looked at the glass, picked it up and drank, then took it to the sink. As she held the glass under the running water, he was fascinated by her long, delicate fingers and almost white nails.

She dried the glass carefully and reached up to put it away in the cupboard. Her satin robe parted, opening to the thigh, and he saw that she was naked beneath it. As she turned back to him, the top of her robe opened just a fraction, and he saw the crease of her breasts.

"What did Rosa tell you about Nino?" Sophia wanted to know. She was twisting her long hair around her fingers.

"Nothing much, just that he had, I think she said, 'ripped you off.' " His legs were shaking, and he squeezed his buttocks together, feeling himself harden. He dropped his hands into his lap beneath the table. His whole body tingled with heat; he knew his cheeks were turning red.

"Well, you could say that. Probably my own fault. I was very foolish. My husband warned me not to trust him."

Luka had changed his position on the hard chair. "Do you"—he pressed his erect penis between his hands—"do you want to tell me about it?"

She bit her lower lip and unconsciously ran her hands down the satin of her robe, outlining her breasts, and tightened the sash. The whiskey and the Valium were making her slightly woozy but completely relaxed. "Not now. I think I'll go to bed. Will you turn off the lights? I think everywhere's locked up, but I suppose you'll check."

As she left the room, he came, soaking his pajamas. The relief made him sigh, a quiet moan of pleasure. Then he hurried to his bedroom, wanting to clean himself, but he remembered to turn off the lights first.

In the darkness of the children's room, hurrying to get out of his semen-filled pants, he tripped and fell to the floor, landing on his bad shoulder. He winced with pain and kicked his pajama bottoms away, angry at his own clumsiness. Then he stripped off the pajama top and checked his wound, easing away the adhesive that held the small dressing in place. It was clean, and he tossed the bandage into the basket.

The gold heart at his throat glittered, and he touched it tenderly, lifted it, and kissed it, as if it were a crucifix.

Luka overslept and found Graziella sitting alone at the breakfast table, but before he could ask about Sophia, she walked in, already fully dressed. He quickly busied himself pouring coffee so she would not see that he had blushed. He could smell her perfume, a soft, powdery smell. He asked if she had already had coffee.

"Yes." She leaned over to kiss Graziella. Her gleaming hair, drawn back from her face and tightly coiled, made her look severe. She wore a smart charcoal gray suit and dark gray stockings; but her white silk shirt was open at the neck, and he could see, as she bent over Graziella, a minuscule portion of her white lace brassiere.

"Will you take care of Mama, Signor Moreno? I shouldn't be more than a few hours. Did you sleep well?"

Luka nodded.

Sophia walked into the lounge and began putting papers into a slim black leather briefcase. Luka pushed his chair back and followed her. He saw her close the case, then open a drawer and take out a bottle. She unscrewed the top.

"Would you like me to drive you?"

She turned with a guilty look, her eyes wide and startled. Three tiny yellow pills dropped to the floor and rolled. Immediately Luka was on his knees, picking them up, his hand close to her slim ankles, her fine kid shoes. He wanted to touch her. . . . When he stood up, he was near enough to feel her warmth and smell again the soft, powdery perfume.

"I have a headache," she said guiltily. Her confusion gave him confidence.

"I'll bring the car around to the front entrance."

He hurried to his room before she could argue. Quickly he combed his hair, changed his shirt, and put on one of the suits he had taken from the Villa Rivera. It had been one of Filippo's, left after the funeral. As he passed the reception area of the building, he noticed the doormen's office door was open and one gray uniform cap was lying on the desk. He took it.

Sophia appeared not to notice the effort he had made. She didn't smile when he doffed the cap, turning to face her in the backseat.

The hat was a little large, but he took it off and stuffed tissues in the inside band, then tried it on again.

"Could we go? I don't like to leave Mama for too long."

She sat to one side in the back of the car, her eyes closed, legs crossed. Luka tilted the rearview mirror a fraction in the hope that she would open her legs a little. Her elbow was propped on the armrest; her hand covered her brow. She sat like that for most of the journey, only occasionally dropping her hand to give him directions.

Sophia was in her lawyer's office for more than three quarters of an hour, and when she returned to the car, her mood was more distant than ever.

"I have to go to Milan. Nino Fabio is working there. You can either drive me there or go back to Mama, and I'll make other arrangements."

"No, I'll take you."

Sophia reached for the car phone and called Graziella to say she would be gone longer than she had anticipated. Graziella assured her she would be all right; she would go out and buy some groceries.

Luka drove out of the city and onto the highway, observing Sophia as she opened the small bar in the back of the car. She drank some vodka and took another of her little yellow "aspirin." Then she caught him watching her.

"I wish you would stop looking at me. It's very unnerving. I can see you doing it, you know. If you're spying on me, it's really not worth it. You can tell Teresa that I take about four Valium a day and a sleeping tablet now and then. . . . I presume that is why she insisted you accompany us to Rome, isn't it?"

Luka pulled over, stopped the car, and leaned his arm along the back of the seat. "Not quite. I'm looking after you and Graziella until we get to New York."

Sophia laughed sarcastically. "Well, that really makes me feel secure. . . . Do you mind driving on? I don't want to be late."

They did not speak again for the rest of the journey. Sophia opened her briefcase and began reading some papers. Then she sighed, made a few notes, and leaned back on the seat, her eyes closed.

When they got to Milan, she directed Luka down the back streets to what had once been warehouses, now converted into luxury apartments and a few offices. They drew up beside a tall building, freshly painted.

Sophia instructed Luka to park and wait. They were in a courtyard where the space that had once been reserved for delivery trucks was chained off for private parking. The chains were painted white, and there were large tubs of flowers all around.

Luka watched her as she entered the building. He waited for half an hour, then left the car and entered the building. It was now past one o'clock in the afternoon.

Luka checked the company names on the door, then walked down the stone corridor and summoned the old freight elevator. At the third floor he pulled the lever to stop the elevator and stepped out into a white-painted cavernous space. A number of doors led off the entry, but there was no indication of which was Nino Fabio's workroom. Only the telltale potted plants gave away the fact that the building was no longer a goods warehouse.

He followed the murmur of voices through a room filled with dummy models to a door at the opposite end. On the other side was a carpeted reception area with a shiny black desk and more potted plants. A flamboyantly lettered sign, in gold, told Luka that he had found "Nino Fabio."

To his left he could hear the low hum of machinery. The voices, louder and more distinct now, led him straight on to where the space had been divided into offices and showrooms painted in bright yellows and peaches. All the doors were glass-paneled, with signs: DESIGN DEPARTMENT, EXPORT DEPARTMENT, SHOWROOM. Luka paused until he heard Sophia's voice. She was in the room at the very end, with Nino's name on the closed door.

Nino threw the rolled-up drawings across the room. "If I let you have the '85 to '86 collection, my reputation will *suck*! All that frilled and swathed crushed fabric is *dead*! I hate those old designs. The answer is no. If you want to open a boutique, fine, go ahead, get another designer, if you can find one. But this one, sweetheart, is not yours to be had."

"You know I don't have the finances for that, Nino."

"Look, I'm sorry, but right now I have my own business to see to. I never expected any favors from you; I worked my butt off for you. Whatever happened has nothing to do with me. What is my business, and the only thing I care about right now, is me, my future, my breaks. You had it like a princess; now go away, play games elsewhere, and I'm warning you, if you go ahead and use those old designs, I'll sue you, my company will sue you. Get off my back, Sophia, you can't win, and if you want some advice, don't bother. You could **never** have made it without me to begin with."

"Please, just release a few of them, so I can start again. My lawyer's drawn up a very fair deal; you'll get a percentage."

"Sophia, please, we've said all there is to say. Everyone will be coming back from lunch. I don't really think you want this spread over every gossip column because you know that's what will happen if these boys get to hear. The walls have ears."

Sophia stubbed out her cigarette. "I don't have any record of the sales of the machines taken from my own premises and from the warehouse you used for your lingerie business. You may not be aware of the fact, but I own the entire warehouse. Where are my machines, Nino?"

He shrugged. "I haven't the slightest idea. I haven't been there since the day I saw you there. Maybe the manager, Silvio, took them. I don't know. I can't help you."

"I see. So you won't mind if I look around? Just to see what kinds of machines your people are using? If I find one, just one, from my company, Nino, I'll be the one charging you with theft, okay?"

"You look wherever you like, be my guest. I don't have your machines, Sophia. I have nothing belonging to you, and I don't want anything, just as I don't want you trying to resurrect your business on my back. You use one of my designs, just one, and *I'll* be charging *you* with theft. Is that understood?"

Nino and Sophia turned in surprise as Luka walked in. He went straight to Sophia and took her elbow.

"Your car, Signora Luciano . . ."

Sophia stood in silence as they descended in the elevator, her hands clenched at her sides, her face set. When Luka raised the iron bar, she ducked under it and hurried out to the car.

By the time Luka was in the driver's seat, Sophia was blazing.

"How dare you interrupt me like that? How dare you walk in like that!"

"You were about to grovel so low, you should thank me." His blue eyes were angry as he leaned over the seat and pointed at her. "You are a Luciano. . . . You and your mama are somebody, understand me? You want that dickhead to sign papers, there are ways of getting him to sign. But you never beg, never beg, not you. . . . You don't need him."

He watched her open her handbag, searching frantically.

"And you don't need those."

"Mind your own damned business! I don't need you or anyone else to tell me how to run my life, you hear me?"

She looked past Luka, and her expression altered. She cowered back in the seat because, no more than ten yards ahead of the car, was the man who had run the illegal sweatshop attached to her company. Silvio was deep in conversation with a small, oily-looking man in a fur-collared coat.

"Don't move the car. You see those two men? Can you see where they're going?"

Luka watched them enter a building farther down the courtyard, too close to Nino Fabio's workshops for there to be no connection. Sophia was tight-lipped with anger as she instructed Luka to drive along the yard and park outside the door Silvio had entered.

She got out, not even sure what she was going to do. But

then Celeste Morvanno, the young woman who used to work
as her receptionist, came out of the same building. She was
wearing a blue print wool maternity dress, and she flushed with
embarrassment when she saw Sophia.

"Signora Luciano, what are you doing here?"

Sophia smiled, and to the watching Luka, they appeared
to be having a friendly conversation. Celeste leaned forward
and kissed Sophia on both cheeks. Sophia remained standing
there as Celeste walked toward Nino Fabio's.

When Sophia got back into the car, she was shaking. "Just
get me out of here, hurry."

"You okay?"

She was white-faced, and as they turned out of the yard,
she said, "Stop the car. I'm going to be sick."

She stumbled out of the car, lurched toward a wall, and
bent over as she heaved and vomited. Luka waited beside her,
then handed her his clean handkerchief.

"Sorry, I'm sorry . . . Will you help me back to the car?"
She was very unsteady on her feet and struck her head as she
bent to get into the car.

"You okay?" he asked again.

She nodded. "I must look like a mess."

Luka passed her handbag to her, then climbed into the
driver's seat. He watched her through the rearview mirror as
she freshened her face and carefully repainted her lips. Then
she lit a cigarette and, sighing, told him to drive around for a
while with the windows open because she needed some
fresh air.

"You know what it makes me feel like? Used, I have been
used, and what is worse, Nino knows I won't do anything
about it."

"Why not?"

"How can I? You tell me, do you think I could go to the
police now? As it was, the place was illegal. They couldn't have
been paying the girls union wages, not to mention the taxes—"

"The business was important to you?"

She sighed and stared out of the window. "Yes, yes . . .
It was important."

"You want to start up here again?"

"Yes, of course. Why else do you think I went to see him?

But I need his designs. I don't have the money to find another designer, a good one. And in Milan everyone knows what everyone's doing; it's very hard to break into the fashion business and be taken seriously."

"But if he did them when he was working for you, then you own them. They must have been part of your company?"

"Yes . . . I don't know anymore."

She sat with her head resting against the back of the seat, her eyes closed. There was a helplessness to her, a vulnerability that made him ache to hold her.

Joseph Pirelli wandered along the Via Brera and paused outside La Scala. He had decided to fly back to Palermo that evening and was simply killing time. He wondered if he could possibly catch half the opera and checked the time, then decided against it.

He was deep in thought, standing on the edge of the pavement. He saw the Rolls-Royce; it drew considerable attention. There were not that many around, and the narrow streets were unsuitable for such a big automobile.

Sophia saw him and gave a smile of recognition. Pirelli had only to walk to keep up with the car; the traffic was virtually at a standstill.

"Signora Luciano, hello . . . What are you doing here?"

"Some business. I used to have a boutique."

"Do you have time for coffee?"

"No, thank you, I have to return to Graziella."

Pirelli paid no attention to the chauffeur in the gray peaked cap. "Please, I am catching a plane to Palermo at seven. Just a coffee."

Sophia looked at her watch. "No . . ."

"There's a good coffee shop on the corner near the Piazza del Duomo. . . ."

There was a break in the traffic, and the car began to pick up speed.

"I'll be there. I'll wait for you—" He watched the car merge with a throng of vehicles and eventually disappear.

Sophia realized she had not had anything to eat since breakfast. She said to Luka, "Take me to the piazza."

"No, we've got to get back. It's late."

"Just take me there. You can get yourself something to eat."

"No."

Surprised, Sophia laughed. "Do as I say, and don't argue."

"What about Graziella?"

"Graziella is perfectly all right. If you're worried, you can call her. And it's Signora Luciano to you."

Luka pulled out of the traffic and parked at the curb. "You don't want to see him. We'll go back now."

Sophia's hand was on the door. "Go get something to eat. Pick me up in an hour, is that understood?"

She was out of the car before he could argue. White with anger, he forced the car back into the stream of traffic, almost causing an accident with another motorist. They began shouting abuse at each other.

Pirelli was waiting inside the coffee shop. When she entered, his face creased into a smile.

He pulled out a chair for her and helped her off with her coat. He had no idea it was sable. He tossed it on a vacant chair.

"You look very beautiful."

She smiled and picked up the menu. "I didn't realize how hungry I was. I've not eaten since early this morning. It was a long drive."

"You drove from Rome today?"

"Yes, Well, my chauffeur did. He was furious that I made him stop."

Pirelli blushed. "I'm glad you did."

They ordered, and he told her he had been on a fruitless mission to Rome and had simply traveled to Milan to check out his apartment. He did not mention that his wife and son were in Palermo; Sophia assumed he was a bachelor.

"How long are you staying in Palermo?" she asked.

"I went there originally for one case, but it has escalated. Could be months, who knows?"

Luka ate a sandwich hurriedly, drank a cup of coffee, and returned to wait in the car. The hour was almost up when the car phone rang. It was Sophia, telling him to go back to Rome without her; she had decided to stay on. She had already called Graziella.

"How are you going to get back?"

"There are flights, trains, I don't know."

"I'll wait for you."

"No, just do as I say, go back to Rome."

Luka was beside himself. "I'll come to the café."

"Don't because I'm not there."

"Where are you?"

"I'm at the opera. See you tonight."

The phone went dead. Luka sat there, unable to believe it. The opera? His knuckles whitened from gripping the steering wheel. Why had she gone with that man? Who was he? Was he her lover?

Thinking it over, he talked himself into an icy calm. He would prove to her that he was the most important being in her life. He reversed the car and headed back to Nino Fabio's warehouse.

Ancora tried to make contact with Pirelli, phoning first his Milan apartment and then the Milan police headquarters. They had not seen him since that morning and thought he was on his way back to Palermo.

Ancora replaced the phone and began to type out a short report on a body, now identified as that of Giuseppe Rocco, a known Mafioso, found in a multistory parking garage. He was a member of the Corleone family.

He had been dead for more than twenty-four hours, his death caused by a blow to the head. There were also deep lacerations to his neck. But what made the discovery of Rocco's body important was that the gun found with him was the weapon they had been searching for, the walking cane with the horse's head that divided into three separate sections, stolen from the Villa Palagonia. In fact, the dead man's trousers had been pulled down to his ankles and the gun rammed up his ass.

The opera was *Rigoletto*, and Pirelli seemed enraptured with it. Sophia sat in the darkness, wondering why on earth she had agreed to come, unable to comprehend why she had even had a cup of coffee with him. The more she thought about it, the more ridiculous she felt. Johnny would be halfway home by now. . . . She began to think of her best way to get back to Rome, and her head began to throb. She turned to Pirelli.

At that moment he turned to her and smiled. She felt strangely comforted by his shoulder touching hers.

"I have to leave. . . . Please, you stay."

He followed her along the row. When they reached the lobby, he asked if she was all right.

"Yes, yes, I'm fine, but I must go home. It was stupid of me to stay. I'm sorry, you go back, please."

Crestfallen, he nevertheless took her arm, and they walked outside. She felt the comfort of him again; his hand on her elbow was firm. She eased her arm away, wrapping her coat around her.

"It's cold. . . ."

Tongue-tied, he answered, "Yes, er . . . My apartment is close by."

She gave him a look and turned away. He coughed. "Er, we could go back there, and I could check on the trains or see if there's a flight."

Before she could reply, he had flagged down a taxi and they were heading she had no idea where. Her confusion growing, she sat as far away from him as she could.

Pirelli said nothing, just stared out of the window. He was just as confused as she was, almost afraid to meet her eyes in case she could see the turmoil he was in.

They walked up the three flights of stairs to his apartment. There was no doorman in evidence.

Once inside, Sophia kept her coat on, standing in the middle of the neatly organized living room while he threw his coat off and checked timetables. Eventually she sat on the edge of the sofa and lit a cigarette.

"Do you have any brandy?"

He immediately brought her a glass of brandy. She seemed uninterested in the apartment, neither looking around nor remarking on the taste. She was simply there. . . .

She cupped the glass in both hands, sipping, not meeting his eyes. He had trouble catching what she said. "I think—I think I should call Mama."

He watched her cross the room to the phone, put her glass on the table. She turned to look at him, and their eyes met; she smiled and continued dialing. Pirelli lit a cigarette and inhaled deeply; his hand was shaking like a teenager's.

"Mama? It's Sophia. . . . No, Mama, I'm still in Milan." Again she turned to Pirelli, seemed to be searching his face for the answer to some unspoken question.

"Something has come up, and I'll be delayed. . . . You okay? . . . No, he's not; he should be back shortly. . . . No! No! Nothing to worry about. . . . Yes."

After another glance at Pirelli, she turned her back on him. "In the morning, Mama, I'll be home then. . . . Yes, plenty of time."

She replaced the phone slowly but did not turn. She began to ease the fur coat off.

Pirelli went to her to take the coat, and as it slipped down to her arms, he bent his head and kissed her neck. Her only response was a slight tilt to her head, as if offering him more of her bare neck. The coat fell to the floor. He stepped back, and she turned.

He was bereft of words. Slowly she cupped his face in her hands. She could feel him shaking. As she rested her cheek against his, all he could say, as if on a sigh, was her name. She opened her jacket and lifted his hand to her heart.

He could feel her heartbeat through his hand, feel the softness of her silk blouse, the curve of her breast. He was drowning in the heat of it. . . . Carefully he slipped her jacket and blouse off, his hands gently brushing her shoulders, then worked the zipper of her skirt down until it fell to the floor. He wrapped her in his arms, holding her softly, nestled in his embrace. He kissed the lobe of her ear.

"I love you, Sophia."

She seemed to collapse against him, and he picked her up and carried her into his bedroom. He laid her down on the bed, and she turned her face into the pillow. She felt as if her mind were not part of her body, not part of her craving. She wouldn't look at him.

Pirelli drew the curtains, unbuttoned his shirt, kicked off his shoes, and peeled his socks off. Then, still wearing his trousers, he moved soundlessly to sit on the bed beside her.

"You know, I never believed it possible to feel this way about someone. The first moment I saw you . . ."

She turned and touched his chest, tentatively at first; then her fingers dug into his flesh, into the thick, dark, wiry hair, and she clawed him, pulling him down. He felt her bite his lip, and he gripped her face, drawing her toward him. He kissed her more roughly than he believed himself capable of. . . . He tore the straps from her slip, pulling it away from her, and gasped at the beauty of her heavy breasts.

She unbuckled his trouser belt, and suddenly he felt her hands on his erect penis, pulling at him roughly, drawing him upward as she lowered her lips around it.

He pushed her away. "No . . . no . . ."

She flopped back on the bed. "What's the matter with you, Commissario? Don't you want me? Don't you want to fuck me?"

He gripped her wrists. "Look at me, look at me! Do you think I want you like this? You think I want this?"

He looked at her scornful face, a half-smile on her lips as if she were laughing at him. "No? You don't want me? What's the matter? Don't you like a woman to go down on you?"

"Jesus Christ!" He moved away from her; he had to because he wanted to slap her. He couldn't cope with the way she had changed. She was a stranger, a whore he had brought back instead of the beautiful dream he had fantasized loving. He snapped, "Get dressed! This was a mistake. I'm sorry."

She laughed. Was she laughing at him? He had never felt so inadequate in his entire adult life. The sneering smile on her face made him turn angrily back to her.

"I can pay for what you offer, Sophia. Get dressed."

Her eyes blazed with anger. "Maybe I can do the same. How much do you want, Commissario? What do you charge for a fuck because that is all I want? I thought that was why you brought me back here."

She reached out and caught his arm, drawing him toward her, but he pushed her away so roughly that she fell against the bedside cabinet. He heard the crack of her head against the wood, and it made him feel worse, even more inadequate.

"I'm sorry, Sophia, I'm sorry."

She wouldn't look at him, but all the sneering anger had gone. She seemed simply to give up.

"Did I hurt you?" he asked. He sat on the bed, at a loss for what to say. His whole body ached for her, wanted her, yet he could not reach out and touch her. She turned slowly to face him.

His expression of concern brought the sweetest of smiles from her, and she whispered, "No, you didn't hurt me. I wanted you because I felt nothing. I have nothing left."

He kept looking at her, feeling her loss, her emptiness, and her need. He felt an overpowering desire to be the one to fill that need; she drew from him a bewildering tenderness. Slowly he moved closer and closer. Like a father to a daughter, he opened his arms, willing her, wanting her to come to him, to take the offer of comfort freely, without fear.

The release when she reached out, when he encircled her in his arms, when he felt the warmth of her nakedness against his own was like no emotion he had ever experienced. Never had he cradled such fragility. He tightened his hold, whispering that it was all right.

His was the first embrace, the first physical comfort Sophia had received since discovering her babies murdered, since burying her dead. She had cried endless tears for her loved ones; now she wept for herself. He encouraged the release, rocking her backward and forward as shuddering sobs swept over her, until at last she was still, her body pressed against his, her heartbeat at one with his own. Then, at that last moment, he lifted her chin gently and kissed her.

He laid her down and began to take the pins out of her hair, loosening it. He smiled down at her. "I dreamed of seeing you like this, with your beautiful hair spread out. I love you, Sophia. I love you."

She closed her eyes, and he stroked her belly, soft, brushing strokes. "I can make you feel loved, make you feel cared for. . . ." Her skin beneath his fingers was like silk.

It was Sophia who placed his hand on her breast, let him feel the erect nipple, let him know that he had aroused her, that she wanted him. They made love, and he came into her within moments.

He smiled down into her beautiful face. "Thank God we've got all night . . . all night. . . ."

And all night they made love. In the early morning he

made breakfast and brought it to her, and they ate it, side by side in the bed. He ran her a bath and soaped her body, toweled her dry, then held her tightly.

"What am I going to do, Sophia Luciano? You have me wrapped around your little finger, you know that? From the first moment I saw you."

She laughed and went back into the bedroom, opened the curtains, flooding the room with light. She dressed while he showered and changed, and she sat in her fur coat, waiting for him. Her Turkish cigarettes made the whole apartment smell sweet. It was as if nothing had happened from the moment they had walked in.

"We will be in Palermo for the hearing. Mama's case comes up this week. Will you be there?"

He nodded, realizing he had not called his office. He checked the time. "I'll get a cab to the airport."

She stubbed out her cigarette. "Can you be there? Mama is afraid of the press, she's afraid, and we only have—" She was about to say "Johnny," but then she said they had only their chauffeur.

"I'll be there. . . . Will you be returning to Rome or staying in Palermo?"

"I'm not sure. It depends on the case."

While he phoned for a taxi, Sophia looked around the room, then stood up to look at a photograph. Her back was toward him while he spoke to the taxi company and thumbed through the timetables at the same time.

"Who are they?" She was holding the photograph.

He touched his lip; it was swollen where she had bitten it. "My wife and my son."

She replaced the heavy frame carefully. "How old is your son?"

"Nine . . . Well, eight, nine next birthday. Sophia?"

She picked up her handbag, refusing to look at him.

"Sophia, Sophia, I would have told you—"

"But you didn't."

Sophia refused to talk to him on the way to the airport. His flight was due to leave first. As it was called, he gripped her arm.

"I have to see you again. I can't leave like this. I can't—"

"You had better or you'll miss your flight."

"Fuck it! I want to see you again."

She shrugged. "Fine, I'll see you in court."

"That's not what I meant. I want to see you, be with you."

She smiled and cupped his face in her hands; but it was a false smile, and her eyes were cold. "Why complicate things, Joe? Whatever happened last night happened. It was good, but forget it. I do not want to be anyone's bit on the side."

"Don't speak like that! Do you think I usually go around doing this kind of thing? Do you? I meant what I said, Sophia."

She stepped back. "They're calling your flight again. You'll miss it."

"I don't want to lose you."

"You want to leave your wife? Your son? Don't play games, Joe. We're both too old for that. Let's finish it before we get more involved. It'll be best for both of us."

Pirelli couldn't argue. He hadn't even contemplated leaving his wife. He walked toward the departure gate without turning back.

When she returned to Rome, Sophia was confronted by an irate Luka, who demanded to know what she had been doing. She tossed her coat over the sofa and looked at him.

"We had better get a few things straight: You work for us, you don't give me orders, and you don't ask me where I've been or what I've been doing because it's none of your damned business."

"I am supposed to be protecting you, looking out for you. If I don't know where you are, how can I do that? Who was that guy you were with?"

Sophia walked into the bathroom without bothering to reply. She ran a bath and stripped, stared at her reflection in the mirror. There were no marks on her body from their lovemaking, but she was changed: She felt calmer and more confident.

Soaking in the bath with her eyes closed, she thought about Pirelli, refusing to admit to herself the possibility that she cared for him, that she could— She picked up the sponge quickly and soaped and scrubbed her body. No matter what he said, in the end he had in some way betrayed her. It was foolish even to contemplate becoming involved with him. Instead, when the time came, she would use him; he could prove useful.

Pirelli took a bit of ribbing from Ancora. His lip was badly swollen, and no one believed he had walked into a gate. But whatever Ancora believed, his bad mood was due to the fact that no matter what evidence they kept coming up with, they were still left with the problem of tracing their man. Officers were being pulled off the investigation, and there was still no sign of Luka.

Pirelli went over the reports of the Rocco murder and examined the walking-cane gun. It had been wiped clean, no prints. At a loss for what to do next, he could have gone home. Instead, he worried at the problem like a dog with a bone, after something, anything, to help.

Pirelli put off going back to his Palermo apartment for as long as possible, not wanting to face his wife. Eventually he was so tired that he had no option. Feeling guilty, he bought some flowers and returned home, sheepishly. Lisa was watching television with her feet propped up.

"Hi, you okay?"

"I suppose so, but you are the limit. You get me and Gino to stay here in this awful place. Then you go to Milan!"

He shrugged, and she stared at him. "What have you done to your lip?"

"Had a bit of a run-in with a couple of guys at the airport; it's okay. Anything to eat?"

She rolled off the sofa and went into the kitchen. "Did you get to the apartment?"

"Yeah, just a quick look in. Everything's fine."

"Good. Can we go out to dinner then? Save me cooking?"

He sighed and agreed halfheartedly. He was so exhausted he could barely stand up. She stood on tiptoe to kiss him, and he gave her a small hug. "Oh, is that all I get? Away for two days? You haven't even asked me about your son."

"I'm sorry, just that things are really getting on top of me. Is Gino okay?"

"He's fine. I'll ask the girl upstairs to baby-sit. Oh, by the

way, you'll have to get Gino a new bike for Christmas. His has
been stolen."

Pirelli yawned his way through dinner, and try as he could
to avoid thinking of her, his mind was full of Sophia. When his
head finally hit the pillow, all he wanted to do was sleep. Lisa
snuggled up behind him, kissing his neck, but he caught her
hand.

"Not tonight, Lisa, I've got a terrible headache."

She rolled over to her own side of the bed. "Isn't that supposed to be my line? You know, the sole reason I am here in
this god-awful apartment is to be with you. What happens?
You go back to Milan. When do I get to see you? Joe? Joe!"

He was deep asleep, dreaming of Sophia with her hair spread
across the pillow. . . .

After a solid nine hours' sleep Pirelli presented himself at
the magistrates' court for the hearing of Graziella Luciano's attempt to murder Paul Carolla.

Luka was cagey about being seen at the courthouse and
had tried to make excuses to stay in the car, but Sophia had
insisted. "You are supposed to be looking after us—well, do
your job!"

He wore his gray chauffeur's cap and sat with Graziella on
a hard wooden bench in the marble-floored corridor outside the
court. He was wary, but the many people hurrying back and
forth paid him little or no attention. Graziella was nervous,
twisting her handkerchief around and around in her lap. She
was not afraid of the outcome, just of being alone.

At Sophia's request, Luka went to get her some water. He
filled a paper cup at the water fountain and returned along the
corridor past another court in session. Posted outside the court
were the lists of the day's hearings and beside them notices
requesting information on bail jumpers and other wanted fel-
ons, arsonists, petty thieves—and there, in full view, was a picture of Luka himself.

The poster asked anyone who had seen Luka Carolla to
contact the nearest police station. There was a brief description
of him: his blue eyes, his height, and that his hair might be
blond or light brown.

A woman was standing directly behind him, reading the notices over his shoulder. He excused himself and went on along the corridor. His bladder felt as if it were about to explode, and his hands were shaking. By the time he returned to Sophia and Graziella, his face was ashen, and his fingers, holding the small paper cup, felt frozen stiff. They were still waiting for Graziella's legal representative to arrive.

"I've just asked how long we might have to wait. Apparently it might be a considerable time," Sophia said to Luka, but her whole attention was on Graziella.

"Why don't I go see about arranging a nice restaurant for lunch?"

Sophia hesitated, looked at her watch. Then she shrugged. "Why not? Also, we can ask the clerk whether we can leave by the back door. I don't want Mama bothered by the press."

Luka stepped back a few inches. "Okay, I'll wait in the car, directly outside the rear entrance."

He hurried away, passing Pirelli, who was deep in discussion with Graziella's lawyer. He didn't even glance in Luka's direction as he passed because Sophia greeted him. He shook her hand, his eyes searching her face.

"Mama, you remember Commissario Pirelli?"

"*Sì* . . ." Graziella took his hand.

"You've got one of the easiest magistrates, Signora Luciano. I've talked to him and just had a long conversation with your lawyer. I don't think there's going to be any problem. I won't be in the court, but I will come by later." He turned to Sophia. "Could I have a word in private?"

Sophia excused herself and left Graziella with the lawyer. She and Pirelli went into an interview room and closed the door.

"Can I see you after the hearing?"

She wouldn't look at him. "There's no point. . . ."

"I see. What do you want me to do?"

She sighed. "It has nothing to do with me. You are married. It's best we don't see each other."

"Do you want to? Just tell me, do you want to? I mean, I don't know where I am with you."

"I don't know what I want, Joe."

He ran his hands through his hair and gave her a helpless look. "What do you want me to do?"

She came to him, touched his face lightly. "Joe, I don't know what I feel for you . . . what I could feel for you. . . ."

He pulled her to him and kissed her. She rested against him, feeling his strength, comforted by it, secure in his arms. "Joe, it would be so easy for me to say yes, I want to see you again, but it would all become a tangled mess."

He gripped her arms. "I can't stop thinking about you. I want you every minute. I want you right now. . . . I love you."

She made no reply.

He released her and leaned against the door. "What if I were to leave my wife?"

"That is your business. Don't expect me to tell you what to do. If you want to leave her, then—"

"Just tell me if that's what *you* want me to do?"

"No, I won't. What happens if you leave your wife and then we—then we don't work out? You'll make me responsible, blame me! I have had enough heartbreak to last me the rest of my life. Don't give me any more, Joe, please. Maybe, maybe I came to you because I needed you at that moment."

"You don't need me now?"

Her eyes filled with tears. "Oh, Joe, I have such a need inside me. You filled me, gave me something, but don't you understand, I don't know if it's love or just the fact that you filled my need. I have to try to make myself whole again. I'm only half alive."

He had to swallow hard to prevent himself from weeping. "I'm sorry, you're right, you'd better get back to Signora Luciano. If you need me, you've got me, with or without ties. I mean that. All you have to do is call."

She kissed his cheek, whispered her thanks, and walked out. He remained in the room, trying to compose himself. He couldn't rid himself of a terrible sense of loss.

Luka sat in the car outside the court. He now knew that Sophia had been with the commissario, the man named Pirelli. What had she told him? Why had they gone into that room to talk together? He was so deeply engrossed in his own thoughts that he cringed when someone tapped on the window of the car.

A court clerk bent to speak to him. "Signora Luciano is just coming out. You take the first left, down the narrow alley; then there's a sharp right turn back onto the main road—"

Luka already had the engine running as Sophia helped Graziella into the backseat, then sat next to Luka.

"There's the paparazzi at the front, so hurry."

The Rolls Corniche screeched along the narrow alley.

As Pirelli had predicted, Graziella had been fined and given a suspended sentence. By late afternoon they were ready to leave for New York. There was no trouble with customs; Signora Gennaro, her son, and her daughter were not even questioned.

Luka and Graziella between them had chosen the passports. The photograph in Anthony Gennaro's passport did not really resemble Luka, but the fact that it was a family passport enabled them to pass straight through the security net and customs.

They would be landing at JFK within ten minutes. It had been a good, quiet flight, and they all had slept, Graziella resting her head against Sophia's shoulder. Sophia, always nervous about flying, had clasped Luka's hand for assurance as the plane had lifted off, then laughed when her stomach churned. Luka loved her deep, husky laugh.

He thought of the surprise he had for her as a result of his late-night visit to Nino Fabio's warehouse: the signed release of all her designs, including some of the 1987 collection. Nino had signed away all his rights and even given permission for Sophia to use his name.

The plane began its descent, and all three leaned over to look out of the window. Graziella made the sign of the cross, praying for their safe landing. Again Sophia reached for Luka's hand, and he was there, beside her, smiling that angelic smile, the soft dimple appearing in his cheek.

When Nino Fabio's receptionist arrived at work, she noticed that the light was on in his office and presumed he had come in early, as he often did.

She opened the mail and brewed coffee before tapping on

Nino's door. Receiving no reply, she opened the door and looked into the room.

The white carpet was covered in bloodstains. Entire footprints of bare feet showed where someone had walked through the blood, the marks disappearing into the black carpet of the reception area.

There were more bloodstains in the small private bathroom, smeared across the mirror, over the sink. The footprints were clear again on the white floor tiles. There was blood on the taps, blood sprayed over the wall.

As the office began to fill with machinists and cutters, the scene became surreal. The police arrived and immediately cordoned off the area while they tried to find Fabio.

Two hours later a young assistant, passing through the area where the life-size dummies were stored, began to scream hysterically.

All she could do was point to Nino's body, almost drained of blood, perched on top of a male dummy. He was as waxen and lifeless as the white plastic body he appeared to be humping.

# 19

Graziella was distressed at seeing the cramped apartment that Teresa and Rosa occupied. She had no comprehension of the high cost of living in New York, and to her the East Thirty-fifth Street apartment was not just rundown but little more than a slum.

She wept, throwing her arms up as she went from room to room, shaking her head at the small kitchen, asking over and over why, why she had never been told, why Filippo had never let her and Papa see the state they were forced to live in.

Graziella called for Sophia, demanded that she find a better place; it would be impossible for them all to stay in such cramped conditions. Sophia could not help agreeing. She was leaning against the front doorframe, gasping for breath, having carried her own suitcase up the stairs.

Luka brought up two more suitcases, and the narrow hallway was full. With Graziella's wailing it seemed like bedlam.

It was late evening by the time they made sense of everything, having allocated rooms and moved furniture to create space. Rosa moved in with Teresa, and Graziella had Rosa's room. Sophia was given a tiny room of her own. Teresa was tight-lipped as they squeezed into the dining room to eat supper.

Luka had fetched and carried, pushed furniture around, and been very willing to assist in every possible way, but he refused to eat with them. He wanted to go out and arrange a room for himself. He would return in the morning. Bidding everyone good night, he edged his way around the stack of suitcases in the hall.

Supper was a noisy affair as they all talked at once, arguing about their accommodations. Graziella made Teresa even more irate by turning her nose up at the food, that if they had to live in the slums, there was no need to eat like the *americanos*.

"Mama, I don't want to hear another word about the apartment or about the food. If you want to cook, it's fine by me, but I just don't want to talk about it tonight."

"I have a house . . . I have one—"

"No, Mama, the villa was sold. You don't have a house, an apartment even."

"Yes, I have a house."

Teresa pounded the table in fury. "Mama, you think we'd be living in this place if there was anything else? We've got no other place. We live as we are until we get things organized, okay? *Okay?*"

"There's no need to shout, Teresa. Mama is confused. We have been in and out of Palermo, back to Rome. . . . Maybe instead of arguing, you should ask how it went in court." Sophia pushed her dreadful hamburger around her plate. "Mama had to pay a fine, or I did."

"I presumed everything had gone well; otherwise you wouldn't be here. Can we talk about what's really important?"

Graziella folded her arms. "You know something, Teresa? What you think is important is not always right. What's most important is the home; that is the place you live from, you grow from. The family and the home are one."

Sophia slipped her arm around Graziella's shoulders. "You are right, Mama."

"Of course, I'm right. I don't like this place. My bed is next to a wall; who wants to wake up looking at a wall, huh?"

"Okay, Mama, you want my room? Take it, have my room."

"I don't want your room, Teresa. I want out of this place.

It closes in on you. Tomorrow, when we have had some sleep, we look for a new place."

Sophia helped Graziella to her feet and was elbowed away.

"And don't treat me like I was an old lady; show me some respect. I have left my home; you think I don't feel it in my heart? Don't you know what I lost, what I left behind?"

"You had no choice, Mama." Teresa was fighting to control her temper.

Graziella leaned across the table. "I had a choice, Teresa. Don't think I did not. That house died, may it rest in peace."

Teresa threw her hands up in the air. "What do you want us to do, Mama, weep for the house now?"

"No, just remember I gave you my home." She walked to the door, then paused. "Where's the bathroom?"

Sophia roared with laughter as she led Graziella down the small, obstacle-strewn hallway.

"Well," said Rosa, "Aunt Sophia seems in better spirits than when we last saw her. I wonder if the pills are working overtime."

"You show respect, Rosa, or you'll feel the back of my hand."

Rosa looked at her mother and continued to pour the wine. As she filled her own glass, she said, "Johnny seems to be a part of the family now. Seems very friendly with Sophia."

Teresa collected the dirty plates, saying nothing, but she did bring up the subject of Johnny when Sophia returned.

"So, how did our Mr. Moreno work out?"

Sophia accepted a glass of wine and smiled.

Teresa leaned closer to Sophia.

"Did anything happen with Johnny? Sophia?"

"He worked out just fine. He drove the Rolls—oh, we left it at a long-term garage, Teresa. We can pick it up anytime, although it is a ridiculous car for Rome, the streets are so narrow."

Teresa was still not satisfied. "Did you find out anything more about him? Like who he worked for?"

Sophia shook her head. "No, but he took care of us. So what's the next move, now that we're all here? What do we do now?"

"I've made contact with Barzini," Teresa said. "He was

more than eager to see us. I said we would meet with him as
soon as you arrived, so if you and Mama get to bed early, I'll
call him and we can go to see him first thing in the morning.
The sooner we have this settled, the sooner we can get on with
our lives."

Luka was still acting as the widows' chauffeur. He had
polished Filippo Luciano's Lincoln in the garage below the
apartment building. He watched as the women headed toward
him and held the door open for Graziella.

Teresa stared hard at Luka. As he reached to help her into
the car, she cringed away.

He flushed slightly, wary that Teresa's reaction would be
noticed, and remained silent throughout the journey to Barzini's, taking surreptitious glances at her through the mirror as
she gave them each their instructions.

Barzini occupied a residential suite at the Plaza Hotel. As
the car drew up, a uniformed doorman moved toward it, but
Luka was out fast, barring the man's way. He made a great
show of ushering the women from the car.

They all were wearing black, and Graziella was veiled. They
looked rich; they looked like old money, their clothes obviously
designer quality. People turned to stare as, one by one, they
stepped out of the limo and crossed the sidewalk. Then, in their
now well-rehearsed group with Graziella leading, they entered
the Plaza Hotel. Ignoring the front desk, they walked sedately
to the elevators and rode up to the sixteenth floor.

A man in a light gray suit and pink-tinted gold-rimmed
glasses was waiting for their arrival at suite 6. He moved toward
Graziella.

"Welcome, Signora Luciano. We met in '79, but you will
have no reason to remember me. My name is Peter Salerno."

Graziella nodded, and he gestured for them to follow him
through the open door of the suite. He guided them into a very
large, sun-filled room.

Pink silks lined the walls, and there was a profusion of pale
oyster-colored sofas and matching chairs. The air was sweet
with the scent of large, ornate flower displays on white marble
pedestals. Small glass-topped coffee tables were placed conve-
niently around the living-room area, and in the center of the

room was a low white marble table with dishes of candy and glasses for the champagne, which waited in silver ice buckets. A white-coated waiter stood by, ready to serve them.

The man they had come to meet, Michele Barzini, was talking on the phone. He was in his late fifties, a small man, no more than five feet five. His hair was sandy gray above a pinched face on which he wore rimless tinted glasses. His suit was a light, shiny gray, and his black shoes were so highly polished that light glinted off them. His rose-colored tie sported a large diamond pin in its perfect folds.

Within a moment he had put the phone down and hurried with open arms to greet his guests.

"Forgive me, forgive me . . . Welcome, Signora Luciano."

He kissed Graziella's hand, then turned to do the same to each of the other women as they were introduced. He patted their hands in condolence, then invited them to sit down. Graziella, about to accept the offered champagne, was immediately silenced by Teresa.

"Thank you, nothing."

The waiter was dismissed, and no one spoke until he had drawn the carved white doors across the archway. Peter Salerno sat in a high-backed chair while Barzini chose a soft one, facing the women. He addressed himself to Graziella.

"Your husband was my dear friend for many years. If you have a problem, I am honored that you come to me."

His small eyes flickered from one to another. He noted how very pretty Rosa was and looked twice at Sophia, with her shining black hair and high cheekbones. The bowed head was almost nunlike, but the curvaceous legs in sheer black stockings were tantalizing.

The white Art Deco phone rang shrilly, and Barzini leaned toward Salerno and told him quietly not to put any calls through. Salerno moved quickly from the room, to return a few moments later, unobtrusively.

Barzini smiled. "Ladies, you have my undivided attention. . . ."

Teresa had opened her briefcase and unloaded a thick folder of documents. Her face was drawn, a little haggard, and when she lifted her eyes, he was surprised at how unflinching the contact was. He knew instinctively that this woman was not

afraid of him. But when she spoke, her voice was totally sub-
missive.

"My mother-in-law used an old family friend, Mario Domino, to arrange our affairs. He was very elderly and, sadly,
incompetent. . . ."

She went on to give Barzini a detailed and concise history
of the women's predicament and financial situation. She gave
very clear estimates of the worth of the main Luciano company.
Salerno made notes of everything she said.

Sophia kept her head down, staring at the ghastly pink
carpet. She found the ornate suite distasteful, cloying, and she
did not like Barzini at all. She could feel his mole eyes undress-
ing her and making her skin crawl.

Rosa was fascinated by the way Barzini's eyes rolled back
in his head. She, too, had felt his scrutiny but became trans-
fixed with the way his small but cruel hands smoothed the creases
of his trousers and fingered his diamond pin.

For her part, Graziella was in a world of her own, trying
to recall where she had met this small, ugly little man. She was
sure her husband had never spoken of him. But there was
something familiar about him.

Teresa was explaining their treatment at the hands of the
Corleones, who had offered nothing more than an insult. She
told him that she was sure that every family in Palermo would
have wanted to lease their properties if she had been allowed to
do what she had intended.

The polished black shoe twitched, and Barzini flicked a
small look toward Salerno. Then he removed his glasses. "Have
you ever had a hand in running an import or export company
. . . Teresa? I hope you don't mind my asking you this. It's
just that without experience you could have been mistaken about
the financial worth of the Luciano holdings. . . ."

Teresa gave him a wonderfully innocent gaze, hesitated,
then sighed. "Facts are facts. There have been, over the past
twenty years, many offers, and they did not decrease. The
company was very profitable and continued to expand until the
death of Don Roberto. The Luciano company was a highly re-
garded legitimate business, and I suspect that the families wishing to buy us out needed the cloak of legitimacy to enable them
to export narcotics. . . ."

Barzini leaned forward. "Believe me, I have no wish to offend any of you. Pray God I don't. But Roberto Luciano was a witness for the prosecution. . . . No matter what vendettas have come between brothers, that was an act of madness."

Teresa's mouth turned down, and she dropped her act of innocence a fraction. "Believe me, we know more than anyone what that madness led to. But we come to you for help, because you loved Roberto Luciano as a brother. He stood against Paul Carolla, a man who, for more than twenty years, tried to force him into the narcotics trade. Carolla wanted our warehouse space, our cold storage facilities, our factories. . . ."

She rattled them off, one after the other, and Salerno wrote them all down. Not so much as a look passed between him and Barzini. The only hint of Barzini's interest in what Teresa was saying was that his hands became still. He appeared totally relaxed, but Teresa was sure he had taken the bait.

Sophia sat half turned toward Teresa, alert to everything she was saying.

Teresa continued. "All we ask is a fair price, what the company is worth. We have come to you, a man beloved of our dear papa, for your help in this matter."

Barzini's hands began to move again as he replied, "I am touched, my dear, that you chose to come to me. In honor of my long-standing friendship with Don Roberto, I will try to help. I will speak to some of my friends, put a proposition to them."

With that, he sprang to his feet and helped Graziella rise, as if she had instigated their departure. He kissed their gloved hands in turn, leaving Teresa until last.

As they walked to the door, he asked her casually if she had brought with her all the documents necessary for a sale. She smiled and said yes, everything, proof of ownership, land leases; only the widows' signatures were required.

She handed the file to Barzini, and he ushered them out, pressing the button impatiently for the elevator.

His small hands clutched the folder triumphantly, and it was not until the elevator was about to close that she mentioned to him that the folder contained only copies of the original documents. The doors closed before she could see his reaction.

Barzini turned to Salerno and smiled. "I think the little blackbird just handed us a gold mine."

Luka was ready and waiting for them outside the hotel, eager to know how the meeting had gone. He had no opportunity to ask because as soon as they all were in the car, Sophia snapped angrily, "How could you do that, Teresa? You never actually said it, but it was clear enough. If Barzini hasn't anything to do with narcotics, he soon will have. If they buy us out, they'll use the company for the very thing that Papa fought against his whole life."

"Do you care?"

"Yes, I care. You may be able to live with it, but I can't."

"You tell me how you're going to live at all because right now we've got *nothing*. You're the one who needs cash to start up in Rome, you! Well, you'll have it."

"Have you no morals?"

"Don't give me morals. Whoever buys the company will do what they like. What do you think the Corleones would do, export Italian candy? Grow up, Sophia, just grow up."

Rosa tapped her mother's knee. "Why Barzini? Why did you choose him?"

Teresa shrugged. Sophia lit a cigarette and opened the electrically operated window. "I've got a damned good idea. . . ."

Teresa pursed her lips. "He was the first in the U.S. to make an offer after Papa's death. Barzini is a front man; he doesn't act on his own but is used by various families as a negotiator."

Sophia flicked the ash from her cigarette. "I read Barzini's original offer; it was an insult. We can't sell to him; it's against everything Papa fought for; it would be sickening."

Teresa said coldly, "We'll need your signature. Are you saying you won't give it?"

Sophia gave her a disgusted look and stubbed out her cigarette. "Yes, I guess that is exactly what I am saying. There's got to be some legitimate trader who'll give us a fair price."

"And what straight guy is going to want to put a cent in a company with our connections?"

Luka had said not a word. Now he stared at Sophia through

the driving mirror and said, "Teresa is right, and remember, you will need Barzini's protection. You cannot start looking around for other buyers, not now. It's too late."

The rest of the journey passed in sullen silence.

Graziella insisted on preparing dinner and nearly blew up the small kitchen because she didn't know how to light the gas stove. She clattered around as she cooked up a huge pot of spaghetti.

Luka arrived, almost hidden behind a bouquet of roses. Graziella took them in her arms, laughing delightedly. He had also brought wine, mozzarella cheese, and fresh-baked bread. He was drawn into the kitchen to taste the spaghetti sauce.

Sophia could hear Rosa calling her. Teresa tapped on the bedroom door and entered.

"Are you coming to eat?"

"I'm not hungry."

Teresa closed the door and sat on the edge of Sophia's bed. "If you want out, that's your business, and we'll see if we can somehow raise enough for you to return to Rome and start up again."

"With what? I have no designs, I don't even have a work-room, and I used every last cent to pay off Mama's fine at the court. I'm broke, Teresa, but I still can't agree with what you're doing."

Teresa sighed and looked at Sophia seriously. "Do you want a word of advice? If I were you, I wouldn't go back into the fashion mainstream. I'd use more off-the-rack designs, you know, chain-store things. That's where the dough is."

"You know about a lot of things, Teresa, but don't tell me how to run my business."

"Maybe someone should have told you a long time ago. Then you wouldn't have bankrupted yourself. Those silk things, you know? Those swathed tops were lovely, but who can af-ford five thousand dollars for them? Your market's too small."

Sophia lit a cigarette. "A lot of women can, Teresa. I used to, and the women I want to sell to spend sixty thousand dol-lars in one season, and that's not accessories, that's just dresses."

Teresa's mouth turned down at the corners, and she snapped, "So don't fuck up our chances of wearing them. If

Barzini arranges a buyer, we accept it and start living. You won't stop me, stop any of us, is that clear?"

Sophia remained silent during the noisy dinner. Graziella had cooked enough for twenty, and she watched and listened.

Just as Rosa was about to clear the table, Graziella asked her to remain seated. "So, Johnny, what do you think about this Barzini deal?"

Luka hesitated, then said quietly, "The deal was discussed in Palermo. Now you change your minds. You are safe for the moment, but if you start shopping around, you could be in a very dangerous position because it will get back to Sicily. They'll know that there is no deal. Take Barzini's offer."

Graziella nodded and turned to Teresa. "So, what do you think? If the price is good enough, what then?"

Teresa was tight-lipped with frustration. "Exactly what we agreed before we came back: We accept it, get out, and cut our losses."

Graziella now looked at Sophia. "But Sophia does not agree. So now you, Rosa. What do you think?"

"I don't know."

"You don't know. . . . So we have two against, one for, and one don't know."

"There's Johnny's vote, if that's what you're taking. He's in for a cut, too."

Graziella nodded. "Since his signature is not required on the documents, I don't think we need to know right now."

Teresa sighed. "So you're against it, too, are you, Mama?"

Graziella pursed her lips. "You are right about certain things: the difficulty of finding a legitimate buyer, for one. Then there is the time factor; it is imperative we move fast. So we are left with the question, Do we let Barzini arrange a buyout by whoever he represents, or do we refuse because of our moral obligation to Don Roberto?"

Teresa had heard enough. She pushed her chair back, but Graziella slapped the table with such force that the plates jumped. "Sit down, *sit down*. . . . Give me the courtesy of at least listening to what I have to say."

"I was just going to put some coffee on."

"The coffee, Teresa, can wait. What we are discussing here cannot, and without my signature and Sophia's you can't sell.

I would rather die than let this man use our name; I would prefer to see everything wiped out."

Teresa was about to interrupt again, but Sophia touched her hand. "Go on, Mama, finish what you have to say."

Graziella continued. "Let us suppose we sell to whoever Barzini brings into the deal; we sell, take our money, your inheritance, and you are free. If the companies are then used by narcotics traders, what would the drug enforcement agencies need? What information would enable them to arrest and charge these so-called importers? Not in small swoops, but with a net that could draw the big fishes as well as the little ones? We could give them the information to set up the trap."

Sophia leaned back and lit a cigarette while Teresa and Rosa carried the plates into the kitchen and whispered to each other.

Teresa returned with coffee. Putting the cups down, she asked no one in particular how risky it would be if it were ever discovered.

Sophia poured the coffee and passed a cup to Luka. "Well, Signor Moreno, since you are getting a cut, why don't you tell us? Better still, save all our skins by offering to give the information to the police."

"All right, if you want me to."

Sophia gave a soft laugh. "I was joking."

"I wasn't. I could see that the right people received whatever information you wanted to give."

Again Sophia laughed. "My God, I think he's really serious."

Luka flushed pink. He couldn't cope with her banter. "At least none of you would be at risk."

"Thank you, Johnny, I appreciate that. We all appreciate your offer, but until we decide what we are going to do, our acceptance would be premature."

Graziella smiled warmly at him, but he looked yet again at Sophia. She was turning her gold cigarette lighter over and over on the cloth, in deep thought. He could see the sweep of her dark eyelashes, so long they seemed to rest on her cheek.

"Okay, anyone want to disagree with Mama's suggestion?" asked Teresa. Nobody did. Teresa drained her coffee cup and rose. "Fine, then it's agreed. If Barzini comes up with a good enough deal, we accept, we do whatever Mama wants."

She walked out, and they all decided it was time for bed. Rosa had hoped to sit alone with Luka and was disappointed when he followed Sophia into the hall.

"I have something for you," he said.

Sophia opened her bedroom door awkwardly; she was carrying her coffee cup, and he held the door for her. There was a small suitcase, closed, on her bed.

"What is it?"

"Something you wanted. Good night."

He closed the door behind him, and she looked at the case, puzzled. She put her cup down and opened it to discover books of Nino Fabio's drawings, loose sheets of his designs, hundreds of them.

Teresa was finishing washing the dishes while Rosa dried the cutlery.

"Where's Johnny?" Sophia called from the hall.

Rosa dried her hands, her face tight with anger. "He's left. He's gone."

The telephone rang, and Teresa froze. "This could be Barzini." She hurried into the small room she used as a study.

Sophia had gone back to her room, where the drawings were spread out on her bed. She was sure she had an entire season there, maybe more. She searched her handbag for her address book, then picked up the telephone.

Teresa was still on the phone in the study, and just as Sophia was about to hang up, she heard a man's voice saying, "That is an awful lot of money, Signora Luciano. I don't know if my friends would be prepared to go to that."

Teresa's voice was clearly audible: "In that case, Mr. Barzini, am I to assume that you are no longer interested?"

"I will have to discuss it further."

"You won't take long? I think I mentioned our financial situation."

"Gimme a few hours, maybe less."

Sophia walked straight into the study without knocking. Teresa put the phone down and looked up with a tiny smile.

"I hope to God you know what you're doing," Sophia said.

"I do. . . . Was that you on the extension?"

"Yes, I'm sorry, I didn't mean to listen in, but I was about to call Rome. Johnny just presented me with a suitcase full of Nino Fabio designs. It's sort of crazy—"

Teresa looked puzzled. "How come? I thought that was what you wanted."

"Because before we left Rome, Nino flatly refused to let me have even one design, and now I've got a suitcaseful. It just doesn't make sense. I mean, how the hell did he get them?"

Teresa agreed that Sophia should call and find out and handed her the telephone. "But don't tie up the phone for too long, in case Barzini tries to get in touch again."

Teresa went into the kitchen. Everything had been put away, and she smiled her thanks to Rosa. She looked at her watch.

"I'm waiting for Barzini to call. Sophia's on the phone to Nino Fabio; apparently Johnny's given her all his designs." She listened and was relieved to hear the extension ping.

Teresa returned to the study just as Sophia was coming out. "Did you call Nino?" But before Sophia could reply, the telephone rang. Teresa snatched it up, then composed herself before she spoke.

"Yes, speaking. . . . Oh, yes. . . . Yes, everything." She looked at Sophia and gave her a thumbs-up, then continued. "Thank you very much, I can't tell you how we appreciate this. . . . Yes, thank you. . . ." She let the phone drop, then clapped her hands. "We did it. Barzini has agreed! Rosa! Rosa!"

"How much? How much, Teresa? *How much?*"

"Wait, wait, *Mama, Rosa, come in here!*"

Rosa appeared with Graziella just behind her. Teresa was half laughing and half crying. "We did it! Barzini has agreed to pay us fifteen million dollars. What a Christmas!"

Rosa hugged her mother and cheered. Graziella beamed and turned to Sophia. "Good news! Now we celebrate, right? We did it good."

Sophia gave a small smile. "Yes, Mama . . . Why don't I go buy some champagne?"

She left the room and paused at the small table in the hall where Luka had left a note of his address. "You want me to come, too, Aunt Sophia?"

"No, Rosa. I won't be long."

Sophia hurried out, and Rosa went to the table. The note was gone. Graziella patted her shoulder as she passed, heading toward her bedroom. "Rosa, help your mama with the contracts; we've got to sign each one."

"Grandma, did you take Johnny's address from the hall table?"

"No. . . . Did you hear me say to help your mama?"

Rosa walked into the study. "Mama, did you take Johnny's address from the hall stand?"

"No. I'm going to need your signature, Rosa, and Mama's—"

Rosa tapped on Graziella's door and peeked around the door. "I think Sophia's gone to see Johnny. She said she was going to get some champagne, but she's gone to see Johnny."

"Maybe she's gone to tell him the good news."

Rosa shrugged and muttered something about Sophia's getting a bottle of champagne.

"I think celebrations are a little premature."

Graziella watched her granddaughter wander around the room, then sit at the small dressing table. She began picking up brushes and combs and replacing them; then she pulled her hair back from her face and coiled it into a bun like Sophia's. She pursed her lips, watching her reflection in the mirror.

"Sophia's very beautiful, isn't she?"

"Yes . . . You know, when I first saw her, she was a few years younger than you, and so thin, her little face so pinched—"

"I like Johnny, Grandma."

"I think we all do; he's a nice boy, hard worker. That's just what he is, though, Rosa, a worker, understand me? When the day comes for you to find someone, he must be worthy of you because you are all we have left, Rosa. Through you the Luciano line will continue; only you can produce a Luciano family, children. That is the most important thing in the world, children, a son. . . . When the time is right, we will return to Sicily and find you a husband, so don't get ideas about Johnny. Stop them right now."

Rosa leaned over the bed and kissed Graziella's cheek. "Yes, Grandma . . . Good night."

She had no intention of obeying her grandmother. When

she got her share of the money, she could do what she wanted; she would be free.

Sophia paid off the cab and wished she had asked the driver to wait. The rooming house was in a run-down area, just a row of bells by the side of a paint-peeled door. Many of the bells were smashed, and garbage bags and broken bottles littered the steps. She pressed the button for room 18 and waited. She pressed again and heard Johnny's distorted voice asking who was there.

"Just let me in."

The buzzer went two or three times before the lock sprang back. Inside, the dark lobby stank of stale, rotting food and urine. Only one naked bulb lit the stairwell. Sophia began to walk up the dark wooden steps.

By the time she reached the third-floor landing he was waiting for her, smiling his delight. He swung the door to his room open wide, then looked at her in concern.

"Is there a problem? Everything all right?"

She brushed past him. "How did you get those drawings? You'd better tell me."

"Does it matter?"

"Yes, it matters. Don't tell me he just gave them to you because I know he wouldn't. . . . He's dead, he's dead!"

"How do you know?"

"I called his workrooms, I called him, that's why."

"Do you want to sit down?"

"No, I just want you to tell me the truth."

"I also got you this. He signed it, just in case there should be any trouble."

She snatched the single sheet of paper from his hand. "What did you do, Johnny? Tell me!"

He skirted the room with its naked, dim light bulb and single bed, as if cowering from her. Eventually he stood with his back to her, looking out of the grimy window over the fire escape. "I thought you wanted the drawings. I thought that was what you wanted."

The neon lights of a hotel sign outside lit his frame with an eerie, bluish light, off, on, off, on. . . . One moment she could see him clearly; the next he was in shadow. She sat on the edge of the bed, rubbing her hand over the rough gray blanket. "I don't believe this is real. I don't think I am here—"

"It's a dump of a room," he said softly.

"I need a glass of water."

He left the room, and she remained sitting on the bed, patting the blanket. Her head was throbbing. She stared around blankly. His clothes, everything belonging to him were neat and tidy.

He returned, carefully carrying a paper cup. She coughed, and he went to take her hand. She drew away from him.

"Please don't touch me . . . Don't . . ."

He seemed hurt. He lowered his head, pouting.

"Stop playing games, Johnny. Drop your little-boy-lost act. Look at me. . . . Look at me, Johnny, because I want the truth."

He lifted his head. His body swayed slightly, and he suddenly appeared to be very young, younger than his twenty-six years. When he spoke, she could hardly hear him.

"Sophia, don't be nasty to me." His eyes pleaded with her like a bewildered child.

"Did you kill him?"

"Yes."

She tried to put the paper cup down on the bedside table, and it toppled over. The next moment Luka was kneeling at her feet, both arms wrapped around her legs.

She protested, "Please don't do this. Please don't."

He pressed his face against her thighs and shuddered. His arms tightened around her.

"I did it for you, to prove that I was important. When I saw you go off with that man, I had to do something to prove to you. . . . I did it for you."

Sophia eased herself away from him, and he sat back on his heels.

"Do you have anything to drink?" Her tongue felt swollen, and she couldn't swallow.

He leaped up and hurried to the door. "I'll get you some more water."

The moment he moved away she stood up. "No, no, I'll be all right. I have to go. They're waiting for me. . . . I said I was going out for champagne. . . . Barzini called Teresa; he's offered a lot of money. *Please stay away from me, don't come near me!*"

"Shussssh, someone could hear you." He opened the door

a fraction and looked out, then closed it and locked it. "What are you going to do?"

"It doesn't matter what I am going to do."

"Yes, it matters. I did it for you."

She felt her anger rising. "What do you think I can do with the designs now? Do you think I could even contemplate using them after I know what you've done? Don't say it, don't dare say it again. I never asked you to do anything for me—"

His voice was plaintive. "But no one can possibly connect you."

"No? Are you stupid as well as crazy? Won't connect me? I was there, *I was there*! The police will want to question me; the people who work for Nino will notice the designs are missing!"

"But there were hundreds. I didn't take them all."

*"Don't you understand, you've destroyed any chance of my being able to use even one of them!"*

He gestured for her to keep her voice down, and she clenched her hands at her sides. "I could have paid him, understand? I could have bought them legitimately."

He sat on the edge of the bed with his head in his hands. She wanted to hit him, slap his face, kick him. She had never known such blind fury against another human being.

"I should go straight to the police and hand you over. . . . Give them the drawings, let them deal with you, you stupid—"

She paced the room, her anger easing the horror of the situation. She stopped in front of him and pulled his hair to make him look up at her.

"As soon as Barzini pays us, you get out of our lives, or so help me God, I'll tell the police."

It was a hopeless threat. She was cornered, and she knew it. Her freedom, her release from the Lucianos, was disappearing fast.

"It was an accident, Sophia. He started saying things about you, and all I could think of was how you had crawled to him, begging him to help you, and he laughed in your face. He made you vomit in the street; he said you were finished, you could never do anything, you had no talent. He kept on and on, and I told him to stop; but he wouldn't. . . . I swung out, hit him with something from his desk, a statue. . . . I don't know, I don't remember. I didn't mean to kill him; but he deserved it, and I would do it again if I had to, anytime. No one can hurt you, no one. I won't let them."

"You—you took my last chance." Her face crumpled, and she sobbed; but as he stepped toward her, she moved away, went to the door, tried to turn the knob. Frustrated, she turned just as he clasped her to him. She tried to break free, tried to claw at his face, but he twisted her arm behind her back.

"You can have everything again, Sophia. I'm going to give it to you. I love you, I love you."

Her dark eyes showed her contempt. "Your love disgusts me. Now, move away from the door and let me go."

Luka kissed her, a passionate, longing kiss, but she did not respond. He could feel her teeth, her lips. . . . When he broke away, he looked into her angry eyes. They were filled with such hatred that he let go of her shoulders and fumbled in his pocket for the key. She stood directly behind him while he unlocked the door.

As she made her way down the stairs, she wiped her lips with the back of her hand. She knew he was following her, but she didn't turn back. She didn't turn until she reached ground level. Then she looked up to see him staring down the stairwell. The light from the naked bulb behind him encircled his head and shoulders, and at that distance she could not see his expression. He was like a statue, so still, his pale skin and blond hair making him appear ghostly.

Sophia let herself into the apartment. As she closed the door, Rosa appeared.

"Where's the champagne?"

"I—I couldn't find a liquor store open." Sophia passed her, heading for her bedroom.

"You went to see Johnny, didn't you?"

With her hand on the doorknob, Sophia sighed. "Rosa, it's none of your business where I've been."

Rosa flushed with anger. "Are you two lovers?"

"No."

"Don't lie to me. He can't take his eyes off you. What happened in Rome?"

Sophia opened the door. "Nothing, and take my advice, stay away from him."

"Because you want him?"

Sophia slammed the door shut and turned on Rosa. "Don't be childish, and don't be so rude to me. I'll forget it this once, but don't you ever insinuate that there is anything between me and that creature. . . . And I mean it, Rosa, stay away from him."

Rosa turned and ran into her room as Teresa came out of the bathroom.

"What's going on?" she asked Sophia.

"Nothing . . . I just want to go to bed, all right?"

"Fine by me. I just thought you and Rosa were having an argument. No need to snap my head off."

"I'm sorry. . . . Rosa seems to think I am having a thing with Johnny."

"What? Are you serious?"

"Don't let her see too much of him, Teresa. Believe me, I know what I'm talking about. The sooner we get rid of him, the better."

Teresa hesitated, wishing she could agree, but Johnny had bound her to him with the Rocco murder. If she were to anger him, his violence could turn against her, against any one of them.

"Johnny's still useful to us, Sophia, but I'll speak to Rosa."

Breakfast was not a happy affair. No one had much of an appetite for the eggs and sausages Graziella had cooked. They all were too worried about the meeting with Barzini, which would take place in a few hours. The weather outside was freezing, and Sophia, generous as ever, offered one of her furs to whoever needed it.

Rosa pulled a face. "I think it's disgusting walking around with dead animals on you. I don't know how you can. You've got about fifty pelts there; that's fifty hearts, lungs. . . ." Sophia lit a cigarette and said nothing.

The telephone rang, but Teresa waited. "We don't want to look too desperate. I'll answer it." She disappeared into the study.

When she came out, she announced, "We're to meet him at a restaurant called the Four Seasons, at one o'clock sharp. Sophia, would one of your coats fit me?"

"Oh, Mama, how could you?"

"Quite easily, Rosa, I'm not going to freeze."

Barzini and the three women sat at his table at the Four Seasons restaurant. They ordered; Barzini was a genial host, refusing to discuss business until lunch was over. He seemed to be a regular customer, acknowledging other diners and being on first-name terms with the waiters.

The women were very formal, fearful, and hardly able to touch their food. Every person Barzini called to seemed a threat, and when he reached over to grip Sophia's hand, she shrank back.

"You are very beautiful, I am honored, but I am puzzled. . . ."

They waited. Rosa's leg, beneath the table, pressed against her mother's. She hated the way his small hands were never still, the way his eyes flicked from one woman to another.

"Where is Signora Luciano? I was looking forward to meeting her again."

"Mama is feeling unwell, Mr. Barzini. She asked me to send you her very best wishes and her apologies."

"No apologies needed. She must be tired. She is staying with you, Teresa? I may call you Teresa?"

"*Sì*, please. We all are staying at my apartment."

He nodded, then touched Rosa's hand. It shook beneath his fluttering little pats. "Good. You see, as I promised, I will ensure you are protected. You must trust me, these are dangerous times, and it is good that you are together, a family, no?"

It felt as if the luncheon would never end, that Barzini would never broach the subject, the entire reason for the meeting. But when coffee was served, he rested his manicured, small hands on the white linen cloth and, looking from one to the next, said quietly, "To business . . ."

Barzini agreed to pay the women in the form of a bank draft, which would be delivered to them within twenty-four hours. In exchange, he would receive the documents relating to all the Luciano holdings in Palermo plus named companies in New York. Satisfied that the meeting had reached its conclusion amicably, with all parties in agreement, the diminutive Barzini hailed a taxi outside the restaurant for their departure.

Sophia was very much aware that he had not mentioned the names of any of the parties involved in the buyout.

Graziella used the women's absence to speak to Luka in private. She busied herself in the kitchen, brewing fresh coffee. Then she called him in. "Please sit down, sit. . . . Now we have no one overhearing us, eh? So now, Johnny, I want to talk to you about Rosa."

He looked surprised. "Rosa?"

"She's very young, and I think she has a liking for you, a crush, as we used to call it in my day. I'm sure you understand what I mean."

"I didn't know."

Graziella smiled. "Maybe not, but I want to make sure that you do not encourage her in any way. You see, Rosa must make a good marriage; we are dependent on her, you understand. Only Rosa can carry the Luciano blood. . . . Only through Rosa can our family survive."

"I have hardly spoken to her."

"But you have become very close to all of us. We appreciate all you have done; I know Teresa has promised you a percentage, and rightly so, but when this is over—pray God, today we will know—but when this is over, Johnny, I think you should get on with your own life. We must; Rosa must. We have to find a suitable marriage. She is a Luciano, you understand? You are a young man; she believes you mean more to her than you do. This must not happen, understand me, Johnny?"

Graziella brushed his cheek with her hand, and he caught it, kissed it.

"I just want to stay with you all. I want to work for you."

She smiled at him affectionately, pinched his chin. "How old are you, Johnny? Twenty-one, twenty-two? How old?"

He swallowed. "I'm twenty-six."

"Oh, so young, but old enough to want to marry and settle down? You got someone special, Johnny?"

"No, I have no one . . . except all of you."

"Then it is time you thought about your life, too. You don't want to be always surrounded by women, and you're too clever to want to be just a driver, huh? You will have money, you make a career for yourself, yes?

He rested his head on his arms. She touched his hair softly. "What of your family? Rosa says you have a brother. Is that right?" She continued to stroke his blond hair. He lifted his head, and she let her hand fall back in her lap.

He pushed his chair back and smiled his soft, intimate smile. Then he rose to his feet.

"I'll drop by later. I have to collect something for Teresa."

Graziella heard the front door close behind him, but she was staring at her hand; her fingers tingled, as if she could still feel the soft silkiness of his hair. She sighed, a long, deep sigh. . . .

Slowly she got up and went to her bedroom. She opened the dressing-table drawer and took out the photograph of Michael. As she stared at it, she could see him clearly, sitting at the old dining-room table, leaning close to Roberto, smiling once more that beautiful smile. . . .

She heard the key turn in the front door and quickly replaced the photo, telling herself she was being foolish.

Rosa was carrying two grocery bags full to the brim. "This is going to be a great Christmas, Grandma. We got everything you can think of . . . turkey and all the fixings. . . ." She dumped the bags on the small table in the hallway and swept Graziella into her arms.

Sophia said nothing, walking straight into the bedroom, and Teresa stared after her.

It was just after four o'clock when the doorbell rang. Graziella was carrying a tray into the dining room. Rosa was in the bathroom washing her hair, and Sophia was still in her bedroom. The bell rang again, and Teresa opened the door wide.

Three men in hideous masks pushed the door so hard that it caught her shoulder and she fell back. The next moment she felt her hair gripped, almost torn from her head, and a gun against her neck.

"Keep your mouth shut and walk . . . move. . . . Get the others."

Graziella came to the kitchen door, and one of the men dragged her out to join Teresa in the hall. When Graziella struggled, he knocked her over. As she fell, screaming, Sophia hurried into the corridor.

"Shut up and put your hands above your head an' you won't get hurt." The man's voice was distorted by a rubber wizard mask with a terrible long nose and wobbling, crooked chin, the whole disgusting thing covered in warts.

Sophia made the mistake of screaming for Rosa. The gun hit her on the right temple, and she fell face forward at Graziella's feet. Teresa was still being dragged along the corridor, hauled so roughly by her hair that her legs went out from beneath her.

"Please, don't hurt us, please . . ."

They were herded at gunpoint into the study. Rosa, still in the bathroom, could hear the screams. Terrified, she dropped the hair dryer, locked the bathroom door and ran toward the fire escape. As she raised the window, she heard shots fired, dull, thwacking noises from a silencer, which split the lock and blew the door open. Hysterical with fear, Rosa hunched against the window, and the man wearing the grotesque clown's mask reached down and dragged her into the study, where he rolled her toward Sophia. She clung to Sophia, while blood streamed down her aunt's face.

The man in the wizard mask trained his gun on them and backed away. "Now keep nice and quiet and nobody will get hurt. You, come here."

He yanked Teresa toward the desk, and her hip banged against the corner.

"We want the papers. Hand them over."

Teresa clutched the edge of the desk. "What papers?"

The wizard backhanded her. "You know, bitch, you know. Now get on your knees. . . . *On your fucking knees!*"

He twisted her arm behind her back, and she sank to the floor. Rosa started to scream and was kicked in the stomach so hard that she retched as she buckled over. The clown took some rags from his pocket and sat on Rosa to tie her hands behind her back. Then he made her kneel beside her mother.

The wizard was pulling out drawers, sifting through the papers. "You know what we want. Don't waste any more time. *Where are they?*"

Weeping, Teresa shook her head. "I don't know what you want. What papers? There's nothing here—"

Rosa shrank back in fear as the third man, wearing a rub-

ber mask with long strands of white hair dangling from the
chin, grabbed her arm. He shook her and shouted, "Tell her to
give us what we fucking want! *Tell her*!" He smashed her head
against the desk, catching her just above her right eye, and she
screamed.

Graziella had been cowering against the wall, holding tightly
to Sophia's hand, but hearing Rosa's screams was too much.
She hurled herself at the man, trying to grab his mask from his
face.

"Don't hurt her! You leave her alone. What kind of man
are you to fight women—"

The clown pushed Graziella away, kicking out at her as
she stumbled. Rosa was sobbing, pleading: "Oh, God, Mama,
give them what they want, please. . . . Mama . . ."

The wizard laughed and gestured to Teresa. "Hear what
she says, huh? Come on, do what your daughter says. You
wanna see her face cut?"

Sophia had to hold Graziella back as the old lady was about
to let fly again. "Teresa, do what he says. Give them what they
want. . . . *Do it!*"

About to ring the doorbell, Luka paused. He had noticed
that the lock was not quite caught. He inched the door open
just as Rosa screamed.

The sound had come from the study. Opening his jacket,
he took out a gun. Now he could hear Graziella. He moved
silently to check out the other rooms, until he was certain they
all were in the study. Then he backtracked down the corridor,
into the bathroom and out onto the fire escape. He followed the
fire escape around the corner to the study window. He flattened himself against the wall and peered through the blind.

Teresa, a gun at her head, was being forced around the
desk. Rosa still knelt in front of the desk. Sophia stood at the
far end of the room with her arms around Graziella. All three
men had their backs to the window. . . .

Luka inched forward a fraction. Sophia and Graziella were
standing to his left; Rosa, tied up, was still on her knees in
front of the desk, sobbing uncontrollably. Teresa, terrified, her
hands shaking, was passing documents to the man in the wizard
mask. He held a gun to Rosa's head.

The clown stood by the study door, a gun in his right hand. The third man appeared to have no weapon; he was sifting through the documents as Teresa passed them over. Part of his rubber mask, the white, trailing beard, had been torn.

Twice Luka took aim on the wizard, but Teresa was in his way. Then the moment came; Rosa, sobbing, cowered lower behind the desk. Teresa bent down to sign a document, and the wizard was in the clear. Luka fired.

The wizard lurched forward, the bullet blowing the back of his head open. He fell, sending the documents flying, his blood spraying the room, covering Teresa. The gun went spinning from his hand. Teresa picked it up, held it in both hands, and fired.

The bullet caught the clown in the right upper arm, and he lost his balance, falling backward. Teresa shouted to Sophia to get his gun, but Sophia had turned to the window, having no notion who was outside.

"*It's me!*" Luka screamed, frantically kicking out the jagged glass, jumping into the room because the man with the white, trailing beard had reached his friend's weapon. The bearded one's fingers touched the metal as Luka fired. The bullet clipped him in the upper thigh. His fingers froze, and he buckled over in agony.

Graziella untied Rosa and dragged her beneath the desk for safety. Luka drew Sophia to his side and gave his gun to her. "Keep it on them. If they move, shoot."

Sophia held the gun while Luka forced the two wounded men to lie facedown on the floor. He kicked the clown so hard in the groin that he howled. The man with the white beard, now splattered with blood, lifted his hands above his head.

"Don't shoot! Don't shoot!"

Luka ordered Rosa to crawl out from beneath the desk. "Gimme the ropes . . . rags, whatever they brought. Lemme get their hands tied."

Graziella moved cautiously around the desk. Her feet crunched on broken glass as she leaned over the wizard, sprawled on the desk. She touched his hand, feeling for a pulse. There was blood everywhere, covering the desktop, splashed on the documents. She gasped to Teresa, "He's dead!"

Teresa stood as if unable to move, both hands still holding

the gun, her eyes wide and staring. Graziella reached out to touch her; her daughter-in-law was rigid and seemed not to hear her name. All she could do was stare at the gun in her hand. Her face and dress were covered in blood. Slowly she began to pant. Then she gasped, "Oh, God, Mama! Oh, my God, Rosa . . . Where's Rosa?" Her voice was a high-pitched shriek. "Oh, Mama, what have I done? What have we done?"

Luka finished tying the second man, then took Rosa by the shoulders. She looked at him with scared eyes, her face streaked with blood, and was about to start screaming—he knew it.

"Rosa, come on! Take Graziella out of here, will you do that?"

She nodded, her eyes flicking around the room and back to Luka.

Graziella led her out of the room. "You come with Grandma, Rosa, there's a good girl." The old lady was shaking with fear.

Luka took his gun from Sophia and stuffed it into his belt. Sophia reached for Teresa's hand.

Tears streamed down Teresa's face, and she was saying over and over again, "I don't know what to do, I don't know what to do. . . ."

Luka snapped at her, "Well, we had better start thinking. Sophia, get some water, bandages, old sheets, anything, These two are bleeding all over the carpet."

Sophia held Teresa, and they both looked at Luka. Teresa's voice was little more than a whisper. "Oh, God, what are we going to do?"

Luka held up one of the documents. "They came for these. First we find out who sent them, and if you don't like what I have to do to find out, then both of you can get out."

Sophia tried to draw Teresa toward the door, but she wouldn't be moved. Luka stepped closer. "We need bandages, get anything to see to their wounds. Sophia, will you do that? I'll take care of Teresa."

Suddenly he clasped Sophia's face between his hands. "You see how much you need me, all of you need me? Now you can trust me; you have to trust me."

There was a chilling ruthlessness in the way he snapped out instructions, as if he were enjoying their dependency.

They huddled in the kitchen, leaving him alone in the study.

They were beyond tears; they sat in mute silence, waiting. Their fear held them together, united them, until Sophia couldn't stand it another second.

"We knew this could happen. So much for Barzini protecting us; they must have been sent from Sicily. We could have this for the rest of our lives. . . . We stop it, now, stop it from going any further. We give them whatever they want. I can't take any more of this."

Luka stood at the kitchen door. Startled, frightened faces turned towards him.

"The dead man is Michele Barzini's cousin, Harry Barzini. He works for Barzini. The other two work as driver and bodyguard. They say no one else is involved except Barzini; he was trying to keep all the deeds, all the money for himself. So you can breathe easy; they didn't come from Sicily."

Teresa was up and out of the room. She ran to the study, kicked open the door. All her fear, her shock had turned to anger. She went into the study and picked up the clown's mask. Before anyone could stop her she was kicking and dragging at the clown to force him into a kneeling position beside the desk.

"You made my daughter kneel, you do it now. You kneel. . . . *Kneel*! And tell me what Barzini told you to do to us. You tell me!"

Rosa followed her mother and saw the terrified man weeping as Teresa pulled at his hair.

The dead man had been shoved from the desk and lay facedown on the floor, his wizard's mask filled with his own blood. Rosa kicked at the bearded man. . . . His eyes rolled in his head.

Luka looked on with interest. The tables were turned; how far would the women go to get their answers, to rid themselves of their pent-up terror? But his speculation was interrupted by Graziella.

"Teresa, Rosa! Stop! Sophia and I have decided, we will go to the police. These men broke into our apartment, so we get the police. It's finished, and you, Johnny— We listen to you, take orders from you, but enough is enough—"

Teresa's face was red with fury. "No, Mama, no! We go to the police and we lose everything."

"There is nothing else to lose, Teresa. We cannot fight

these people; they are animals. And look at you, you behave like an animal; you make your daughter behave like one. I say enough."

Teresa clenched her fists. "You don't have the right to do that, Mama!"

Sophia came into the room. "She has every right. This has gone far enough. I want no part of it."

"You never did, Sophia. You have been against everything I have tried to do from the beginning."

"Now you see why! Look, Teresa, look at this room. There's blood on the walls, on our clothes, over your daughter's face! For God's sake, Teresa, face reality. This time we were lucky, but what happens next time? What happens when Johnny is not around?"

Luka tried to reach out to her. "I'll always be around."

Sophia pushed his hand away. "Stay out of this, Johnny, or so help me God, I'll tell them the truth about you. You go, get out, go away from us!"

"I just saved your life! Is this the thanks I get? You think they would have taken the deeds and just pissed off?"

Teresa was trembling with anger. "Listen to me, Sophia, just listen. If Barzini has the money—"

Luka nodded. "He's got it. Sophia, Barzini has the bank draft to pay you off. He got greedy; his gamble didn't come off, but he's on his own. No one else is in on this."

Sophia turned on Teresa. "You think you can trust what these men say, what Johnny says? Can't you see what is happening to us? Look at us now, standing here in this room, men tied up, one dead . . . and we are *arguing*! It's madness!"

Luka ripped the gag from Barzini's driver's mouth, gripped him by the hair, and yanked his head up. "Tell them!"

The man stuttered with fear, his eyes on Luka. "Peter Salerno got the bank draft, I swear on my life. He gave it to Barzini. I heard them saying it was to pay you off. I swear . . . Oh, Jesus Christ, I swear on my kid's life, I am telling you the truth! Barzini's got the dough; he was just trying it on—"

Luka looked at Sophia. She turned away. He jerked the man's head up again. "Tell them what Barzini told you to do."

The man started to cry. "He said you wouldn't cause trouble. We was to scare you, just frighten you off so you wouldn't talk, make it look like a break-in."

Luka pulled again. Tufts of the man's hair were coming away in his fingers. "What else?"

"He said Luciano was scum, he acted as a witness, so anything we did to his women would be okay, no one would help them."

Luka shoved him away in disgust and looked at Sophia. "Barzini thinks he's in the clear, he's alone in the apartment." He kicked the man at his feet. "He's alone, yeah? *Yeah?*" The man nodded and rolled back in agony.

Getting no response from Sophia, Luka turned to Graziella. "We can get straight to him, walk right up to his door. Borrow these punk masks, so if he looks through his peephole, he thinks he's seeing his friends."

Graziella shook her head. "We Lucianos will decide what to do. Johnny, you stay with the men. . . ."

They sat together in the kitchen as Teresa pressed for a confrontation with Barzini.

"We can get the layout of the entire apartment, if necessary, and if Barzini is alone, why not? We wear the masks, like Johnny suggested, to get in. Sophia, please . . . At least talk to Barzini, give him the chance to hand over the money. I think we should take Johnny with us."

Sophia shook her head. "No, if we do this, it's just us, with one of those men's guns—for our own protection. Nothing else, Teresa, understand? And if we have trouble, we get out, and for good, agreed?"

For a moment no one spoke. Teresa pursed her lips. "It'll work. It has to. Mama, do you want to come?"

Graziella looked first at Sophia, then Rosa, and slowly nodded her head. "I will go. I want to speak to this man face-to-face! Then after, we do the right thing, what Sophia suggests."

Teresa rose from the table. "So it's all agreed, no police? Not yet anyway. I'll tell Johnny."

Luka sat kicking his heels against the edge of the desk. Teresa entered the study door and closed it behind her.

"No police, we'll go to see Barzini."

"Yeah? Just like that, huh? Well, first, what are you going to do with this guy with his head blown off? And these two, bleeding to death over your carpet? What are you going to do about cleaning this place up? The walls need washing down, carpets, desk. . . ."

Teresa nodded. "I'll get the others."

"No, wait. First let me work out what we're going to do with these guys."

"Don't they need to go to the hospital?"

He looked at her, his head to one side. "Yeah, I'll arrange it. First we get the body out." He bent down to one of the men. "We'll get you to a hospital. You got transportation? You come in a car?"

The man nodded, his eyes popping out of his head because of the gag still stuffed in his mouth.

"Okay, they got their own transportation. Rosa, see if you can borrow that old lady's wheelchair, the one from the floor above, and I'll get the dead guy ready to leave."

"What do you want the wheelchair for?"

"He's a big man, you want to be seen carrying him? Just do what I tell you, and get a move on!"

As soon as the door closed behind her, Luka moved around the desk, heaved at the body. The wizard mask was still in place, still bloody. But the man's clothes were in disarray, his shirt open, his trousers loose. Luka smiled at the two terrified men.

"Better get him all tidied up. Don't want to upset the ladies, do we?"

The two men watched in mute, terrified silence as Luka dressed Harry Barzini's body.

The women looked at drawings of Barzini's apartment, made by Luka from a description by one of the captives. They knew now which room was his wife's and that she went to bed early.

Rosa returned with the wheelchair. Luka had the body ready. It was covered by a blanket, a scarf around the neck and lower face, and one of Filippo's hats crammed on the bloody head. Luka, Rosa, and Teresa lifted the corpse into the wheelchair.

"No one goes into the study. Stay away from the men until I come back. Teresa, check if there's anyone downstairs. Rosa, you guide from the front, I'll take the weight from behind. I'll dump him in an alley a few blocks away; we'll have to get rid of the clothes we put on him, we don't want anything traced back here. Okay, Rosa, let's go!"

Teresa went ahead to check out the stairs while Rosa and Luka heaved the dead weight into the chair. Then Rosa stood outside the apartment building and watched Luka wheel the chair down the street. It was almost six o'clock, rush hour, and people crowded the sidewalks, but Luka seemed self-assured, almost cocky. After half a block he turned back to see if Rosa had gone inside, then made a U-turn and headed back almost to the entrance of the apartment building. He wheeled the chair down the ramp into the underground garage. He passed a few residents; but there were cars reversing and parking, and no one paid him much attention.

He passed Teresa's Lincoln, then stopped by a new silver Lincoln Continental. Barzini's car.

Luka rang the bell and waited. Rosa opened the door, and he tapped her on the cheek.

"You must always ask who's at the door, Rosa! Now, go over this chair for any blood. I'll need the hat and scarf again for the next man."

Teresa was in her robe. She had put all her bloodstained clothes into a garbage bag.

"Where did you put him?"

About to go into the study, Luka paused and smiled. "Like I said, in an alley. Forget it. Come help me get this guy ready to go down to their car."

At six-forty Luka guided the bearded man down the stairs. The overcoat was draped over his shoulders to hide the fact that his hands were still bound behind his back, and he wore the hat and scarf to disguise that he was gagged. Luka spoke quietly, encouraging the man to hurry, telling him the sooner he was in the car and waiting, the sooner his friend could join him and they would be taken to the hospital. The man was in agony, limping badly, and he leaned heavily on Luka.

The man was panting, his breath hissing through his gag,

when Luka finally helped him into the backseat of the Lincoln. When he was settled, Luka leaned in and smiled.

"Everything'll be okay, but I need your hat." As Luka reached for it, he fired a single shot to the man's temple, using the man's own gun and silencer. Then he propped up the body and returned for the clown. Luka draped him in the coat and scarf, put the hat on his head. The man's arm was streaming blood, it ran in rivulets down his fingers, and he sobbed in agony as he was hustled out of the apartment.

It was now seven-fifteen. Luka told the women he was taking the two men to a hospital. While he was gone, the women worked at cleaning the study, washing the walls, rolling up the stained rug. All bloodstained clothes had to be discarded, so they stuffed everything into black bags, ready for Luka to carry to the incinerator in the basement.

But four hours later Luka had still not returned. There was nothing else for them to do; even the wheelchair had been taken back. The women's nerves were at the breaking point.

Teresa paced up and down the hall. She was sure something had gone wrong. Perhaps the men had escaped. Four hours!

Sophia sipped a cup of coffee and checked her watch for the hundredth time. She had been on the point of telling them about Luka's part in Nino Fabio's death, but had not, because if Michele Barzini did have their money, they could pay Luka off and get rid of him. Then she could find her own freedom.

"It's eleven-thirty, Teresa. Barzini might have gone out. Or he could be halfway to Tokyo. Where did Johnny say he was going?"

Teresa gasped. "Oh, my God! You don't think he could have gone to Barzini's alone?"

Graziella, wearing her hat and coat, stood at her bedroom door. "What are we waiting for? Are we going to Barzini or not? I've had my coat on for an hour."

"We're waiting for Johnny, Mama."

"Why? You said we go alone. So why don't we go?"

At that moment Luka knocked on the door and called to them to open up. He had changed into a clean shirt and jeans, and he handed Teresa a black bag containing his stained clothes, together with the hat and coat they had used. He made no apology for keeping them waiting but suggested they get into the car while he took all the bags down to the incinerator.

They were ready to leave when Luka swore. The garbage bag containing the carpet had begun to split. Teresa stayed behind to help him while the others went on down to the garage. Together they tried to stuff the bloody carpet into a spare bag Luka had brought with him.

"Johnny, we're going to need another one. They're in the kitchen, under the sink."

She tipped out the contents of the bag Luka had brought and found his shirt, drenched in blood. Her hands were covered in it. . . . She opened the bag further; his jeans and sneakers were also caked with blood. She looked up at him in horror as he came back with the fresh bag.

"What have you done? Johnny?"

"Go wash your hands. I'll take this down to the incinerator and see you at the car. Oh, I got you this: It's a simple mechanism, just withdraw the safety catch, and it's ready to fire. It's loaded, so don't mess around with it. Just put it in your purse."

She grabbed the .22 and hurried into the bathroom, leaned against the door. Her hands were stained with blood, and the gun felt slimy to the touch. Gritting her teeth, she forced herself to wipe it clean, then scrubbed her hands nearly raw under the running water.

She took a last look around the apartment to make sure it was clean. Only the shattered window gave any indication of the nightmare that had taken place. She collected her purse and the gun, then locked the front door and hurried down the stairs.

As she reached the basement door, she could hear someone whistling. She paused, then crept closer, panting. . . .

It was Luka, seeming totally unconcerned. He stopped whistling when he saw her, smiled, and opened the door with a flourish. All she could think of was the bloody shirt, the stained jeans, the sneakers caked with blood. Were the murders never to end? She swayed, gulped for air, and was about to faint when Luka clasped her elbow. His fingers pinched, hurting her.

"I did what had to be done. Now straighten up, pull yourself together, okay? Okay now?"

She nodded, and he slowly released his hold. They went on into the garage.

\*  \*  \*

It was eleven forty-five as they drove away from the apartment. Teresa sat up front with Luka, who was at the wheel. In the backseat sat Graziella and Sophia, with Rosa between them. They held the mask of the clown and the torn one with the wispy beard.

Luka drove carefully, unhurriedly. Teresa could feel the outline of the gun in her bag, and slowly, gradually, the terrible feeling of panic subsided. The gun comforted her, gave her confidence.

Luka, after a sidelong glance, reached out to stroke her hand. "Okay?" he whispered, and she nodded.

"We're here." Luka pulled on the parking brake and was out before the uniformed doorman had time to step forward.

Teresa turned to the backseat. "Hide the masks under your coats. Are we ready?"

They nodded, and the passenger door swung open. Sophia stepped out first, followed by Rosa. Then Luka helped Graziella. Closing the door, he turned to Teresa. "You sure you don't want me to come with you?"

"Stay with the car!"

The four well-dressed women merged easily with the many people thronging the reception area. They separated as they approached the elevators.

They made it to the door of the suite without seeing anyone. As Rosa pressed the buzzer, Graziella and Sophia put on the masks. Teresa, a fraction behind them because some of the wispy gray hair on her mask had caught on her handbag, jerked it free and only just had time to get the mask in place before they heard the lock on the door click.

Barzini peered through the peephole, and they could hear him swearing at them for being so fucking stupid. Then he swung the door wide. Before Teresa could even start her well-rehearsed speech, Graziella began a tirade in Sicilian.

Barzini was so startled that he stumbled backward and overturned a small Venetian urn. The floral display cascaded over the floor.

Teresa moved Graziella firmly aside. "Good evening, Mr. Barzini."

She ripped off her mask and threw it at him. Sophia closed the door and put the chain on it. Her hand was shaking so much that twice she missed the small aperture.

Teresa watched Barzini squirm as he tried to assimilate what had happened.

Rosa cut the telephone wires and replaced the scissors in her bag. She then followed her mother and aunt into the living room.

Graziella went in the opposite direction, looking for Barzini's wife. She locked the bedroom door from the outside, then returned to the living room and held up the key.

She sat on the sofa, and her appearance gave Barzini some hope. "Come on, girls," he said, "I don't know what these men told you, but—" He still had the mask in his hand. He tossed it aside.

Teresa put a hand on his shoulder. "Pay us off, Mr. Barzini, and you won't get hurt."

He shrugged again. "Is this some kinda sick joke?"

She grabbed him by the hair. "You give us the bank draft, and we leave."

"I swear I don't know what you're talking about. I don't know what this is all about. Now why don't I get you ladies a drink and we can talk about this?"

Teresa bent down and whispered to Rosa to give her the scissors. Rosa slipped them from her bag as Barzini turned his attention to Sophia, declaring that he knew nothing about the men who attacked them. Sophia asked how he knew they had been attacked, and his eyes rolled frantically as he pointed out that they had bruises and Sophia had a bad cut.

Teresa was at his side, and as he looked around to see what she was doing, she snipped at the lobe of his ear with the scissors. He screeched and backed away, his hand to his ear.

"What the fuck! Are you crazy?" Blood trickled down his hand, and he took out a white handkerchief, pressed it on the wound.

"We just want the bank draft, Mr. Barzini."

"Jesus Christ, you cut my ear, you cut my fucking ear!"

Teresa gestured to Sophia, who got up and went to Barzini's desk. She began to pull the drawers out and tip the contents on the floor.

Barzini turned on her in fury. "You leave those alone. Don't touch anything—"

Teresa opened her bag and took out the gun. He stood

helplessly watching, dabbing at his ear with the handkerchief. "I can't believe you women could be so stupid! You know what you're doing? You think you'll get away with this, think I make the decisions? I got partners."

"We know you do, Mr. Barzini. Did you ever think that we might have, too? And we're not taking anything that your partners weren't prepared to give."

Teresa handed the gun to Rosa and joined Sophia in searching through Barzini's papers. She picked up a small book and flicked through it.

Barzini moved to the desk to try to take it. "You crazy bitches!"

With both hands shaking, Rosa pointed the gun straight at him. He froze, afraid to move even a step, while Teresa flipped through the book.

When she spoke again, her voice was very calm. "Empty your pockets."

Barzini took off his jacket and flung it aside. "I tell you, you're making a mistake. Believe me, this doesn't stop here."

Teresa searched the pockets of his jacket and opened his wallet. She took out a folded white envelope, and just by the look on his face knew she had found it. The draft was for fifteen million dollars, but it was made out to Barzini.

"You get the documents when you've cashed this draft. That was a nice restaurant you took us to; book another table there, say, one o'clock tomorrow. We don't want any drafts, just the cash, and in return you'll get exactly what we agreed to. If you don't turn up—"

Suddenly Teresa had lost it. What if he didn't turn up? What if he cashed the draft himself and took off?

Graziella rose from the sofa and walked sedately toward Barzini. "If we do not receive the money, we will ask for a meeting with my husband's associates. We will tell them of our treatment. We will tell them, do you understand? You made a grave error of judgment. Do not believe we are alone."

As they walked out of the hotel, Luka was already opening the door for Graziella.

They were still describing to Luka what had been said and who had done what to whom when they let themselves into the apartment.

Luka asked to speak to Teresa alone. They went to the study and closed the door.

"How do you know he'll stick to the bargain now?" he demanded.

"We couldn't do anything else; the draft was in his name."

"There're all-night banks. . . . You shouldn't have walked out. I told you to take me in with you. You fucked up. You could get every one of those women hit, you know that, don't you?"

Teresa felt her legs shaking. Luka leaned close, but his eyes were so pale and dead that she backed away from him.

"You needed me. He had to be scared, understand? You have to put the fear of God in him. You needed me. Why won't you trust me? I saved your life, all your lives, for chrissake."

Teresa clutched the desktop to give her strength. "And we' saved yours, so I guess we're quits. You're going to get a slice of the fifteen million, and you've earned it. But then what happens? What happens next, Johnny? Are we going to live under the threat of blackmail? Is that what we can expect?"

"Has Sophia been talking to you?" Teresa shook her head, and he went on. "Then why? Why are you turning against me? I don't understand. You need me."

She gave him a hard look and adjusted her glasses. "How come you know so much, Johnny? You're just a kid, and we keep on trusting you, but we know nothing about you and . . . you made us accessories to murder."

He lifted his hands in a gesture of amazement. "You know why I had to do that! What did you want me to do then? Run? Why won't you admit I saved your lives?"

Teresa sighed. "I know, I know. . . . But it's all getting out of control, Johnny. I keep listening to you, but—"

He was sitting on the edge of the desk, swinging his foot. "Reason I know so much is that I was a runner, you know, a messenger boy. I kept my eyes and ears open. My father was small-time, but part of the mob. I was running messages before I was thirteen, cleaning the cars, that kind of thing. But because I could keep my mouth shut, they liked me."

Teresa took her glasses off. " 'They,' Johnny? Exactly who?"

"Well, sometimes it was the Gennaro family, and they kind of passed me around. They shipped me out to Sicily almost a year ago. I was supposed to be a courier, you know, bring stuff back for them. By then my father was dead. I was in deep trouble over the Dante thing; I mean, I can't go back, I blew it, they'd have me shot. It was heroin, I told you, and so without you I wouldn't have stood a chance of getting out of Sicily. I guess I need you! So, *you* hire me now, I work for you. You own me because if you wanted, you could turn me in at any time."

"That works both ways, Johnny."

"Right, but I don't want to take over. I'll take whatever orders you give me. I want to work for you; you've become my family. I've got nobody else."

Sophia walked in, and he turned. She leaned against the doorframe. "It's two in the morning. I think we all should get some rest. I think Johnny should leave."

Luka was off the edge of the desk fast. He didn't look at Sophia, just muttered that he could come back to drive them to the meeting with Barzini.

"I'll walk you down, Johnny. I need some air," Teresa said.

Sophia watched them standing in the street below. She closed the curtain and turned to Graziella. "Do you have any pills? I've run out."

Graziella opened her bedside drawer and held out the bottle. As Sophia reached for it, she saw Michael's photograph.

"He was your favorite, wasn't he?"

Graziella closed her eyes. "He filled my soul and broke my heart. They always say the firstborn is the one, the one that touches you most, lives inside you more than the others. Maybe because the first one is so frightening and so wonderful—"

She stopped. Sophia had left the room.

Sophia poured a glass full of whiskey, then sat at the kitchen table. She took the first pill, then a second, and felt a hand on her shoulder. Graziella took the pill bottle, carefully screwed the cap back on, then pulled out a chair and sat down, reaching for Sophia's hands, but she could think of no words of comfort for her daughter-in-law.

"I want to sleep, Mama, and never wake up. I don't think I can take any more. It's as if we're caught in madness."

Graziella sighed. "Yes, sometimes I lie awake, and it is as if I am in a different world."

Sophia reached for her hand. "Mama, there is something I have never told you. You remember that night when Filippo brought me to the villa after the accident? I had come to Palermo from Cafalù because—"

She stopped because Rosa had appeared in the doorway.

"Where's Mama?" she asked. Her face was drawn and pale. Graziella patted her knee, and Rosa climbed on it like a little girl and buried her face in her grandmother's shoulder.

"Grandmama, I am so glad you are here."

Graziella smiled. "You know, I guess we all are hungry." She kissed Rosa's cheek.

"You know what day it is today? Grandmama? It's Christmas Day."

Rosa felt her grandmother's arms tighten around her, and she snuggled closer.

"You know, Rosa, Christmas at the villa used to be so special. We would put lights all over the big tree, you know, the one by the kitchen garden? Full of lights, and Papa would climb to the top and put up the holy saints that the children from the local school made specially each year. And when the boys were little, after we checked to see they were asleep, we would creep out and hang up their stockings. Only they weren't real stockings but old pillowcases with the boys' names printed on them in big red letters. Michael, Constantino, Filippo. I would put Papa's gifts underneath the tree, but never, never did he put one there for me, no! He would hide it, like I was a little girl. Sometimes it was under my pillow, sometimes in the pocket of my robe, and once I found it under my napkin at breakfast, a string of pearls. Oh, Rosa, each one perfect, each one chosen by Papa. Years and years he had waited because to find pearls the same size, the same color is very, very difficult. There was one for each year of our life together, one for each of my sons. . . ."

"Can I see them, Grandma?"

Graziella whispered, "They're gone, Rosa, all gone."

"I will buy you some more."

"Some things, Rosa, you cannot buy. Mama just put it into words." Sophia gave the sweetest of smiles; it was that smile that had touched Graziella's heart the day Sophia had been carried into the villa. Now it touched her again, because all the sadness and the madness surrounding them had not destroyed the sweetness in Sophia's soul.

Sophia knew then that she could not, would not ever tell Graziella about Michael's child; it was too late.

Teresa wrapped Sophia's coat around her. Luka tucked his hand under her arm.

"You should go back!"

"No, I couldn't sleep. Besides, I wanted to talk to you. You're a strange boy, and sometimes you scare me. I trust you, then I don't, but I want to trust you, Johnny, because—"

They stopped, and Luka drew the collar of the fur coat closer to her neck, protecting her from the cold night air. It was a comforting, kindly gesture. He cupped her face in his hands. "Teresa, you mistrust me because you, and only you, know what had to be done. But you know that I can take care of you, all of you. In every family there has to be one to protect you; that is all I have ever done."

They had walked all the way to the trucking company. It was still locked and barred, with lethal-looking wires threaded over the tops of the walls.

"This is where my husband used to work. It's the only part of our business that I didn't include in the sellout. I also kept the leasing rights to Pier 3 at the docks. It's one of the biggest."

Luka looked up at the unlit warehouses and shoved his hands deeper in his pockets, feeling the cold himself.

Teresa smiled. "I want to plow my share of the money into starting this place up again. I need help, of course, people I can trust."

Luka stamped his feet, feeling really cold now. "How are you going to find these people? For starters, you'll have the unions on your back."

She wasn't listening to him but was looking up at the huge warehouse doors. "This is where all the gasoline used to be brought. The Lucianos were paid a percentage of every gallon they sold. Did you know that? They had so many fake companies it was a full-time job just keeping track of the names.

Old Papa Luciano was always going on about his legitimacy, but I know for sure that he made millions out of the gasoline scams."

Luka cocked his head to one side, looking at her hunched in the cold, her thin nose red. He was touched by her earnestness.

"You want the Lucianos back in business, is that it?"

She nodded, looking down at her shoe, and kicked at the street. "I need to know who Barzini's partners are, if they are American or Sicilian, what business they're in. Could you find out?"

Luka had not the faintest idea of how to go about it, but he said, "Sure, I'll find out for you. Go on home, Teresa, I'll take care of it."

Exhausted, Teresa climbed the stairs. She hoped they all would be sleeping; she couldn't face any further arguments.

She heard them as she turned onto their landing. At first the high-pitched wail frightened her. Then she listened in disbelief as the three voices, off-key, warbled together, "*Adeste, fideles.* . . ."

# 20

Commissario Pirelli spent Christmas in Milan, and it was the worst Christmas he had ever had. The investigation into the murder of the Paluso child had, to all intents and purposes, been forced to end. It had to be admitted that Luka Carolla had probably left Italy. There had been no fresh evidence for six weeks, no further sightings. The judge in overall charge of the case decreed that Carolla would remain on the wanted list, with the right of extradition if he was found in the United States. The case, as with hundreds of other Mafia-linked cases, would remain open on file.

Pirelli, with his wife, Lisa, and son, Gino, had returned to Milan on Christmas Eve. They had shopped for a tree and gifts. When they finally arrived home, Lisa sent Pirelli out to fill a bucket with earth for the tree, while she unpacked.

One of the cases was full of dirty laundry that she hadn't had a chance to wash in Palermo. As she tipped it into the laundry basket in the bathroom, she noticed the pair of sheets she had put on the bed before she left.

Although it was against the rules, Pirelli dug the earth from a flower bed. When he carried it back to the apartment, Lisa was waiting.

She threw the dirty sheets across the room. "Since when have you bothered to change a bed? I'll tell you when: The day you brought a whore back here, you bastard!"

Pirelli said nothing, and Lisa's voice rose to a screech. "You call yourself a detective? No wonder that guy got away. You can't even bring a woman here and clear away the evidence! Well, you spend Christmas here, get your whore to keep you company, because that's all the company you'll have! I am leaving. . . ."

Pirelli slumped into a chair and lit a cigarette, still saying nothing. Lisa faced him, hands on hips, eyes blazing. "Well, aren't you going to say something? Even try to make an excuse?"

He shrugged, refusing to look at her. Frustrated by his silence, she stormed into the bedroom and slammed the door. He could hear her crying. Slowly he stubbed his cigarette out and followed her.

She was curled up on the unmade bed, sobbing. He sat beside her.

"Lisa, Lisa, listen to me. . . ."

"How could you bring someone into our bed? How could you do that to me?"

"I have no excuse, it was unforgivable, and I'm sorry."

Lisa sat up. "Who is she? Do I know her?"

He lit a cigarette. "You don't know her."

"How long has it been going on?"

"It happened only once. I'm sorry."

"Who is it?"

"You don't know her. I couldn't understand it myself; all I can say is that I'm sorry. I am ashamed, if that makes you feel better."

"Are you still seeing her?"

To Lisa's astonishment, he appeared close to tears. He shook his head, unable to meet her eyes.

"Do you love her, this woman? Joe?" She pushed his shoulder. "Are you in love with this woman, whoever the bitch is?"

He caught her hand, and she tried to pull away; but he

held on tightly. "Listen to me. It's over, but I can't talk about it."

"Oh, fine! You bring a woman back here to our apartment, sleep with her in *my* bed, then tell me you don't want to talk about it! Well, fuck you."

She broke free and slapped his face. He turned his head away, then gestured toward the door. Their son was peeking into the room, his face scared.

Lisa snapped, "Go to your room, Gino. I'll come and see you in a minute. . . . Gino, do as I tell you."

The boy slunk away, and Pirelli got up and closed the door. He stood with his back to his wife and sighed. He asked. "What do you want me to do, Lisa? You want me to leave?"

She took a tissue from the box on the dressing table and blew her nose. "I don't know. . . . I just don't know how you could have done this to me."

She seemed so helpless. He went to her and rubbed her shoulders.

"Don't you love me anymore?"

He stroked her cheek. "I do love you, Lisa, I love you. . . ." He flushed guiltily and gave her a sheepish smile. "Look, we'll go on that vacation, the three of us. Now that I'm through in Palermo, we can go right after Christmas. What do you say?"

"I don't know, Joe. Right now I don't know what I want, I'm so mixed up, so . . . I still can't believe you lied to me."

His face tightened. "I haven't lied, Lisa. Believe me, I haven't lied to you. It is over. I won't see her again."

He held her in his arms, kissing her hair, her neck, as she clung to him, crying. He hugged her tightly.

"Don't, Lisa, please don't."

Christmas was strained, with Lisa referring to his "one-night stand" at every possible opportunity. Pirelli was torn by guilt and a sense of failure. Luka Carolla was out there somewhere; thinking about him brought Pirelli back to Sophia as if the two were somehow linked.

He had decided not to return to work after the Christmas break but to take the two weeks' vacation due him. Then he received a call from an old friend.

Detective Inspector Carlo Gennaro was in charge of the

Nino Fabio homicide, and he asked Pirelli's help in tracing Sophia Luciano because he needed to question her. Pirelli agreed. He had no way of knowing that Sophia was in New York.

Michele Barzini was a worried man. He knew that the men who had supplied him with the cash to pay off the widows were now waiting for the documents giving them full rights to all the Luciano holdings.

He left his suite at the Plaza and walked two blocks to his underground parking space. Engrossed in his own thoughts, he walked down the ramp and headed toward his car, fumbling in his pocket for the keys.

As he opened the car door, the parking attendant called out something to him. He looked around, but the attendant had bent down out of sight. Barzini slammed the door and started the engine, then turned and slung his arm along the back of the seat as he reversed. He heard something fall off the rear seat, and after pushing the gear lever to the park position, he leaned over to see what it was.

In the dim light of the garage he could not see clearly, so he opened the glove compartment, took out a flashlight, and shone it on the floor behind his seat. Still unable to see, he put his hand down to feel what had fallen. He grasped some kind of fiber and pulled.

The material was human hair, attached to the severed head of Harry Barzini, his cousin.

Panic-stricken, a scream strangled in his throat, Barzini struggled out of his jacket and threw it over the dismembered head. Then he fumbled to open the trunk of the car.

The stench made him retch. He became hysterical, gibbering and shaking, and the head slipped from his shaking hands, rolling like a ball beneath the car.

Barzini had to get down on his hands and knees on the oil-streaked concrete floor to retrieve it. His fingers inched toward the ghastly, glaring face. He drew it close by some strands of hair. Panting with the horror, he threw it into the trunk and slammed the lid down, but it sprang open again. He forced it down until the lock caught, then ran back to the elevator.

The parking attendant looked at Barzini, then back to the Lincoln, parked halfway across the exit lane.

"Mr. Barzini? Sir, you want me to move your car? Everything okay, Mr. Barzini?"

The elevator door closed, and the attendant made his way slowly to the Lincoln. Barzini's keys were still in the ignition.

He opened the door and drove the car the few feet back into the bay. He climbed out, locked the door, and was about to return to his duties when he looked at his hands. They were sticky, stinking. . . . Slowly he walked around the car to the back and bent down to see dark fingermarks all along the bodywork where Barzini had tried desperately to shut the trunk. He looked at the elevator, then back at the car, the keys dangling in his hand. . . .

The hysterical Barzini got back to his apartment just as Salerno was about to let himself in. He dragged Salerno inside. "Get some guys, have my car towed away, dumped, set alight. Where nobody can find it, understand me?"

"What happened, you had an accident?"

"Just fuckin' listen . . . The Luciano women are crazy motherfuckers. I've gotta pay them."

"What? I thought they were paid off by now."

"Just do what I tell you."

"The deal was a straight cut. What's gone wrong? You try something?" Salerno knew by Barzini's face that he had and shook his head. "When are you gonna learn, Mike? They already got stuff bein' shipped from Colombia into Palermo, but they got noplace to store it and ship it, so you're in shit if they don't get the Luciano property. What the fuck did you try?"

"Just get out of here and do what I tell you. Get my car towed out."

As Michele Barzini climbed into a taxi at the front of the Plaza Hotel, police cars were arriving at the entrance to the underground garage. His car was cordoned off, and a sheet covered the open trunk, concealing the remains of his relative.

Salerno turned tail as soon as he saw the cops. He tried to call Barzini from the hotel lobby, but just missed him.

The police were already at Barzini's apartment by the time Salerno returned to it. He overheard Elsa Barzini telling them that her husband was lunching at the Four Seasons. . . .

*          *          *

Barzini was ten minutes late arriving at the Four Seasons. He seemed composed as he walked up the wide staircase, carrying a black leather attaché case, but when he sat down at his table, the sweat showed on his forehead.

Teresa smiled and said everything had gone smoothly. She passed him the thick folder of documents.

Barzini gestured to the wine waiter and asked Teresa, "You want wine? Mineral water?"

"White wine."

Barzini looked over the wine list, snapped the leather-bound pages shut. "Gimme a large bourbon on the rocks and number seventeen." He turned to Teresa again. "What'll you have?"

"The fresh salmon, please."

He examined the menu and looked at the still-hovering waiter.

"Dish of the day, no appetizer, thanks."

Then he moved his cutlery aside and opened the folder. He perused each paper, checking it thoroughly, not giving her a hint of what he felt. But the sweat formed a shining film across his upper lip.

His bourbon was placed on the table. His eyes glued to the documents, Barzini picked up the drink and all but downed it in one gulp. The wine waiter brought the bottle, and Barzini gestured to him to open it, not even looking to check the order.

He paused over one paper, flicked back to see if it connected with another, then continued, satisfied. He looked up as the waiter filled his wineglass, and then he stiffened.

Two uniformed police officers had entered the restaurant and were walking up the wide staircase. One called to the maître d' to join them. Barzini's eyes, behind the glasses, blinked furiously. The maître d' turned toward his table and pointed; the officers headed toward Barzini.

He turned, with a look of loathing, to Teresa. "You bitch, you set me up, you fucking whore!"

Barzini erupted into motion, hurling the big table up, sending the glasses and crockery cascading to the floor, and made an insane dash for the stairs.

He ran into the street, into the traffic, zigzagging among the cars as they swerved to avoid him. As the police officers gave chase, he ran directly into the path of a yellow cab. . . . His body was thrown into the air, over the front of the cab, and into the path of a delivery truck coming the opposite way. He bounced like a rag doll.

Luka, sitting in his parked car waiting for Teresa, watched the accident in stunned amazement.

Teresa saw it all through the vast windows overlooking the street. She slipped the documents into Barzini's case and clasped it under her arm, putting her handbag on top. In the commotion, with people running in and out of the restaurant, no one noticed her leave.

She walked straight to the waiting car and slipped into the backseat. The engine was already running.

As they pulled away, Luka said, "You see that guy get it from the truck. Looked like a dummy being chucked about."

"It was Barzini. Cops walked in, and he ran for it."

Luka grinned. "How come? Is the food that bad?"

She smiled and clutched the briefcase.

"Convenient, eh?" Luka said as he drove out into the main stream of traffic.

"You could say that. Our money's in here, and I've still got the documents. I think we'd better get home."

Pirelli was in the middle of a coughing fit, his face gradually turning puce. His office door opened, and Inspector Carlo Gesù Gennaro smiled at him.

Pirelli gesticulated wildly. "Oh, man, I'm giving up smoking before it kills me."

"You said that four years ago when we worked together. Any hope of some coffee?"

Thick black coffee was brought in, and the two men lit up, filling the air-conditioned office with fine blue smoke that drifted out through the air vents.

Gennaro offered his condolences on the Palermo situation, and Pirelli shrugged. "I'll get him one day. How're things with you?"

Gennaro shrugged. "Oh, so-so. As I said, I'm on the Nino Fabio case, and I need to find Sophia Luciano. Seems she sold her apartment in Rome. On December 16, 1987, the day of the murder, she had an afternoon appointment with Fabio, and everyone within earshot heard them having one hell of a row. She accused Fabio of bankrupting her, and she wanted to use some of his designs to open up her business again. He refused to help her. Interesting now; all Fabio's drawings, designs, whatever you call them, are missing, as is Signora Sophia, and I got no joy at the old Luciano headquarters. Place has been torn to the ground . . . So, what can you do for me? Know any way I can get in touch with her?"

Pirelli poured more coffee. "You think she had something to do with it?"

Gennaro shrugged and accepted a refill. He heaped sugar into the cup, stirring it slowly with a plastic spoon already bent from use. "I doubt it. Looked like a real sicko at work, and it appears that Fabio was into being beaten and chained, liked his rough trade. Maybe the drawings were stolen to put us off the scent. All the same, I'll have to talk to her, just for elimination, you know."

Pirelli nodded. "I know she was in Palermo just before Christmas, for Graziella Luciano's court hearing. But I don't know where she is now."

Gennaro spilled coffee on his shirt and swore. He took out a grubby handkerchief to dry the spot.

"That suspect you're after, still no idea where he's run to?"

"Carolla? If I knew, I wouldn't be here."

Gennaro gave Pirelli a sidelong look. "Well, it's because of him that I'm here, that and trying to trace Sophia Luciano."

Pirelli was like a bird of prey. "You got something on him?"

"Maybe . . . We questioned Fabio's employees. There were more than thirty, but one of them, Celeste Morvanno, was in the hospital having a kid, so I didn't get to her until two days ago. She saw Sophia Luciano outside Nino's building, talking to a chauffeur."

Pirelli sighed. "Get to the point."

"Well, she's sitting in my office, right? I ask her to describe the guy so I could check if it was the same man the other witnesses saw. Well, she starts to hem and haw, then she gets up and walks over to the bulletin board. She points at the picture of Luka Carolla."

"What?"

"Hang on. 'I think this is him,' she says, 'but this photograph is more like him.' The photograph, Joe, is the one you sent around after the composite; they're both pinned up on my board."

Pirelli rocked backward and forward in his chair. "How much can you depend on this witness?"

"Not that much. It was a good three weeks after the event, but she came in of her own volition. There's no material gain. I mean, she doesn't even work at Fabio's anymore."

Gennaro rummaged in his briefcase, eventually pulled out a dog-eared folder. He tossed over some large black-and-white photos of the corpse. "Like I said, the guy that did it was a real sicko. You can see by the stains on the carpet Fabio bled to death. We found him parked among his dummies."

Pirelli stared in distaste at the photos, and Gennaro suggested that perhaps a real drink was in order.

It was not until Pirelli had downed a beer that he told Gennaro he had actually been with Sophia on the night Nino Fabio was murdered.

Gennaro gaped, and Pirelli gave him a dirty look. "We went to the opera, okay? But she was with me at the time you reckon Fabio was murdered."

Gennaro gave him a sly look. "Did you see any sign of the chauffeur?"

Pirelli's mind reeled. He lit a cigarette. He had seen the chauffeur but not paid him much attention, could not recall seeing his face. His started to sweat. Jesus Christ, had Luka Carolla been driving Sophia Luciano's Rolls?

His voice gave no hint of his turmoil. "No, I never saw him."

"How about when she took her mother-in-law to the trial? Any sign of him then?"

Pirelli dragged at his cigarette. He couldn't remember. At the time he had been too involved with his feelings for Sophia. "No . . . No, I didn't see anyone with her but her mother-in-law, Graziella Luciano."

Gennaro watched Pirelli order another drink, a brandy this time. "You okay, Joe?"

Pirelli smirked. "Yeah, like someone took a shot at my belly. I'm trying to keep my head from falling off. . . . You sure about this chauffeur guy?"

The drinks were brought, and Gennaro sat silently until

the waiter had gone. "Joe, I'm asking you straight, and you'd better tell me because if I unearth anything, you'll be left covered in shit. . . . You and this Luciano woman, don't give me any crap about opera, you got something going with her?"

Pirelli stubbed out his cigarette. "I was investigating the murder of her two kids, for chrissake. Of course, I saw her, on more than one occasion, but it was on the level. I happened to be in Milan the same time as she was. We met accidentally and . . . that's all there was to it. If it wasn't, I'd tell you, okay? I guess I'm her alibi. She couldn't have been anywhere near Fabio's place when he was murdered."

Gennaro sniffed. "That's not to say she didn't get someone to do it for her."

Pirelli's assistant in Milan, Eugenio Muratte, worked through his lunch hour while his chief and Gennaro sat in the bar. He joined them after an hour. He had been unable to trace the whereabouts of Sophia Luciano or her mother-in-law. But he could try Teresa Luciano in New York to see if she could help them.

Pirelli gave the go-ahead to call the NYPD and also suggested that he take the file on Nino Fabio and run it through the computer to check for any other homicides of a similar nature in the past five years.

The two men continued their liquid lunch. By the time they returned to Pirelli's office they realized they were hungry and sent out for some sandwiches.

There was a memo on Pirelli's desk to say that they would soon have Teresa Luciano's phone number in New York. When Eugenio returned, beaming, they both presumed he had it. But what he actually had was something far more important to Pirelli.

Pirelli scanned the telex from Palermo, then slumped back in his seat. "Listen . . . I've got the proof I needed. Luka Carolla's surfaced in the U.S."

He paced the room as he read aloud, " 'Aware that you are,' et cetera, et cetera, et cetera 'Manhattan State Bank, private boxes, one box listed as number four-five-six . . . after extensive inquiries was found to be owned by Paul Carolla, now deceased. The last will and testament of Paul Carolla,' et cetera, et cetera, 'New York City, named his son, Giorgio Carolla, as his sole heir. On December 28, 1987, the ownership of the box was transferred by court order to G. L. Carolla, to await collection. G. L. Carolla took possession of the contents of private bank box four-five-six, property of the Manhattan—' *Jesus Christ*! 'December 28, 1987.' That was one week ago!"

Gennaro thought Pirelli was about to kiss him. "What the hell does it mean?"

"G. L. Carolla is Luka Carolla, and I've got to be there before those bastards let him slip away. . . ."

Gennaro returned to his own headquarters, hoping to squeeze a flight to New York out of his bosses. Pirelli also harassed his superiors. He was granted an economy-class ticket to New York, plus three days' expenses. When Gennaro received his go-ahead, the two men arranged to travel together.

In New York the women divided the money, but not without argument. Rosa insisted on having her share separate from Teresa's. Then Graziella said she wanted to divide hers among them all; she wanted nothing for herself. In the end Teresa banked her money, and Sophia and Rosa banked theirs, insisting that Graziella take at least a quarter. They each traveled to a different bank, but only Teresa knew that they still retained the documents.

Luka made a call from a pay phone to Peter Salerno, requesting he arrange a meeting with Barzini's so-called partners. He was careful to make no mention of the Luciano women, sure that Barzini's phone would be tapped. Teresa stood beside the phone booth, listening.

"My clients are still interested in doing the same deal. They still have the documents and wish to do business." Luka could not repress a smile as he continued. "You see, they still have no cash, so they need to move quickly."

Salerno was sure that Barzini had cashed the banker's draft and paid the widows, but he didn't say so. He simply stated that he would contact the parties involved. It would take a few days to set up a meeting. And he added, quietly and courteously, that he would require payment for his efforts.

Luka finally agreed to 2 percent of the final sum.

Teresa inched the door farther open and whispered, "Make sure he knows we don't have the documents at the apartment."

Luka gave her a thumbs-up. "My clients wish it to be known that all the documents are in a safety-deposit box and not at their apartment. Is that understood? I have the key, so it would be a waste of time trying to get them—"

"Who is this?"

"That is no concern of yours; I am simply acting for my clients. Please do not delay. I'll call you again, on this number, in three days."

Putting the phone down, he smiled at Teresa. "You hear? I think he's gonna play ball. He's got no option. . . . Put it there!" He held out his open hand. Teresa laughed and slapped it; then he hugged her tightly. "We did good, huh?"

She looked into his face. "I want you to promise me something. Swear to me, Johnny, there will be no more killing. I want your word, it has to stop."

Luka stepped back from her and crossed himself. "Before almighty God, it's over."

It began to snow lightly as they walked along Fifth Avenue arm in arm. Teresa stopped at a furrier's window and pointed. "I want to buy something for Rosa."

"Not a fur. She won't wear a fur. It's against her principles."

Teresa laughed. "Not mine, though. What do you think? Shall I try it on?"

Teresa arrived home laden with boxes, twirled around in her new fox fur coat, and began handing out parcels.

"Happy belated Christmas, Rosa, Mama, Sophia. . . . These are from us."

"Us?" repeated Sophia.

"Yes, Johnny and I bought them. Well, aren't you going to open them?"

Sophia took her Bergdorf Goodman parcel. "Where is the boy wonder?"

Teresa smiled. "He said he would be by shortly. I think he's arranging a surprise for us, a trip, he said. It's a good idea. We should get away for a couple of days, just in case any more men in masks decide to pay us a visit."

Teresa was in such high spirits she was almost hysterical.

"Open your present, Sophia," said Teresa. "We spent hours choosing it."

Sophia's box contained a Ferrucci cream silk shirt. It was worth a fortune. She smiled. "Thank you, I'll go try it on."

Beaming, Teresa handed the two largest boxes to Graziella and Rosa. "Come on, open them."

Suspicious, Sophia paused in the doorway. "What did Salerno say, Teresa?"

"He has to discuss it with the others. We are going to call back in three days' time."

Rosa ran her hand down Teresa's coat. "Mama, this is not Sophia's. Did you buy it?"

"Yes, but please open your gift. Come on, Mama, open your box, too."

Sophia lingered at the door. "Why did he speak with Salerno and not Barzini?"

"I don't know." With a shrug, Teresa changed the subject. "Aren't you going to try your blouse on?"

Sophia was sure Teresa was up to something. She watched as Graziella and Rosa lifted the lids from their big boxes.

Rosa's face fell. "Oh, Mama, how could you? I won't wear it!"

Teresa snatched the coat from the box and shook it out. "Oh, yes, you will, because it's a fake."

Graziella held up her own fake mink jacket. "What is it?"

Teresa tried to help Graziella into the coat. "It's supposed to be mink, but it's a fake."

"What's fake? I don't understand—"

"It's a fake fur, Mama, you know, it's not real? And this isn't fox fur; it's a fake, too, a fake."

"Fake? What animal is a fake?"

Teresa threw her hands up in despair. "Man-made, the animal is man-made. . . . What do you think, Rosa?"

Rosa's face was a picture; she loathed her coat. "Well, Mama, it still means that it looks real, and someone will throw a pot of paint over me. It's just as bad as wearing a real fur because it still encourages—"

Teresa snapped, "Fine, forget it. I should have known there's no pleasing you. Take the receipt and change the goddamn thing!"

Graziella stood looking at her reflection in the hall mirror, a deep frown on her face. She gestured for Sophia to come to her side. "Fake? This is a fake, you mean, like a painting is fake?"

"*Si*, Mama, it's because so many people don't like to wear the real thing."

Graziella nodded and adjusted the collar. "It's okay . . . Teresa, *grazie* . . . You think it'll be warm enough? It's very light—"

Just then the front door opened, and Luka walked in, wearing a fur hat. Sophia collapsed laughing. Luka doffed his hat with a bow.

"It's not real, Rosa. It's fake fur, see? It says, 'man-made fiber.' " He looked from one smiling woman to the next. "Teresa bought it for me. . . ."

Luka was beaming. He had brought flowers and champagne. He told them proudly that he had hired a limo for a surprise trip early the next morning. Stern-faced, he instructed them to be ready before eight.

He excused himself for not staying; he wanted to get everything ready for tomorrow. Before he left, he went to Rosa's side and whispered, "This is for you. I knew you wouldn't like the coat, but she wouldn't listen to me."

He handed her a small jewelry box and left quickly. Rosa flushed as she opened it. Then she gasped. The diamond was in the shape of a tear, on a fine, thin gold chain. She hurried after him.

"Johnny . . . Johnny, wait!"

He turned and watched her as she ran down the stairs. "It's so beautiful, it's just lovely, thank you. . . ."

"I'm glad you like it, I picked it out myself."

She stopped two steps above him and leaned down to hug him tightly. "Thank you."

She tried to kiss him, but he took her hands, held them tight. "It's just a friendship gift, Rosa, because I like you. . . . Don't read anything into it."

Rosa looked into the clear blue eyes. "Has Mama been talking to you?"

He released her hands and turned away. "I have to go. I have things to do."

She ran down the stairs and caught his arm. "Wait, please—"

He jerked himself free. "No."

"Johnny, please." She grabbed him again, pulling him back. He resisted at first, then relaxed as she said, "You know how I feel about you. You do, don't you?"

For a moment he seemed confused, and she cupped his face in her hands and kissed him tenderly. He didn't respond, and she looked at him questioningly. His eyes were those of a child. She held him tighter, kissed his neck, his cheek. . . . As she found his lips, she felt his arms squeezing her roughly.

"Rosa, Rosa, come back here."

Luka released her and pressed his back against the wall. They both looked up at Sophia, standing above them, eyes blazing. "You'd better go, Johnny."

He ran down the stairs and out of sight. Rosa marched back up to the landing to confront Sophia. "What's the matter, jealous?"

Sophia pushed her into the hallway. "Don't be childish. Teresa, you'd better talk to your daughter. I found her on the stairs with Johnny. Talk to her. Make her see sense—"

Rosa turned on her aunt in fury. "Why don't you mind your own damned business? I'll do what I want. You don't have the right to tell me what to do; nobody has—"

The telephone rang, the shrill, insistent ring striking fear into them. With a glance toward the study Teresa said lightly, "So, the telephone's ringing; it could be my hairdresser." But no one made any attempt to pick up the phone.

Finally Teresa answered. She turned her back on the others, who were waiting impatiently to know who it was. "She's not at home right now. . . . Yes, she is staying here. . . . Of course, yes."

She covered the mouthpiece and said to Sophia, "It's someone asking about you. It's a detective from Milan. Gennaro. Do you know him?"

Sophia shook her head, and Teresa said into the phone, "Yes, yes, I'll tell her as soon as she returns. Do you have a number where she can call you?"

Teresa wrote down the number on a used envelope. As she did, she covered the mouthpiece again. "He's in New York. . . ." Then she asked Gennaro, "May I know what this is about? . . . Oh, I see. . . . Well, then, I will get her to call you."

Sophia was at her side. "What does he want?"

Teresa gestured to her to keep quiet. "Yes. . . . I will, thank you."

Replacing the phone, she turned to Sophia. "He's been trying to contact you, something to do with Nino Fabio. You'll have to get rid of him. The last thing we want right now is the police coming around. What do you think he wants?"

Sophia sat down and lit a cigarette. She was shaking, and her face had lost its color. Teresa told Graziella and Rosa to stay in the kitchen. Then she shut the study door.

With a searching look she asked, "What's it all about?"

"I'll show you," Sophia replied. She went to her bedroom and returned with the suitcaseful of Nino's drawings. "Johnny gave them to me. I tried to tell you about them."

"Yes, I remember. But why would he come all the way to New York to talk to you about them? Oh, shit, did Johnny steal them?"

Sophia bit her lip. "I think so. . . ."

Teresa tore off her glasses and rubbed her eyes. "That stupid boy . . . My God, this is all we need. It's your fault, you know. He's got this thing about you, never mind about him and Rosa. . . . It's you he's always staring at, has been since you came back. Did anything happen between the two of you in Rome?"

Sophia slammed the case case shut. "Don't be ridiculous. . . . Do you think I would encourage him? I was the one who wanted you to get rid of him at the very beginning; he's the one who got us into—"

Teresa interrupted. "I don't want to hear that now, Sophia. If it weren't for him, we would all have been shot. Anyway, are they worth money? The drawings? Is that why the detective is here?"

"*Yes!* They are worth a lot of money. It's almost his entire collection, but—"

She was trapped. If she told Teresa about Nino Fabio's murder and Johnny's part in it, Teresa would know that the detective wasn't in New York just to inquire about the theft of designs. Sophia's mind was so scrambled that she couldn't think what she should admit to knowing. . . .

Teresa was pacing up and down the cluttered room. "Okay, let's take it step by step. Do they know about your connection with Fabio?"

"Yes, of course." Sophia rubbed her head. "I went to his factory when I tried to buy them from him. Johnny was with me; he was driving the car. I told you that."

"Did anyone see you there?"

Helplessly Sophia shrugged her shoulders. "I don't know. I can't think."

"Well, start thinking. Who saw you there?"

"No one, I didn't see anyone. Wait, when I was leaving, I saw a girl who used to be my receptionist. She was still working for Nino. I talked to her outside the building."

"So she also saw Johnny?"

"Yes, of course. He was driving the car."

Teresa sighed. "Okay, first of all, get rid of the drawings: Burn them, do anything, but get rid of them. They mustn't be found anywhere near us. Next, call this detective, seem very willing to see him, and tell him you saw Fabio but you left. Come on real innocent."

Sophia sat immobile.

"Are you listening, Sophia?"

She nodded. "Yes, yes, I'm listening."

"Okay. You have to call him before he calls again. Otherwise it'll look suspicious. Tell him you don't know anything about anything, admit you wanted the designs, but when Fabio refused to let you have them, you gave up your business and came to the States. It all makes sense, doesn't it?"

"Yes . . . Yes, when should I call?"

"I don't know." She looked searchingly at Sophia, then asked again, "That is all there is to it? You sure there isn't anything else you need to tell me?"

Sophia picked up the suitcase. "I'll go down to the basement."

Luka lay on his small bed, staring up at the light bulb. He had arranged every detail of the weekend trip with care. The small satchel containing all of Paul Carolla's papers was stashed by his bed, and he put his hand out to touch it, then slid his hand inside to feel the folded papers and bundles of bank notes. Then he rolled over onto his belly and pulled the pillow over his head. Paul Carolla's dream of the good life was now contained in one small bag.

He saw clearly the potbellied man who had foolishly tried to be his father, could smell the cigar smoke, feel the way the fat hands used to grip him, hold him in that bear hug. . . . He giggled, hugging the pillow.

# 21

Pirelli unpacked his overnight case and went down to the lobby of his hotel, then down farther into the bar.

Gennaro was already sitting on a stool. He ordered a beer for Pirelli and munched on a handful of peanuts from a bowl at his elbow.

"I put in a call to the Luciano place. They didn't know where Signora S. was, but she's in New York. I left the number here for her to call. . . ."

Pirelli sat on a stool and flicked open a new package of Marlboros. He searched his pockets for his lighter, then picked up a strip of courtesy matches from the ashtray. He struck a match and looked at his hand; it was shaking.

It was after ten, but Pirelli couldn't sleep. He picked up his book and tried to read, but he couldn't concentrate. He was going to see her and didn't know how to handle it. He and Lisa were arguing more than ever, especially since he had canceled the promised vacation.

He threw the sheets off and took a miniature brandy from

the fridge. As he unscrewed the bottle top, the light on his phone blinked.

The operator informed him that the caller had asked for Gennaro, but there was no reply from his room. "He requested that in his absence any calls should be passed on to your room, Mr. Pirelli. Do you wish to take the call?"

Pirelli reached for a cigarette. "Sure, who is it?"

"The caller would not give her name, Mr. Pirelli."

"Put the call through."

A husky voice asked if he was Detective Gennaro.

"No, it's me, Sophia. It's Joe."

There was a long pause. Then: "Joe?"

"Yes. I'm here on an investigation; we came together."

"I was asked to call; he wants to see me."

Pirelli paused and inhaled deeply, letting the smoke drift from his nostrils. "I want to see you, too."

She did not reply. Eventually he asked, "Sophia, are you still there?"

"Yes . . ."

"I can't discuss Gennaro's case, you understand?"

"Of course . . . Well, I'll call him tomorrow. I'm sorry I called so late."

"It's not that late. . . . How are you?"

"I'm fine."

He had to warn her. "Sophia, he'll ask your whereabouts the night we went to the opera. He knows we were together, but nothing more. . . ."

Again he waited. When she spoke, her voice was faint. "Is it about Nino Fabio?"

"You know about him?"

"I know. I called his office. They told me."

"I guess that's what he wants to talk to you about."

"Why?"

"I can't really discuss it."

"No, I guess not."

"I'll come to see you with him."

"Oh, are you on the case, too?"

"No, but I'll be with him."

"When does he want to see me?"

"As soon as possible."

"Tomorrow?"

"Yes . . . about nine?"

Again there was a pause. "Make it a little later. My sister-in-law and mother-in-law are going out shopping later, so the apartment will be empty. It will be easier to talk."

"Okay, how much later?"

"About eleven?" said Sophia.

"I'll tell Gennaro."

There was another long pause. Then Pirelli said, "I have missed you, Sophia."

Silence. "You hear me?" he said.

"Yes, I hear you. . . ."

"I'll see you tomorrow morning then?"

"Is there a reason for you to come tomorrow?"

"Yes, I have some questions I need to ask you."

"What about?"

"It would be best to tell you when I see you."

"Until tomorrow then." Her voice was very soft.

"I still love you," he said quietly. But she had hung up.

Teresa stared hard at Sophia. "Well? That wasn't Gennaro?"

Sophia shook her head. "No, it was Commissario Pirelli; they're together. They are coming here at eleven."

"Yes, I heard. Did he say why they wanted to see you?"

Sophia lit a cigarette. "Nino Fabio's been murdered."

Teresa gasped, "What? They think you had something to do with it?"

Sophia shrugged. "They think it was robbery, but I was seen at his warehouse, so I guess they have to question me."

Teresa squinted. She was not wearing her glasses. Sophia's face seemed blurred. "What are you going to do?"

"Well, be here, you heard me. I can join you wherever you're all going for the weekend. Right now I'm tired. I'm going to bed."

Teresa watched her leave the room. Sophia never ceased to amaze her; she appeared unruffled by the fact that the police were in New York. Teresa was relieved that she, for one, would have left by the time the police arrived.

*     *     *

Sophia tossed and turned, unable to sleep. Finally she crept from her room and went to make herself a cup of tea. Did they know about Johnny? She knew they couldn't suspect her . . . or could they? They? This was Joe, Joe Pirelli. . . . She thought of the comfort he had given her, the warmth of him, the gentle way he had made love to her. Was she the real reason he had come to New York? Did he really love her? Love . . . The very word seemed alien. Too much had happened in the past year to contemplate being loved.

The kettle boiled, and she was about to pour the water into the teapot when she heard a sound. Turning, she saw Rosa creeping down the hall, fully dressed.

"Rosa?"

Rosa was so startled she froze. When Sophia came out into the hall, she gasped, "You frightened me."

"I couldn't sleep. I'm making a cup of tea. Do you want one?"

Rosa whispered guiltily that she was just going for a walk and started toward the front door. Sophia caught her hand.

"No, Rosa, don't go to him."

Rosa jerked her hand free. "I don't know what you are talking about. I just wanted to go for a walk!"

"It's after twelve, you shouldn't be in the street alone."

Rosa's face hardened. "You want to tag along with me?"

"No, Rosa, but you are not leaving the apartment. If you try, I shall call Teresa."

Rosa sighed angrily. "It's like a goddamn prison in here, everyone watching every move you make."

"It won't be for long. Besides, you're all going on a trip tomorrow."

"And you're not coming?"

"No, I'm staying behind. I have to talk to this Detective Gennaro."

"What do the police want?"

Rosa followed Sophia into the kitchen.

"It's about Nino Fabio, you know, the designer I worked with. He was found murdered, and they have to question everyone who saw him the day it happened."

Rosa leaned against the wall. "It seems you're unlucky."

Sophia poured two cups of tea and opened the fridge for the milk. "What do you mean by that?"

"Well, it's obvious, isn't it? Everyone near you gets bumped off."

"Is that supposed to be funny?"

Rosa's eyes glittered. "I'm not laughing. I'd say it was unlucky that you had a scene with Nino."

Sophia banged the sugar bowl down on the table. "I was not having a scene, as you call it, with Nino, nor am I interested in Johnny. And if you had any sense, you wouldn't be either."

Sophia looked at the girl's moody face and could have slapped her. Instead, she sat down and began to drink the hot tea. Rosa joined her, grudgingly, but did not drink hers. For a time they sat in silence. Rosa twisted the chain with the diamond teardrop at her neck, then rubbed the cold stone across her lips.

"That's very pretty."

"Yes . . . Johnny gave it to me."

"I know." Sophia reached out to touch Rosa's arm, but the young woman moved away. Sophia sighed. "Rosa, maybe you feel something for Johnny, but—"

Rosa interrupted. "What business is it of yours?"

"None, but I do care for you, and . . . just listen to me."

Rosa pushed her chair back, but Sophia gripped her hand. "Maybe it's because we have been so trapped in this place, so closeted together, that you feel more for him than you would in normal circumstances."

Rosa's voice was a hoarse, bitter whisper. "Normal? You think it's normal for a girl my age to be a virgin? To have a marriage arranged for her? To know you were sold like a side of meat . . . And to know that as soon as all this is over, Grandma and Mama will try to marry me off to someone else they think suitable. Well, I am going to be free! I have my own money, and I can do what I like when I like. I can go with whoever I like, and nobody can tell me any different, not you, not anyone. I just want someone, I want—"

Her face crumpled, and she bit her lip. She hugged herself, rocking slightly. "I thought Emilio loved me, the way he kissed me. . . . He said he loved me when all the time he was just doing what Grandpa told him to. . . ."

Sophia slipped her arms around Rosa. "He did love you,

you know it. I remember the day we went into Palermo, do you? The day before the wedding, the day before—"

Rosa turned her face away. "Am I likely to forget?"

Sophia shook her head, and her voice filled with pain. "No . . . I mean, when we all were going shopping and you didn't want to come. As we drove out of the villa, we saw the two of you, sitting close together. . . ."

Tears spilled down Rosa's cheeks, and she clung to her aunt. Her voice was choked with tears. "He touched me, he touched my breasts, he touched me, and I wanted to feel him. . . . I unbuttoned his shirt, and I slipped my hand inside. . . ."

Sophia kissed the top of Rosa's head, with soft, whispered sounds of comfort, then knelt beside her. "You are so beautiful. . . . Let me tell you, those feelings, that warmth running through your body, the heat, as if it were going to burst your heart—"

Rosa nodded. "Yes . . . Yes, he was so warm . . ."

"I'll tell you a secret. I have never told anyone this before, and you must promise me never to tell anyone. Promise?"

Rosa nodded, and Sophia pulled her chair so close that their heads almost touched. "I used to be a waitress, did you know that? It was when I was even younger than you, fifteen. I had to work because my mother was an invalid. I was so skinny, my clothes were all hand-me-downs, and I don't think I had a new pair of shoes until I was eighteen. . . . Anyway, I worked in a coffee shop, and one day a group of young boys came in. They were teasing me, and one of them put out his foot to trip me when I was carrying a loaded tray of dishes. I fell, and all the plates and cups shattered. They laughed, it was so awful, because I couldn't help crying, as I crawled around on the floor picking up all the pieces. . . . I knew the manager would make me pay for the damage."

"But it wasn't your fault!"

"I know, but that's the way it was. And after work, sure enough, he deducted the breakages from my pay. I was crying my heart out, leaning against the wall near the bus stop. . . . Then this boy—I had seen him once or twice; but the customers were mostly rich kids with their flashy Lambrettas, and they never noticed me. But this boy did. He came up to me and put

his hand on my shoulder, asked if I was all right. I was embarrassed because I had really seen him, you understand? He was
the handsomest boy and well known, his family very rich. . . .
I used to dream about him, and there I was, all red-eyed from
weeping. He was so caring, so understanding. The next day I
discovered he had paid for the damage, so the manager had to
repay me.

"He used to come every day after that and sit outside, and
he'd always smile at me. He left me very big tips. . . . And
then, one day, he asked if I would like to meet him when I was
free."

Rosa realized that Sophia was no longer telling her the story;
she was talking to herself, looking straight ahead.

"We used to meet in an orchard. I'd ride my bicycle, and
he would be sitting on an old, tumble-down wall, waiting for
me. He was my first love. I loved him. . . . Mama tried to
persuade me to bring him home to meet her, but I was ashamed
of the apartment, even ashamed of my mama. . . . But I
wouldn't let him make love to me because in my dream he married me, in my dream I was accepted by his family."

Rosa waited. Sophia was still, her hands clasped, resting
on the table in front of her.

"What happened?"

Sophia slowly flattened her hands on the tabletop. "One
night he came to see me. He threw pebbles at my window, and
I crept out to join him. I was wearing just my slip, and I was
barefooted, but I went because I was afraid he would wake
Mama and the neighbors."

Rosa leaned forward. "Did he sleep with you?"

Sophia turned to her. Two tears, as clear as the diamond
Luka had given Rosa, trickled down her cheeks. "Yes, yes, he
did. . . . He'd come to tell me he was going away, perhaps for
two years. He promised to come back for me, promised to write
to me. . . . He gave me a keepsake; it was a little gold—"

She lifted her hand, and it was as if she were seeing the
little gold heart on its fine chain.

Rosa touched Sophia's hand; it was ice cold.

In a soft, low whisper, Sophia continued. "He never came
back, never wrote to me. I never saw him again." As if waking
from sleep, she turned slowly to Rosa. "I loved him, I loved

him so very much. His touch, his kisses are still inside my heart; they never fade. . . ."

"But you loved Constantino; you married him. Was it the same?"

Sophia smiled and shook her head. "No, but it was a sweet love, a good love. And believe me, it was returned. . . ."

Rosa smiled. "He was rich, he was a Luciano, so in the end your dream did come true. You married and were accepted by the great Luciano family. . . . Was this boy's family as well known?"

Sophia didn't reply, and Rosa smiled and whispered, "Tell me how you met Constantino."

Sophia shook her head. "No, I think I have told you enough for one night. You must go to bed. Sleep tight. . . . Maybe you will have sweet dreams now."

Rosa kissed Sophia's cheek and yawned, but it was not until she was almost out of the room that she turned back and whispered, "Thank you. Shall I turn the light out?"

Sophia nodded, and the room went dark. She waited to hear Rosa's door close. Then she stretched her arms out across the table and rested her cheek against the cold surface. She could feel her heartbeat against the table. All the years in between vanished as she whispered, "Michael, we had a beautiful son, a perfect baby—"

She sat up suddenly, her hands pressed against the table. He would be a grown man now. What did she think she could do for him? Give him money, make him a Luciano? She said aloud to the dark room, "You are still dreaming, Sophia. Stop it, stop it right now. . . . The past is over. Forget it. Live your own life."

Her hands clenched into fists. Tomorrow, after Pirelli had been to see her, she would leave, leave them all. There was no possibility of her involvement in Fabio's murder. She had a perfect alibi: She had been in bed with Commissario Joseph Pirelli and would not hesitate to admit it if necessary. She no longer cared what anyone thought. She was no longer Signora Luciano; she was Sophia Visconti.

At eight the next morning Luka was there with the limo to take them to Long Island. He ran up the stairs two at a time.

All their bags were ready and waiting, and Luka began to carry them down to the car, shouting back that they should hurry because he was double-parked.

Rosa rushed to change when she decided she didn't like the dress she was wearing. Teresa helped Graziella into her new coat, then went into Sophia's bedroom. Sophia, still wearing her bathrobe, was creaming her neck.

"I don't like leaving you alone. Are you sure you'll be okay?"

"Yes, Teresa, I'll be fine. Now go on, they're all waiting. Johnny has some great surprise in store for you all. Call me when you get there, tell me where you're staying, and I'll join you."

Teresa hesitated, then suggested that Sophia could always get the train. Sophia marched her to the door, saying she could also rent a car and drive herself.

When Teresa had gone, Sophia leaned against the door and sighed. She had done it. It had been so easy, a simple promise that she would join them. Already the empty apartment, the silence felt good.

The doorbell rang, shrill and continuous.

It was Luka. He stood like a man possessed. As Sophia opened the door, he struck it hard with his fist.

"Why aren't you coming? Why?"

She backed away from him. "Because I have to stay here. Didn't Teresa tell you?"

"You have to come with us! I have it all arranged. You have to be there; you can't stay."

He tried to drag her to the door, but she pulled her arm away.

"I can't."

"You don't understand. I have something for all of you. You have to come."

"Johnny, I don't *have* to do anything."

"Yes!"

"No!"

"Yesss . . ." He dragged her toward the door, and this time she pushed him forcibly away from her; but he still wouldn't let go. Finally she hit him, and he fell against the door; he kicked it in anger.

After a moment he controlled his tantrum. With his back

to her he muttered, "I have something for you."

"Johnny, I can't come. I have to wait here."

When he turned back to her, his eyes were vivid blue and crazy. "What'll you tell him?"

"Enough so he won't come back again. I burned the drawings."

He glared furiously at her. "You shouldn't have done that."

"I had to. If he found them here . . . Don't you understand? He's coming to question me about Nino. . . ."

"I'll come back for you. Wait for me."

"That won't be necessary."

"Why not?"

"Because I will find my own way to wherever you're going."

"You're not thinking of leaving us?"

"No . . ."

"Remember, he is your enemy. Keep saying that to yourself. He's the enemy."

"I'll remember that."

She turned and walked into the kitchen, pausing a moment because she did not hear the door close behind him. She retraced her footsteps to the hall and found him just coming out of the study. He was holding a small gun.

He came to her side. "I bought this for Teresa. You see the small lever at the trigger? Lift it, and it's set for firing. There are only four rounds."

"I don't want it."

"Take it."

"Please, why don't you leave?"

He held out the gun again. "You must be protected. He is the enemy. Always remember that."

She finally took it and smiled reassuringly. "I'll be all right."

He seemed unable to drag himself away. Gently he lifted a stray curl from her face. Then he bent his head and swiftly kissed her lips. She averted her head.

"Don't, please don't. . . ."

Her thick terry-cloth robe was open in a deep V, and he could see the crease of her breasts. He pulled at the belt and stepped back as the robe opened. Slowly she turned to look at him, trying to stop him with her glance as he lifted the fabric from her breasts. His hand was cold, his touch light.

"You are so beautiful," he whispered.

He got down on his knees, kissing her belly, moving the thick robe aside to rest his face against her stomach. "I love you, I love you. . . ."

She shivered, wary of his next move, but he clung to her like a child.

"They are waiting, Johnny. You have to go."

He got slowly to his feet, leaned toward her, kissing her as her sons had kissed her. "I'll come back for you. Wait for me. Promise you will wait for me?"

"Yes, I'll wait. . . ."

She sighed with relief when he left but made no attempt to cover herself. She let the heavy gown fall to the floor and stared at her reflection in the hall mirror. As Luka had done, she lifted a stray curl and patted it into place.

Sophia lay in the deep, soapy bath. The silence soothed her; the perfumed oils relaxed her. . . .

Her hair washed and wrapped in a towel, she returned to her bedroom. With studied concentration she chose each garment she would wear, laying it out on the bed.

She stared in the mirror at her nakedness, then picked up the little gun from the dressing table. She ran the cold metal over her skin, tracing her thigh, her belly, her breasts. Then she held the gun to her temple, drew the silver barrel slowly across the high bone of her right cheek until it rested against her lips. The soft, childish kiss from the crazy, foolish boy had felt as cold as the gun.

One bullet and it would be over. She was in control of her life; she could end it if she wanted.

Slowly she put the gun down. She began putting her makeup on, carefully smoothing the foundation over her perfect skin. She brushed her cheeks with blusher and lightly powdered her face before outlining her eyes and applying mascara. Lastly she painted her lips. . . .

Joe Pirelli shaved, brushed his hair, and changed his shirt twice. He dabbed on some cologne, put on his thick, long leather coat, and was still surveying himself in the mirror when Gennaro walked in.

"You ready?"

Pirelli turned with a boyish smile. "Yeah, I'm ready." He locked his room, then said, "I'll see you outside the Luciano apartment at twelve, then, and don't be late."

Gennaro nodded, unaware that Pirelli had lied about the time of the meeting with Sophia. He wanted to be alone with her first.

Gennaro walked into the elevator. "How do we work it? I talk first? Hit her with the element of surprise et cetera?"

Pirelli nodded, pocketing his key, and they stood in silence while the elevator descended to the lobby. Gennaro watched as the *commissario* checked his appearance in the mirror.

"You're certainly making a great effort. What are you after, another night at the opera?"

Pirelli laughed. "Nah, I want to impress the law over here. I've got a meeting with the New York attorney general. He's supposed to be one hell of a guy, Italian. What are you gonna do?"

"Oh, I'll do a bit of shopping, get the wife something. I'll see you at twelve."

The pair of them walked silently past the reception desk and out into the street. It was thick with slush, and more snow was falling heavily.

Sophia checked her watch. It was still only ten-thirty, and Pirelli was not due until eleven. All she had to do was to get dressed. She had already packed her suitcase and arranged for a flight to Rome that afternoon.

The doorbell rang, dispelling her good mood. Was he back? Had Johnny changed his mind?

"Who is it?"

"It's Joe."

Sophia looked through the peephole and could see he was alone. She opened the door.

"You're early."

"Yes, and I've also lied. I told Gennaro to come at twelve. Is that all right?"

She hesitated, then gave a slight nod to confirm that it was. "Do you want coffee? I was just about to dress."

He stood leaning against the door. The snow had wet his

hair, and it formed small curls on his forehead. His thick fur collar was turned up around his ears.

"Yes, coffee would be fine."

She gestured for him to take off his coat and to follow her into the kitchen. He left the coat on a chair in the corridor and ran his hands through his hair.

"Are you sure you don't mind my coming without Gennaro?"

She turned and smiled. "I suppose you have a reason. Black or with milk?"

"Black, no sugar. Oh, I got you some cigarettes, the ones you like."

He tossed a package of her Turkish cigarettes on the table and pulled out a chair. She smiled her thanks and continued filling the percolator.

He sat awkwardly in the kitchen chair, feeling foolish, knowing he should not have come, as he watched her getting cups and saucers, putting them on the table in front of him. As she passed him, he caught her hand.

"I had to see you, to find out if everything was all right. Where are the others?"

"I told you they were going shopping. Do you want to see them?"

"No . . . Are they all together?"

"Yes."

"You've had no trouble?"

"No. Should I have?"

He smiled suddenly. "I've missed you, Sophia."

He turned her hand over and kissed the center of her palm. She withdrew it quickly and gestured toward the coffee. He lifted his hand in a gesture of apology. "Sorry . . ."

"What does he need to ask me? Did he tell you?"

"Better wait for him to tell you himself. By the way, I told him I was having a meeting with the attorney general. . . . It's only partly a lie; I am having lunch with him."

"Is that why you're here, in New York?"

Pirelli nodded. "I got a possible lead to Luka Carolla. He's here in New York. I got a tip. Someone using his ID picked up the contents of a safety-deposit box previously owned by Paul Carolla."

She seemed uninterested. He continued. "I was virtually off the case. I'd already returned to Milan—"

She turned. "You mean, they closed the case? Even though you hadn't found the killer?"

"Not exactly, but we aren't looking for anyone else. The case is still open, but since this tip . . . Can I help at all?"

She stepped back quickly as if afraid he would touch her again. "No, I won't be a minute."

But when he again reached for her hand, she gave in, leaned against him slightly. "Don't, Joe. Whatever happened between us was a mistake. It is over."

He still held her. "Didn't it mean anything to you?"

Tentatively she touched his head. "Yes, at the time, of course, it did."

Pirelli looked up at her. "I'll leave my wife. Is that what you want?"

She drew away. "What I want shouldn't make any difference. If you want to leave your wife, that is your business. It has nothing to do with me."

He snapped, "Of course, it does!"

Equally angry, she turned to him. "No, it hasn't. You're married. I don't want anything to do with breaking up your marriage. That would put the onus on me, wouldn't it? What you're saying is, if I want you, you will leave your wife."

"But if I left her, where would we be?"

"There is nothing between us."

He felt as if she had slapped his face. "I see. Well, I'm sorry. I believed you felt something, maybe even wanted me, because I wanted you—"

"Then you were mistaken. I'm sorry, too."

Pirelli stood up. "Look, I'll leave, come back with Gennaro."

With some semblance of control, he asked if he could make a telephone call. Sophia nodded and pointed to the study. He made sure he didn't touch her as he passed.

The coffee percolator bubbled and frothed, and she poured herself a cup, then went back to the hall, unintentionally able to overhear his phone call. She heard the name Barzini and moved closer to listen.

"Yeah, well, I'm sorry, but if you could check out Barzini's associates, in particular over the last five years . . . You can contact me at my hotel. I'll be back there about three this afternoon, local time. . . . Thanks a lot, bad timing. . . . Okay, thanks!"

Pirelli let the phone fall back onto the hook. He had just been told that Barzini had been buried that morning. He was glum-faced as he walked into the corridor.

"Everything all right?" asked Sophia.

He nodded and went down the hall to get his coat.

"Your coffee's ready."

"What?"

"Your coffee . . ." She waved toward the kitchen.

He gave her a lopsided smile. "I'd better skip the coffee. I'll see you later."

She walked to the front door and reached for the lock. He was close; as she turned, he drew her into his arms. She struggled slightly, resisting as he kissed her neck.

"No . . . No, please don't."

He grabbed her hair roughly, pulling her head back, and kissed her lips. She couldn't stop herself, couldn't prevent her arms from encircling him. . . . He lifted her off her feet.

"Where's the bedroom?"

She clung to him, and he didn't wait for a reply. He crossed the hall, kicked open a door, and laughed. "First time lucky!" He carried her to the bed and laid her down.

"Do you want me the way you tried before? You want me that way? You call the shots because I'll have you any way you want, take anything you want to give me. . . . Just tell me, tell me you want me."

She held her arms out to him, and he knelt on the bed, holding her gently. His voice was muffled with emotion. "I love you. You know that, don't you? I love you. I ache with it, hurt with it. . . ."

She was close to tears. "It can't work, it can't. . . ."

He tilted his head and looked at her as he loosened his tie, threw it aside, and began to unbutton his shirt. When he reached the third button, he tapped his chest. "You know how to knife a man in the heart, kill him? Want to know exactly where to place the knife? Here, third button of the shirt. You hit the bull's-eye the first time I laid eyes on you."

She couldn't stop herself from smiling up at him, wanting him closer.

"I want you," she whispered.

He smiled and took her face in his hands, kissing her sweetly. Then his tongue traced her lips, and she pulled him to her, feeling him against her, the rush of heat sweeping over her until her legs wanted to open for him, curl around him. . . .

The coffee was cold, but he didn't care. He gulped it down, then looked at his watch. He was dressed only in his shirt and shorts, and she laughed.

He grinned. "It's not funny, I've got to get out of here and down to the street before Gennaro arrives. It's almost twelve now."

"Go just as you are. He'll never suspect anything."

Pirelli laughed, a wonderful, infectious laugh, and it made her want to hold him. She giggled as he stumbled around trying to get into his trousers.

"Get dressed, woman. This is all your fault."

"No, it's yours. You came early."

He kissed her. "Do you have any idea what it did to me, seeing you in just that robe? I could smell you, fresh from your bath. You drove me crazy within seconds."

She laughed, then looked around the room. All her carefully chosen clothes had been thrown in disarray on the floor. She picked up a silk shirt.

"Never mind what I do to you. Look what you've done to my beautiful shirt! And get your pants on, Commissario. Your friend will be arriving."

He was suddenly serious, almost as if he were rehearsing her. "You just have to tell him the truth; we met in Milan by accident and went to the opera, had supper—"

"What if I were to come clean, tell him what we did? What would happen?"

He slipped his shoes on. "He'd want the graphic details and then get me in the shit. Can you see my tie anywhere? Besides, he's not really interested in you. I've already given you an alibi. He's just after the driver of your car."

He located his tie and bent to retrieve it. He saw her expression change; she looked puzzled. He knew he should leave, but he hesitated, quickly knotting his tie.

"It's your chauffeur he's trying to trace. Right, I'm ready. I look okay?"

She took two steps away from him. "My God, why didn't you tell me this before? Before you made love to me? Why?"

"Because what just happened was more than I believed possible."

She folded her arms. "Why are you here, Joe? To fuck me, or what?"

He turned on her, his face flushed with anger. "I am here in New York to continue the investigation into the whereabouts of Luka Carolla. I am hunting a killer, Sophia, the possible murderer of your two sons. But I am in the bedroom with you, right now, because I had to see you. To put it simply, my priority is to track down a murderer. That I happen to be in love with you complicates—"

She snapped, "I'm a complication now, am I? You came early to soften me up?"

"That's not true, and you know it."

"Then tell me why you will be coming here with Gennaro? Tell me."

He stared at her, feeling the fear behind the anger as she asked again why Gennaro wanted to know who was driving her car.

Pirelli opened the front door. "I'm sorry, I can't discuss it. You'll have to wait for Gennaro; this is not my case." The look on her face made him close the door again. "Okay, you win. Gennaro believes the driver of your car was Fabio's killer."

Sophia gasped, staring wide-eyed in faked amazement. "What?"

Pirelli looked at her and gave a dispirited shrug. "That's why I was so afraid for you, for your family. . . . Who was he, Sophia?"

"We just hired him. There must be some mistake."

It was late. Pirelli walked out, saying over his shoulder, "I'll see you in a few minutes."

Sophia closed the door, her heart thudding. They knew about Johnny. She shook with panic, then got a grip on herself. The trembling faded as she reapplied her makeup. *They just want to question me about the driver of the car—* They? Joe . . . Had he told her the truth?

She hurled her lipstick across the room. Was there more that Pirelli hadn't told her? Had he simply used her, betrayed her? She reached for the Valium to ease her confusion but let the bottle fall into the wastebasket.

*There's nothing more anyone can do to you, Sophia, she told herself. Tell them just enough to get rid of them and then go . . . get out.*

Pirelli stamped his feet. It was cold; the snow was still falling, the light flakes making the sidewalk wet. Slush filled the gutters.

Gennaro was late. Pirelli checked his watch, then, with relief, watched the yellow cab draw up.

Gennaro paid off the driver. "Sorry, I took the stuff I bought back to the hotel. Everything go all right?"

Pirelli nodded. "Barzini was killed in a road accident; he was buried this morning. I tell you, this case is some crazy scene, created to torment me." He checked his watch. "We should go up, we're late."

Pirelli and Gennaro walked up the stairs side by side. As they reached the apartment, Pirelli ran his fingers through his hair.

When Gennaro was introduced to Sophia, he flushed to the roots of his unruly mop of dark hair. Pirelli had not exaggerated her beauty. . . .

Pirelli sat in silence, listening as Gennaro took Sophia's statement. Her voice was quiet, and she hardly looked in his direction once.

"And you didn't see anyone at Fabio's workroom?"

"No, I think it was lunchtime. There was no one in any of the workrooms—or perhaps there was, but I didn't see anyone the whole time I was there."

Gennaro tapped his notepad and shifted position. "If I was to tell you that someone saw you and you were actually accompanied by—"

Pirelli watched the way she smiled, shaking her head. "They must have been mistaken. I presume there must have been someone in the offices or you wouldn't have known that Nino and I were arguing. . . . Nevertheless, I saw no one, and I was not accompanied."

Gennaro asked her where she was between the hours of ten-thirty and midnight on the evening she had visited Nino.

Sophia didn't even give a flicker toward Pirelli. "I met Commissario Pirelli, quite by chance, and we went to the opera together. The opera was *Rigoletto,* and we left halfway through, before the last act. We then dined together, until after midnight."

Gennaro raised an eyebrow to Pirelli, but he was staring down at the carpet.

"Do you know a Celeste Morvanno?"

"Yes, she used to be my receptionist. When I closed my company, she went to work for Nino, although I didn't know that at the time. In fact, I was not aware of it until I went to Nino's workshop. She had actually told me that she would not be working after she had left my firm because she was pregnant. She obviously lied, but then I am getting used to people using me, lying to me."

She did not look at Pirelli, but he coughed and shifted his position slightly.

"How did you arrive at Fabio's workroom?" asked Gennaro.

"By car, a white Rolls Corniche. It used to belong to my father-in-law, Don Roberto Luciano."

"Did you drive the car yourself?"

"No, I used a chauffeur."

"Did you know the driver well?"

"No. He had worked for my mother-in-law for some time, at the Villa Rivera."

"Do you know his name?"

Sophia hesitated, then nodded. "His first name was Johnny, but I can't recall his other name. I am sure my mother-in-law could give you his full name."

Pirelli looked up, his eyes narrowed. The name Johnny struck him as being one hell of a coincidence. He waited to hear what Gennaro would ask next, but Gennaro did not seem to pick up on Luka Carolla's alias.

"Did your driver enter the building at any time?"

"He came to collect me and take me down to the car."

"Do you know if he returned to the building?"

"No."

"You seem very sure?"

"Well, I can't say he didn't, I mean, I don't know his exact movements, but he had no reason to return. When I told him to go on to Rome, after I had agreed to meet Commissario Pirelli, He returned directly, or so I presume."

"You don't know what time he arrived in Rome?"

"I'm sorry, I don't. But perhaps my mother-in-law, Graziella Luciano, can give you the time."

"He was staying at your apartment?"

She hesitated, licking her lips. "No, he was not, but I did ask him to check if she was all right. I don't like to leave her alone for long, after everything she has been through. I cannot give you his address, but again, perhaps my mother-in-law can provide it."

"Do you know if he knew Nino Fabio?"

"I doubt it. He was simply a driver."

"So when you went to the opera with Commissario Pirelli, what happened to the car?"

"As I said, the chauffeur returned to Rome, to my apartment there."

Gennaro closed his notebook. "I will have to question your mother-in-law, and I would also like to trace the driver. Do you have any idea of his whereabouts?"

"No, I'm sorry. I presume that after we left Italy, he got work elsewhere."

Gennaro looked at Pirelli, and the room was silent for a moment. Pirelli got up and leaned against the side of the desk.

"Do you know how Nino Fabio was murdered?"

"No. I discovered he was dead when I called from here to suggest the possibility of renegotiating the purchase of his designs."

"I have already discussed with you my need to trace Luka Carolla, the adopted son of Paul Carolla—"

Sophia nodded, then turned away, unwilling to look him in the face. He continued. "You are also aware, I think, that I believe Luka Carolla was involved in the deaths of your children?"

Her hands clasped and unclasped. "I am sure you and your associates are doing everything possible to— Would you excuse me? I need a glass of water."

Both men stood as she left the room; then Gennaro moved

to stand beside Pirelli. "She's too cool. Nothing seems to register, and she doesn't ask the right questions. I think she is covering something. I'm not through with her yet, but I want you to have a go at her, so I can sit back and listen."

Sophia came back into the room carrying her glass of water and a chilled bottle of wine on a tray, with two glasses. "Can I offer you some wine?"

"No, *grazie*." Pirelli stuffed his hands into his pockets. "Would you prefer to come with us to the local precinct? We have been given an interview room. Perhaps it would be more convenient—"

"Will that be necessary? Surely, if you need to question me further, then I should contact my attorney. Is there any need for me to do that?"

Pirelli crossed his legs, his hands still in his pockets, and looked at Gennaro. "As far as I am concerned, whatever I have to discuss with you does not require the presence of an attorney. Whether Detective Gennaro thinks differently . . . He is taking your statement, but if you are satisfied—"

Sophia gave a small shrug and sat down. Gennaro glanced at her perfect legs as she crossed them neatly, patting her tight skirt into place. She gave no indication of how nervous she was. Her eyes did not waver when she looked at Pirelli.

"There is really nothing more I can tell you."

Gennaro closed his notebook. A look passed between the two men. Pirelli lit a cigarette and pulled an ashtray closer, then started talking. "Sophia, I sincerely believe that you, and perhaps your relatives, are in danger. I want to make you aware of the facts. If after that you wish to call an attorney to rethink your statement, it is entirely up to you. . . ."

Sophia swallowed and glanced at Gennaro. Pirelli went for it. "I am sure Luka Carolla killed your children, just as I am sure that he was involved in a number of other homicides. I am also sure that he is a very sick young man."

There was no reaction; she kept her eyes downcast. Pirelli realized that he should try to be more relaxed. He poured himself a glass of wine.

"I want you to understand that you do not have to say anything. I also give you my word that anything you do say, outside your statement to Detective Gennaro, will be strictly between us. All I want is to find Luka Carolla before he kills again, and there is no doubt in my mind that he will kill again. From what I have managed to piece together about his life with the aid of the Palermo psychiatric unit and a radiologist from the Holy Nazareth Hospital who saw him when he was five or six years old, I know that Luka Carolla has the classic background for a psychopath. We can only presume the worst, that he has a compulsion to kill."

The snow was falling, thick and heavy, the windshield wipers screeching under the load. Luka drove into the private road and smiled at Graziella through the mirror. She was looking excitedly out the window of the limousine, and Teresa, in the front, sent her window gliding down.

"What is this, a hotel?"

"No, it's a private residence."

The neatly clipped hedges of the drive opened onto a sprawling, snow-blanketed lawn before the white-pillared house. It had belonged to Paul Carolla, although he had never actually lived there. It had been his dream, his step into high society, his proof of his success.

The house had been ready for occupancy the week before he fled the States. It had remained waiting for more than a year and a half, and now Luka had inherited the estate, Carolla's dream home in the exclusive Hamptons on Long Island. He owned the house, the vast gardens, the stables and yards, outright, although he had been unaware of this until he had opened Carolla's safety-deposit box. He had never been interested in the contents; he had simply wanted to put his percentage from the Barzini deal into safekeeping.

The women stepped from the limo, wide-eyed with wonder and delight. Luka was almost weeping, so thrilled was he with his secret. His excitement was marred only by the fact that Sophia was not with them.

The snow swirled around him, and he laughed, wiping it from his face. With an elegant, sweeping bow, he proudly handed Graziella the front door key.

"It is my gift, my gift to you all. And here is the deed, signed over to you, Mama Graziella Luciano."

Graziella clapped her hands to her face and said that she

couldn't possibly accept such a gift, but Teresa, at her side, laughed and said that if Graziella didn't want it, she, for one, would gladly accept on her behalf. All Graziella could say, over and over, was "*Bella, bella* . . ."

They stood in the domed hallway, looking up at the chandelier. Teresa slipped an arm around Graziella. "Well, Mama, this is more in your line, isn't it? Do you think this place is fit for the Luciano women?"

Graziella nodded, the tears streaming down her face. "This is what Papa would have wanted for you all . . . Oh, yes, this he would be proud of. *Bella, bella* . . . Johnny, come, let me thank you."

She took him in her arms and held him, kissing his face until he drew away. "For you, Mama, it's all for you, and for Sophia, too. Now, let me show you around."

Teresa slipped her arm through his. "This must have cost a fortune. Are you serious? I mean, are you giving it to us?"

He nodded, looking more boyish than ever. "We can be a family, all of us together. . . ."

Teresa smiled, but as they walked up the stairs to see the bedrooms, she tried to calculate the value of the property. "Who did it belong to? It looks as if it were recently renovated," she said.

Luka smiled happily. "It belonged to some rich banker who died before he could move in. It was sold lock, stock, and barrel."

"Is it rented, Johnny? Have you taken a lease on it?"

He shook his head. "No, I bought it. . . . Now, this is the master suite. . . ."

The women followed him from room to room, but Teresa began lagging behind, touching the tapestries, looking at the chandeliers, the paintings, and feeling the thick wool carpets beneath her feet.

Nothing appeared to have been used, even in the vast kitchen. Every pan and plate was new; some things even had price tags on them. Teresa calculated that the contents of the house were worth a hundred times more than they had given Luka, so how had he come by the house? If he did own it, as he said, why had he given it to Graziella? Nothing made sense. It was all eerie. Something was wrong. . . . She wished Sophia were with them.

While Graziella and Rosa continued to the next floor, Teresa returned to the front hall and opened the envelope containing the deed. It was, as Luka said, in Graziella's name. She carried it into the living room, pausing to take in the wonderful antique furniture, the floor-to-ceiling windows overlooking the lawns. She listened for the voices upstairs, then hurried to the telephone. All she had to do was call the real estate agents, who could tell her. . . . But the phone had not yet been connected.

Pirelli had been talking for almost two hours. The bottle of wine had been consumed, his cigarette pack emptied. Sophia had not interrupted once, just sat with her eyes downcast, as if concentrating on a small spot on the carpet. Her glass of water was still half full, and although Pirelli had offered her cigarettes, she had smoked only the one she had lit at the beginning of the interview, stubbing it out after a few moments. Her hands remained clasped in her lap.

Pirelli had told her everything he could possibly recall about his search for Luka Carolla. Now he felt drained; his voice was hoarse. He had left nothing to her imagination, describing in detail the strength the killer needed to inflict such wounds. Even Nino's bizarre death seemed to leave her unmoved. He had expected more, and now he felt depressed and sickened, so emotionally drained that his head throbbed. He wanted to shout at her, but all he could do was look helplessly at his friend.

The silence within the room was ominous, and he sighed. Slowly she looked up to meet his eyes; then she looked down again. After what seemed an endless delay she smoothed her skirt, pressing her palms flat against her thighs. "I—"

He leaned forward, waiting.

"Everything you have told me shocks me, frightens me more than I can put into words, but I cannot see how I can help you. Believe me, I sincerely wish that I could, but even knowing everything, I am still unable to give you any assistance. I have never to my knowledge met Luka Carolla; however, I will most assuredly take precautions and warn my family."

Pirelli met her eyes; they seemed so expressionless that it was hard to believe they had shone with love only that morning. He moved a fraction closer.

"Sophia, we are sure you had nothing to do with Nino Fabio's murder. . . ."

She continued to stare into his face.

"You have stated that you met Celeste Morvanno outside the building. But what we have not told you is that Celeste, when brought in for questioning, saw a wanted poster and a photograph on the wall of the police station and stated that the man in the photograph and the man driving your car were one and the same. She swore this under oath, and that is why we both are in New York."

Sophia continued to look directly at him, waiting.

"Sophia, the photograph, the picture Celeste picked out, was of Luka Carolla."

A reaction at last, a sharp intake of breath, the only sign that his words had affected her. She seemed to shake her head slightly; then, as Pirelli waited for something further, she bowed her head again, once more concentrating on her hands in her lap.

His voice became very quiet. "The other piece of information I have withheld until now is that Luka Carolla is known to use an alias. When he checked into a hotel before Paul Carolla was killed, and when he booked a flight out of Italy, he used the name Johnny Moreno, the same Christian name, at least, as your driver."

Both men watched her intently. She was unnervingly still. When she spoke, her voice was huskier, even deeper than before, but without a tremor. She lifted her beautiful head.

"Do you have this picture, the police composite? I think, if I could see it, I would be able to tell you if the driver—if the driver was—" her voice faded, and she almost whispered the name—"Luka Carolla."

Gennaro took the photograph from his briefcase and passed it to her. She studied it, then handed it back. He passed her the composite, and again she spent some time looking at it, giving Pirelli the opportunity to watch her.

Her profile seemed carved in stone; but her full mouth with the dark lipstick was open a fraction, and he saw her tongue lick her top lip. It was a small movement; he would have missed it if he were not watching her so closely.

Suddenly she looked up, her eyes so dark they seemed all pupils. "I am afraid there is no resemblance between my driver and this man in the drawing. Celeste was mistaken. But then I am sure that while we were talking, the driver was actually in the car. It has a tinted windshield."

Pirelli leaned closer. "Please look at the picture again, Sophia. The police composite was made up from a number of witnesses' descriptions, but it is the man we want. Look at it closely. Was he the man you hired to drive for you?"

She bent her head to look at the picture of the man who had killed her babies, Luka Carolla alias Johnny Moreno. Both detectives sat poised, waiting.

*Why isn't she answering?* Pirelli thought. *Why?* His head throbbed with tension.

Gennaro coughed, breaking the awful, tense silence. It had lasted only a few seconds, but in that time Sophia made her decision. There would be no turning back. She knew where Luka was, knew who he was, and he belonged to the Luciano women.

She set the composite down with care. "No, this is not my driver. His hair was reddish, he was perhaps younger, but I am sure when I speak to my mother-in-law, she will be able to give you his name and no doubt the address of his family."

Gennaro looked to Pirelli for his lead; there was nothing more. He rose to his feet, placing his empty wineglass on the tray.

"Thank you for your statement, Signora Luciano. I presume if it should be necessary for me to contact you again, and Signora Graziella, I will find you at this address?"

Sophia stood up and told him she would be staying with Teresa until she found alternative accommodation and would certainly forward any new address. She walked them to the door, thanked them both for coming, and shook both men's hands.

Gennaro was too close for Pirelli to say anything personal. All he could do was smile; he received, in return, a frozen stare. Sophia was untouchable; her hand resting in his was cold, alien. He felt he would never be allowed to come close to her again.

The men walked slowly down the stairs, hearing the door close behind them. Sophia had waited until they were almost halfway down before she slid the chain across the lock.

Unhurriedly, as if in a trance, she went into the bathroom. She didn't retch. The vomit seemed to spew out of her belly in one long stream. She brushed her teeth and returned to the bedroom, put the phone back on the hook. Then she sat at the study desk and waited for Luka Carolla, alias Johnny Moreno, to call. And she feared for the women.

More than an hour later the ringing began. She picked up the phone.

"Sophia, is that you?"

"Hello, Teresa."

"Are you all right? Did everything go okay?"

"Yes, where are you?"

Teresa told her about the house, how strange it was that Johnny had said he owned it. "Sophia, it's worth millions, and he's given the deed to Graziella."

"Where is he now, Teresa?" Sophia tried to keep the panic from her voice.

"He insisted on driving back to pick you up. Listen, we all brought our gowns, you know, the ones we wore at the Sans Souci, kind of for a celebration dinner—"

"Teresa, is the phone cut off at the house? Why are you calling from a pay booth?"

"It isn't connected yet. We're at a local supermarket. When we're finished here, Rosa wants a bathing suit. We're filling up the pool. . . . Hello? Are you there, Sophia?"

"How long will he be? When did he leave?"

"Hours ago. Are you okay? You sound kind of uptight. Did it go okay with Pirelli?"

"He stayed for hours. I had to leave the phone off the hook."

"I know. We couldn't get through. . . . Listen, I don't know about this house. . . . Sophia, is anything wrong?"

"No . . . I'll explain everything when I see you. Now can I speak to Mama for a moment?"

Graziella came on the line and began to describe the house they were staying in, but Sophia interrupted her. "Mama, listen to me. You once had a gardener, a young boy with reddish hair who used to work for you. Can you recall his name?"

"What?"

"A gardener, Mama, he had red hair—"

"Oh, *sì*, Giulio! He is Adina's nephew. Now he has a taxi

firm in Palermo. You know the Excelsior Hotel? Papa bought him his first car . . . Giulio Bellomo."

"*Grazie*, Mama, give me Adina's telephone number in Mondello."

Graziella didn't have it, but she instructed Sophia to look for her telephone book in one of her dresser drawers in the bedroom.

Sophia searched the drawers and found the photographs that used to adorn the piano at the Villa Rivera. She looked at each one in turn: her little boys; her wedding to Constantino; another of Teresa and Filippo holding Rosa's hand when she was a toddler.

She found an old photo, brown with age, of Roberto Luciano as a young man. The black eyes stared, unsmiling, from a handsome, arrogant face that was very different from the photo of him and his wife on their wedding day. Last was the familiar face of Michael, the same as the one that had hung on the walls of the Villa Rivera. She touched it fleetingly with the tips of her fingers before she turned to the little worn book.

Adina answered the phone and wept as soon as she heard Sophia's voice. She grew quiet when Sophia assured her that they were fine but needed help. Very slowly Sophia outlined the favor she wanted, the debt that could be repaid to Don Roberto's widow. She simply required Giulio Bellomo to fix his payment books to show himself as the driver of the Lucianos' Rolls-Royce. She also wanted him to go to Milan and familiarize himself with the route from her apartment to Nino Fabio's warehouse. She was not satisfied until Adina had repeated the instructions three times. Then Sophia told her that she must prepare herself for possible questions from the carabinieri, that Giulio must not deviate from the story told by Sophia. It was imperative; it could affect Graziella's life.

Sophia then placed a call to Pirelli's hotel, knowing that he would not be there. She left a message for him to the effect that Graziella's recollection was that the driver was called Giulio Bellomo, nicknamed Johnny, and supplied his address.

Sophia began to remove all the personal papers from Teresa's study, packing anything that seemed to be of importance into her briefcase. She then went to each room, searching drawers and bedside tables, removing everything she thought necessary. She did not want to take too much; it was imperative she did not make Johnny—Luka—suspicious, but she had to make sure she took everything important so they would never have to return to the apartment again.

Sophia's hoped-for freedom was over. She knew now she would never be free of the Lucianos; they would cling to her like a curse. But now she no longer felt dragged down by the fact; it was as if she were standing outside herself, watching, gently denying any fear.

Pirelli opened a new package of cigarettes. Gennaro, sitting next to him on a barstool, gave him a sidelong glance. In front of them stood a row of empty glasses.

"Maybe we should grab a sandwich? What do you think?"

Pirelli gave him a sour look and gulped his whiskey down without bothering to reply.

"What's the next move, Joe? What's next?"

Pirelli hunched over the bar. "I don't know."

Gennaro stared into his drink. "You know, the only time I saw any kind of reaction from her was when you said the name Johnny Moreno. She seemed to kind of tense up, but I couldn't see her face. But say it was him at Fabio's place, I mean, if he had somehow wormed his way into driving for her, do you think even after everything you told her, she still would have denied it?"

Pirelli sniffed and hunched further over the bar. "You got any kids?"

"No."

"Well, I've got one, a boy, and if he had been shot and my wife were told who had done it, even if she'd robbed a fucking bank with him, you think she wouldn't do something, say something?"

"Maybe your wife would, but then she's not a Luciano."

"Jesus Christ, what the hell difference does that make? Sophia's a woman, a mother. You should have seen her when I first met her. She wanted the killer then, even accused me of not trying to find him because she was a Luciano. . . . Well, now she knows all there is to know. If she wanted him caught before, stands to reason she wants him even worse now. If she'd recognized him, do you think she wouldn't have said? Wouldn't have reacted? Your witness has to have been wrong."

He ordered another round of drinks. Gennaro shook his head, refusing the refill. "You still gonna see what you can get from the Barzini tip?"

With a nod Pirelli knocked his drink back. "Yeah, while I'm here, I'll do whatever I can. You gonna hang around to see the old lady? Do you need to now?"

Gennaro shrugged. "Nah, it's not worth it. I can get the next flight back. With the expenses that cheap bastard handed out, I can't afford to stay. Besides, I reckon you'd like an excuse to go back and see the beautiful Sophia, huh?"

"What?"

"Come on, you still expect me to believe your meeting was accidental? A quiet supper, and you didn't even try to make her? I would have if I were in your shoes. Christ, what a pair of legs—"

Pirelli interrupted by waving his hand to the bartender. He snapped, "You've got it wrong. You don't make women like Sophia Luciano."

"Maybe, but I wouldn't blame you for trying."

Pirelli glared and turned back toward the bartender. He tossed some dollars on the bar to cover the tab, then picked up his coat. "Don't push it, Gennaro, or you'll get that bowl of peanuts rammed down your throat. Call the hotel, see if there's any messages, and I'll grab a cab."

It was freezing, the snow pelting down. Cab after cab splashed past, and Pirelli, frustrated, turned his fur collar up around his ears. Every cab that passed was taken or had the off duty sign up. He was actually standing within yards of the entrance to the Luciano apartment, but he couldn't bring himself to look in its direction.

Heading down the street, no more than a hundred yards away and hemmed in by the traffic, Luka Carolla impatiently inched the rented limo forward. He was within moments of the apartment block when an empty taxi turned out of a side street, its availability sign lit up. Pirelli stepped into the road to hail it as Gennaro, holding a newspaper over his head, ran from the bar.

"Hey, Joe, she's already called the hotel."

Halfway into the taxi, Pirelli stopped and turned. "What?"

"Sophia Luciano—she left a message."

Pirelli's heart stopped. "For me?"

"No, it's the name and address of the chauffeur."

Two cars behind in the traffic, Luka Carolla had his hand on the horn, urging the cab to move on. He swore at the delay.

Pirelli climbed into the cab and slammed the door shut. Gennaro banged on the window. "Hey, what about me?"

Pirelli yelled, "I've got to see the attorney general."

The taxi moved on, almost causing an accident with the car behind. The cabdriver yelled abuse while Gennaro shouted to Pirelli, "I thought you'd already seen him?"

Pirelli opened the window and stuck his head out. "I lied! I was making passionate love to Sophia Luciano! See you back at the hotel."

Gennaro, his newspaper disintegrating on his head, gave him the finger. "Lying bastard," he muttered, getting his feet soaked as a stretch limo passed him.

The limo took a left turn into the underground garage beside Teresa Luciano's apartment block, passing Gennaro by inches.

If Pirelli had looked out of the back of the cab, he would have seen him. It was as close as he had come to finding Luka Carolla. He took out his handkerchief to wipe his face dry.

"You have a good Christmas?" the cabdriver adjusted his mirror. "Gonna be freezing tonight."

Pirelli nodded but made no reply. He didn't want to get drawn into conversation, and the lump in his throat wouldn't have made it any easier. . . . He sat back and closed his eyes. Maybe she had no feelings for him; maybe she had been hurt too much; maybe she was simply out of his reach, beyond him. He knew he would never forget her. Perhaps when he was an old man, he would dream of her, remember the passion, her wondrous hair across the pillow, her sweet smile when she reached up to him. But he knew it would not happen again; he would make no attempt to see her; it was over.

"Sophia . . ." He said her name just once, without emotion, and there was none left. It felt as though a missing part of him were being compressed back into shape. As soon as he returned to Milan, he would take the vacation that was owed him, and he would make it up to Lisa. Just thinking of his family gave him a sense of security, a sense of how much he had almost lost.

Sophia had lived her life with secrets, weaving lies so that her past would not catch up with her. It was therefore not difficult to lie to Luka; it was easier than she had anticipated because she no longer felt any guilt. At her suggestion Luka returned the rented limo, and they drove to Long Island in the Lincoln.

The more lies she wove into her report of her interview with Pirelli, the more she saw Johnny, or Luka, relax. As the snow continued to fall, she felt wrapped in a cocoon, a private world she alone controlled.

# 22

The snow was thicker than ever as Sophia and Luka drove up to the Groves. She looked back to the gates to see them ease shut electronically.

Luka deposited her at the front porch and drove around the back to park. She hardly had time to shake the snow from her coat before Graziella threw open the door. She clasped Sophia to her, drawing her into the impressive hallway.

Rose hurried down the wide, sweeping staircase, wrapped in a bath towel. "There's an indoor swimming pool. I've been swimming," she said delightedly.

Sophia was pulled this way and that, and all the while Luka hung back slightly, blushing and smiling with pleasure. Sophia said all the right words.

They all seemed to have had great weights lifted from them, and nothing in Sophia's manner gave even a hint of what was to come.

As soon as Luka drove off to shop with Graziella's extensive grocery list, Sophia called to Teresa and stopped Rosa on her way back to the swimming pool.

"Go and get Mama. I want to talk to all of you, and hurry, we don't have much time."

They converged on the hallway from various parts of the house. Sophia stood at the door of the living room and gestured frantically for them to come inside. She then shut the doors as if to keep them all in the room.

"Is this about Pirelli, Sophia?" Teresa demanded.

"Yes, and you'd better sit down, all of you because I don't know how to make what I have to say any easier."

Her husky voice held them all. "You must keep calm. We have to work out exactly what we are going to do and how we are going to do it."

They waited expectantly as she paused a moment, then plunged straight in: "Johnny Moreno is not who he says he is. He is Paul Carolla's adopted son. His real name is Luka. He is Luka Carolla."

Luka loaded two more bags of groceries into the Lincoln. He could hardly close the trunk; there was enough food and wine to keep them for months. He checked the list to make sure he hadn't missed anything. Then, satisfied, he drove to a gas station. He had been out nearly two hours.

Sophia stood with her arms folded, her fingers gripping her upper arms so tightly she could feel the nails cutting into the flesh. The atmosphere was tense now; she was surrounded by panic-stricken faces.

She continued. "He must not have any idea that we know. Mama will begin cooking, and we will prepare dinner as if nothing has happened. Keep him occupied; keep him out of the way. Teresa and I will make sure every exit from the house is locked. There must be no way out, no escape. As soon as we know he can't move out of the house, we eat. We all sit down together as planned. He may not seem dangerous, but remember, Pirelli said he must be exceptionally strong to cut his victims so viciously. . . . If you waver, if at any time you feel afraid, you, Teresa, remember Filippo, Rosa, your Emilio, and you, Mama, think of Papa, my babies, Constantino. . . . All of you keep remembering what he has done and know we will, as we have prayed, at last get justice. And we all want it, we do all want this? Don't we?"

Her face was like a beautiful mask as she looked from one woman to the next. Rosa wiped away her tears with the back of her hand, afraid to meet Sophia's penetrating gaze.

"Rosa? Rosa?"

Rosa swallowed and half rose from her seat as Sophia loomed over her. "Do you want to leave? Rosa, if you want to leave, you had better say so."

"No . . . No!"

"Fine. Then dry your eyes. Are you all right?"

"No, of course I'm not, because you could be wrong about him. You don't know for sure."

"Then he can prove it. We'll give him that chance. Now go get dressed. You all were expecting to dine in your best, so dress—and act—as if nothing has been said."

Graziella remained seated, her hands on her knees, her eyes closed as if in prayer.

Teresa whispered shakily, "Maybe you shouldn't have told Mama?"

But Sophia shook her head. "We need her; she'll have to slip the stuff into his dinner; she always serves."

Graziella spoke, and there was not even a tremor to her voice. "I pray to God you are not wrong, and I thank God if you are right. Then I can die in peace."

Sophia knelt by Graziella, held her hands. "Mama, he'll have the chance to answer all our questions. We won't do it until we are sure, and we will be sure when we do it."

Teresa was afraid, she knew it. For all her bravado, every-thing seemed to pale against Sophia's cold, calculating de-meanor.

Sophia was still bending close to her mother-in-law. "I'll bring you the pills, Mama. Maybe if we crush them into pow-der. . . . You always have a handkerchief up your sleeve; you can empty it like so. . . ."

Sophia slipped a lace-trimmed handkerchief from Graziel-la's sleeve to demonstrate how Graziella could empty the pow-der into Luka's dinner.

Teresa asked, "Sophia, how are we going to do it?"

The beautiful, masklike face turned in Teresa's direction. "He is guilty, Teresa, I know it. In some way I have always had this feeling about him, but I never knew what it was, why he made me feel the way he did. He has to die slowly, painfully."

"Which one of us will do it?"

"All of us, we'll all do it. . . ."

They heard the tooting of the car horn, and Teresa crossed to the window. Her whole body was shaking as she said, "He's here. It's him. . . . He's driven around to the back of the house."

Sophia looked at Rosa. "Get the keys as soon as he leaves the car, and you, Teresa, use the electronic lock for the main gates."

The tire tracks could still be seen, although the snow was still falling. Rosa waited, trembling, in the stables. Luka passed her three times, unloading the groceries. She heard the lid of the trunk slam down; then he passed her a fourth time, whistling. She peered over the stable door in time to see him going into the kitchen.

She hurried down the long gravel drive to the big iron gates and slipped a padlock and chain around them. Then she ran back to the car, took the keys from the ignition, and went into the kitchen, her heart pounding. She quickly removed her coat and shook the snow from her hair.

Graziella had already covered the kitchen table with the provisions from the brown grocery bags. As Rosa slipped the car keys into a kitchen drawer, Graziella asked her to put a pan of water on the stove to boil for the rice and then to chop mushrooms, onions, and tomatoes.

The knife was sharp as a razor, and the pattering of Graziella's feet on the tiled floor as she bustled about seemed unreal. The old lady was behaving as if nothing untoward were about to take place. She was simply cooking dinner, their first dinner in their new home. The tears streamed down Rosa's face, and suddenly she felt her grandmother's soft hand on her neck.

"Onions always make such tears. . . . You know, if you place a bowl of hot water at your side, you won't cry. Did you know that, my little one?"

Rosa nodded and wiped her cheeks. Graziella put a steaming bowl of water beside her, and her soft voice calmed Rosa. "Remember that night, when you were all dressed up in your wedding gown that Sophia had made especially. . . . It was so beautiful, and you were so happy. . . . Remember, Rosa, remember?"

Graziella's eyes held her granddaughter's, and it was not until Rosa nodded that Graziella turned back to her cooking.

Graziella began to sing an old Sicilian ballad. It was eerie: the soft voice singing, the bubble of food on the stove, and the onion tears that continued to stream down Rosa's face. Rosa started to remember, to see again the night she danced for them in her white wedding gown, and the quick chopping of her knife became firmer as her sweet young mouth set into a thin, hard line.

Teresa was wearing the black dress Sophia had given her for their dinner party in Rome. She came out of her bedroom just as Sophia was passing.

"I think that's a good idea, Teresa."

He appeared from nowhere, his blond head resting on his forearms as he leaned on the banister rail. Teresa watched as Sophia went to stand close to him.

"Johnny, don't you think Teresa looks lovely?"

"You look beautiful, Teresa. Turn around and let me see. . . . What a dress! Is this one of Nino Fabio's creations, Sophia?"

"Yes . . ."

Luka laughed, giving Sophia an intimate look, and started up the stairs. Teresa couldn't stop shaking; she hurried down the stairs, leaving Sophia alone on the landing. Luka paused and turned back, looking down at Sophia, as he pulled his T-shirt over his head. His gold heart caught in the cloth, and he twisted his head to free himself from the chain. When he looked at her again, she was staring at his body, and he flushed, wanting to cover his chest.

She could see how tight and muscular he was. How strong he must be; Nino Fabio's wound had been so deep the muscles of his back had been cut through. . . . He turned and ran on up the stairs, thankful that she could not see the effect she had on him. His body seemed to be on fire for her.

Sophia could see the welts on his back as he disappeared from view. Pirelli had forgotten nothing; he had repeated the description of Luka given him by Father Angelo. It was yet further proof of his identity.

Rosa met her mother on the landing. Teresa looked furtively toward the floor above and whispered, "Are you all right?"

"Yes, Mama."

"Did you get the keys?"

"Yes . . . Mama, I can't bear it. I can't—"

Out of the corner of her eye Teresa saw him, wrapped in a bath towel and peering down at them. Teresa's dress was still creased from the suitcase, and she tried to smooth it with nervous hands.

Rosa's voice wavered as she tried to make conversation. "Why don't you play the piano, Mama? It's a Steinway. Go and play the piano, I'll go change . . . Mama?"

Teresa looked upward, but Luka had disappeared. "I'll wait with you, Rosa."

Rosa whispered, "No, go downstairs and play for us."

Obediently Teresa entered the living room.

Graziella could hear the piano in the kitchen, but she did not recognize the melody. She stood with her head slightly cocked to one side. . . . She could remember Roberto's voice, laughing when he said there was never any time for him to have his bath because the bathroom was always full; she could remember the children's voices as they played on the landing. . . . She moved to Sophia's side as if for comfort.

Sophia was squashing tablets, a mixture of Valium and Seconal sleeping tablets with the garlic press. "Where's your handkerchief, Mama?"

Graziella took the clean lace square from her pocket and handed it to Sophia. The piano stopped abruptly as they heard a scream.

Sophia ran from the kitchen, snatching up the knife Rosa had been using.

Luka, wearing a strange frock coat and an old top hat, was swinging a cane and laughing as Sophia entered.

Teresa was still sitting at the piano, trying to cover her nervousness by leafing through old sheet music. "He gave me such a shock!"

Luka laughed. "I crept up behind her. I was going to break into song. . . . I couldn't remember the words."

Sophia hid the knife behind her. Fixing a smile on her face, she asked Luka where on earth he had got the clothes from. Luka said they must have belonged to the previous owner; they were in an old trunk in his room.

Sophia backed to the sofa and slipped the knife between the cushions. "Why don't you play something that Johnny could dance to for us, Teresa?"

Sophia stared hard at Teresa, who fumbled frantically through the sheets of music. "I can't play by ear. I have to have music. . . ."

Luka did a quick imitation of Charlie Chaplin, shrugging his shoulders and twirling the cane, scuttling around the room with his feet splayed out. He seemed in very high spirits, and Teresa couldn't stand it. She slammed down the lid of the Steinway.

"I'll go help Mama. I'm not in the mood."

Luka tossed his hat and cane onto the sofa and looked at Sophia.

"Aren't you going to change for dinner, too, Sophia?"

"Yes, as soon as I have a moment."

Sophia was relieved when Rosa came in, carrying a tray of champagne.

"Where is Mama?" she asked, the glasses rattling as she put the tray down. When she offered a glass to Sophia, her hand shook visibly.

"Helping Graziella in the kitchen." A look passed between them as Sophia took her glass, her dark eyes urging Rosa to offer Luka a glass.

He refused a drink and picked up his hat and cane, saying he wouldn't be a moment; there was something he had forgotten. As he left the room, he gave Sophia a strange, unfathomable stare.

Sophia barged into the kitchen and spoke loudly in case Luka was listening. "Is everything all right in here, Mama?"

Graziella nodded as she put some serving dishes in the warming oven. The door opened suddenly behind Sophia and pushed her forward. She froze, then looked around fearfully. She sighed with relief when she saw it was Rosa.

\* \* \*

Luka knew something was going on. He sat on his bed and gripped the sides of it with his hands. It was Sophia; she was different. . . .

Had Pirelli told her more than she admitted? Could it be that she knew how Nino Fabio had died? Was that it? He moved to his bedside table and looked through one drawer after another. He had left his knife there. . . . If she were to tell the others . . . Would she tell on him? Someone had been in his room, searching his belongings.

The door handle was beginning to turn, and his eyes were transfixed in a wide stare. . . .

"Didn't you hear me calling you?" Sophia demanded.

She could see the sweat on his forehead and the stains in the armpits of his shirt.

"Are you all right?"

He backed away, a single, small step.

Sophia turned and he could see that the back of her dress was open. "Would you zip me?"

He edged toward her, and she felt how cold his hands were as he eased the zipper upward.

"You look very beautiful."

She turned to face him. "Thank you. . . . Don't you think you should change? Dinner's almost ready. Everyone else is downstairs, waiting."

He seemed so unsure that she moved closer. "What is it? Don't you feel good? Don't you want to eat?"

His hand was wet with sweat. His fingers tightened on her hand. "I—I got all sweaty dancing. I need to wash."

"Well, don't be long. This is a special occasion."

Suddenly he confronted her. "You've changed. Something has happened. You're different."

"It's just your imagination."

Sophia closed the dining room door behind her. "He knows something is wrong, and that's your fault." She nodded to Teresa. "He's very strange, and his room stinks. He's sweating like an animal."

Teresa put her fingers to her lips to silence Sophia; she had heard something. Sophia pulled her chair out, saying loudly, "Well, Mama, this looks wonderful. Can I help you?"

They all listened; then Rosa asked if everyone wanted wine. Teresa held out her glass, and their hands shook so much that between them they spilled a fair bit. Behind them the door creaked, and Luka, having changed his shirt, came into the room.

"Now, Johnny, you sit at the head of the table there, in the carving chair, as you are the man of the house." Graziella smiled at him as she set down the warm soup plates, then opened the serving hatch to bring a tureen to the table. She began to serve the steaming vegetable soup with a large silver ladle. Luka was silent, his eyes guarded; he sat like a naughty child forced by an adult to behave at table.

After the soup was served, Graziella folded her hands in prayer: "For what we are about to receive, we thank the good Lord. Amen."

Sophia raised her glass and smiled. "To Johnny, for providing us with this wonderful house; for this dinner, too."

They toasted him, and he seemed slowly to relax. He sipped his wine, and now his behavior was more like that of a young boy allowed to dine with the grown-ups. Somehow they managed to talk about everyday things.

The soup plates were stacked, and Graziella bustled into the kitchen. Rosa assisted her grandmother, carrying all the serving dishes for the main course and putting them close to Graziella's place at the table.

Teresa, her face flushed with wine, suggested that the first thing they had to do was hire some servants. Adina was latched onto gratefully as a subject for light conversation. Graziella lifted the lid of a serving dish and leaned over, closing her eyes to smell the aroma.

"It's good, good. . . . Now, Sophia?"

They watched as she served each of them with the fresh pasta with its thick seafood sauce, leaving Luka until last.

"I'll pass it to Johnny, Mama!" Sophia leaned across Graziella, taking the plate from her. Teresa tasted the pasta and congratulated Graziella on her culinary expertise. They all were tasting and murmuring their approval, but none of the women, it seemed, could eat more than a few mouthfuls, although the clatter of cutlery and the continuous refilling of wineglasses at least gave the appearance of a jovial dinner party.

Suddenly Teresa leaned directly across to Graziella. "Mama, you have dropped your handkerchief."

Sophia bent quickly to retrieve it, and while hidden from view, she checked that all the crushed tablets had been used. She shook it slightly, and as she sat up again, she saw Luka wiping his plate clean with some bread.

She turned to Graziella. "Mama . . ." She held out the handkerchief.

"*Grazie*, Sophia." Graziella slipped it into the sleeve of her dress. "Johnny, are you still hungry?"

The main course finished, Graziella cleared the table and brought fresh fruit and several cheeses. She was just setting down a thick cheesecake with fresh raspberries when Sophia asked her to sit with them. They could wait for coffee.

By the time Graziella had walked back into the dining room she could see that Luka was drowsy. He was sitting well back in his chair, his face flushed, and he didn't seem to notice that Graziella locked the double doors behind her as she returned to her seat and placed the key in front of Sophia.

The room fell silent, and the women looked at each other furtively. Then Sophia picked up a knife. "Would you like fruit and cheese or some of Mama's homemade cheesecake? Luka? Luka?"

Their faces were staring at him through a distorting mirror; they had elongated noses and wide cheekbones, and their mouths flapped at him. He giggled, and it didn't even register that Sophia had called him Luka.

No one moved, no one made any attempt to continue talking. They fell silent, watching him, waiting for him to sleep. It seemed an interminable time before his head rolled forward.

Sophia took one of the leather belts she had collected and tied his right leg to the chair. As Rosa did his left leg, Teresa pulled at his right arm. His left arm hung limply at his side, and he muttered, trying feebly to free himself. But the next moment he was trapped, with both arms and both legs shackled to the chair.

Sophia examined the buckles. "Make sure he can't get them undone. He's strong. Make sure they're tight."

They eased the chair a fraction away from the table and tied a scarf around his eyes. His head was now slumped on his chest. To ensure that he was completely trapped, Rosa wrapped yet another belt around his shoulders.

After they cleared the dishes and removed the tablecloth, they dimmed the huge chandelier to candlelight level. Sophia gestured for them all to leave the room.

Teresa whispered, "Shouldn't one of us stay with him?"

Sophia shook her head. "No, he can't move, look at him. We wait until he wakes."

Rosa brought coffee into the living room and passed it around with chocolate mints. On the surface everything appeared natural, yet the tension in the room was electrifying. They had succeeded in phase one; they had him trapped. Now they had to move on to phase two. When Luka woke, could they get him to talk? Would he?

Teresa, feeling chilled, rubbed her arms, and asked Rosa to light the gas fire. They all watched as Rosa knelt by the ornate marble fireplace and turned on the gas.

Graziella spooned sugar into her coffee, stirred it slowly. "Do you think there is any doubt at all, Sophia?"

Sophia shook her head, then stared into the flames as she explained how Pirelli had described him to her.

"I am *so* sure I brought along all the papers we left at your apartment, Teresa. We need never go back. If this place is really ours, we can live here, but we'd better check just how much of it we actually own. We cannot trust a word he has ever said to us."

"It's not rented," Teresa said. She walked into the hall and looked into the darkened dining room, seeing the shrouded figure still bound to the chair. His head, still wrapped in the Hermès scarf, lolled forward. She returned with the deed and handed it to Sophia.

The flickering fire attracted their attention, made a focal point for the room. Graziella watched the blue and red flames curling and weaving around the fake logs. She sighed; perhaps the fire reminded her of the massive stone grate at the Villa Rivera, but she spoke to the room, softly, without direction. "This must be a lesson to us all. How easily we have been used. Papa never allowed anyone outside the family to stay at the villa."

She turned to Sophia, watched her a moment as she read through the deed to the house. "Do you remember that time, Sophia, how angry Papa was because Constantino brought you to the villa. . . ."

Teresa was on the defensive immediately. "Mama, there were reasons for allowing Johnny into the villa, reasons we don't want to go into now."

Graziella nodded acceptance. "I had my own reasons for not being more suspicious." She smiled sadly. "He always reminded me of Michael; sometimes he looked just like Michael."

Teresa snapped, "Mama, we don't want to hear about Michael now, okay? If it weren't for him, none of us would be in this situation."

Sophia said sharply, "This is not the time to argue among ourselves."

Graziella went on. "I am not criticizing you, Teresa, just stating a fact. We must learn to protect ourselves, never allow anyone to get so close—"

Teresa's voice rose. "We all agreed to let him stay at the villa; it wasn't just me. It wasn't just my decision; you can't put the blame on—" She was red-faced with anger. "Tell her, Sophia, we all agreed."

Sophia's voice was cold but soft. "Not quite, Teresa, but what is done is done. As Mama said, we should be more careful in future."

Close to tears, Teresa left the room, flinging a last remark over her shoulder: "We have a future then, do we?"

Graziella and Rosa looked fearfully at Sophia, who could feel the tension building up in the room. She held up a small red book. "What's this?"

Rosa looked at it. "We took it from Barzini's desk, I don't know what it is." She flicked through it. "It's full of numbers, and at the back there's a list of names."

Sophia handed Graziella the deed to the house.

"Check this over, Mama," she said, then bent close and whispered in Sicilian, "Leave Teresa alone."

Graziella whispered back, "But you know what I am saying is true. You know it."

"Because he's blond and blue-eyed? He has nothing to do with Michael, Mama, and this is not the time to start thinking about Michael."

But Graziella would not leave it alone. "We just accepted him, but you know, I still can't believe what you say is true. I go over and over it, but it can't be true. All you know is what some detective told you. Don Roberto never put any trust in the police—"

"We are going to find out the truth, Mama. That is what this is all about." Sophia kissed the top of Graziella's head and patted her shoulder.

Her hand was gripped tightly, then released. "I'm sorry, I'm sorry."

Returning to her chair, Sophia began going through the folders and documents. Her head was aching, but she would not take anything—no more pills, nothing more to drink. She knew she had to remain in control of herself.

Teresa walked back into the room, and Sophia gestured for her to come to her side.

It was the thick folder of documents that puzzled Sophia. "These were supposed to be handed over to Barzini. Are these the originals?"

Teresa flushed. "Yes."

"But I thought Barzini had them?"

Teresa was shaking as she told them what had taken place at the meeting with Barzini and why she had not discussed it with them. She also told them of Luka's part in contacting Salerno.

Sophia looked hard at Teresa. "In the future you do nothing without consulting the rest of us. We were paid for the Luciano holdings, the fifteen million, yes? So why didn't you hand these over to Barzini?"

"I was going to. You see, I felt it was important to make contact with Barzini's partners, make sure they knew we weren't trying to cheat them. But at the same time we still own a New York waterfront pier, not included in the deal, and two warehouses right on the dock. I would like to continue working, with that property as a base. There are vast opportunities—" She stopped suddenly, as if everything she was saying had no place, no meaning. Not now, tonight.

Sophia stared into the flames of the gas fire. "You start running, Teresa, and your legs will be slashed off. We have to walk this one, very slowly. Maybe you're right, it is a good basis for a business, and the money split four ways doesn't in the end amount to a fortune, but . . . If we were to start up, we would have to settle with Barzini."

Teresa hesitated, then quietly, guiltily, explained that Barzini was dead. She described how he had been killed the day she met with him and that was why he had not taken the documents.

Sophia rose slowly to her feet and gripped Teresa's arm. "And you never told us? Are you mad?"

"I was only doing what I thought best."

"For whom, Teresa? We are what is left of the family. . . ." She released Teresa's arm, leaving a red impression of her slender fingers. Then she continued calmly. "Commissario Pirelli came to New York to meet with Barzini. He had had some information, a tip that linked Barzini to the murder of our men. Barzini could have been the one who hired Carolla. If they discover what we have done, we could be in trouble."

"But it was an accident. He ran straight into the street."

Sophia nodded. "Maybe we can use his accident to our advantage."

Rosa sat as if at a tennis match, looking from her mother to her aunt. Were they arguing? If so, it was very subdued.

Graziella, sitting in a low chair close to the fire, interrupted them. Her quiet voice made Sophia bend low to hear what she was saying.

"They are like wasps in a nest. Kill one, and the others will swarm around in retaliation. I used to place a jar of honey on the step, part filled with water. A lot would die because they wanted the honey. But the heart of them was in the nest. Not until the nest was set on fire were they gone. . . . Shouldn't someone check on Johnny?"

Teresa hurried from the room without being asked. Sophia looked with renewed interest at Graziella, a soft smile on her lips. Graziella warned Sophia to be careful with Peter Salerno and his willingness to cooperate. "We have the honey, Sophia, but never forget the nest."

Rosa cleared the coffee cups. As she carried them toward the kitchen, Teresa was easing the dining-room door closed.

"He hasn't moved," she whispered.

Luka's breathing was loud, as if he were deeply asleep; he had been that way for an hour and a half.

Teresa helped Rosa stack the dishes. Rosa asked, "What were you and Sophia talking about?"

"The deal with Barzini."

"I thought you were arguing."

"No, just clearing up a few things."

"She's changed; she's different."

Teresa dried her hands. "I think, under the circumstances, we all are going to change."

"Mama, if we find out, you know, if we get him to talk, what's going to happen?"

"You'd better ask Sophia. I've made so many mistakes, Rosa. I should have listened to her from the beginning. We should have gone to the police as she wanted, handed Johnny over to Pirelli when he came to the villa. But we didn't, Rosa, and I was the one who persuaded everyone to keep him safe so he could work for us. I keep seeing the blood on his clothes at the apartment: It was thick; it covered my hands."

Even now Teresa could not tell her daughter of the part she had played in Rocco's murder. At the time she had forced herself to accept it as a necessary evil. But the guilt was now manifesting itself, and it weakened her, made her vulnerable. She tried, hesitantly, to explain this to her daughter.

"Everything I did was for you and for me. I felt we were owed; I didn't care about the others. Sophia is right, I have made so many mistakes."

Teresa's face crumpled, and she wept openly, holding out her arms pleadingly to Rosa. They held each other tightly, Rosa trying to soothe her mother, whispering that no one blamed her.

"You know who's to blame, Mama, so why do we wait? If it weren't for him, I'd be married; if it weren't for him, none of this would have happened. Sophia is right: We must take our justice. He began it himself. Now we should finish it; we shouldn't wait any longer."

Teresa watched, stunned, as her daughter pulled open one drawer after another. Then, shouting, "What are you going to do? Rosa!" she rushed forward, but Rosa had torn the diamond from around her neck and was hacking at it with a meat cleaver, trying to smash it on the wooden chopping board.

Luka stirred, but he could barely lift his head. He moaned softly, then slipped back into his drugged sleep. They both heard him.

Rosa whispered, "We have to kill him, Mama, for what he's done. I want to."

Sophia had come to the kitchen door. They spun around

as she spoke. "That's right, Rosa. Now, come into the living room. I think the notebook we took from Barzini is important."

Mother and daughter hurried past Sophia, who was about to follow them when she saw the chain, the diamond teardrop, and the cleaver. She gave a slight nod of her head as if in confirmation and picked up the diamond.

She returned to the living room and bent to lay a gentle hand on Rosa's shoulder, whispering, "Diamonds are hard to destroy, Rosa. Keep it; it is valuable; we may need it."

Rosa looked up into her aunt's beautiful face. "Grandma had a pearl for every good memory of her life. Do I get a diamond for the bad? I don't want it!"

Sophia slipped the diamond into her pocket. "You will have pearls, Rosa, I promise you." She crossed to Teresa, who was flicking through Barzini's notebook.

Teresa muttered, "I don't understand this. It could be some kind of code for keeping cash records. If Barzini handled the payout to us, then maybe he used to pay off others. . . . I don't know . . ."

Sophia took the notebook and turned to the last page. "You see this? It's just a list of names. You heard of any of them?"

Teresa shook her head, and Sophia passed the book to Graziella. "Mama, these names in Barzini's book, have you ever heard of any of them? They have to be important. Remember his face when we took the book?"

Graziella held it at arm's length to read. "I've got to get some glasses. . . . Ah! You remember, I told you Mario Domino was in Papa's study, all his papers were gone? You remember, Sophia? Three men, and two of them are listed here: E. Lorenzi and G. Carboni. These men were in papa's study—"

As Sophia moved to Graziella's side, they all heard the awful sound, half cry, half howl, like that of a crazed dog.

Sophia was out first, running across the hall to the dimly lit dining room. She heard, mingled with the screams, the frantic banging of the chair as Luka tried to free himself, his body twisting and jerking the chair almost off the floor. His head thrashed from side to side, and it looked as if at any moment the chair would fall over backward.

Luka's terror cut through his throbbing head, his hazy,

drugged mind. His screams were interspersed with crazed curses, some in Sicilian, some in English, crude, foul gutter language that a child might use.

Sophia walked calmly into the kitchen and returned with a large pan of cold water. "Throw this over him; he's hysterical."

The cold water made him gasp. He stopped thrashing and sat, head down, his chest heaving as he panted.

They sat around the table, confronting his pitiful figure, not sure how to begin. They looked to Sophia for guidance.

She opened the large manila envelope and placed on the table the photographs of her children, of Constantino, Filippo, and Don Roberto Luciano. Then she returned to her seat. The pictures were not for Luka but for the women, a reminder.

The other women waited for Sophia to speak. Finally she said, "We want to know the truth, we have to know, and we do not care how long it takes us to find out, how many days, how many nights. We will wait for you to tell us what we need to know."

Unable to see her through the scarf, he turned his head as if to hear better. It was *her* voice; it was Sophia. . . . He moaned her name pitifully, asking why she was doing this to him. . . .

"Sophia is not alone. We are all here, all of us."

That was Graziella, or was it Teresa? His chest began to heave again, and panic-stricken, he started to wail. Graziella whispered to Rosa, and she slipped out of the room. Another pot of ice-cold water was thrown over him. It hit him with such force that it jerked his head back. As before, his howling stopped.

"Why don't you tell us who you are? We know you are not Johnny Moreno."

He went still and gave a shuddering sigh. The scarf, soaked, clung to his face like a second skin.

Teresa looked at Sophia and bit her lip, then cupped her hand over her mouth and whispered, "Remember how he always hated being locked in his room at the top of the house. Maybe we should lock him in now?"

Sophia nodded and gestured for Teresa to lock the door.

His head jerked as he tried to hear what was going on: first the sound of chairs scraping, the echo of footsteps. His body twisted toward the sounds. They were taking over, growing louder. . . . His nails scratched at the arms of the chair, and he stiffened as if in preparation for the sound that terrified him the most: the sound of a key turning in a lock.

The fear eclipsed all rationality. He fought it, rubbing harder against the back of his chair, trying to loosen his blindfold. But the memory swept over him; he was back in the suffocating, dark, airless cupboard, his face pressed against the door, his small body hunched as he tried to find a tiny crack of light, a small aperture he could see through, breathe through. But in that chink of light he had seen the men brought into the room, seen them pay over their money; then came the sickness in his stomach, knowing that the door would open and he would be dragged out. . . .

His bound feet pressed harder against the floor, his fingers clawed at the chair, but he was so small, so tiny, nothing he did could stop them. No one ever came to help him; no one stopped them; there was no one but himself. The wringing, twisting motion of his body ceased, and he sighed as he listened to the rhythm of his breathing, concentrating on hearing only that sound. He could float away from the pain; he didn't feel the whippings; the lacerations crisscrossing his back hurt him only momentarily. He could be suspended in a sanctuary of his own making, a place where he was free from the darkness.

Giorgio Carolla had been the only one who had understood Luka's darkness, who knew Luka's suffering, because he himself had suffered. The two boys had needed each other, been entwined with one another. The night Giorgio died, the night he had held Luka in his arms, his gentle hands tracing the white scars across his back, the dying child had comforted his sweet, tortured friend. As his heart weakened, he had thought not of himself but of encouraging Luka to talk, to release the darkness he was so terrified of. In whispering sobs Luka had put into words the nightmare, and when at last he had slept and the nightmare returned, he had screamed himself awake, the terror as vivid as always. But then came relief because his beloved friend was beside him. Smiling, he had reached out for comfort, but Giorgio was cold. . . .

The death of Giorgio had taken from Luka the only love he had ever known, and try as he would, he could not breathe through the overpowering darkness that had descended. It swallowed him, swamped him, and he gave way to it.

The women had unknowingly locked Luka into his past, and now he was experiencing again the pain he had hidden inside him for so long. They watched in sickened fascination as Luka's body relaxed, momentarily, as he gasped for breath. Then the chair banged, his body twisted, and a blubbering, infantile voice shrieked ceaselessly as his head rolled from side to side, the mouth hanging open. . . . If he was speaking, the words were unintelligible.

Graziella was unable to stand another moment; her body strained as if to go to him, comfort him. Sophia gripped her hand tightly. Rosa covered her face, whispering, "Oh, God, stop him! What's the matter with him?"

He couldn't hear her. The straps binding his arms and legs were the ropes they had used to tie him down. . . . He was hearing the chanting, the susurration of feet in leather-soled sandals, smelling the incense. . . . He whimpered and in a small, plaintive voice began to speak, the words clearer but half formed.

"It hurt me . . . hurt me. . . . No, no, please, no. . . . Please . . . please . . . please . . ."

On and on the voice whispered, pleading, as Luka became still, his head bowed. Suddenly Teresa leaned across the table and took the key, got up, and unlocked the door. Rosa followed her and, after a moment, Sophia. Only Graziella remained in the dining room, still sitting opposite Luka.

In the living room Sophia poured brandies, handing a glass to Teresa. "This all could be an act."

"What if it isn't? We don't know."

Sophia snapped, "We know he's lied to us; we know everything that Pirelli told me. We know he is a killer; we knew that back at the villa. And we protected him, so don't look at me as if I have done something wrong now. The only crime I want to know about, care about, is the murder of my children, my husband, because whoever killed them didn't just end their lives; they took mine, too. They took everything that made me a person; they took everything that made my life worth living, everything I had—"

Teresa interrupted, shouting, "We all lost, Sophia! We all want to know; we all want justice! But not this way . . ."

They heard Graziella's voice, talking so softly they could not decipher her words, but she was talking to Luka. Sophia went back to the dining room but paused in the doorway, her hand raised in warning to the others. They moved silently to look over her shoulder.

Graziella was sitting next to Luka, holding his hand. She stroked it, patted it. One by one the younger women crept farther into the room.

Graziella spoke so quietly that they had to strain to hear her. She was asking his name, over and over, asking him who he was.

"It's all right, you can tell me. No one is going to hurt you. Tell me, you can tell me."

The child's voice answered, "My name is Luka, but you must not tell him; he mustn't know I've told you."

"Who mustn't I tell? Who mustn't know who you are?" Graziella looked to Sophia, warning her to remain silent.

Luka tensed, his blindfolded head jerked, and he cowered back again. Graziella asked him over and over who he was afraid of, and now she was stroking his head, standing close to him, bending down to hear as he whispered his own name, weeping.

"Luka, Luka . . ."

Graziella gave a small look to Sophia, not understanding. He had said he was afraid of Luka, yet he also said he *was* Luka.

"Are there two Lukas?" Graziella asked gently.

"Yes," he whispered, "there are two of us."

He began to relate a long, rambling story about stealing a chicken leg, nothing that made sense to the waiting women. The tension of watching him was exhausting. The sweat glistened on Graziella's face, her body was stiff from standing in such an awkward position, and her hand ached from his unrelenting grasp; but she did not leave his side.

"Was Luka a bad boy when he was older?"

"Yes."

Not one of them dared move as the strange, high-pitched voice described how Lenny Cavataio, the man Roberto Luciano had replaced as a witness, had died. Graziella patted Luka's hand, interrupting his description of knifing Cavataio.

"Was Luka given orders? Did someone tell him to do these bad things?"

Eerily the voice suddenly deepend in tone. He spoke rapidly, "He is a professional, do you understand? No one can catch him, no one knows who he is. . . . Riding a bicycle, little boy on a bicycle. He felt no pain, no hurt. The innocent must feel no pain, must be done quickly."

Sophia sat back in her chair and closed her eyes as Luka continued to describe how the child had been offered an ice-cream cone, a raspberry-flavored ice-cream— She knew he was talking about the Paluso child, could remember the photographs of him lying in the gutter beside his bicycle.

Facing them all was the man Pirelli had tried to trace for so long, the dangerous psychopath, the mass murderer, the cold, calculating killer. Yet here was a pitiful, cowering boy, talking in the high-pitched voice of a child no older than her elder son had been. She could not even contemplate revenge; justice was a meaningless word.

The women had no anger left, felt no satisfaction in having the insane being before them trapped like an animal. Their faces registered their feelings. As Sophia glanced covertly at them, she could feel their wretchedness.

The click of her gold cigarette lighter broke the silence. She inhaled deeply and let the smoke drift from her mouth. They all could smell the heavy Turkish tobacco, and like a dog, Luka lifted his head, sniffing. . . . His body stiffened.

Sophia spoke loudly, "So now we know you killed the Paluso child, do you hear me, Luka?"

Luka's grip on Graziella's hand tightened, hurting her; she had to wrench herself away. She looked angrily at Sophia. "Why did you say that?"

"Maybe, Mama, we need to speak to his other self, tell the child Luka to go to hell. He's acting; he's playing with us."

Graziella eased herself away from him and turned to look at the scattered photographs on the table. She reached out and drew them into her arms. She didn't want to hear anymore, did not think she could bear anymore. Slowly, holding the photographs to her chest, she moved toward the door. Teresa, seeing her sway slightly, got up to assist her from the room.

Rosa pushed back her chair and followed the others. Sophia remained sitting, smoking, each breath labored. Then she drew the ashtray close and stubbed out the cigarette. She studied her perfectly manicured nails resting on the edge of the table and wanted to gouge the shining surface in which her own face was mirrored.

Luka's head lifted, and he turned sideways, listening intently. "Sophia? Sophia?"

She waited, but he said no more. Eventually she replied in a whisper, "You murdered my sons. They were innocents. Why? Why did you kill my babies, Luka?"

His head twisted, and his hands curled, making wringing motions as if he were trying to free himself. He remembered them, lying together, that was how he had first seen them from outside the window. His orders had been to radio in to the men waiting when the Lucianos left the villa, no more, no less, but the picture of the two children innocently sleeping with their arms entwined had stopped his heart. To him they were not Carlo and Nuncio Luciano; they were Luka and Giorgio. Hidden by the darkness, drawn to the soft, glowing light from the children's room, Luka had watched, then like a thief in the night had crept into the room. His gun was heavy, unwieldy, and he had winced as he attached the silencer, sure the scraping of metal on metal would wake the boys. Perhaps if they had woken, the murder would never have happened, but their steady breathing continued and assured him that what he was doing had to be done.

Even when he slid a pillow from the bed, the brothers did not wake. Neither made a sound as he covered their faces with it. Pressing the gun into the pillow, he had fired quickly, once, twice.

When at last he lifted the pillow, the gaping wounds in their heads upset him, so with great care, he had turned the children to face each other, their wounds hidden from view. He was still not content until he had laid Nunzio's arm across his brother's heart. These two boys would always be together.

Luka had stood there awhile, unable to leave them, because that was the way it should have been for Luka and Giorgio.

"Who gave the order, Luka? Who told you to murder my children?"

He made a guttural sound. She moved beside the table until she was close enough to smell his sweat. He cowered in the chair.

"You will die without a prayer unless you answer me.

Your soul will remain in hell, burn there. . . ."

He murmured something unintelligible through the wet scarf. After a while Sophia gave up and walked out. Luka listened for the door to close, but all he heard was her footsteps. Was he alone? Beneath the scarf his lips stretched into a smile. . . .

Rosa, sitting on the stairs, saw Sophia walk from the room and pause beneath the chandelier in the hall. For a moment Sophia tilted her head back, closing her eyes, and she was so still, so unnaturally still, that Rosa could say nothing. She watched as Sophia crossed the hall to the coatrack, threw a coat around her shoulders, and went out, closing the door quietly. The cold draft made Rosa shiver.

Suddenly Rosa was afraid. What had her aunt done? She crept toward the open doorway and switched on the lights.

He was still sitting there, still trying to free himself. Rosa felt drawn into the room.

"Johnny? It's Rosa. Are you all right now?"

She needed to know for herself: Had he been involved in Emilio's death? So far nothing she had heard made sense, and Sophia seemed to care only about her children.

She untied the damp blindfold and Luka blinked, trying to adjust to the light. She stared into his face, then gasped and stepped back, almost falling. He was smiling, an angelic smile, but his eyes were crazy.

His voice was wheedling, plaintive. "Help me, Rosa. Untie me, please . . ." Then softly, as if he were making love to her: "Rosa, Rosa . . ."

She straightened, and for a moment he had a faint hope. Her pretty young face was confused, and he tried smiling to encourage her forward. But his eyes betrayed him, made her fear him, and she closed the door behind her.

Rosa hurried across the hall to the living room. He called her name again, just once. "Rosa!" Then he was silent.

Rosa sat with her mother. "I went in to see him. Did you hear him calling my name?"

"Yes, yes, I heard." All Teresa could do was hold her daughter's hand.

Sophia joined them, closing the door purposefully, and

looked toward Graziella's chair by the fire. "Where's Mama?"

"She wanted to be alone; she's in her room."

Sophia nodded, then drew the curtain back from the window, rested her head against the ice-cold pane and stood there with her back to them.

After a long silence she said softly, "We can bury his body in the garden. I've marked out a place, beneath a tree, where the ground is not so hard. There are spades in the garage. We must be careful to remove the top layer, the grass, and replace it after—" She turned to face them. "Do you understand what I am saying?"

Teresa was shaking, and her voice wavered. "Are you going to— Who's going to do it?"

The curtain swished back into place. The way Sophia patted the fabric back into its folds was unnerving. "I am. All you have to do is help me when it's over. I don't want Graziella downstairs, but I will tell her we have decided."

Teresa smoothed her skirt, a strange, futile gesture, and Rosa put her arm around her mother's shoulder. "It's all right, Mama, but we'd better change; it's cold outside." She gave Sophia an almost defiant look before leaving the room.

Sophia smiled sadly. "Rosa is a Luciano, Teresa."

"I hope to God you know what you're doing, Sophia."

Sophia's voice was icy. "It is what all of us are doing, Teresa. Because we are all that's left."

Teresa and Rosa headed across the lawn to the area Sophia had marked out for the grave. Their footprints were clear in the snow. They began to dig, working hard, in unison. They did not speak as they laid the frozen turf carefully to one side and dug into the hard dark soil.

Sophia had changed into a cotton nightgown, having brought few clothes with her. She had decided that whatever she wore would have to be burned. She was barefoot and moved silently around the house, hoping Graziella would not hear her. She collected an armful of towels and took a sheet from one of the beds.

As she crossed the landing, Graziella opened her bedroom door. She looked at Sophia, at the white gown and the towels, and walked back into her room, knowing Sophia would follow.

"Are you all right, Mama? Can I get you something to help you sleep?"

Graziella shook her head. "So you have decided. I knew it would be you. I am sorry. You must be very sure, Sophia. Did he talk to you?"

"No, Mama, I think he is in a world of his own—maybe hell, who knows? He certainly put us there."

"Don't say that. . . ." The pale blue eyes searched the dark, hooded ones; then she reached for her daughter-in-law's hand. She held it tightly and lifted it to her lips, kissed the soft skin. "Stop his heart for him. The boy is so sick. I saw some poison on the top shelf of one of the kitchen cupboards. . . . Do you need me?"

"No, Mama."

"I'll pray for you, for us all."

"Yes, Mama."

Sophia went down the stairs and listened at the door. She went into the living room and felt between the cushions, brought out the knife. She could not hesitate, could not think about what she was doing. She opened the dining-room doors.

Luka sat with his head resting back on the chair. His eyes were closed, but the fact that his blindfold had been removed unnerved Sophia. She had not wanted to see his face.

Soundlessly she moved across the room. She let the sheet drop to the floor and placed the towels around the legs of the chair. The third button of his shirt was where she would knife him, but the strap Rosa had tied around his shoulders had worked down and was covering his heart.

She put the knife on the table and began to unbuckle the belt. She had to take it off, leave his chest bare.

Suddenly he turned, opened his eyes. "Sophia? I knew you would help me. I knew you would be the one." There was no trace of the child in his voice. He was Luka. She pulled the belt away, found it wet with his sweat. She went back to the table and picked up the knife.

He smiled, convinced she was going to cut through his straps. The knife was poised, held in both her hands. The tiny gold heart on the thin gold chain was like a glowing target. She gasped, and her eyes widened. . . . Then she blinked and stepped back.

Luka tilted his head to one side. Confused, he watched her put the knife down on the table. She turned to face him, staring at him with almost his own confused expression. She came closer, closer, lifted her right hand. . . . She was trembling so much her fingers quivered; she was looking not at him but at the gold locket around his neck.

Suddenly she snatched at the heart. He pulled back, and she jerked the chain harder, harder, until it snapped. She held it for a moment in her clenched hand as if afraid to open her fingers. Then she moved away from him into the shadow of the room. Her thumb rubbed at the heart, but her eyes did not leave his face. She could feel the telltale teeth marks and knew without looking that it was her heart, it was Michael's heart, it was her baby's heart.

"Where did you get this? *Where did you get this?*"

With the heart still clenched in her fist she hit him directly in the face. The chain cut his lip.

"It's mine," he said.

"No, no, you stole it, you stole it." She turned, shocked, as the door was rapped sharply. Teresa's frightened whisper asked if she was all right.

"Leave me alone, *don't come in.* . . ."

Her breath rasped. She felt as if someone were strangling her. She pressed her face against the heavy wooden doors until she heard the footsteps going away across the marble hall. With her back to Luka, her face hidden, she uncurled her hand, then clenched it tightly again.

To Luka it seemed an age before she turned to face him again. He watched, now afraid, as she slowly circled the table. When she was at the opposite end, he saw her open her hand and look again at the heart.

Sophia could hear Graziella saying how much Johnny reminded her of Michael. Could this insane boy be her son? Michael's son?

He watched as she came closer; he could see the small beads of sweat on her brow, her upper lip, the sheen of her cheeks. He looked into her eyes, preparing himself, but it wasn't the same. There wasn't that look on her face, the one he remembered, the look in their eyes just before they hurt him.

"Please, tell me, where did you get this?"

"It's mine."

He could see the outline of her body through the thin cotton gown. She was naked underneath; strange, it was all he could think of: *She is naked.* There was something in her voice. Was it fear? What was she afraid of?

"Where did you find this, please tell me?"

"It's mine."

She moved closer to the table. "It is very important. You must tell me. Please . . ."

She reached out and touched his face, then withdrew her hand. Still frightened, he pressed his body back against the chair.

Sophia scrutinized his face, then suddenly spun around, her eyes darting about the room, looking for the envelope she had brought the pictures in. Graziella had taken the pictures that had been on the table, but Sophia knew there was one more. She saw the envelope on the floor and ran toward it, snatched it up, and withdrew the last photograph.

Luka watched, fascinated. Why was she behaving so strangely? He saw her take the photograph out inch by inch, then turn her back to hide what she was doing. A soft moan escaped her.

Standing directly in front of him now, she looked into blue eyes that registered only confusion and fear.

"Tell me the names of those who wanted the Luciano family destroyed, and in return . . . in return I will tell you the name of your father."

He gave her nothing but an angelic smile of disbelief. She moved closer "I swear on the Holy Virgin that I am telling the truth. I know, Luka, I know."

His whole body was poised in an unreal stillness. He did not believe her; his pale eyes were accusing, unwavering. . . . He could not be tricked. He had no father, no mother. He had been born of the devil; that was why he had to be punished, why they had locked him away.

"You ran away, didn't you? From the holy sisters? They looked for you at the fairground."

His face became a mask; only his eyes registered the torment of confusion, one moment accusing, the next, fearful. How did she know about the fairground? And his refusal to answer made Sophia doubt. Could she be wrong?

She leaned closer. "Did you go to a fairground? Were you in Catania, Luka? Do you remember?" He looked upward; his eyes rolled back in his head.

"Tell me who ordered the deaths of my children. Give me that at least. . . . Luka?"

Silence. His eyelids fluttered; he blinked rapidly; then he stared at her, through her, an unnerving, steady gaze. He seemed to be mocking her, forcing her to be the one to look away, and it made her angry—at last, angry again.

*He is not my son*, she told herself. *Thank God. He is not my child*. Somehow he had found the heart, stolen it. He was a thief, a killer, and she was wasting time.

"It was the slide, big, high slide. You came down head-first, on a little rough mat. . . . I wanted another turn on the slide."

Her breath caught in her throat. Dear God, was he lying to her? Why had she mentioned the fairground? He was clever; he always lied; he had to be lying.

She held out the gold heart in the palm of her hand. "Where did you get this?"

"I don't know," he said matter-of-factly.

"Did you steal it from another child? Find it? Why do you have it?"

"Because it belongs to me. I like to swing it in front of my eyes; it helps me sleep." He seemed to be playing a game; he showed no fear of her. Instead, he asked slyly, his head tilted to one side, "How do you know about the fairground?"

"I'll tell you, Luka, if you'll give me the names, tell me who ordered the deaths of the Lucianos."

He smiled. "Okay!"

Outside the room, Teresa, still wearing her overcoat, rested her head against the door, trying to hear what was happening. She whispered to Rosa that Luka was talking.

"What is he saying?"

Teresa put her hand up to silence her; then she straightened. "I can't hear."

Rosa sat by her side. "It's stopped snowing."

Teresa looked at her, not understanding.

"It means the grave will show clearly."

*   *   *

Sophia leaned on the table, about to write on the back of Michael's photograph. Luka, still bound to the chair by his arms and legs, strained forward.

"Barzini."

"You are giving me a dead man's name, Luka. I know Barzini is dead."

He continued quietly, as though he hadn't heard her. "Barzini carried the message to Sicily; that is why his was the first offer to buy out the Lucianos. He was nothing; Peter Salerno is more important, but three, maybe four families were involved. They were out to make sure that no man as high up in the organization as Don Roberto should be a witness."

"Just give me the names, Luka!"

"Okay, okay. I can give you the names I heard. But I was not important enough to be told anything. I only know what I know because I was Paul Carolla's son."

"Adopted son, Luka."

Luka snapped out three names, names that meant nothing to Sophia, and she wrote them down on the back of the photograph. She waited for the fourth, pen poised. . . . She turned to him, and he sat back in the chair, looking directly at her.

This was the child she had abandoned, then searched for, and in her mind had given up again. He was Michael's son; he was her son, the rightful heir to the Luciano family. Now it was up to her to kill him. Yet she believed that he had just spoken the truth, that he had played no part in the murder of the Luciano men. But what about her children?

"Luka, you admitted you killed the jailer's child; the same gun killed Carlo and Nunzio—"

He snapped at her, "No! I have answered your questions. Now it is your turn."

She turned, refusing to give him the photograph. "Tell me, Luka, the two children."

His eyes blazed with impotent fury. Trapped helplessly in the chair, he rocked backward and forward, shaking the chair. "Yes! Yes! Yes!"

"You admit it?"

"Yes! Now, keep to the bargain. Did you lie to me? You know about the fairground." He clenched his teeth. "Who told?"

"You killed them?"

"Fuck you! *Yes, yes, yes!*"

She turned the photo of Michael Luciano over, leaving it directly in front of him on the table. He laughed, leaning forward to see it.

He shook his head in disgust, his eyes narrowed. "You lied to me. I spit on this kid."

"You spit on your father, Luka. He was Michael Luciano. The photograph was taken just before he died. He was twenty-two years old."

He hissed, spitting like a cat at the photograph, then looked at her as if for some reaction, smirking. She saw now the Luka who could kill innocent children, the man who could mutilate and violate his victims with such ferocity; madness had turned his eyes to glittering stones. He was shackled by his legs and arms, yet she had the terrifying feeling that he could, if he desired, break free.

His voice was mocking. "You always were cleverer than the others. I knew it, I always knew it. And I know you'll be the one to cut me loose." He laughed as she turned toward the knife.

"I know you are lying, Sophia, but I'll say I am Michael Luciano's son if that's what you want. I'll do anything for you. The rest of them mean nothing to me. You will have everything I promised you, remember?"

Her fingers tightened around the wooden handle of the knife, her body shielding her actions. Her voice was no more than a whisper.

"I didn't lie to you, Luka."

She had to force herself to turn back to him. She had to do it now, now while she could still hear that hideous, sneering voice.

The blade went straight between his ribs into his heart. She needed all her weight, all her strength, to push it farther. She forced his body against the back of the chair until she was leaning over him, her knee pressed against his thigh. He made a soft, gurgling sound in his throat.

As she pushed herself away from him, her hand seemed frozen to the knife, as if her son were gripping her tightly, and she pulled hard until she stumbled backward.

He remained upright because his arms were still tied to the chair, but his head had rolled slightly to one side. A trickle of blood ran from his mouth and down his neck. She felt for his pulse; it still flickered. Then she cupped his face in her hands and kissed his still-warm lips. She could taste his blood in her mouth, could feel his soft hair, his skull between her hands. . . . Slowly the pulse stopped, and it was over.

Sophia slipped the gold heart on its broken chain into the pocket of her bloodstained gown. She unbuckled the straps from his legs and picked up the sheet to cover his body. Then she unbuckled his left wrist, seemingly calm, strangely methodical, but as she started on the right hand, the buckle would not unhook. She pulled it tighter, and his hand moved. . . . She sank to her knees.

His blood began to color the towels beneath him. It became a spreading stain on the sheet covering him. There was a light tap on the door.

"Sophia, are you all right? Sophia?" She heard Teresa's frightened whisper and forced herself to stand. The distance between the chair and the door was only a matter of yards, but each step felt like a terrible weight. Her limbs ached. She reached the door, gasping for breath, and it was a considerable time before she could turn the key and open it.

Teresa and Rosa stood like children, Rosa holding a thick blanket. They did not have to ask if it was done. Sophia's face was ghostly. She opened the door wider.

"I can't unbuckle the belt on his right—his right . . . wrist."

The two women inched into the room, looking at the shrouded figure, the bloodstained sheet. Covered, he was not the nightmare they had expected. But they, too, seemed unable to move. . . .

"Rosa, lay the blanket down, and, Teresa, help me unstrap his wrist." Teresa's hands were shaking as she jerked at the strap. As it came away, his arm, released, lolled over the side of the chair.

Sophia turned to see if the blanket was ready and looked to Teresa. "We'll need all three of us to lift him out of the chair."

Rosa wrapped the sheet tightly around Luka's head and shoulders, then gripped him by the armpits. Sophia and Teresa took his trunk and legs, staggering. They carried him to the blanket and laid him down.

"What about the knife?" Teresa demanded. "Sophia, the knife?"

Sophia got down on her knees. "Pull the sheet down, Rosa. We have to get rid of the knife."

Rosa forced herself to move the sheet away; Luka's head was almost in her lap. She gasped, "Oh, my God, oh, God!"

"Help me, Rosa," ordered Sophia.

"No, no, I can't touch him, please don't make me touch him. . . ." She began to make a strange sound, like a mewing kitten, and cringed as Sophia used both hands to pull the knife out. The blood oozed thickly, and Teresa covered his face quickly.

"Now wrap the blanket around him, hurry, Sophia."

Sophia obeyed.

"Roll him over. We'll have to roll him over."

Her face stricken as she stared now at the rolled blanket, Rosa was still making that noise. Sophia turned on her.

*"Stop it! Stop it!"*

"Don't. Don't shout at her!" Teresa held her hand out to her daughter. "We need you to help us. You don't have to see him, but you must help us."

They bound him in the blanket, using the straps to make sure it was secure. Then all three lifted him, carried him through the kitchen and out into the garden.

The grave had been dug beneath an oak tree at one side of the snow-covered lawn, according to Sophia's instructions. It was deep but not long enough. "Bend his knees," Sophia whispered.

He lay on his side, his knees curled up like a baby in the womb. The mother who had given birth to him now scraped at the earth with her bare hands while Teresa and Rosa used the spades to refill the grave. It seemed to dominate the vast white area of lawn. Their breath streamed out in front of them in the freezing cold, but they didn't appear to feel the chill. Sophia was still barefoot, wearing just the bloodstained cotton shift.

The grave filled, Teresa surveyed their work.

"Quickly, shovel snow across the top."

"We won't have to," Sophia said. "Look at the sky."

It was gray, and almost as Sophia spoke, the snow started again. Sophia turned back to the house, leaving Rosa and Teresa to shovel the last of the soil into a wheelbarrow. Together they tipped it onto a flower bed.

The snow fell thickly now. Suddenly feeling the cold, they ran back to the house. Rosa, pushing the wheelbarrow, slipped and fell facedown in the snow. She began to sob, and Teresa turned back.

"Are you hurt? Did you hurt yourself?"

Teresa ran to Rosa as her daughter's sobbing rose to a hysterical pitch. She dragged her to her feet. "No! No! Rosa! Rosa!"

She had to slap Rosa's face, then held her tightly, talking her down, calming her, as Rosa gasped, "I'm sorry, I'm sorry. . . . I'm sorry, Mama. . . ."

Her face was streaked with soil and blood. The wet snowflakes made her cheeks shine. The murder they had played a part in, the covering of the corpse, the zigzag road mother and daughter had skidded along like a roller coaster since the murder of the Luciano family were an unreal, distant horror. All Teresa could think of or see at this moment was her daughter's beauty. She cupped Rosa's face in her hands and kissed her lips.

"Rosa, everything will be all right now. It's over."

Graziella slowly drew her curtains. From her window she had watched them digging the grave, watched them carry the shrouded body, watched them bury him. Her heart had reached out to Sophia, in her bare feet and bloodied nightgown, forced to commit a murder that numbed her senses to such an extent that she did not feel the freezing night. She had seen her granddaughter fall as she hid the evidence of the murder, heard her cry and understood the hysteria, wept when she witnessed the gentle kiss between mother and daughter. She had remained watching until there was no trace left of the freshly dug earth or the grave.

It was not over; they had to clear away any incriminating evidence. Each had been allocated tasks, and it helped them to be forced into making sure it was done.

Rosa started a bonfire in what was once a walled vegetable garden; with the house left empty much of it had grown wild. Rosa discoverd a stack of old newspapers left in the garage and used them to kindle the fire.

Teresa carried Luka's clothes and few personal belongings from his room, stuffed the pockets of his clothes with paper soaked in turpentine and tied them into parcels with string. Sophia washed down the banisters, Luka's bedroom and the bathroom he had used, putting his toothbrush and comb in a bag. Then she put the bag into the garbage compactor and turned it on. From the kitchen window she could see smoke rising from the fire outside.

Teresa threw Luka's clothes into the fire. As the flames lifted and crackled, she hurried back to the house to check that she had missed nothing. Rosa remained by the fire, prodding it with a stick to keep it burning. Looking around, she noticed a row of canes stuck in the earth in a sheltered corner. She turned back to the flames, remembering that sunny morning when Luka had kissed her, when he had laughed with Graziella, pointed out where he would plant new seeds. She watched now as his clothes turned to ashes.

Sophia still wore her blood-soaked nightdress. From the kitchen door Teresa said, "Take it off. I'll burn it. . . . Sophia?"

Teresa had to repeat herself. Sophia's feet were blue with cold. Slowly she lifted the gown, remembered the heart in the pocket and took it out.

"The gown, Sophia, give it to me. I have to burn it." She looked for something to wrap around Sophia, but there was nothing. She took her own coat off and accepted the blood-soaked nightdress from Sophia. "Put this on, take a hot bath . . ."

Sophia nodded but just stood there. Teresa went to her and tried to put the coat around her, but Sophia pushed her away.

"Don't touch me. Please, don't touch me."

Sophia stumbled up the stairs and into her bedroom. She locked the door after her and lunged across the room toward the bathroom. She almost fell into the white-tiled shower, hitting her shoulder on the wall, but she turned on the water, tried to wash away the bloodstains on her body, her hands . . . and still she clasped the little gold heart.

The icy water hurt her, as if someone were slapping her face, her body. But still she made no attempt to turn on the hot water. She put the heart in her mouth and bit into it; her belly heaved, the pain ripping her apart as it had done at her son's birth.

She hit out at the tiles until her fists bled, banged her head against them, yet she would not allow herself to make one sound. This was her punishment, her silence; no one must ever know what she had done. Nothing anyone ever did to her, nothing she could ever do to anyone, would alleviate her guilt. She had committed the utmost crime: She had given birth, rejected her own blood, and, in the end, slaughtered it. She and no one else had destroyed the heart of the family. The child she had discarded for her own greed had become a monster, but the secret would remain as silent as Luka's grave. She would protect all that was left with the ferocity and, if need be, the violence she now knew herself capable of.

The day after Luka's murder, Teresa, Rosa, and Graziella went to bed. Having been up all night, they slept through the day, overwhelmed with fatigue. Mercifully their exhaustion blanked out the horror in which they had participated.

For Sophia there was no sleep. If she closed her eyes, she saw her son's face. She wandered around the house, unable to sit, unable to rest. Her only solution was to occupy her mind with the family papers.

She left the lights off in the drawing room and read by the glow of the fire, studying Michele Barzini's notebook, checking his figures against the missing sums of money from the Luciano estate, the multiple accounts, the fortune that had so mysteriously vanished. Time and time again, the amounts listed by Barzini, with strange markings beside them, matched those of the stolen money. She couldn't break the code, but she wondered if the few initials beside the figures were the first letters of the banks' names. She turned to the list of names printed on the back page. Graziella had recalled two of them, but Luka had know three. They were members of different families, in diverse businesses. If they all had joined forces, agreed on the

Luciano assassinations, and, at the same time, reaped vast financial rewards . . .

She was too tired to think further. She gathered all the documents together and returned to her bedroom.

At six-thirty that evening she went to sleep for a few hours. By the time she had dressed again she could hear the others talking together in the living room.

They fell silent when she walked in. Then Graziella, with a warm smile, indicated her own chair by the fireside, inviting Sophia to sit in it.

Graziella held out her hand. "This is for you, Sophia. We want you to wear it; we give it to you for your bravery. We love you and trust you, and I kiss you, in the hope that you will receive it and wear it."

She kissed Sophia on both cheeks, then took her daughter-in-law's hand and placed on her wedding finger Don Roberto's embossed gold ring.

"Mama, I can't. . . ."

"Please, Sophia, wear it, in the name of my husband, my sons, my grandsons. I ask one thing from each of you. I ask you to swear on the Holy Bible never to speak of Luka. His name must never be mentioned. We are held together by his death; we need nothing more. *Omertà* . . ."

She kissed her small, worn leather Bible and made the sign of the cross, closing her eyes in prayer. Then she passed the Bible to Teresa, who laid her left hand flat on its cover and crossed herself with her right.

"I swear, by almighty God . . ."

They waited in silence for Sophia to take the oath and show that she accepted Don Roberto's ring. Her hands were folded in her lap, the ring hidden from view. Her mind was in turmoil; instead of asking her to head the family, they should be casting her out.

Graziella touched her hand. "Sophia, please . . ."

Wearily Sophia rested her hand on the Bible. "I swear by almighty God, Mama." Then she rose to her feet. She clasped Graziella and kissed her on both cheeks, then turned to Teresa, and last she cupped Rosa's face in her hands, kissing her.

Rosa noticed the small gold heart that Sophia wore on a

chain, and asked if it had belonged to Luka. Sophia answered simply that it had belonged to one of her sons.

It was as if Luka continued to help them from the grave. Even before his death rumors had begun to circulate about who exactly was behind the widows; the rumors spread an insidious fear. Revenge was expected, but from where?

The murders Luka had committed, the decapitation of Barzini's cousin, even Barzini's own coincidental death were discussed. It was whispered that perhaps not all the Lucianos had died that fateful night in Palermo, that one of them had ordered the death of Paul Carolla.

As the silence continued, suspicions mounted. A contract was out on Carolla's crazy son, but he had disappeared. Peter Salerno repeated innumerable times the telephone conversation he had had with the unnamed man who claimed to represent the widows. Old ground, past history, was dredged up, and a few came to the conclusion that if there was not some big name family behind the widows, then there *was* a Luciano still alive. If so, revenge would come; it had to; it was their law. But until it could be proved, no one wished to make a move. Orders passed from one family to another: wait.

Peter Salerno waited patiently, sure he would be the first to be contacted. The call he had been expecting came two weeks after Luka's death.

Sophia Luciano requested a meeting with Salerno and the men behind Barzini. Salerno agreed to arrange it and quickly checked out the address Sophia had given. The Groves, he discovered, had been owned by Paul Carolla and had been handed over to the women by Luka Carolla. The hit on Luka Carolla was upped to one hundred thousand dollars.

Three weeks after the murder of Luka and five days after the call requesting the meeting, Salerno traveled to Long Island in a chauffeur-driven limousine. The three men with him were high-ranking *consiglieri* of three major families, the families that had been named by Luka as instigating the Luciano assassinations.

The men with Salerno were Tony Castellano, the U.S. representative for the Corleones, Johnny Salvatore, for the

Gambino family, and the hugely fat Nuccio Miano, the pay-master for the Chicago-based Avellino family. They were gray-haired, smartly turned out, and determined to gain control of the Luciano empire.

They fell silent as they reached the impressive avenue of The Groves, partly in admiration but also with anger that they had let this prize piece of property escape their attention.

The sun shone, showing off the house to full effect. The heavy clang of the electronic gates locking behind them made one man turn, and the hair on the backs of his hands prickled.

Graziella preceded Teresa and Rosa into the room, where they were introduced to the others by Salerno. Then Graziella gestured to Rosa to leave the room.

When Rosa had gone, Graziella gave a small nod for Teresa to offer the visitors the most comfortable chairs. "My other daughter-in-law will join you shortly. I have wine, a favorite of my husband's: Brunello di Montalcino. It would be an honor for me to serve you and toast the memory of Don Roberto."

They could not refuse, and the small glances they passed among themselves was confirmation. The wine was uncorked, wrapped in a fine linen napkin, and Graziella poured it into the fine crystal glasses. She carried a silver tray, a small silver bowl of crackers, to each man. She was servile, charming, murmuring, "*Grazie,*" as they accepted their drinks. She then replaced the tray but did not pour herself a glass. Instead, she stood next to Teresa.

Peter Salerno lifted his glass. "To Don Roberto!"

Graziella crossed herself, murmuring "*Grazie.*"

The men made no attempt at polite conversation. They could feel the tension in the two watchful women, yet there was no antagonism. Teresa opened a box of Havana cigars, Graziella gave a nod, and Teresa offered them to the guests.

Rosa tapped on Sophia's door, then opened it slightly. But Sophia seemed not to notice her niece's presence. She was standing by the closed shutters, half in shadow, and was talking softly to herself. When she finally became aware that Rosa was there, her body froze, her face still in profile, her lips slightly parted.

"They are waiting, Sophia."

Sophia did not move, did not answer. As Rosa slipped out of the room, she didn't see Sophia lift her hand and touch the small gold heart.

Rosa closed the double doors into the living room and joined her mother and grandmother silently. The men exchanged glances among themselves, wondering why they were being kept waiting.

At last they heard the click of high heels across the marble of the hall. The door handles turned slowly, and then the doors swung open wide. Sophia paused a moment, framed in the doorway. Her sleek black hair was coiled in a bun at the nape of her neck; her plain black dress was open at the collar. High-heeled black shoes and black stockings made her look stark but demure. The only color was her lipstick, a slash of crimson. She gave them the sweetest of smiles and walked serenely to the center of the room.

Graziella quietly introduced each of the men. They had to rise from their seats, cross the room, and kiss Sophia's hand; she made no move toward them. As they kissed her right hand, they could see that she wore Don Roberto Luciano's ring, the ring that had once belonged to Joseph Carolla.

Sophia gestured for her guests to be seated, then sat, crossing her legs, and not a man there could resist looking at them.

"Gentlemen, I have been named Don Roberto's heir. I am now, and wish it to be known, the head of the Luciano family, and as such I have every intention of running *il Papa*'s companies, apart from those we have already agreed to sell."

Peter Salerno looked at the other men. They sat back, bemused expressions on their faces. Sophia Luciano appeared to be asking for membership in an establishment that had never in its history allowed a woman to take the oath.

Sophia's husky voice continued. "I am fully aware of my father's organization connections, and I leave it to the commission either to ignore my existence or to agree to let me run my business without harassment."

Miano sucked at his cigar, spit, then picked a piece of tobacco from his fat lip. With a dismissive gesture he said, "Signora, no one is going to harass you. What occurred with Michelè Barzini was most unfortunate—"

"Forgive me, signor; you say unfortunate. Perhaps that is not a good description. We were treated without respect, almost robbed."

She looked at Graziella, then back to Miano. "Signor, we are no longer interested in negotiation. We still retain the legal rights to the properties under consideration, but now our price has tripled. Furthermore, we will agree to sell only if certain conditions are adhered to. I am against the trade in narcotics, like my father before me, and unless we can be assured that his wishes are respected by the new owners, we will not sell."

Salerno found himself tapped on the arm and pulled close by Salvatore, who murmured to him, keeping his face averted. Salerno, his eyes on Sophia, held up his hand, excusing the interruption. He nodded his agreement; then Salvatore turned, ignoring the women, and discussed something in a hushed voice with Miano and Castellano. The three huddled close, then separated and leaned back.

Salerno was given a small wave of Salvatore's heavily ringed hand. He obviously spoke for them all.

"Signora, there must be some mistake. You have, to our knowledge, already been paid a considerable amount for the businesses."

"You are mistaken. Barzini hired men who physically attacked all of us in an attempt to secure the legal titles to our company without paying for them. Perhaps you should look to those working on your behalf for the return of the funds you wrongly believe to be in our hands."

She touched the gold heart at her throat, as if feeling for a pulse, but her eyes moved from one man's sweating face to the next, finally resting on the shifty-eyed Peter Salerno.

He in turn watched her warily, detecting the anger behind the mask of her face and puzzled by her repeated gesture of raising her hand and placing her index finger on the gold locket at her neck.

"Within ten days you will receive the full transcripts of Don Roberto Luciano's statements that were prepared for the trial in Palermo. They show, clearly, that until the end he was a man of honor, a man who could have been trusted but, tragically, was not. We feel it our right to be given compensation; this, I believe, is your law. If we cannot expect this from you, then we will take whatever action is necessary to ensure that Don Roberto Luciano is given the justice he deserves."

Salerno looked at each man present, then eased forward in his chair, resting his elbows on the carved arms.

"Signora Luciano, all of us here offer you and your family our deep condolences regarding your tragic losses. But we do not have the right to offer you compensation, even if we wished to do so, because that would indicate that we were in some way involved when nothing could be farther from the truth. We are simply businessmen, no more, no less. Nevertheless, we cannot dismiss Michele Barzini's treatment of you, and we wish you to know that he acted without our knowledge. We agree to pay you an extra twenty thousand—"

Sophia interrupted. "Twenty? Twenty thousand?" She smiled coldly. "Your gift is most acceptable, but what we need is assistance in discovering the identities of those men concerned in arranging our beloveds' murders. And financially, we feel we are entitled to Paul Carolla's estate. After all, Joseph Carolla named Roberto Luciano his heir, and now that Paul Carolla is also deceased, we—"

Salerno interrupted. "But Carolla has a son."

Sophia turned to face him, held his eyes, and he gave way, looking down at his hands.

"Luka Carolla is wanted for the murder of my children, Signor Salerno. Furthermore, he was adopted; Paul Carolla leaves no blood heirs."

Graziella signaled that she wished to speak to Sophia, and with a small inclination of her head as if to apologize to her guests for the interruption, Sophia went to her side, unintentionally bending away from the men, listening and masking Graziella's whispered words. Salerno took the opportunity to confer with Miano, who was becoming impatient.

The four men waited as Sophia returned to her chair, but they remained standing. Salerno coughed. "Signora, we are aware that this property was owned by Paul Carolla and was recently signed over to Signora Graziella Luciano. When there is a meeting in the near future, we can discuss Paul Carolla's estate, but until that time I am unable to say if any of it can be handed over to you."

Nuccio Miano cleared the phlegm from his throat and adjusted his vest, refusing to say anything at this time, but he had listened long enough. He wanted to leave.

Tony Castellano picked up on his associates' agitation and gave a barely noticeable nod to Peter Salerno. With Miano irritated by the women's audacity, Castellano knew there would be repercussions from Sicily when he reported back.

Sophia thanked each man cordially for coming to the meeting, then turned to Graziella and smiled. But it was the smile of Luka that Graziella saw on her face. All sweetness had gone, and her eyes telegraphed a warning to each woman to remain silent. Their visitors must get no hint from any of them that she was about to lie.

Sophia then continued. "What none of you realizes is that there remains an heir to the Luciano estate, an heir who wants only what is rightfully his. If he is refused, you give the family no option but to look elsewhere. . . . *La spine della rosa sono nascoste dal fiore.*"

The other women watched Sophia as she insisted on serving more wine to her guests with her own hands, handing Peter Salerno his glass last. She smiled at him above the rim of her own glass, lifting it as if in a toast. Then she turned her attention to the three other guests, speaking to each man in turn and saying that it was sad that the Lucianos were not given the respect of meeting the two other families interested in negotiating with them. She spoke the two names without any show of emotion.

She ended the meeting as abruptly as she had opened it: courteously and without a trace of fear. Her voice had been soft and persuasive and never at any time less than cordial.

Now, as the three men walked from the room, she rested her hand on Peter Salerno's arm, gave him yet another smile, and this time leaned toward him and kissed him on his astonished lips.

"*Arrivederci,* signor, we thank you."

The men agreed it was farcical of Sophia to believe there was even so much as a possibility of her becoming part of the organization. Yet there remained the fact that to date the women had already got away with fifteen million and still retained the entire Luciano holdings in both America and Palermo.

Sophia's demand for Paul Carolla's estate furthered the rumor that someone was behind the Luciano women, someone who had schooled them well, and someone who was prepared to kill for them. And who was the heir she claimed? Miano spit in disgust at the thought of men willing to take orders from four women, one of them just out of school, another a grandmother.

The car passed through the wrought-iron gates, which closed soundlessly behind them, and the hidden video cameras swiveled back into place. Peter Salerno, sitting in the backseat, could not resist a last look back at the impressive house. He looked up at the top-floor windows; a woman, clothed in black and partially hidden by the security bars, was watching them leave. She was in the shadows, but he was sure he recognized her.

"I think Sophia Luciano's different, a different kind of woman from what we're used to. She's—"

The men in Salerno's car admitted that she unnerved them; she was, they joked, an unknown commodity. None of them had ever had any dealings with a woman like her, in business or bed. They all agreed with less humor than before that she was *bella . . . bella mafiosa.*

But Salerno didn't laugh. He stared from the car window. What had made her so different?

The slush spattered the road and the gleaming sides of the limo. The cigar smoke made him feel sick, and he pressed the button to lower the window, gasping for the freezing air. How had she known just which of the families were involved? He went over the meeting virtually word for word, picturing her face as she quietly listed men who didn't even know of one another's complicity. This meant she had to know every man involved in the murder of her family. Salerno was chilled by the ramifications because if she knew who they were, she must also be aware of the money transferred from Sicily, the Luciano fortune.

Someone asked him to close the window. He reached for the button; the pain in his gut was like an explosion, blowing his bowels apart. The burning sensation swept up through his chest and into his throat, choking him, and spittle ran from his lips. His mouth flapped soundlessly as if he were trying to warn the other men, but he never uttered another word.

*        *        *

Peter Salerno's name was scratched from the back of the photograph. The photo of Michael Luciano was set back in its place of honor. Graziella Luciano, widow of Don Roberto Luciano, Teresa, widow of Filippo Luciano, and Rosa, the tragic bride-to-be, waited expectantly to hear the outcome of their meeting, unaware that Sophia, widow of Constantino Luciano, mother of little Carlo and Nunzio Luciano, had already acted. The seeds of the vendetta that had begun with the murder of Michael Luciano would continue. *La spine della rosa sono nascoste dal fiore.* The thorns of the rose are hidden by the bloom.